Pr...

M...

"Cherie Priest is supremely gifted and *Maplecroft* is a remarkable novel, simultaneously beautiful and grotesque. It is at once a dark historical fantasy with roots buried deep in real-life horror and a supernatural thriller mixing Victorian drama and Lovecraftian myth. You won't be able to put it down."

—Christopher Golden, #1 *New York Times* bestselling author of *Snowblind*

"*Maplecroft* is dark and lyrical, haunting and brined in blood. It is as sharp as Lizzie Borden's axe—and Borden herself is a horror heroine bar none. Cherie Priest is our new queen of darkness, folks. Time to kneel before her, lest she take our heads."

—Chuck Wendig, author of *Blackbirds* and *The Blue Blazes*

"With *Maplecroft*, Cherie Priest delivers her most terrifying vision yet—a genuinely scary, deliciously claustrophobic, and dreadfully captivating historical thriller with both heart and cosmic horror. A mesmerizing absolute must-read."

—Brian Keene, Bram Stoker Award–winning author of *The Rising*

"Cherie Priest has long been a favorite author of mine, but with *Maplecroft* she has outdone herself. Grim, impeccably written, and deliciously disturbing, it's nothing less than a gothic masterpiece, and represents Priest at the height of her power. Easily my favorite novel of the year so far."

—Kealan Patrick Burke, Bram Stoker Award–winning author of *Dead Leaves*

"The best damn Cthulu novel you've read in ages . . . a wild, awesome page-turner. . . . Priest has taken the real-life historical details of the Borden murders . . . and turned them into one of the best Lovecraftian stories I've ever read." —io9

"[A] terrifying and powerful series launch by fan favorite Priest. . . . Readers will be intrigued by the weird monsters and nineteenth-century science, but the story is really carried by the characters' emotional dynamics."

—*Publishers Weekly*

"The historical and paranormal interweave beautifully and the dread just seeps through the pages. This is a lovesong to Lovecraft and a very fine example of effective horror writing." —Badass Book Reviews

continued . . .

"*Maplecroft* is probably [Priest's] best work so far . . . a beautifully written story of horror, [the] genuine stuff of nightmare . . . a truly unique macabre masterpiece of fully realized characters given weight through historical accuracy." —My Whole Expanse I Cannot See

"Priest excels at exploring some of our deepest, darkest fears by weaving together a realistic setting and historic events with a frightening, visceral supernatural element." —Bitten by Books

"A superb work [that] wields both mastery over the classic forms of Lovecraft and Stoker and the keenly honed blade of modern sensibilities." —Mania

"A stunningly good horror tale, driven by the characters' own impending sense of doom. Reminiscent of Stephen King's *The Shining*, *Maplecroft* delves into the madness that lurks just beneath the surface." —CK²S Kwips and Kritiques

"*Maplecroft* is timeless horror–dark fantasy crafted by an absolute master storyteller . . . a towering literary achievement. It's a macabre masterwork." —Paul Goat Allen

"A brilliantly done Lovecraftian horror filled with monsters that provoke absolute dread. It truly is horror at its finest." —The Nocturnal Library

Praise for Cherie Priest
and Her Novels

"Priest kills as a stylist."
—Charles de Lint, *The Magazine of Fantasy & Science Fiction*

"Cherie Priest kicks ass!"
—Maggie Shayne, *New York Times* bestselling author of *Deadly Obsession*

"Cherie Priest has created a chilling page-turner. Her voice is rich, earthy, soulful, and deliciously Southern as she weaves a disturbing yarn like a master! Awesome—gives you goose bumps!"
—L. A. Banks, author of the Vampire Huntress Legend Series

"Wonderful. Enchanting. Amazing and original fiction that will satisfy that buttery Southern taste, as well as that biting aftertaste of the dark side. I loved it." —Joe R. Lansdale, award-winning author of *The Thicket*

"Fine writing, humor, thrills, real scares, the touch of the occult . . . had me from the first page."

—Heather Graham, *New York Times* bestselling author of *The Betrayed*

"Priest can write scenes that are jump-out-of-your-skin scary."

—Cory Doctorow, author of *Homeland*

"Give Cherie Priest fifteen minutes of your time; trust me—you won't look back."   —Bookslut

"Priest masterfully weaves a complex tapestry of interlocking plots, motivations, quests, character arcs, and background stories to produce an exquisitely written novel with a rich and lush atmosphere."   —*The Gazette* (Montreal)

"Priest has a knack for instantly creating quirky, likable, memorable characters."   —*The Roanoke Times* (VA)

"Cherie Priest has crafted an intriguing yarn that is excellently paced, keeping the reader turning pages to discover where the story will lead."

—*San Francisco Book Review*

"Priest's haunting lyricism and graceful narrative are complemented by the solemn, cynical thematic undercurrents with a tangible gravity and depth."

—*Publishers Weekly*

"With each volume, Priest squeezes in several novels' worth of flabbergasting ideas, making each story expansive as hell while still keeping . . . tight control over the three-act structure."

—The Chicago Center for Literature and Photography

"Cherie Priest has mastered the art of braiding atmosphere, suspense, and metaphysics."

—Katherine Ramsland, bestselling author of
Ghost: Investigating the Other Side

"Priest does an excellent job of building tension throughout the novel . . . up to and including the satisfying ending. Writing that can simultaneously set a mood, flesh out characters, and advance plot is a force to be reckoned with. With writing this good . . . I have no doubts that we will be hearing from Cherie Priest again and again."   —SF Signal

"[Priest] is already a strong voice in dark fantasy and could, with care, be a potent antidote for much of what is lacking elsewhere in the genre."

—Rambles

Also by Cherie Priest

Maplecroft

chapelwood

THE BORDEN DISPATCHES

CHERIE PRIEST

A ROC BOOK

ROC

Published by New American Library,
an imprint of Penguin Random House LLC
375 Hudson Street, New York, New York 10014

This book is an original publication of New American Library.

First Printing, September 2015

For more information about Penguin Random House, visit penguin.com.

LIBRARY OF CONGRESS CATALOGING-IN-PUBLICATION DATA:

Priest, Cherie.
  Chapelwood: the Borden dispatches / Cherie Priest.
    pages cm.—(The Borden dipatches)
  ISBN 978-0-451-46698-3 (softcover)
  1. Borden, Lizzie, 1860–1927—Fiction.   2. Serial murderers—Fiction.
  3. Good and evil—Fiction. I. Title.
  PS3616.R537C48   2015
  813'.6—dc23 2015009666

Printed in the United States of America
10 9 8 7 6 5 4 3 2 1

Set in Horley Old Style

Penguin
Random
House

For Karl, even though he's not in this one.

ACKNOWLEDGMENTS

I'm always terrified when it comes to acknowledgments and thanks, because I feel like I'm virtually guaranteed to leave out someone important—by virtue of my own cluelessness. So, although there are approximately a thousand people I'd like to mention here, I will try to keep it relatively short and sweet.

Therefore, I offer copious and oversized thanks to the usual suspects: my editor, Anne Sowards, who helped bang this thing into shape, and wonder publicist Alexis Nixon, who helped launch *Maplecroft* so grandly (in preparation for this here follow-up); my agent, Jennifer Jackson—who also serves part-time as my bottle rocket of fiery justice—and likewise to all the other fine folks at the Donald Maass agency, who make my life easier each day; my husband, J. Aric Annear, who hears all about these projects in what must surely be excruciating detail but never pushes me off a cliff or anything; and, of course, to everyone else on the production and marketing teams at Roc. Even though I don't know all your names. You rock. Yes, *you*.

chapelwood

Leonard Kincaid, American Institute of Accountants, Certified Member

❧

I escaped Chapelwood under the cover of daylight, not darkness. The darkness is too close, too friendly with the terrible folk who worship there.

(The darkness would give me away, if I gave it half a chance.)

So I left them an hour after dawn, when the reverend and his coterie lay sleeping in the hall beneath the sanctuary. When last I looked upon them, taking one final glance from the top of the stairs—down into the dim, foul-smelling quarter lit only with old candles that were covered in dust—I saw them tangled together, limb upon limb. I would say that they writhed like a pit of vipers, but that wasn't the case at all. They were immobile, static. It was a ghastly, damp tableau. Nothing even breathed.

I should have been down there with them; that's what the reverend would've said if he'd seen me. If he'd caught me, he would've lured me into that pallid pile of flesh that lives but is not alive. He would have reminded me of the nights I've spent in the midst of those arms and legs, tied together like nets, for yes, it is true: I *have* been there with them, among the men and women lying in a heap in the cellar. I have been a square in that quilt, a knot in that rug of humanity, skin on skin with the boneless, eyeless things that are not arms, and are not legs.

(I dream of it now, even when I'm not asleep.)

But never again. I have regained my senses—or come back to them, having almost fled them altogether.

So what sets me apart from the rest of them, enthralled by the book and the man who wields it? I cannot say. I do not know. I wanted to be with them, to be like them. I wanted to join their ranks, for I believed in their community, in their goals. Or I thought I did.

I am rethinking all the things I thought.

I am fashioning new goals, goals that will serve mankind better than the distant, dark hell that the reverend and his congregation seek to impose upon us all. They taught me too much, you see. They let me examine too many of their secrets too closely, and taste too much of the power they chase with their prayers and their formulas.

When they chose me for an acolyte, they chose poorly.

I take comfort in this, really, I do. It means that they can misjudge. They can fail.

So they can fail again, and indeed they *must*.

In retrospect, I wish I had done more than leave. I wish I'd found the strength to do them some grievous damage, some righteous recompense for the things they've done, and the things they strive to do in the future. Even as I stood there at the top of the stairs, gazing down at that mass of minions, or parishioners, or whatever they might call themselves . . . I was imagining a kerosene lantern and a match. I could fling it into their midst, toss down the lighted match, and lock the door behind myself. I could burn the whole place down around their ears, and them with it.

(And maybe also burn away the boneless limbs, which are not arms, and are not legs.)

But even with all the kerosene and all the matches in the world, would a place so wicked burn? A place like Chapelwood . . . a place that reeks of mildew and rot, and the spongy squish of timbers going soft from the persistent wetness that the place never really shakes—how many matches would it require?

All of them?

I stood at the top of the stairs and I trembled, but I did not attempt any arson.

I did nothing bolder than weep, and I did that silently. I can tell myself I did something brave and strong, when I walked away and left them behind. I can swear that into the mirror until I die, but it isn't true. I'm a coward; *that's* the truth. I was a coward there at Chapelwood, and I am a coward every day I do not descend upon that frightful compound with a militia of righteous men and all the matches in the world, if that's what it would take to see the place in ashes.

Not that I could muster any such militia.

Even the most righteous of men would be hard-pressed to believe me, and I can only admit that my case against the reverend may well sound like nonsense. But the strangeness of my message makes it no less true, and no less deadly. No less an apocalypse-in-waiting.

In time, perhaps, they will reveal themselves as monsters and the city will rise up to fight them. And the one thing working in my favor is that, yes, there is time. Their mechanizations are slow, and that's just as well; what horror would the universe reveal if mankind could alter it with a whim and a prayer? No, they need time yet—time, and blood. So there is time for the men of Chapelwood to make a mistake, and I will be watching them. Waiting for them.

Stalking them, as they have stalked others before.

Which brings me to my recent resolution, and why I'm writing of it here.

Do I incriminate myself? Fine, then I incriminate myself. But I will incriminate the reverend, too. I will incriminate them all, and when my time comes, I will not go down alone. I will not go quietly. And I will not have the world believing me a fiend or a madman, not when I am doing God's own work, in His name.

(If He should exist, and if He should see me—then He will know my heart, and judge me accordingly. I have tried to pray to Him, again and again. Or rather, I have tried to listen for Him, again and again. He does not speak to me, not so that I can hear it. It is one thing I envy the reverend and his followers: Their god *speaks*.)

(Or is their god the devil after all? For it is the devil who must make his case.)

This must be how the Crusaders felt, when tasked with the awful duty of war and conquest. A necessary duty, and an important one, to be sure. But awful all the same.

My duty is awful too, and I will not shirk away from it. I will confront it.

ℑ said before that they showed me too much, and they *did*. They invited me into their confidence because of my training and my aptitude for numbers; I've always had a head for sums, and I've worked as an accountant for the city these last eleven years. They needed a mathematician, a man who could see the vast tables and workings of numbers and read them as easily as some men read music.

I was flattered that they considered me worthy of their needs. I was proud to assist them, back when I was weak and eager to please.

I took their formulas, their charts, and their scriptures, and I teased out the patterns there. I showed them how to make the calculations themselves, how to manipulate the figures into telling them their fortunes. I *believed*—do you understand? I believed that the reverend had found a way to hear God speaking, and that when He talked, He spoke in algebra.

I was right about part of it. *Someone* is speaking to the reverend in proofs and fractions, but it's not the God of Abraham. I don't know what it is, or what else it could be . . . Some other god, perhaps? Is that blasphemy? No, I don't think so. It *can't* be, because the first commandment said, "Thou shalt have no other gods before me." It did not say there *were* no other gods; it said only to eschew them.

Would that the reverend had obeyed.

Would that I had figured it out sooner, that I was hearing the wrong voice when I scratched my pencil across the paper, tabulating columns and creating the tools the church would need to hear the voices of the universe without my assistance. It is not so easy to live, knowing that I may have given the reverend a map to the end of the world.

So I will do what I can to thwart him. I will take matters back into my own hands, and take the formulas out of my head and commit them to chalkboard, to paper, to any surface at hand, and I will beat them at their own game.

It won't be any true victory on my part. Too many innocent people will die for this to be any great triumph of justice and virtue; and they will die at my hand, because if they do not . . . they'll die at the hands of the church, and worse things by far will follow. So I am to become a murderer, of a man or two. Or three. Or however many, until the reverend makes enough mistakes and attracts enough attention that someone, somewhere, rises up to stop him in some way that I can't.

Or else until he succeeds.

I must account for that possibility, and I will write it in as a variable, when I compile my equations and build my graphs. This string of numbers will haunt me until I die, or until we all do.

I have determined the reverend's next target: an Italian woman who lives down by the box factory, and works there with her mother and sister. She is an ordinary woman, thirty years old and unmarried. Her hair is brown and her eyes are brown, too. She goes to Saint Paul's on Sundays and Wednesdays, too, if her work and health permit it.

I will try to catch her on the way back from her confession, to leave her soul as clean as it can be. I will try to grant her that much, but if the reverend forces my hand, then I will have to take measures—so I can only pray that she prays, and prays often.

She's done me no wrong, and her death will cause great

sorrow, but it could be worse, and that's what I must remember when I take my weapon and hide it in my coat. I must remember the equation written at the top of my slate in my hidden little flat, and I will tell myself as I strike that it is this woman tonight . . . or the whole world tomorrow.

It's a terrible sum.

Father, forgive me—for I know *precisely* what I'm doing.

Ruth Stephenson

❧

BIRMINGHAM, ALABAMA
SEPTEMBER 4, 1921

(LETTER ADDRESSED TO FATHER JAMES COYLE,
SAINT PAUL'S CHURCH, BIRMINGHAM, ALABAMA)

I've been thinking about what you told me, about demons and God and everything else we can't see—but still take for granted. You can't be completely wrong, and I know that for a fact because I've seen it myself, and I'm so afraid I just don't know what to do. You don't know my daddy, sir. You don't know what he's like, or how he gets.

You don't know what he's gotten himself into, but I'm going to try to explain it, and maybe you can help me . . . since you *did* offer to try.

It started back in January, when Daddy got caught pretending to be a minister so he could marry people, down at the courthouse.

Our pastor saw him, asked what he was doing, and got a straight answer out of him, more or less. I'd give him credit for telling the truth except that he'd been caught red-handed, and he would've looked stupid for lying about it.

(Daddy hates looking stupid. I guess everybody does, but you know what I'm trying to say. He takes it personal when you call him out.)

So when Pastor Toppins caught him pretending to be something he wasn't . . . they started arguing, and then before you know it, Daddy had to find a new church. He said he might as well make up his *own* church, if it was going to come to that, and at first, I thought that's what he was planning. But then he got drinking and talking with some man from the True Americans, who said maybe we ought to try out the Reverend Davis's new flock.

Daddy said no at first, because he ain't no Baptist, but this fellow (I can't think of his name, but it was Haint, or Hamp, something like that) said it didn't matter, because it was supposed to be a meeting of like-minded men, and anybody who wanted to hear the word straight from the Bible with a patriotic Southern bent ought to come on out to Chapelwood for Sunday services.

I didn't want to go, because I know what it means when somebody says "patriotic Southern." That just means it's made for angry white men, and to hell with everybody else, me included.

My daddy's been angry and white his whole life, and it's gotten him nothing but mean. It's gotten me and my momma beat, and it's gotten us broke, and it's gotten him nice and drunk a whole lot—which gets him even more ornery.

And that's about *it*.

But he made me and my momma go with him, out to Chapelwood where all the other angry men go. Some of their wives were there, too, but I didn't see any children anyplace. Come to think of it, I was probably the youngest person there, and I'll be twenty-one in August.

So we went, and I haven't been able to shake the bad feeling it gave me ever since.

We rode up to the main house, or lodge, or whatever it is, in a cart because we don't have a car, but that was okay with the reverend. He had somebody put our horse up, and greeted us warmly—like this was just any Sunday service—and I think Momma felt a little more at ease about it when she saw him acting like everything was fine.

The reverend was wearing all black, like you do . . . but it wasn't like a priest's black or a pastor's black. It was something like a Klan robe, done up in black instead of white. It had this strange gold trim on it that almost made the shape of a star when he held still and it hung down off his shoulders. You couldn't see his feet at all, and his hands were covered in black gloves—not leather riding gloves, but cotton, I think. Under those long arm sleeves, his hands looked strange. Like his fingers didn't have any knuckles or joints . . . they moved like an eel moves, all smooth and just about boneless.

Please don't read that and think I'm crazy.

He invited us up the stairs of that big building, I guess it was a house, come to think of it. Probably the biggest house I ever been inside in all my life—even though we didn't see too much of it, just the church part in the front. It was shaped funny; it made me think of a cross between a castle and the courthouse. There's lots of stone, lots of columns. Several towers. But it don't look like a church, that's what I'm saying. The stairs were wide but not too tall, and I had to make little tippy-toe steps to get up them without tripping myself. The whole thing was just so damn uncomfortable, if you'll pardon me saying so. I knew it from standing outside, from pausing there and looking up—or from looking down at my feet, trying not to fall when I followed everybody up inside . . . that's not a church, and it's not meant to make people feel safe or comfortable. It's not meant to be a friendly place that welcomes people from outside. It's a prison, and it's meant to keep people *in*.

I figured that out for sure once we went through the door. It was a little door, not something big and open that swings back and forth to let the spirit of God come and go with His people. And everything inside was dark. Not dark like *your* church, when the lights are down and all your candles are lit. That's a warm, nice kind of dark, and I can still see where I'm going. In your church, there's all that light from the colored windows, and it glitters off all the gold and the wood. Your church *glows*. This place . . . it didn't give off light. It ate light.

When I was a little girl and I told my momma I was afraid of the dark, *this* was the dark I meant.

I couldn't see my own two feet at first, when the door closed behind us. Hardly even my hands, if I waved them in front of my face. I blinked a whole lot, and after a few seconds I could see a bit, but I didn't see nothing that made me feel any better about being there.

The pews and the altar up front, all of it was painted black—and not a shiny black, like the kind that gets polished. This was black like a slate, without any gleam to it at all. There were colored glass windows up high, but they were real dark. The glass wasn't red and blue and yellow, it was dark purple, dark green, and I don't know what else. Maybe it was more black. For a bunch of fellows who don't like black people, they sure do like black everything else.

Folks started moving around—I know because I heard them,

not because I saw them. I think they were all wearing robes like the reverend's . . . or they were wearing something real dark, anyway. I stood out like a sore thumb in my Easter best, like Daddy had insisted. I was wearing pink and yellow, even though it wasn't spring at all.

Then my parents disappeared, or I thought they did, and I thought about yelling—but my momma grabbed my arm and told me she was right there, and everything was all right. Someone had come up behind her and put one of those robes over her, and I guess they did it to Daddy, too, but he didn't say anything about it. I think he left. I think they took him someplace else to talk with the reverend.

Someone took me and my momma to one of the pews and had us sit down, so we did. I was shivering, partly because I was scared, and partly because it was hardly any warmer inside than it was outside—and it felt real damp. It felt like the inside of an icebox with a block that's mostly melted, so it's all cool and wet inside.

I held my momma's hand tight, and she held it back, but she didn't really strike me as being too worried. I don't know if Daddy had a word with her beforehand and told her what to expect, or if she's just so used to being scared of things that this wasn't any big deal to her.

Anyway, the reverend started his sermon, if that's what it was.

Mostly he talked about how our idea of heaven isn't right, because most people think of heaven as being some pretend place, or something that happens to us when we die—but he says it's *not*. He says it's a *real* place, and it's out beyond the stars . . . so far away that if we looked up with the biggest telescope in the whole world, we wouldn't be able to see it. He says the constellations are a map, and that there's a God, yes, and there are other things that aren't exactly angels, or not angels how we've always thought about them. He says that a whole lot of years ago, these other kinds of angels lived here on earth. They lived in our oceans, and they ruled everything, and people served them. Eventually, they left us and went back to the stars, and someday, they're coming back. The reverend knows this, because he says they talk to him. He says he's found more maps, not just the constellations, and not just the things buried in rocks that are a million years old.

I don't know, Father Coyle. It all sounded like craziness to me—and if that's the kind of god who's coming back to call us all home, I don't think I want to go with him.

(But while he was talking, I got the weirdest feeling that the windows up above, near the ceiling, were moving around somehow. Maybe not the windows themselves, but the patterns— like they were swirling or spinning, I'm not sure. Maybe there were clouds overhead, and the light was doing funny things. Maybe my eyes were just playing tricks because it was so dark in there, and I'd been there for so long.)

Finally, the reverend was finished and I thought it was time for us to go. I said a little prayer to the regular God, telling Him thanks for letting me out of there because, I'm telling you, it was so dark I could hardly breathe. Does that make sense? Well, maybe it don't. But that's how it felt.

We stood up to go, me and Momma, and something touched my arm. I want to say some*body* touched my arm, but it didn't feel like a hand grabbing me—it felt like a snake, wrapping around my wrist. Cold and smooth, all muscles and no bones, like the reverend's fingers inside his gloves (but much bigger). It was real strong, and it squeezed me real tight, so I let out a little yell and jumped back, and it let go of me.

The church door was open, and a little bit of light came

inside so I ran toward it, and I practically threw myself out onto the stairs. I stumbled down them and I was breathing heavy, trying to catch my breath even though I hadn't run very far.

I'm telling you, I couldn't get out of there fast enough.

But I couldn't get as far as I wanted. I felt dizzy and tired, even as scared as I was. I didn't know where they'd taken the horse or the cart, so I didn't know which way to go in order to get myself home. I wasn't thinking so clearly. I was almost dizzy from all that darkness, all that being inside someplace so closed up and crowded. I wasn't sure what to do, so I stopped at the bottom of the steps.

That's when I heard them talking, my daddy and the reverend—or I guess it could've been someone else. Everyone had those robes on, and they still had their hoods up, so it was hard to tell who was who (but I knew Daddy's voice when I heard it). They weren't quite whispering but they were chatting all quiet-like, just inside the church. I couldn't see them, but their voices came floating down in bits and pieces, and mostly what I gathered was that they were talking about *me*.

I don't like that place, Father Coyle. I don't want to go back there, and I don't want to see the reverend again—but Daddy's already talking about heading there next Sunday and I don't think I can stand it. Please, sir, if there's anything you can do, anybody you can talk to . . . I need a friend.

I need *help*.

Lizbeth Andrew (Borden)

❦

I was making tea when the newspaper arrived this morning, hitting the porch steps with the usual graceless ruckus and startling the cats who gather there waiting to be fed. Sometimes I think the paperboy aims for them, and it's some stupid, childish sport; but if that's the case, then his aim is worse than his manners when he comes to collect his fee on Tuesdays. Thus far, no cats have been struck, and they are content to sit in a row and watch him ride past on the new red bicycle his parents bought him last month. They stare at him with lazy, narrowed eyes, but ears and whiskers on high alert.

They know a brat when they see one.

I finished the tea and poured myself a cup with just a dusting of sugar, and gathered the scraps and kibbles the cats have come to expect. Then I made my donation to the feline breakfast fund, and took a seat in my rocking chair to watch while they politely cleaned their plates and licked their little chops.

They have no idea who I am, apart from their personal kitchen staff—and they wouldn't care if they did. They are forever tidy, civil, and gracious, and I am charmed by their tendency to climb into my lap and purr . . . working in tandem with the tea to keep me warm on the chillier mornings.

This morning, it was chilly but not so bad that I did not sit with them for a while in companionable quiet—the paperboy notwithstanding.

I'm not being fair.

I'm sure it's just the boy's job, that he's been told a thousand times to aim for the front door. I've made that impossible for him, haven't I? When I rebuilt the front porch a few years ago, I made sure to give myself privacy, and the cats some shelter for the nastier days of winter. He couldn't hit the front door unless he came inside and stood before it. I suppose he does the best that he can.

But I've heard him whisper, when I've gone to town. I've seen him, and his nasty little friends. I know what they call me. I know what they say, when they think I'm out of earshot. It's nothing new, and by now you'd think I'd be accustomed to it, but sometimes it gets under my skin all the same.

I ought to be too old to give a damn.

But I *do* like the cats.

Emma, when you were alive, I hated to shoo them away—through no fault of their own, they made you sneeze, and you had problems enough breathing without their accidental interference. Now that you're gone, I can lure them as close as I like, and even let them inside if they're amenable to it. Most of them are content to remain outdoors, but one or two prefer the fireplace around January. Who can blame them?

Now that you're gone, and Seabury's gone, too, I take my friends where I can get them.

Sometimes even now, especially late at night, I think I can hear you, Emma—up in your room, which I've made into an office. I awaken in the wee hours to the sound of a bell, like the one you used to ring when you needed me. In my dreams your voice is no longer feeble; it doesn't struggle for volume, or crack when you raise it. It's the voice of a stronger, younger woman than I knew you last: the woman you should've been, and might have been, if things had been . . . different.

So if anyone haunts this place, I know good and well it's you. And yet, despite my esoteric interests, I'm afraid to make any effort to find out for certain.

I wonder if Doctor Owens haunts *his* old home anymore.

I thought I saw him there once, after his funeral. I attended in black and a veil—not that it concealed my identity in the slightest—because I wished to show my respect for a man who was such a fine friend and ally in difficult times, never mind that his mind was so badly troubled in the end. I needn't have bothered with my civilized disguise. Only three people attended the service, he was so far gone to the community by the time he left it for good.

He lingered until 1899, barricading himself into that grand old house he once shared with his wife; and then he left to join her in the cemetery by the old Presbyterian church on Eighth Street. I'm not sure who found him, but he hadn't been gone very long—I know, because I'd seen him only a few days before.

(He'd been much the same . . . distracted and disheveled, scarcely recognizing me but seeming to appreciate my presence. We sat in the parlor and had tea, while he told me stories about the lights in the water, or fish-pale things with starfish hands that he'd seen in his dreams. Disturbing, as always. But I owed him, so I listened to him and I let him talk so long as he was willing.)

At any rate, someone found him and extricated him from that house—stuffed to the brim with all manner of things he'd collected. In the end, the place was only navigable by a series of paths he'd either created or worn with his own foot traffic.

I thought perhaps someone would burn it to the ground and build something new in its place. I couldn't imagine anyone cleaning it out and restoring it, for the doctor had no family left who might inherit it and feel some sense of obligation to it.

But I've been wrong before, and I was wrong again.

Someone bought it for a song, cleaned it out, and listed it for sale. I forget who bought it the first time, and I forget who bought it the second, third, and fourth times, too. No one ever keeps it for long.

Which is why I wonder if he haunts the place.

I think he might. As I said, I remember walking past his house before anyone had emptied it and made it habitable again . . . I remember I was still wearing the black of his funeral, so it must've been that very day. (Forgive me, it's been so long. I forget the finer details, and only remember them by way of other minor particulars, which for some reason remain more firmly fixed.)

I stood outside his house and looked at it, very consciously not looking across the street at that *other* house—*our* old house, you know the one. (There are some memories I can't unfix, not for all the trying in the world.) And inside I saw, just for a flash, a tall shape with a shock of white hair. I would swear to you, this flicker was faster than a gasp—but there was a streak of maroon to it, like the color of the old smoking jacket he used to wear. He practically lived in that thing, in those last years. It smelled terrible. I wonder if they buried him in it. I bet someone buried it, at any rate.

I am not entirely certain that I believe in ghosts, but there's no good reason not to, considering.

I would like to think—and I know you don't wish to hear this, Emma—but I would *like* to think that if anyone was going to haunt me . . . that it would be Nance.

God, just writing her name.

I shouldn't have done it. I'll cross it out. After all this time, it's still too awful. No, after all this time, the worst part is not even knowing how awful it really is. For all I know, she isn't even dead.

That's not true, though, is it? In some form or another, she's definitely dead. Or she's so far gone, so far removed from me that she might as *well* be dead. I can only hope and pray that wherever she is, whatever became of her . . . she's happy, or free from pain at the very least. I can only hope, if there's any God of any merit whatsoever out there, that He'd grant her that much.

But what do I know of God? Not a damn thing.

Wait. I was going to write about the newspaper, and I almost completely forgot to.

The newspaper, it makes me think of you. Remember how you received so many of them, and so many periodicals, from so many places? Every time I collect the paper, and every time the mailman comes, I think of you.

I still order papers from out of town. I still order magazines, though not the technical ones you always preferred, with all the diagrams and Latin in them. I am but a layman, from a biology standpoint. That was always your field of expertise, my sister.

The things I order these days are either more mundane, or much more strange.

On the one hand, I gather gossip and follow the goings-on of the suffragettes and their continued push for women's rights. On the other, I order religious treatises from many different faiths, I follow their conferences and their research, and I keep up with where they stand on a variety of issues. (There's more overlap between the two than you might expect.)

On a third hand, someone *else's* hand, perhaps, I've become terribly interested in the spiritualism movement. Do I agree with every jot and tittle of their sprawling and flexible views? Not at all. But the fact that their tenets sprawl, and are flexible . . . that's meaningful to me. Almost as meaningful as their admission that many things happen that are unexplainable by science, or traditional (Christian, one must qualify) religious inquiry.

I know precisely what you'd say to it all—something about me taking my superstitious inclinations too far, right off the deep end. That's what you'd tell me, if you were here.

Well, you're not. And if you were, we'd only quarrel about it anyway.

So I watch with interest—and without interference—what becomes of their little enclaves such as Lily Dale in New York, and Cassadaga in Florida, Sunset in Kansas, Chesterfield in Indiana, Pine Grove in Connecticut, Etna in Maine, and so forth, and so on. In some ways, they are so progressive! And in others, I am not so certain. But that's to be expected, isn't it? Balance, always balance.

Regardless, I appreciate the broad scope of their search for meaning. I like the way they don't stick to the usual paths in pursuit of truth. Heaven knows the usual paths never got me anywhere, though in the name of balance I should add that the *un*usual paths mostly brought me sorrow.

One day, I mean to visit one of these camps.

I'll do it quietly—it shouldn't be hard. No one recognizes me anymore; thirty years will do that to a woman. That's one small grace granted by Father Time, in my case if none other. I am not anonymous here in Fall River, but should I leave, no one elsewhere should have the faintest idea who I *used* to be, and what I did (or did not) get away with.

The question then, I'm sure you're asking yourself . . . is why I've stayed.

I wish I had a decent answer, but you know I don't. I have instead a host of *in*decent answers, each one more frail and ridiculous than the last. I stay because this is my home, and it always has been, despite everything. I stay because I love this house, even without you in it. I stay because you're buried here, and Doctor Owens is buried here. I stay because Nance left me here, and what if she were to return only to find me gone?

I stay because I like the cats.

The point is, I *stay.*

You probably thought I wouldn't. You probably thought that once I was free of you and your infirmity, I'd take to the wind like a dandelion seed. But then again, you were always wrong about that one thing—I never thought you were a burden. You were my beloved sister and dearest friend. I wish I could've convinced you of it.

I wish even in my head, right now as I natter in this journal as if you'll ever read it, that I could not hear you arguing with me. In my head, you're waving Nance in my face, and it's unkind of you, really. I wish you wouldn't.

Maybe it's not the house you haunt. Maybe it's me.

As I mentioned, I turned your bedroom into my office. After I walled up the basement, that is.

I couldn't stand to be down there anymore, not after everything that happened; and once Zollicoffer was gone, the monsters stopped coming. So I emptied the basement of all the books or notes that might be of some use to someone, somewhere, and dragged the other contents out into the yard to burn them with the fall leaves. I would've burned the basement itself, if I thought I could've done so without destroying Maplecroft altogether—so I settled for sealing everything shut from the outside, and having some discreet handymen remove the door in the kitchen. They replaced it with a wall of such fine quality you'd never know there was once a passageway there.

Most of the time, even *I* forget.

But the rest of the time, when I wake up drowsy in the middle of the night and wander downstairs for a drink of water or to stretch my legs after a nap . . . I look toward that blank space and I'm momentarily confused. It's times like those that I worry for myself, afraid that my own mind is starting to slide like Doctor Owens's did. Or worse yet, like Doctor Zollicoffer's.

But I'm not a doctor of any sort. Perhaps the madness will leave me alone, then, if it exclusively pursues those who aspire to higher degrees.

So I took your room, and now it's an office—a fairly ordinary one, considering. To be sure, some of the books and papers are strange, but who cares? No one ever sees them but me. I've got a desk in there now, and I've moved your bed out into the spare room past the water closet. It took me all afternoon to do it by myself, but the damn thing is heavy as hell and I wanted it out.

Then I was sad that I'd moved it, because the room didn't smell so much like you anymore. These days, it barely smells like you at all—there's just a whiff of you, once in a blue moon . . . a tiny current will carry you back to me, a hint of that lavender perfume you always liked, or the jasmine soap you preferred. A note of your own personal chemistry, the scent of your hair carried to me light as can be, out of nowhere . . . and there you are, like you'd never left.

It's always you, and never Nance.

I've sniffed the whole house for her, on more than one occasion—closing my eyes and following my nose up and down the halls, all over the guest room where she last stayed, and all over my room, where she stayed more often. But there's nothing at all, only me, and sometimes one of the stray cats, and then that last ghost of you trailing behind, saying you'd told me so, all along.

It doesn't matter. I miss you both terribly.

In my heart there are a pair of holes, one shaped like each of you. No cat can fill it, and no one else even tries.

But I've done it again, haven't I? I've forgotten about the newspaper.

I receive one from Atlanta, a city so far distant that it may as well be in another country—and come to think of it, for a brief stint in the sixties, it *was*. Sherman may have burned it down, but it's coming right along so far as I can tell. Its newspapers are good, if that says anything in its favor. They cover events well outside the city, in other parts of the short-lived Dixie and beyond it, too.

But obviously, it was not the *Atlanta Journal* that landed on my doorstep . . . it was our own gazette—and our own gazette has run a story that I first spied in the Southern paper. Thus the connection in my mind. I made it immediately, and you'll understand why. Here's the pertinent bit of text:

> Still no leads in an ongoing crime wave in Birmingham, Alabama, perpetrated by an armed assailant the locals have dubbed "Harry the Hacker." To date, some eight people have been assaulted, six of them fatally—by an unknown man with a hatchet. The victims include city residents of every stripe: business owners, pedestrians, and young revelers out for entertainment.

Harry the Hacker . . . that might actually be as bad as the nursery rhyme some fool composed about yours truly. And dubbed by the locals? I strongly doubt it. That handle stinks of a junior journalist who wants to sell papers, and it's bound to work.

But whatever facts our local source has noted are dated and incomplete. The fuller story (or some version of it) is available through the *Atlanta Journal*, and I've recently mailed a request to receive the Birmingham paper of record as well. Not purely due to some morbid fascination with axe murders, I hope you believe me when I say that much . . . but because I want the details that were left out of our local coverage. The *Fall River Gazette* mentions the story only as an afterthought, a blurb of nationwide interest to fill a few column inches when nothing else is going on.

From what I've gathered via the Georgia rags, the case is much stranger than a set of simple assaults that fit a general pattern. There's talk of weird churches, anti-Catholic demonstrations, and eschatological street corner preachings. All this, in the midst of a city already plagued by the Ku Klux Klan—a group more sinister and suspicious than most people have any idea, and their public face is troublesome enough without any secret agenda hiding beneath their ridiculous robes. I tell you, they're stranger than the Freemasons and not half as well thought out, but they're radical, blind believers of awful things.

I don't enjoy researching them, not in the slightest, but how am I to confront evil if I can't accurately identify it?

This is what I'm trying to say: Something about the case feels familiar to me. Or maybe "familiar" isn't the right word . . . but I do *recognize* it, something about the details, something about the things left in between the cracks of what's reported. There's a shape to it that frightens me, even as it occurs a thousand miles away.

After what happened here in Massachusetts back in the nineties, is a thousand miles enough distance to feel safe? No, I shouldn't think so. Not a thousand. Not a million, either.

I wouldn't feel safe on the moon.

So I'll watch the matter, and I'll collect my newspapers, and I'll tack my clippings up around your old bedroom and we'll see how big the story grows. Maybe the whole thing will peter out and nothing will come of it, and that's an eventuality devoutly to be hoped for. But in case it doesn't . . . in case it spreads, and sprawls, I should really keep an eye on it.

Maybe I ought to go there for a visit. Let some idiot dubbed Harry take a swing at me with an axe, if some lone maniac explains the crisis. It's been a while since I've swung an axe of my own, but I think I could give him the surprise of his life all the same.

Father James Coyle, Saint Paul's Church

❧

Ruth has run away again, or at least I pray that's what occurred.

She hasn't come here yet, in any case . . . and it's clear that she's come to think of this church as a refuge. Maybe she's found some different refuge, farther outside of her parents' grasp. I'm not sure what to hope for. I'd like to know that she's safe, but I'd also like for her to *be* safe. The truth is, she might be safer somewhere other than here.

We've had to hire guards, for the first time in our recorded history. I can scarcely imagine it; who would've thought we'd see such a day? But the Klansmen come to Saint Paul's, and their brethren come, and at night they try to set little fires and throw little stones, and so we've gotten ourselves a tiny army to keep them at bay. This is a place of worship, for pity's sake! We have children here, learning their letters and their catechism—we feed the poor, and shelter those who lack all shelter otherwise. Why would they harass us like this? Why would they drive us from their city, when we've done our best to serve it all these years?

The worst part is this: I know it's only the beginning. The election looms, and it looks like George is on the way out. Without him, you can safely bet Police Chief Eagan will be sent packing, too . . . and then what? Then who is left to stand between us and the unruly mob?

Nathaniel Barrett's campaign is a study in horrors. He would make us illegal, in essence—he would starve us out of town if he can't run us out. His new laws would ban any business from employing any Catholic, a prospect enforced by a series of "vigilance committees" that would, one must assume, terrorize the locals until there's no place left for our people to earn their daily bread.

For God's sake, they even let the negroes work . . . and they firmly believe they're less than human. So what on earth do they think of *us*?

It all ties together, somehow . . . Ruth and the strange church, Reverend Davis and his "True Americans" . . . I suppose the reverend is the lynchpin there. The bigots have financed Barrett's campaign, and the bigots are led by the shadowy minister— who likewise lures the Stephenson family out to Chapelwood, where Ruth is subject to scrutiny, abuse, and threats presented like promises.

There's something black about it. Something dark and nasty, I know it in my heart . . . though the heart is deceitful above all things—that's always and overwhelmingly true. I have prayed and prayed and prayed, and listened for all I am worth; but at night, when the scurrilous men in their dumb white sheets sneak about the grounds, I look up to the heavens for some kind of answer and I see nothing, not even the stars.

I've concocted half a plan, with regards to Ruth. She must escape her father, and I must help her. I promised, and I will see it through . . . though my powers are tightly limited, given the circumstances. What can I do, other than offer her a haven that's under assault? I can pray for her, I can teach her.

I can marry her off.

Pedro and I were talking about this, after he returned from delivering one of the messages that Ruth and I pass between us. (For the last year or so, he's performed odd jobs for the family—as they've repaired and restored their house. He assisted them with some roofing work, and with some windows—I think he also paints, and probably does any number of other useful things. It rouses no suspicion for him to come and go from their home.) Pedro is old enough to be Ruth's father, and a widower at that. His care for the girl is less that of a lover than a friend, I believe, but he too is concerned for her. He's seen the fear in her eyes, and heard it in her voice. I'm sure he's seen it in her handwriting, which shakes more wildly with every missive. The poor dear is falling apart at the seams.

But if she runs away to get married . . . her father has no more authority to drag her back home, or to church, or anywhere else. Pedro is willing. I am willing. I can perform the service— and it would be legal, and binding, no matter what any incoming politicians would care to think.

Now all we can do is hope that she turns up safely.

If she doesn't, perhaps by tomorrow afternoon I'll go over to Chapelwood myself. Into the pit of vipers, yes, but I have the cross on my side, and a promise to fulfill. The girl needs me.

God, she needs *someone*.

––––––––

I've spent the last few weeks collecting information on this strange church in the forest, on the reverend's old estate.

There isn't much to collect, I'll be honest—what I've found through public records amounts to a hill of beans. Chapelwood is registered with the county as a Christian congregation, under the banner "Disciples of Heaven," which is as vague and meaningless a description as I've ever heard. Is it formally authorized to perform weddings and baptisms, all the ordinary things I can do here at Saint Paul's? Yes. The property was once part of a private farm, which was sold off piecemeal after the war, and Reverend Davis's father purchased the bulk of it.

(I think the church Ruth describes might actually be the original farmhouse, strangely augmented over the years. Or then again, maybe it's one of the barns, having undergone a conversion of its own.)

It is now privately owned by the reverend, though parts of the surrounding property are held in trust by a private firm . . . and on the board of this firm, I've spotted two names that are prominent in the Klan, and three others you'll find in the front row of every True Americans meeting.

The coincidences are piling up. The overlap, I mean . . . between Birmingham's corrupt politics and the Chapelwood Estate.

It might well be argued that bigots sit at the top of the power structure here, and so you might well expect to find them at the top of the churches, the businesses, and the political heap. But these newer groups, the True Americans and their Guardians of Liberty in particular . . . their rise coincides with this sinister place of worship.

I may believe in divine contrivance, but I don't believe in coincidences.

(Yes, I think there's a difference.)

My notes are thin on the ground, but I'll make a point to send them east, regardless—to Boston, and an old friend of mine there. He's an inspector, that's all I'll say about his job. A man about my age, or a little younger, with a head for peculiar facts and a nose for the weird.

Then again, maybe I ought to restrain myself. I've been sending him letters and clippings on the axe murders since the start of August, and I've heard nothing from him in return. He could be off on a case, and therefore out of the office. I hope he's well, at any rate. I'm sure I'll hear from him soon enough. He's not the kind to leave a man waiting, not on purpose.

I'd like to see him again. He's a jovial fellow, as strange as the Good Lord ever dared to make one—but a stalwart friend in times of difficulty. He's also tough to scare, and I could use his stouthearted assistance right about now.

Well, if the axe murders aren't enough to lure him out for a visit, I'm sure the Chapelwood matter will bring him around. I sense that it's more to his taste.

Ruth Stephenson

SEPTEMBER 19, 1921

I shouldn't have done it, but I'm glad I did.

Daddy wasn't home—he'd headed off to a "prayer meeting" and left me with Momma to set up supper for him. It wasn't quite dark yet, but dark was coming, and we had just turned all the lights on and fired up the stove when my momma saw the neighbor's dog digging in our backyard garden. She's been swearing and throwing shoes at that dog for ages, and it made her mad to see him stroll right on up and start making a mess—so this time, she took off her apron, threw it on the table, and said she was going to go smack that thing silly.

I didn't really think she'd catch it, but it was halfway funny watching her try. She ran around the yard with a rake, swiping it back and forth, never noticing that the dog was having a grand old time. He figured they were playing a game, and she figured she was going to beat him blue, and maybe go over to Mr. Marks and start swinging at him, too, since it was his dog after all.

Not much has been very funny, lately. Not halfway, or even a quarter way. Birmingham has become a city full of men in hoods, or men with axes. It's a place where dark churches swallow people up whole. It's not a place where too much happens to make you smile.

So I watched her for a minute, and then I heard something.

A thump, and maybe a sliding noise, like something heavy being dragged around. I tried to tell myself it was my imagination, because that's what you ought to do when you know you're inside a house by yourself—but you hear something heavy moving around in your momma and daddy's bedroom. Their bedroom . . . that's where it was coming from. There was something in there. I listened hard, and it wasn't my imagination at all. And it wasn't funny, neither.

It wasn't no happy dog playing tag. It wasn't my sister, because she had the good sense to be married and living someplace else. It wasn't anybody.

It didn't sound like a person, anyway.

It's hard to explain, but I felt that weird thing again, that dizzy feeling I've been getting a lot, especially since Daddy started dragging us all to Chapelwood. Almost like I'm sick, but not quite. Almost like I've been spinning around with my arms out, or hanging on to the merry-go-round while a big man shoves it faster and faster, and it spins so hard, so fast, that it almost throws me off into the sky.

Momma calls them my little spells, and says it's nothing to worry about, even when I tell her I can hear her long-dead momma trying to tell me something from someplace far away. But she's got her blinders on so thick, it's a wonder she can see the end of her own nose. Whatever's going on, she either knows and doesn't care, or she can't see it, for not paying attention. Either way, it's hard to respect her. It's hard to trust her, too. Whatever's happening, she's no ally of mine.

(Father Coyle says I shouldn't be so hard on her, because it's not really her fault. I know he's kind of right, but I don't think he's *totally* right. Sure, she's gotten used to Daddy and his ways; and yes, I know, she's doing the best she can to muddle on through this life like everyone else. But at some point, a full-grown woman has to be accountable for her own self, and for the choices she's made. That's how I see it. And I see my momma just closing her eyes, and pretending that none of this has ever been her fault, and none of it has ever been up to her. And that just isn't true. She's had plenty of chances to choose one thing or another, one person or another, one church or another. But she lets him choose for her, and that's a choice, too, isn't it?)

But I had myself a little spell, and that's a good way to talk about it, I think.

A spell is a magical thing, and not always a good thing . . . that's what I learned from the library books I used to sneak home, before Daddy caught me one time too many. My little spells are magical, and they are bad. Like I've pricked my finger on a spindle (and I don't even know what a spindle is, but apparently it's something sharp) and gone to sleep for a thousand years . . . or that's what it feels like I'm trying to do.

These spells . . . it's like there's a dark fog creeping in, coming at me from all sides, making it hard to see. It sneaks up and wraps itself around my eyes. It feels like the lights have all gone out—I couldn't see the light on the stove, or the gaslights we had just lit up, even though I could hear them hissing. I *knew* they were on, but I couldn't see them.

After a few seconds, I couldn't really see much of anything. I staggered around, holding on to the chairs to keep myself from falling, and I closed my eyes—because when you can't see anything, at least it ain't weird if your eyes are closed, and maybe that's dumb, but that's what I thought. So that's what I did.

Usually, when I have a spell, this is the part where I start hearing voices. Most of the time, it's nobody I know, but sometimes it's Grandma or our neighbor Mr. Miller, who died when I was thirteen. I never knew him well when he was alive, so I don't know why he's so chatty now that he's in the ground.

But I didn't hear any voices. I was all alone with other noise.

I closed my eyes and I saw that sparkling black light—you know, the kind when you've held your breath too long, or stood up too fast after being half asleep. Some people say it's like seeing stars, but it isn't. The stars don't move, not in those darting, fizzling patterns. Stars don't wink on and off, and go out altogether when you shake your head, trying to fling that spell away.

In the big bedroom, I heard it louder and louder: that thump, slide, and drag . . .

I thought I was taking myself away from it, but I must've got turned around. I found a doorknob and I turned it, thinking it'd let me outside—and I don't know why I wanted to get outside, blind like I was from the spell, and from closing my eyes. But I turned the knob and shoved the door and I knew, even without being able to see, that I'd just opened up the bigger bedroom where Momma and Daddy slept.

I opened my eyes, for all the good it did me. I saw only the shadows of their furniture, the bed, the two chifferobes next to each other up against the wall, and a little bedside table where my momma used to keep a Bible—but I bet she doesn't anymore.

And I saw something else, too. Another shadow, one that shouldn't have been there. Something about as big and long as an oak root, coming right out of the wall, swaying back and forth along the floor.

I rubbed my eyes and didn't see anything no clearer, and maybe that was for the best. I didn't really want to look at it, anyway.

I tried to move away from the thing, to get myself back out of that room, because it was the last place on earth I wanted to be. I found the doorknob behind me, grabbed it, and ran—slamming the door behind me—but then the damnedest thing happened, and it don't make no sense, but this is what it was: I wasn't in the parlor, like I oughta've been. I was *back* in the bedroom, or *still* in the bedroom—I couldn't say. I was so confused, so scared. All I know is I went through the door and I didn't go anyplace, and I was just about to stop breathing, I was so afraid.

Then the thing on the floor, the tree root, or snake tail, or whatever it was . . . it came for me.

It took me by the ankle and it wound itself up tight, and I started screaming—but it only squeezed harder until I thought it was going to take my foot off. It slipped up my leg, up to my knee. And the more of me it touched, the more I could see again . . . but what I saw . . . it *couldn't* have been real.

I saw stars, when it held me. *Real* stars, not the fuzzy kind your brain makes. I saw heaven, so far away and so strange . . . it was heaven—it must've been. Somewhere out past the clouds, past the stars—they went by me so quick it was like they'd turned into streaks, into long white lines. I was moving through the universe and it was all so bright and so dark, too, that I didn't even notice I wasn't breathing anymore. I couldn't breathe. There wasn't any air. There was only the feeling of being squeezed all over my whole body, and watching the stars stretch and explode and fade away.

I could hear my daddy's voice somewhere, even though he wasn't with me. I heard him and the reverend talking. I heard my momma talking, too, but not to the dog in the yard and not to me. I heard a thousand voices, all up inside my ears, and I was all alone in my parents' bedroom except for the thing on the floor that I couldn't see—but I could feel it, and it was trying to tell me something, but I didn't know *what*.

That's true, I think. It was trying to talk to me, using the words of all the people I ever met, ever talked to . . . It took the words from one person, and mixed them up with the words from another person . . . mixing and matching, lining up letters and voices that were so scrambled it was like listening to a thousand preachers all telling different sermons at the same time, as loud as they could.

No, wait. It wasn't quite so personal as that. It was more like standing in a hall with a thousand Victrolas, each one playing a different record. The words I heard in my head didn't come from real people, living and speaking. They were just recordings cut up into pieces.

Sweet Jesus, it's hard to explain.

I caught single words here and there: *lost, falling, come, why, drop, star, water, here.*

If I hadn't been so scared spitless, I might have written some of them down—maybe if I could write fast enough, I could catch enough of them to mean something. I'll start carrying a notebook and a pencil, in case it happens again. (I hope it doesn't happen again. But if it *does,* I'll be ready.)

I don't know what it wanted, and I don't know what it was saying, but I felt my whole body going limp from not breathing. I don't know how long I wasn't breathing . . . I just plain forgot to do it. But when I remembered—then I took a little breath, and a bigger one. Then a real deep one, and I started screaming my head off.

If these are little spells, like Momma says, then I broke this one with the screaming. Just remembering to breathe, remembering I could scream and shout and kick and fight . . . it *did* something. It shook me loose from the thing in the room, and there was this feeling of moving so fast—so fast that it made my skin ripple and my eyes bleed—and there were stars shooting by like gaslights.

And then I was just in the room again, all by myself.

Outside, my momma was calling for me. I guess she heard me yelling.

But I didn't want to see her or talk to her. I didn't want her to come after me. I wanted out of that house, and that's all I wanted.

I still couldn't see too good, but my sight was coming back. I felt my way to the door, and this time it let me out—it didn't send me right back in, so yes, this spell, I broke it my own damn self. I'll remember that next time: I'll tell myself over and over again, "You just have to breathe, that's it. Breathe, and then make a whole lot of noise." (So if there's a next time, when there's a next time . . .)

I have a handbag in my room. There's not much in it, only a little money I've earned and some personal things, and a little pocketknife I carry in case I need it. I grabbed it, and I grabbed my coat, even though it wasn't so cold that I really needed it.

So help me God, I ran.

I ran to the edge of town and right through it, right across it, where the axe murders have been going on for the last year or so, right there down by Five Points where the Italians have their shops and their restaurants, and the Jews have their family banks and their movie theaters, and the girls my age don't walk home by themselves—or with colored boys, neither, because there are awful men who will hurt you if they catch you together, that's what everybody says.

I ran and ran, and I just hoped that anybody carrying something so heavy as an axe wouldn't be able to catch me—but to be real true with myself, I wasn't that worried about it. I had bigger worries, and stranger things to be scared of than some angry folks with weapons.

So help me God, I ran.

(So help me God. So help us God. So help everybody God, because there's only so much we can do to help ourselves.)

I ran to Father Coyle because I didn't know where else I should go, and when I talked my way past the guard with a gun, and got myself up into the sanctuary where he was praying over his candles and his books, he looked real happy to see me.

He gave me some tea and something to eat, and he let me talk. He let me ramble about the Victrolas and the stars, and when I was finished—when I'd run out of words, and sat there shaking . . . then he told me he had an idea.

It was a crazy idea, but these are crazy times and I've got nothing better.

So help me God, I'm going to do it.

I'm scared, though.

I don't think it's going to be so easy that Daddy will let me go—and Chapelwood will let me leave and never come back—just because I take a husband. The law may respect it, or then again the law may not (around here, you never know), but that church in the woods sure as hell won't, and my daddy won't, either.

Father Coyle is a good man, and Saint Paul's is a good church, and it deserves better than what this city is throwing at it. But people don't always get what they deserve, now do they? Sometimes they get a lot better, or a lot worse . . . and I'm afraid for how it's going to go for my friend the priest, once word gets around.

He's drawing up a wedding license for me, and he's going to sign it. I'm just praying—to my God and his God, in case they're listening—that he doesn't sign his own funeral slip while he's at it.

He says he's not worried, that we'll put ourselves in heaven's hands, and all things will work together for good. Well, maybe they will, and maybe they won't, so I'll worry for the both of us. I've seen heaven, I think. It hasn't got any hands, and I don't think it cares one way or another how much we trust it.

Inspector Simon Wolf

BOSTON, MASSACHUSETTS

SEPTEMBER 23, 1921

Axe murders.

Apparently we need one great round of them per century, but at least this time they've happened relatively early and well away from New England—taking place down south in these reunited states. This particular spree occurs in Birmingham, Alabama. Named for an Old England city, I suppose, not that it's much of a connection to anything . . . and there's no sense in overselling it: These particular axe murders haven't held any real interest for me, or for the organization that continues to pay my bills—even after all this time, and my habit of offering bombastic, semiannual resignation notices.

These axe murders appear at a glance to be clear and boring as day—small shop owners and assorted pedestrians, often of immigrant stock, terrorized as part of some thuggish racket. Then, after the first few deaths, the demographic broadened to include young couples . . . particularly young couples whose skin tones weren't quite the same. Another easy guess, not worth too much time: The Klan has not so much a toehold as a choke hold on the city, and likewise it has a grudge against such mismatched unions. The math added up neatly enough. The Birmingham murders were (are?) hardly of sufficient caliber to involve our Quiet Society.

But then I got word today of another death, more mundane even than those that preceded it: a man shot to death, in front of witnesses. A priest, standing on the steps of Saint Paul's. Murdered in cold blood, for reasons yet unclear.

I knew that priest. His name was James Coyle, and we investigated a case together, back around the turn of the century. He was a good, decent man—levelheaded and prone to calm, methodical processes. He was not by any means the sort of fellow you'd expect to find gunned down by an enraged madman with a personal vendetta. I simply can't fathom it.

Then I got further word from . . . oh, let's not call Drake a "superior," for he's more like a traffic director than a manager.

Suffice it to say that I heard from our resident traffic director that we'd actually received several letters from this same priest over the previous month asking us to investigate the axe murders in his city. I was irate—these letters were addressed to me! And I'd never laid eyes on them! But then I calmed myself, for it was true that I'd been out of the office most of that time, peering into a potential poltergeist pestering people in Providence.

I'm sorry, I don't mean to be funny. (It wasn't funny at all.)

What I *mean* to say is that I was out of the office, and the letters were rerouted through a secretary who handles such things in the absence of operatives like myself. He's a different sort of traffic director, you might say. It's his job to open letters and packages to check for anything untoward, and also to prioritize requests and appeals. When I cornered the lad about his handling of the priest's letters, he trembled and told me precisely what I said above: The only unusual element in the axe murders . . . was the presence of the axe. There was no indication that this was something for the Quiet Society to investigate.

I hated him, because I knew he was right.

If *I'd* been the fellow processing the copious mound of correspondence we get in a month, and if *I'd* read about the Birmingham case with half my brain turned on . . . then I probably would have done the very same and disregarded it as a strange case, but not a *weird* one.

I collected the letters that remained—only two had yet been spared from the fire, and the second of those arrived after the good man's death. The first was a general recounting of the more recent deaths by hatchet, and the second was more of a personal note. It had not yet been opened, so I sliced it with my desktop blade and read:

I wish you'd send me some reply, but I understand how much you travel, and how much you must have to read in the homebound intervals. I almost fear you've not received these missives at all, and perhaps they've been dragged into some hole, lost by the postal service, forgotten by your clerks . . . but I have faith that the important parts will find you yet. I must have faith. And I must impress upon you, things here are odder than they seem—far odder than the papers would lead you to believe. I fear for the safety of this city, and for my own safety, too, yes.

Bad things are coming together, and it's sickening my soul to watch them join forces against us.

It isn't just the Klan, though God knows they're bad enough; but there are others like them, the "True Americans," they call themselves, the "Guardians of Liberty." Also there is a church, if one could be so gauche as to call it that. I've known many fine Baptists in my day—men with whom I could chat and cooperate for the greater good—but this is nothing like that. This is something altogether weirder and worse, and it calls itself Chapelwood. Between this unholy triad, they will see Birmingham burned to the ground. Or worse.

I'm afraid, Simon. For everyone. Please come, won't you? I'm afraid, and I am too alone to save everyone who might need saving.

He signed the letters "JC," as a gentle, sacrilegious joke between us. Jesus Christ or James Coyle, either way the initials worked and that's one reason I liked him—one thing we had in common: a propensity in private toward inappropriate humor. (Though I prefer to think of it as a finely honed sense of ironic awareness. Is that different? I don't know.)

I held the letter in my hands and rubbed those initials with my thumb, marveling that he was dead already before his hand-writing ever reached me—this fine man, assassinated on the steps of his own church, by a madman who . . .

. . . who I knew nothing about.

I had only the Huntsville office's descriptor to go on, and it wasn't much. Mad, and a man. That was the whole sum of what I knew.

But I would learn *more*, goddammit.

I packed myself some paperwork of the official variety—the kind that opens doors and loosens tongues—and I went down the hall to Drake's office. He sat within it, tired and old-looking, with a glass of scotch in one hand and a pen in the other. He took a sip of the former and asked me what I wanted.

"I want Father James Coyle to be alive and well, and tending his flock at Saint Paul's in Birmingham. In lieu of that, I want to go there myself and find out who murdered him. And *why*."

He sighed heavily, and for a moment the whole room reeked of scotch. This was not his first glass of the afternoon, nor surely his last. He folded his arms and leaned forward on them, using his elbows to hold himself up. "It *is* a shame about the man. I know you liked him."

"He sent me some letters before his demise, regarding the recent axe murders in that city, among other strange occurrences."

"Jesus," he said. I thought he'd take another swig, but he only gazed longingly at the glass. "You didn't get enough of axes with that Borden woman?"

"Can one ever *really* get enough of axes?"

"Now you're being an ass."

"You began it, sir. I'll end it by catching the next train to Birmingham, since we're both agreed that this conversation should take a different course."

He went ahead and took that swig after all, downing the contents in a hearty gulp. "You think there's some connection between this case and the Borden case?"

"Not really, but you never know. It's been thirty years," I said, almost tripping over the number. Had it really been so long? Yes, good heavens. Thirty years since the Hamilton murders, and the disappearance of the actress Nance O'Neil. Thirty years since the stink of death and fetid tidewater. Was Lizzie Borden still alive? I hadn't heard anything about her passing, so I assumed she must still be among the living. I cleared my throat and swept away the cobwebs in my brain. "The fact is, I don't really care if this is something within our purview or not. Coyle was a friend—an able academic and a fierce ally. He reached out to me for help in his last days, and I did not respond. So I will respond *now*, with or without the authority of this institution."

"I figured as much." Drake opened his top desk drawer and pulled out an envelope. He shoved it across the table at me.

"What's this?"

"A train ticket and a stipend, but don't get too excited about it. It'll only last you a week, and then you're on your own dime. I've already drawn up a file for this one—just direct your telegrams and notes to number 88193. That's also the code to start your phone calls."

I took the revelation in stride. He's not the chief traffic director because he's clueless; he's chief traffic director because he's more than a little bit clairvoyant. Sometimes, it's actually useful. I deflected the fact that I was a tiny bit impressed by saying: "Don't tell me *you're* going to start answering the phone."

"Me, personally? No. I don't like those damn things. Creepy, is what it is—talking to someone when you can't see them face-to-face."

"Says the man who consorts with mediums."

He frowned, but without any real vigor. "It's not the same thing."

"If you insist."

"Just call us if you need to, and mail your paperwork when it comes to that. We've got Gavin on phone duty, and during business hours, yes, he will damn well answer it."

"And after business hours?" I asked, one eyebrow aloft.

"If I hear it, I'll pick it up. Otherwise, you're out of luck." He opened another drawer and pulled out a cigar, and that was my cue to leave.

I thanked him with a short bow, even though bows are difficult for a man of my girth. I hoped he appreciated the gesture, and took it in the spirit I intended—rather than a gesture of mockery. In retrospect, it might've looked like I was making fun of him, but I didn't mean it that way.

I didn't think about it long.

I stuffed the envelope into my satchel and grabbed my coat from the rack beside the front door. I donned it, and likewise my hat. It's only fall, but it's been cold for fall. I try to be prepared.

I could have walked the distance to my flat; it's less than a mile, but I prefer to take a cab, so I flagged one down with a wave. I don't mind the expense. My expenses are few and my pay is substantial. I don't have to walk if I don't want to.

I wondered after the weather in Alabama. Not every corner of the Deep South is a hellhole of overheated air, after all. How far south was Birmingham, anyway? I'd never been before, but I had maps at home—and when I checked my train ticket, I was happy to note that it didn't set me on the rails until the next morning.

There was still time for a good night's rest, a few investigatory phone calls, and a carefully packed suitcase full of cotton rather than wool.

George Ward, Birmingham City Commission President

BIRMINGHAM, ALABAMA

SEPTEMBER 23, 1921

I am going to lose.

There's no sense in pretending otherwise at this point; Barrett has run a rich and disgusting campaign for City Commission president, and Birmingham has eaten it up—gobbled it up, really, and I just don't understand it. Well, that's not true. I *do* understand it, but I hate it—because it makes me bitter. It makes me think that maybe the city deserves whatever it gets with this scoundrel, if it's going to vote him in and give him rein to do as he pleases.

Ignorance and bigotry and money. This is what it buys you: Nathaniel Barrett.

The True Americans have purchased the office for him, and even if the voters don't hand it to him on a silver platter, I'm sure they'll see fit to have him installed. One way or another. Over my dead body, I'm sure—if I were to suggest it. They'd be delighted.

No, tempting as it may seem to surrender, I can't let it come to that.

I can't just *die*, and let them have this place. There are too many others who need an advocate, now more than ever as their voices are stripped and silenced, block by block. Good men remain here still, though our numbers dwindle in the face of constant abuse, threats, and harassment. If we all give up, then what's to come of the colored men and women? The immigrants? The Catholics and Jews? And for God's sake, when I lay it out like that, you'd think we'd have greater ranks to call upon. Our troops are not legion, but they are not . . . they're not *nothing*, either.

But when all's said and done, they're not enough.

The election is tomorrow, and I will lose it, and nothing will stand between that miserable bastard and the decent people I've served to the best of my ability. I am outraged, yes. I am sorrowful, yes. I feel betrayed—by those whose support I thought I deserved, and by those who damn well ought to know better.

Also, and here's the thing I mustn't say aloud: I'm frankly *terrified*.

Something is happening here, something worse than mere politics—these filthy tricks are the tip of some iceberg of awfulness, the scope of which is yet unclear. But I do not doubt, not for a single second, that the recent deadly incidents and the impending ballot box disaster are related.

The targets are the same, after all.

The immigrants. The blacks. The poor. Those who would dare to intermingle.

The first axe murder happened over a year ago, depending on how you figure it—because some say that the *true* first incident was almost a year before that, and maybe it's so; there was an Italian woman whose death I suspect that I ought to include in the roster, but so many people die every day . . . more of them by the blade of a hatchet or axe than you'd really expect. But this much is certain: Once Adam Besler was killed, the other assaults came quickly after. So if his death was not the first of all, it was definitely the first of a cluster.

Besler was a clerk at a haberdashery belonging to the Mangione family, down at the juncture where the streetcar lines cross and connect at Five Points South Circle. It looked like a robbery gone bad, and a poor attempt at cover-up, besides. The man was hacked about the head and shoulders, the store's cash was removed, and the place was set on fire. Fortunately for investigators, the fire was none too expertly set—and it was easily extinguished before all evidence was lost to us, including the axe itself. Whoever attacked him left it on site to burn with everything else.

Therefore, our police chief, Martin Eagan, set off looking for a murderous burglar. The neighborhood went on alert, the streets were given greater patrol, and everyone trusted that this unfortunate (but surely isolated) incident would be brought to a satisfactory solution before long.

Except that it wasn't.

One week later, Joe and Susie Baldone were killed in a similar manner while closing up their small restaurant, just a few blocks away from where Besler died. There was no fire this time, and no murder weapon obligingly left behind, but the crime bore all the same hallmarks of the Besler killing. Then two days later, at the other end of Five Points, Gaspera Lorino was attacked—though he survived, and still struggles to recover his full capacities, or so his sister relayed when I inquired last month. He was not able to describe his attackers, though witnesses put the blame on a pair of black men who'd leaped out of an alley, and we received a similar report in the wake of what happened to Carlo Canelli and his wife, Anna. (Anna survived, but Carlo did not.)

It sounded suspicious to me, and not purely because Eagan told me in confidence that he thought the witnesses were lying.

There's rumor of an organization, you see—they call it "the Black Hand," and it's known to give grief to immigrant business owners, extorting money and favors by threats (and application) of violence. Up to that point, all the victims had been Italians, or in the employ of an Italian, so that was the focus of the investigation—and the accusations of negro attackers sounded like a quick story, concocted to throw suspicion aside and prevent retaliation by any Black Hand members.

But then the victims changed.

There was Will Conway and his girlfriend, Betsey Frye, walking home from the pictures—both attacked, both killed. No witnesses. Neither one an immigrant, but Betsey was a mulatto, and there'd been some talk about Conway stepping out with her. Next came Mellie Hayes and her beau, Travis Foster. Same as Will and Betsey, though Travis did survive—and remembered nothing about the incident, or so he says. Likewise Jennie Heflin, who made it out of the fray alive, but injured.

None of the later victims had any ties to the immigrant community, and all were what could politely be described as engaged in "mixed" relations. It was an entirely different population under siege, and there were no witnesses to confirm or deny the reports of black men on a rampage—but again, I never really believed that in the first place, and neither did Eagan.

We didn't believe the whispers that came next, either . . . though I confess that sometimes, at night, lying alone in my bed and praying to God for guidance . . . I wondered. The stories couldn't possibly be accurate, but there was a certain . . . *symmetry* to them. A sense that they may not be precisely accurate, but they say something true nonetheless.

I'll put it this way: This is how I first realized we were up against something worse than a man the papers called "Harry."

I knew it when Eagan came into my office after a particularly long day. He drew up a chair before my desk and dropped himself heavily into it, sighing as if he were letting all the air out of his body—and with it, the taint of whatever he'd seen or heard over the course of his duties.

I had a bottle of whiskey in my second drawer, and a pair of glasses beside it. I served us both a drink and we sat in companionable silence for a while, listening to the sounds of the city's evening unfolding outside my window. Horses stomped and clattered on the side streets, and automobiles cranked and puffed up and down the lanes; storefront doors shut with the chime of a bell and the turn of a lock as they closed for the day; people called greetings to one another as the last of the streetlamps came on with a gassy hiss; and somewhere a block or two distant, a telephone rang.

"Must have been a hell of a day," I finally said, in case he wanted to talk about it.

"Hell of a day, and you don't know the half of it," he replied, each letter seasoned with the Irish brogue he never quite lost in the American South. "Good way to put it, though. Hell of a day. These axe crimes, you know . . . I've never really seen the like of 'em—not so many like this, all in a bunch. And none of our witnesses ever see anything of any use to us."

"Rogue negroes. Harry the Hacker."

"Horseshit, all of it. But I've been keeping the latest here," he said, patting his chest with one hand, and raising the glass to his mouth with the other. He swallowed. "Or in your office, if anyplace else. It can stay between us, can't it? Because I'll be damned if I know what to do with it."

"From your lips to God's ears, and no place in between," I assured him. He didn't really need the reassurance, I didn't think. I don't know why he asked for it.

He stared hard into the half-empty glass that he balanced on top of his knee. "This most recent one, the girl who got jumped last Saturday . . ."

"Jennie Heflin," I supplied the name.

"I went to speak with her at the hospital, for the nurse sent word she was finally awake. And she *was*," he mused. "She *was* awake. Her head was all shaved, and covered in stitches or bandages—as was a spot on her shoulder. She was all wrapped up like a little Egypt mummy. Her eyes were big as quarters, and her mouth was still swollen up from where she'd hit the curb when she fell."

"But she lived."

"But she lived. And she didn't want to speak to me, hardly at all . . . but I was patient with her. She's about Ellen's age, so I sat with her like I would my own daughter and I waited, and with a little time and patience, she opened up. Except . . ."

"Except?"

He shook his head and finished the drink, but held the empty glass upon his knee without asking for another one. "Except I can't say how much of her story had any grain of truth, and how much of it came from being hit so hard on the head, so many times. Four times," he clarified. "Four hard strikes to the head, then the one to her shoulder—or her back, depending on how you measure it. Someone hit her hard, and nearly killed her. That can rattle a body, can't it? And rattle a mind, too?"

"Absolutely."

"That's what I've been thinking, and telling myself over and over since I spoke to her. So this is what she told me: She said it was early evening—much like now—and that's when they tend to strike, isn't it?"

"Sure is," I said, offering the bottle, even though he hadn't asked for it. He seemed to need it, and he didn't fight me—he just poured himself another slug, though he didn't take a swallow just yet.

"She was walking home to her mother's house, after working in the laundry on Ninth Street, bringing home supper from the Jew's shop, 'cause it was right on the way. The weather was nice, and the night wasn't too cool, and she was just thinking how pleasant it all was, when everything went dark."

"You mean, she was knocked unconscious?"

"No—" He swung his head back and forth. "She said the lamp went out overhead, and so did the one at the other end of the street, and the one behind her—all at the same time, like a switch had been pulled. She looked up and saw the windows above her, in the flats and the hotels, they were all dark, too; she said she saw the outlines of the roofs and gutters up against the sky . . . but there weren't any stars, either. No moon. No light from the sky or anyplace else, and she could only tell it was the sky at all because it was a different shade of black."

"That's . . ." I couldn't find whatever word I meant to give him.

"That's what I mean—" He fumbled, too. "Sounds to me like

someone conked her on the head, and it happened so fast she didn't feel it, didn't know what it was or what had happened. But she insisted that wasn't it—she insisted she was awake, and alive, and she was looking up at the sky but it wasn't there anymore. Then she said she smelled something funny, something like the fish stalls down at the market, at the end of the day when the ice is melted and things are starting to stink. She said it snuck up on her, so strong that she could feel it—she told me she felt it," he asserted. "Felt it crawling around her ankles as she stood there, stopped and staring up at the sky."

I took a drink. All of it, in three long draws. I poured myself another. "Someone hit her on the head, Marty. That's all."

"Her eyes . . . they were all black, too. She said the smell crawled up her legs, up under her skirts, and it wrapped itself around her waist, and shoulders, and around her neck like a snake that was going to choke her—and she couldn't move, not for love or money. She couldn't break loose from whatever it was. She said she looked up at the sky, that was all she could do—stare up at the place where the sky ought to be, but wasn't. That's how she put it, George . . . *that's* how she put it. And that was the last thing she remembered."

I held the bottle in my hand. I'd been meaning to pour another round for us both, but I hadn't gotten to it yet. I sat it back down on the desk without giving myself another drop. "All right, then," I said, trying hard to be rational about it. "If you don't think she's made it all up—by accident, I'm sure—then what do you think happened to her?"

"Can't say. But I tell you why it sticks with me: Lorino, you know, the Italian fellow who survived. He said something about the smell, too. In that strange way, you know—he doesn't really talk right anymore, not even in his own mother tongue. He talks so fast, but none of it makes much sense. But he said that before he was struck, he smelled the ocean real strong. Like something dead lying on the beach, when high tide has gone and left it to bake in the sun. That's a funny detail, isn't it? A funny thing for two folks to offer up, after something like this happened to them both. They wouldn't have seen it in the papers. Nobody reported it, because I didn't tell anyone about it."

"That *is* a funny detail," I agreed. "But what does it mean? We're looking for a murderer with poor bathing skills?"

"I don't know, but it means *something*."

He left, and I left, and we went our separate ways for the night, but it's still tugging at me, hanging about in the back of my head. It's an uncomfortable feeling, almost like I'm forgetting something—but not quite.

So when I say that the dirty politics of Nathaniel Barrett and the axe murders of the past year are connected . . . I have absolutely nothing to bolster the statement except an uncanny feeling in my gut.

There are murders, and there's a police chief who's stumped and—so far as my opponent claims—is doing absolutely nothing about it. They've even implied that he might be at the root of the attacks somehow, which is preposterous; but then again, fools like Barrett and his "True Americans" believe a Catholic capable of almost anything. Their thoughts on that old church, and the pope, and everything associated therewith . . . well, they're far more ridiculous than a girl with a head wound who thought the sky was missing one night.

It's a tenuous connection at best, I know. It's a conspiracy at worst, and that makes me every bit as bad as the Klansmen and the True Americans. But I have nothing else, just a bad feeling about the timing of it all, combined with a horror of the elements that are pushing Barrett into power.

I fear for Eagan, after this vote tomorrow.

I fear for the city, and everyone in it.

Inspector Simon Wolf

⮜◈⮞

BIRMINGHAM, ALABAMA

SEPTEMBER 25, 1921

Through a convoluted series of events, I arrived in Birmingham, Alabama, later in the evening than I'd hoped. Train schedules in this part of the country seem to be more like general suggestions than hard-and-fast guidelines, and this observation does not immediately speak well of the place—and the legendary politeness I've found somewhat cool in tone. Then again, I am (as they still say, so help them God) a "Yankee," and therefore deeply suspicious . . . to the engineer from whom I asked directions, to the driver who asked a thousand questions about my accent, and to the woman at the hotel who looked at me through narrowed eyes when I confessed I was visiting from Boston. I may as well have said Hades, but she smiled and blessed my heart, and gave me my key without incident.

You'd think the war hadn't been over for sixty years.

Well, the food is good. I'll give it that. Mrs. Becker—that's the name of the hotel lady—told me that supper was served at six thirty sharp, and what she really meant was "something closer to seven," but yes, it was *very* good. Everything full of butter and salt, everything fried, baked, and seasoned expertly, and a side to go with every course. Biscuits, corn bread, toast. Puddings, potatoes, and pickled vegetables. I might have gained another five pounds just from looking at the table, but on a frame like mine, it's not as if it'd show.

I'm prepared to forgive myself.

First thing this morning, I collected the local newspaper from the mat in front of my door—and realized that my visit's timing is less than stellar. I read quickly while I ate another large meal—a breakfast whipped up with more syrups, jellies, and flapjacks than a man had any right to hope for in a week—and I learned that I'd arrived on the far cusp of a local election. I'd say it was a hotly contested one, but by the sound of things it was bought and paid for with a significant margin, if the editorials can be believed.

They are triumphant, these editorials. Not even pretending that their political victory had come from something other than the Klan's coffers. You'd think they'd have the decency to demur, but no—it's out in the open here. The Klan is very public, and very active; the paper reports on them like a local sports team. It's appalling, and frankly a little strange. I mean, they have a great number of negroes and Jews about. You'd think the hooded devils would be run underground by sheer population density.

Or not.

They're bolstered by wealth, privilege, and the momentum

of history. They wield authority by the force of a habit no one knows how to break.

Anyway, it's chaos out there on the streets of Birmingham, as far as I can tell.

It was chaos in the police department, that was for damn sure. I arrived at eight o'clock and helped myself to a cup of coffee, after a bright-eyed receptionist suggested I might take one from a sideboard in the spot that functions as a lobby. I stood still, sipped my beverage, and watched people argue, swarm, and come and go with boxes of belongings and sour expressions. Quickly enough, I gathered the gist: People were being removed from their jobs and replaced by a new staff—as a result of the election, no doubt.

And to think, this was the day I chose to seek an interview with the local authorities.

I finished my coffee, and having divined the location of the office I needed, I flashed the receptionist my badge and papers and set off down the hall.

The name on the glass read, "Martin Eagan, Chief of Police," but it wouldn't for long.

The chief in question was emptying his desk drawers into a crate, swearing under his breath, and ignoring a telephone that rang and rang and rang. He was an older man, probably a decade older than me—so perhaps his early seventies—but he was the blocky, sturdy sort. A boxer in his younger days, I would've wagered. His arms were thick within the sleeves of his suit, which was pressed to perfection with all its buttons gleaming. His hat was perched precisely; he wore it like a crown. His mustache was as fluffy and gray as two kittens tail to tail, but tamed with a touch of wax.

I rapped gently on the doorframe and said, "Chief Eagan?"

"No," he shot back. "Not anymore."

"But you've been the chief for a while now, isn't that correct? For the last few years?"

"Since 1917," he confirmed, never looking up. I liked his voice. It reminded me of some of the Boston lads—quite a few Irish among them, farther east from here. He sounded less like a yokel, and more like my idea of a policeman . . . if I must confess to a certain snobbery in that regard.

I tried another approach. "Sir, I realize I've come in the midst of a difficult transition—I assume you've been . . . let go, due to the recent elections?"

"I was offered a job as a patrolman, so yes—you might as well say I've been let go. *Patrolman*," he muttered, each syllable dripping venom. "After all my years of service."

"The offer was an insult, to be sure. My apologies on all fronts, but I do hope I could beg just a few minutes of your time." Before he could order me out the door, I added swiftly, "My name is Simon Wolf, and I'm an inspector from the Boston office—I was a friend of Father Coyle's."

He stopped packing and looked at me, starting at my shoes and working his way up to my eyes. It took him a few seconds. I'm a big fellow, that's no secret. Maybe not the tallest gent in a room, but likely the widest—and I, for one, am quite comfortable with that. I fought it when I was young, and now I don't. Now I buy bigger clothes, and look better wearing them.

"You were a friend of Father Coyle's?"

"Yes, sir," I said, keeping that professional deference firmly in place. "I heard about his passing, and wished to come pay my respects—and also, to see if I could lend a hand with the investigation into his murder."

He wasn't sure if he believed me or not—I could see it in his eyes. "You can pay your respects at the boneyard at Saint Paul's, but there's no investigation, Inspector. We know good and well who killed him. Even if half a dozen people hadn't watched the bastard do it, he confessed quick enough."

"He did?"

"Aye, he did. Finished shooting, and walked calm as you like . . . over to the courthouse steps and sat down, waiting for someone to bring him the irons."

"But why?" I asked.

"Because Edwin Stephenson is a hateful little wretch. Not entirely stupid, though. He knows where his bread gets buttered, and he knows he's going to walk, instead of hang."

"Even though . . . everyone knows he did it? What excuse could he possibly have?"

The former chief of police sighed heavily. He planted his hands on the desk, leaned forward, and looked at the crate filled with his belongings. "It's a long story. No, it's a short one— Coyle was Catholic, and he did something Edwin didn't like. Now the murderer will put his hand upon a Bible and call his actions temporary insanity, if you ever heard of anything half so preposterous. His insanity didn't come temporary, and it wasn't sudden, either. Maybe . . . maybe you ought to walk along with me. There's a bit of a story to it, and I need to be gone before Shirley gets here."

"Is that the new police chief?"

"That's him, and a filthier bastard you'll never set eyes on. He's crooked head to toe; the man must screw his socks on in the morning. If I meet eyes with him, I'm likely to take a swing, so it's best that I be on my way. You can join me, since you're not the sort who's afraid to talk with a papist."

"Thank you, sir. Perhaps I can help carry something?"

I took one box, he took another, and he slammed the office door behind him. As he passed, many of the patrolmen stopped what they were doing and removed their hats, seeing him off with regret, respect, and (if I read their eyes correctly) no small amount of fear. Whoever this Shirley was, it didn't look like his presence would be altogether welcome among the uniforms.

Outside, the morning sun was coming up hot and I wished I could wear a little less fabric, but such is the standard of decency among grown men. I blinked against the light and Martin Eagan ignored it, stomping toward a jalopy parked by the door. He yanked it open, threw one box onto the seat, and then asked me for the other so he could cram that one inside, too.

"There's no sense in driving, and the pair of us won't fit anyway," he said with regards to the little two-seater. Even without the crates, the pair of us might not have fit on the seat, but he was too polite or distracted to say so. "We may as well hoof it."

"To Saint Paul's?"

"It's not so far from here, and I can give you the story, if you want it. But," he said, and that rolling grumble of a voice was all vowels and dissatisfaction, "you aren't going to like it much."

He kicked the jalopy's door shut and walked away, pulling a cigarette from his inside jacket pocket. I was already sweating, and couldn't imagine adding a stick of fire to the mix—so when he offered me one, I declined.

"No, thank you. There's plenty of heat out here already."

"Heat? It's rather cool today, Inspector. If this is what you call heat, you'd best stay away in July."

"Duly noted."

He struck a match, and his mustache twitched as he sucked the cigarette alight. "But you're here about Father Coyle. How much do you know about what happened?"

"Almost nothing. I know he was murdered by a man named Edwin Stephenson, who expects to walk free due to temporary insanity. And *you* told me most of that. Word in Boston was only that he'd been killed, and details were thin."

Eagan cleared his throat and nibbled thoughtfully on the cigarette as we walked side by side through a pretty part of town. It was a lovely city, with clean streets, tall lamps, and signs freshly painted—everything in good repair. Southern charm, I suppose you'd call it. But so far, most of that charm appeared superficial.

"Father Coyle was a good fellow, and I'm not just saying that because he was a priest," the old chief finally said. "He was a man who cared about the people in his church, and everyone else, too. In the end, that was his downfall."

"There are worse things to go on a man's tombstone."

He chuckled without smiling. "True, but no one wants it carved too soon. Father Coyle was only trying to help that girl, and should you ever encounter the despicable Mr. Stephenson, you'll understand *why*."

"What girl?"

"Stephenson's daughter, Ruth. She'd been trying to escape that miserable old goat for half her life. As soon as she could walk, she did her best to run away from him; and recently, the girl'd reached an age where it was hard to keep her at home. I'm not saying she's a bad sort, because she isn't—she's a sweet young woman, and a damn sight brighter than her old man."

"So what did she do?"

"She eloped," he said simply. "With a man plenty older. But that wasn't the problem."

"No?" I asked, but I was already making guesses in my head.

"There were two problems, really. Two problems at the root

of it, anyhow: Her new husband's a Catholic for one thing, and a Puerto Rican for another."

Well, I'd guessed one of them right.

"The fellow's a day laborer who'd worked for her family in the past. Hung wallpaper, built windows, that kind of thing. I don't know him well, but I've seen him around and thought he wasn't so bad. Quiet, competent. Not the sort to beat her. She could do worse, I suppose."

"But her father didn't think so. And oh . . ." I made another guess, one I would've bet the bank upon. "Father Coyle was the man who, shall we say, *facilitated* this elopement?"

"Correct. She'd befriended Coyle somehow, and her father had warned her away from him—with a belt, I expect, or something harder. But she kept coming around the church to spite him, or maybe she was thinking about trying on a different hat, when it came to how she worshipped Our Lord and Savior. Maybe the street preaching and the shouting wasn't for her."

"What was her father's affiliation?"

"Methodist, of a kind."

"There's more than one kind?"

He sniffed, and blew a small stream of smoke through his nose. "I'd hate to sully the name of that church at large, and paint all the Methodists alike with a tar brush, you hear me—and to the upstanding local congregation's credit, when they found out what he was up to, they gave him the boot."

"What does it take to be ousted from one's congregation in the Methodist faith?" I asked. I really knew almost nothing about it.

"He was hanging about the courthouse, telling folks he was a minister—and offering to perform marriages for a small fee. Made himself a little killing on it, over time."

"There's . . . there's a market for that sort of thing? Sidewalk unions?"

"Well, say you're in a hurry for some reason or another. Say you're headed to the justice of the peace, and all you plan to do is sign a piece of paper to make it legal. Then say some nice fellow offers to perform you a service, on the spot—blessed by God as well as the county. Plenty of people have been romantically inclined enough to take him up on it. I think he was asking less than the courthouse fee, anyway—but I wouldn't swear to it. The point is, he was out there pretending to represent the church, and pretending he had the authority to marry people off. And he didn't, either way."

"So these couples . . ." I asked slowly. "They aren't properly married?"

"They filed their certificates like everyone else, but with Stephenson signing them . . . who knows? Maybe he's legal by now. Before he shot down the priest, he left the local Methodist flock in a huff and joined some other church outside of town. Not a church I'd want any part of, if it was me." He scowled straight ahead, then yanked his cigarette from his mouth and tossed it onto the ground half smoked, in a waste of perfectly good tobacco. "It's just another arm of the Klan, is all. No business mixing God and politics, much less God, politics, and hearts full of nothing but hate and fear. I don't want to know what kind of god thinks those fools are worshipping him, when that's all they've got to offer. Hate and fear," he said again, then drew up to a halt outside an ironwork gate with a sign announcing we'd reached Saint Paul's.

The church wasn't the largest I'd ever seen, but it was clean and well kept, and so were the grounds within the fence—which might have once stood for decoration, and now served to give the little patch of land the look of a fortress. Which, after a fashion, I suppose it was.

"This is it, and those are the steps right there. That's where Edwin Stephenson shot Father Coyle, in cold blood, in front of God and everybody. It wasn't right, and it doesn't matter. The Klan has bought his trial just as surely as they bought the election that's sending me home today. Me and George." He shook his head. "We weren't the only thing standing between this town and the . . . the *darkness* I feel coming . . . but people looked to us, and people thought we had some power to protect them. We did the best we could, damn it all to hell. And now there's . . . now there's hardly anybody decent—and anyone who *is* left will be out the door, just as soon as Shirley and Barrett can figure out who they are. This is the start of a terrible time, I can feel it in my soul."

He gave this soliloquy to the church steps, never once looking at me while he spoke. I felt awful for the man, so stalwart and aged. Dignified and furious, and helpless . . . his legs swept out from under him by an election that sounded about as upright as a patch of crabgrass.

A flash of pink cotton flickered at the corner of my eye, and when I turned to get a better look, I saw a young woman. She was brown of hair, blue of eyes. Had a bit of a corn-fed look about her, I think that's how you're supposed to put it when you're trying to say "plain, but not ugly." She was thin and nervous, her hands squeezing repeatedly at a small handbag, and her feet shuffling with hesitation as she approached.

"Chief Eagan?" she began, one hand reaching out for the man. She changed her mind, and used that hand to clutch her shawl closed instead.

"No longer, girl."

"So it's true?" If she looked unhappy before, she was positively crestfallen now. "They sacked you, just like that?"

"They might as well have. And look at you, speaking of the devil."

"Ruth?" I hazarded a guess. "Ruth Stephenson?"

She lowered her eyes and said something about yes, sir, and it was nice to meet me. I introduced myself as Inspector Wolf, and she then looked at me quite keenly. "An inspector? But not one of ours, not from around *here*."

"No, ma'am. I'm visiting from Boston."

Before I could tell her more, Eagan asked, "Ruthie, dear— what are you doing, coming around the church? You won't help the case, if anyone sees you here."

"I was looking for *you*," she told him. "At the station . . . they said they thought you'd come this way. I was hoping you could tell me something, *anything*, about the trial. Daddy's lawyer won't talk to me, and there's no prosecutor lined up yet."

"Barrett'll shoehorn some rat bastard into the spot soon enough. He just took office today, and he's still getting his ducks in a row."

It wasn't quite terror in her eyes, but you could see it from there. "Barrett? He's the one who decides?"

"It'll all depend. The case is going up in front of Judge Holt, I do know that much—so it's brave of you, girl." His voice softened. "But you mustn't get your hopes up, and you mustn't feed his defense by coming around looking like a convert. We all know how this is going to go."

Stubbornly, she said, "I don't care. I'm testifying anyway."

"Against your father?" I asked.

"Damn right. He's a pile of shit from toes to temple—and if he gets away with murder, then all right, that's what happens.

But it won't be because I sat down and didn't say a thing, when I could've said my piece against him."

"Brave indeed," I echoed Eagan's sentiment.

"Why are you visiting from Boston, anyway? Has this got something to do with Father Coyle?"

I nodded, hoping to reassure her. "He was my friend."

"And you're some kind of policeman?"

I hesitated.

She was the first person to ask me so far. Not even the chief had bothered, and as often as not, I can proceed with an entire case without ever having to lie about my office of origin. But sometimes I can't, so I told her, "It would be more accurate to say that I work for the federal government. I came here to help, if I could." The former a lie, the latter the truth.

"Then I'm glad to meet you, well and truly. We need all the help we can get."

The chief wasn't quite so enthusiastic. "No amount will be enough, not since the election. There's no one left who really wants to charge your daddy properly, and there are plenty of folks with money who want to see him turned loose and sent back to that pretend church of his."

Ruth made a face like she wanted to spit on the ground, but was just barely too ladylike to give it a go. "It ain't no church. I've spent a lifetime in churches, some of them better than others. What's going on at Chapelwood, that's just a gentlemen's club for men in hoods."

"Chapelwood . . ." I made note of the name. I remembered it from Coyle's last letter. "That's what they call the church?"

"I don't know what the reverend calls it on his taxes, but that's the name of the old estate. Listen, sir—if you really mean to help, I'd be happy to talk to you, but the chief's right. We shouldn't do it here." She glanced around nervously.

Eagan agreed. "I need to get home. My wife will be wondering if I'm still alive and if I've killed anybody on my way out the door—but, Ruthie, you might want to take this fellow over to George's. I expect they'll have quite a lot to talk about."

Ruthie shook her head. "I've got a husband to get back to myself. But this afternoon, sir," she said to me. "Perhaps you'd like to join us for supper."

"That's a very kind invitation, and I'd be delighted."

She gave me an address, and we agreed on six o'clock.

Then we all parted ways—Eagan back to his vehicle, the girl back to her new husband, and me to find a corner where I might flag down a car. I had no intention of walking back to the hotel in the increasing warmth.

Honestly, I don't know how anyone stands it. And if this is September, ye gods—what the hell can be said of their summer?

Leonard Kincaid, American Institute of Accountants (Former Member)

~~~~

I'm so very tired of the front page. I can't escape it soon enough, and, I mean, really, you'd think they'd run out of room or interest at some point. Right now, my escapades compete only with the elections and the upcoming trial of that man who murdered the priest.

God, I wish one of those stories would usurp me.

As for Stephenson . . . I knew him. Not well, but well enough to know I'd prefer to keep some distance from the man. He's always been an unpleasant fellow, nasty to everyone—especially his own family. I've seen his wife and daughter around town, quiet and browbeaten, except for how the younger daughter kept running away.

I've heard rumors that he's become one of the Chapelwood

men. If that's correct, it's no surprise to me; but he joined the group after I escaped it, so we never worshipped together.

I almost want to talk to him. I almost want to visit him in his cell, ask him questions about their progress and their plans. Would he talk to me? Maybe he doesn't know that I'm banished and hated. Maybe they stopped talking about me, after a while. Of course, it might be the other way, too—they may warn every newcomer about the mad accountant who left his place at the reverend's side, and now creeps through the streets to rob Chapelwood of its sacrificial lambs.

That's more likely, isn't it?

I think it probably is.

I should avoid the jail, and the angry father who waits there for his reckoning . . . not that it'll be much of a reckoning. No one expects a conviction. It's a jury of his peers, after all—most of them Klansmen, or True Americans, or men who are wholly sympathetic to those causes. I say this not because I know it for a fact, but because you may as well count on it. It's just been announced that Hugo Black is the attorney on the case, and that says everything you need to know right there.

This is not a jury that will hang a man for shooting a Catholic, certainly not when his daughter had run off unexpectedly to marry one. Furthermore, certainly not when he was surprised with a son-in-law from Puerto Rico, as brown as the octoroons who used to work the laundry by my office.

I haven't thought of those women in months. They were lovely, and they used to sing while they stretched out the hospital linens along the lines. I liked their voices, and by proxy, I even learned some of their songs. I wonder if anyone has noticed I'm gone. I wonder, if one of their numbers comes up, would she recognize me in her very last moments?

The laundry women. Good heavens, that feels like a life-time ago.

𝕴 ran the equations again last night, twice for good measure. I was extra thorough because I'm *always* extra thorough—I'd hate to get it wrong, not when someone's life and death hangs in the balance. But let me be honest: I'm looking for Edwin Stephenson's name or position.

Wouldn't that be nice, to find him in the digits? What a relief, if I could kill someone terrible, for once. I'd love to feel like my unfortunate reign over the front-page news is helping the city in a concrete way, and not merely a metaphysical one.

But I did not find Edwin Stephenson in the numbers. Alas, I never *do*. Instead, I found a woman who is not likely to be missed—if I am careful. And I am learning to be as careful in my murders as I am thorough in my math.

At first, simple success was all I hoped for . . . but with time and experience, I'm acquiring a skill set I never wished for, and never expected. My pen shakes as I compose this, but it's true: *I'm getting good at this.* So good, in fact, that I wonder how I ever managed to escape capture after those first few deaths. I was sloppy and stupid, and if my victims had been wealthier, more prominent in the community, more socially valuable . . . I think the authorities might have hunted for me harder. It isn't a fair thing, but it's been a fortunate thing for me.

Now they seek me in earnest, yes, because I've become famous and it makes them look bad. But now, I'm capable of evading them.

———

"My victims."

I wrote that, only a few lines ago.

I'm starting to think of these men and women that way, though rationally I know I shouldn't. Rationally, I know they are victims of Chapelwood. I am no murderer, I am only a soldier struggling to save the world—and this is what Chapelwood forces me to do in pursuit of that goal. And I *am* forced. It is either this terrible spree, or the reverend makes his summons and then . . .

. . . then, would it be the end of the world?

Well, I think it'd be the end of *this* one.

What I would give to be free of this equation, snipped off the graph, erased from the slate where I adjust and readjust all the particulars. Every night, with every stroke of the chalk and every tally of the sum, I ask the universe: *Why me?* And it's stupid of me, because I already know the reason. It *must* be me, because there is no one else who knows what's truly at stake. No one else who awakens with equations scrawled on strange surfaces, in his own handwriting—but no memory of how it all arrived. And there's no one else I could convince, either.

But there is a new number on the board, and this time the woman in question is an itinerant streetwalker. She plies her trade near the rail yard, and while she is known to the men who work there, I doubt anyone will notice if she vanishes.

So she will vanish. I can make that happen, with a little planning. Before, I would've only run from her corpse; now I am so numbed by experience that I can picture myself handling it, adjusting it, and disposing of it.

Obviously, I don't picture it with anything but disgust. But I can picture it all the same—and this is a new development, not one I'm particularly proud of. It is revolting. *I* am revolting, and becoming more so by the day.

There really is no hope for me. Maybe there is no hope for anyone else.

Chapelwood has gotten its way, and rather than make any helpful mistakes, it grows in power. It allies itself with the organized fiends of government and thereby lends itself credibility and strength among the hateful rubes who are so plentiful here. We are at a stalemate, that church and I—and I fear with all my soul (or what's left of it) that this is the new normal. I will kill and kill and kill, and Chapelwood will plot and plot and plot, and all that happens is nothing except for death upon death upon death.

How cruel it is, that I'm the one doing the killing.

All I ever wanted was to talk to God.

Lizbeth Andrew (Borden)

⮜⭑⮞

FALL RIVER, MASSACHUSETTS

SEPTEMBER 25, 1921

What the hell is going on in Alabama? From this distance I can only speculate, and speculation isn't terribly helpful for anyone, anywhere . . . not that anyone is asking for my help or suggesting that I interfere. I am merely a long-distance spectator.

For now.

I add "for now" because I'm beginning to feel a certain . . . calling. As if something there is luring me, drawing me . . . trying to seduce me into coming closer. Ordinarily I'd write this off to curiosity and boredom, for I have an ample surplus of both; but there's a familiar element at play . . . something that hints at things I've felt before, in darker, more desperate times.

You'd think that'd be all the excuse I'd need to withdraw entirely—quit subscribing to these papers, quit seeking more information from my journals, and from the more helpful tomes I borrow at the library. You'd think the familiarity would be enough to keep me quietly at home with my own silent ghosts like you, Emma. It damn well ought to be.

But somehow it isn't. Somehow, the dreams I've had in the last few weeks, they're . . .

. . . No, I won't. I can't remember them very well, so long after waking.

As for last night's, I only remember a sky gone perfectly dark, and a sense that something pooled around my ankles, and climbed them. It's not worth trying to write it down now. Maybe I'll leave some paper and a pencil beside my bed at night. Maybe these aren't dreams so much as messages—as ten thousand years of seers, clairvoyants, and witches have sworn is perfectly possible.

I'm none of those things, but I'm prepared to hope all the same.

Perhaps I protest too much. After all, isn't that what the boys in town whisper, when they think I'm gone? They call me a *witch*, and they say it like it ought to be a secret, as if it's true. As if I sit at home with my eyes closed and my hands upon a planchette—a board across my knees—summoning spirits and communing with the devil, not that I've ever done either such thing.

So far.

And so *what* if that's what they think? A cursory examination of Maplecroft would give their theories a fat measure of support, wouldn't it?

Two hundred years ago someone would've found a stake and burned me by now, for the cats alone.

Speaking of witchcraft, the awful boys, and the cats . . . there's a new kitten in the mix: a scruffy little gray fellow with eyes the color of sunflower petals. I acquired him down by the grocery. Two lads whose faces I know, but whose names I don't . . . they'd put him in a bucket and were rolling it down the street, kicking it into a spin every time he tried to climb out.

I stopped the bucket with my foot.

The boys ran toward me as if to reclaim it; then one of them grabbed the other's arm; he drew up his friend in a sudden stop, a halt of panic. He'd recognized me, and in doing so, he nearly scrambled backward to get away. You'd think I carried the axe around still, waving it willy-nilly to show my displeasure.

I retrieved the dizzy, dazed kitten and held him up against my bosom, where he silently quivered, ducking his head beneath my shawl.

The boys whispered fiercely back and forth, until the bolder of the two said loudly to the other, "I know who she is—who cares? What's she going to do, cut our heads off?"

"No." I held perfectly still, because I've learned that it unsettles people, and makes me seem more solid, more strong than I really am. I've become keenly fond of illusion, in my old age.

The street was quiet now. There were a few onlookers, their interest piqued by the commotion the boys had made, and their interest held by realizing who it was the children had trifled with. The ordinary background patter of voices and cars, bells on shop doors, cartwheels squeaking . . . it had evaporated.

I couldn't do much, but I could hold their attention. I could hold that small cat, trembling against me. And I could hold still while the boys worked each other up, to either threaten me or flee from me.

"What do you care about that cat? Is it yours? Witches have cats, don't they—are you a witch?"

"You'd better hope not." I let my voice sink low, and kept it steady. Not raising it at all. I might've been teaching them their multiplication tables when I said, "You'd better hope I'm not a witch, and here's another thing for you to hope: You'd better hope this animal is unscathed entirely, because whatever you've done to him, will be done to you *doubly* in return. And not just this one kitten, I promise you," I continued, eyeing them hard, trying to keep down the anger that rose in my chest as the tiny heartbeat fluttered in my hands. "But any cat or dog, squirrel or bird . . . any living thing you have ever tormented for the sake of torment. It will come back to you *double*, you little monsters. Any tooth you've broken, two of yours will be smashed from your mouths. Any head you've cracked, yours will be cracked twice as hard. Any damage you've ever done, pain you've ever caused—any fear, any sorrow, any misery . . . rest assured, it will be yours again. *Twofold*."

Behind me, and rather nearby, someone gasped. I didn't look around to see who it was. I didn't care. "And that, my boys, is why you'd better hope and pray that I'm not counted among the witches. *Their* words have power, you know."

I left without my groceries; I'll send the neighbor boy, Thomas, after a few tomorrow. I took the kitten home, bathed it, fed it, and left it in the sunroom to nap its fear away. There's a great ginger queen who comes around every night, a lean, powerful cat who I think must be too old to have her own kittens anymore—but she's been known to take others under her wing.

I'll see what she makes of this one.

I really *do* like curses.

They can't fail, that's the beauty of them. Any bad thing that happens to either boy, from now until Kingdom Come, they'll attribute it to my curse. Should the devils survive to adulthood, they'll tell their children and grandchildren about it. They'll blame me for everything from their ingrown nails to a fall in stock prices. They'll swear my name at every paper cut, every death of a child.

It's more power than I have, and more power than anyone deserves. But they're the ones who give it away, so to hell with them.

But Birmingham, Alabama.

My attention wanders so much these days. I must be getting old, or maybe I've only lived alone too long. You've been gone for twenty years, Emma, dear—and you must remember how strange we old folks can become, when we have no one left to answer to, no one left to talk to. Who knows how strange I've become without even noticing—since there's no one here to offer me an outside opinion on the matter.

Well, the postman probably thinks I'm batty, but he's too much a professional to say anything about it.

Over these last few weeks he's brought me two dozen newspapers and magazines from Alabama, and I'm fascinated by every tidbit I encounter about the axe murders there. The local politics are likewise fascinating, but in another way—or maybe not another way at all, because it's the same dread I feel on behalf of the population.

An axe murderer runs amok in their midst. The Ku Klux Klan buys their elections. Is there anywhere on earth more bereft of hope than that small city?

I feel for them, I really do.

Here are some of the more pertinent clippings I trimmed out from the paper:

HAS HARRY THE HACKER STRUCK AGAIN?

Birmingham Daily News
September 6, 1921

Another vicious attack occurred last night sometime after 9:00 p.m. and prior to midnight, when at least one assailant—possibly two or more—leaped from an alley. Struck down were railway worker Will Conway and laundress Betsey Frye as they were walking home from seeing *The Hound of the Baskervilles* at the Cherry Street Playhouse. Both victims were murdered by a heavy blade, presumably that of an axe. Although Conway was a white man, he was walking the town with Frye, a darkie from the Scratch Ankle neighborhood, and there was much talk of disappointment and disgust. Whether or not a man should face violent death for his preferences, the events have frightened the city afresh.

ANOTHER HATCHET VICTIM

Independent Press
September 12, 1921

For the second time this month, a young couple has been assaulted—perhaps by the fiend "Harry the Hacker," or possibly by several assailants, as reports are not yet clear. At some point before midnight last night, Melinda Hayes and Travis Foster were violently attacked as they walked together on Third Street. Melinda, a negress who worked for a Jew's shop in the Five Points neighborhood, was killed. Travis, a plumber's apprentice, was alleged by his family to be merely a concerned friend who was no doubt walking her home. Whether or not this is the case, he survived the attack, though he is not yet available to present his side of events. He remains in the hospital.

There are several others, but they all read more or less the same. The earlier ones imply that the previous victims of "Harry" tended to be immigrant shop owners or workers . . . and for some reason, the later victims were often mixed couples. One must wonder if the original Harry hasn't left, died, or become imprisoned—and some local fiend has picked up where he left off, targeting an unpopular segment of the population.

It is difficult to infer from the articles that too much police power has been directed toward finding the murderer. It's a sensational case, to be sure, and the press is clearly quite delighted to have the bloody fodder for headlines . . . but so long as the hacker sticks to the negroes and Italians, the deaths are more a curiosity than a concern. A curiosity, and a means to line the newspaper coffers.

I've seen it before.

There's other excitement in the Southern city, too. In particular, there's been an election that sounds like a terrible deal for almost everyone, and the papers don't even pretend that it wasn't produced by the Ku Klux Klan. If anything, they seem downright proud of that organization's sponsorship, as if the rightful order has finally been restored, and now all can return to normal; but then again, this distasteful glee could be a matter of self-preservation, everyone hailing the new regime before anyone can fall prey to it.

I can't help but judge them, anyway.

The most recent news out of Alabama comes smaller in scale, but makes for equally grand headlines—or revolting ones, as the case may be.

Apart from the axe murders and the local election, some terrible maniac has murdered a priest, shot him dead on the steps of his own church. I'll be the first to admit I was raised with a bit of bias against the Catholics—though I've overcome a measure of that, as I've learned more about the faith and its intricacies; but even prior to my awakening in that regard, I surely would've frowned upon anyone taking aim at a minister purely for his cassock.

Sadly, that seems to be the case here, if the papers can be believed. The killer was angry about his daughter's recent elopement with a member of the priest's flock. What a horrible reason to shoot someone, as if any decent god gives a damn how he's worshipped, so long as it's directed heavenward with love? What foul deity is summoned with bigotry and rage? I wouldn't want to guess.

If there are indecent gods, then maybe this "minister" serves one of them instead.

Did I mention that part? It comes up again and again in the clippings. The killer professes to be a Methodist, so I know he's a filthy liar and no friend of the faithful. I know too many fine Methodists, and while they might not prefer a Catholic neighbor, they'd fiercely protect any man with a gun unjustly aimed in his direction.

Minister, my hind *leg*.

STEPHENSON TRIAL DELAYED

Birmingham Sun
September 23, 1921

Edwin Stephenson is eager to demonstrate his innocence
before the courts, but due to the recent elections, his trial
has been pushed back to next week—when a prosecuting
attorney can be assigned by incoming commission president
Nathaniel Barrett. Although former president George Ward
showed significant interest in prosecuting immediately,
his failure to secure the election means that this is no
longer his decision. In the interest of justice, this is likely
for the best. It's well known that Ward was an Episcopalian,
and if that was not enough to confirm his papist leanings,
he installed the (now dismissed) police chief Martin Eagan—
a confirmed Catholic.

Could any true justice be found for Stephenson, a
respected Methodist minister, when the whole of the city
government was allied against him? It seems unlikely.
But now that the new administration has assumed control,
this poor man has a fair opportunity to see his case heard
and understood by a jury of his peers, rather than a
select group of unsympathetic men with more compassion
for a member of the Vatican elite who'd betrayed the public
trust.

A member of the Vatican elite? They're speaking of a small-
city priest, for pity's sake. His only betrayal of public trust was
to perform a wedding for a pair of adults who wished to be thusly
joined. It's not as if he mounted a secret campaign to steal and
baptize Protestant children. I assume.

No, I don't have to assume anything. If he'd done anything more scandalous than perform an unpopular wedding, I'm quite confident that the newspapers would've been more than happy to crow it from the rooftops. If the worst they can say of him is that a Protestant girl liked him, and liked a member of his congregation well enough to marry him . . . there's not much to condemn him at all.

I fear there's little chance of any justice. For the priest, or for that poor girl—the killer's daughter, who is set to testify against him. Bless the poor girl, she'll have quite the life if she stays there. A traitor to her race, her faith, and her family. That's how they're playing it, since she married an island man. Her father wants the world to know that she's an ungrateful wretch who willfully defied him in the worst fashion possible, again and again.

She'd run away several times before, according to some stories.

God Almighty, who could blame her?

Today, I received my monthly copy of the *Journal of Arcane Studies in the Americas*. Within it, I found an article that gives me true pause, true concern, for the good people of Birmingham . . . assuming there are a few, somewhere in the mix.

(**No**, that isn't fair. There are *some*. I detect them in the background, in the ousted commission members, the stalwart daughter of the murderer, the innocent men and women minding their own business when the hatchet found them. I assume they were innocent. I might be wrong, but at the very least, they were not actively seeking to harm anyone.

My standards for "innocent" might be slipping.)

𝕴 realize that it's not precisely the *Wall Street Journal* or the *New York Times*, but I honestly believe that the contributors . . . they honestly believe in the subjects they research and report upon. Though some of the stories and their details seem salacious, they're no more so than anything I've seen out of Birmingham over the last month; so it's not that I give equal weight to the journalism, necessarily . . . it would perhaps be more accurate to say that I view it all with a similar balance of suspicion and credulity.

And that's why this piece about American cults and communes leaped out at me.

(Excerpted for relevance.)

ON THE RISE OF ISOLATED RELIGIOUS COMMUNITIES IN THE GENERATIONS AFTER THE GREAT AWAKENINGS

Journal of Arcane Studies in the Americas
September 1921

. . . Throughout history and across the globe, groups of people have set themselves apart due to their social, political, or religious beliefs. Generally speaking, such groups are benign or even of a positive nature, planned primarily to form an association of like-minded fellows, or even generate an earthbound Utopia—one could point to the Amish and Mennonite communities as groups of spiritually inclined people whose communities are private, but scarcely scandalous, and likewise the Shakers in New Lebanon, who are thought to be peculiar, but hardly dangerous. In the middling territory reside the Theosophists,

Christian Scientists, Perfectionists, Seventh-Day Adventists, and so forth—with Mormons presenting a somewhat trickier edge case, given their propensity toward plural marriages and a purportedly Christian faith that feels improbable to more traditional Christians.

One step farther into troublesome territory (so far as mainstream worshippers are concerned) are the Spiritualist communities, which despite the resistance from outside forces, have nonetheless succeeded in creating a number of long-lasting and well-established gatherings. These groups may begin and remain small, as in the case of Reverend Highs and his "circle of faith" in the 1890s (incorporated into the Red Pines community in 1901); or they may eventually establish fully fledged townships, springing forth from grand annual camp meetings (leading to the incorporated communities of Lily Dale, et al.).

But most troubling of all, from an outsider's perspective, are the quiet, insular groups that speak not to Christ, not to the Hebrew god Jehovah, to the dead, or even to any of the somewhat unfamiliar (but well-established) Eastern gods or spirits. There may be elements of all these things present, but more often the group is founded around a singular prophet who professes ancient knowledge on behalf of some other culture: Egyptians are popular at the moment, as are Etruscans, Assyrians, and Celts. Through force of personal magnetism, these prophets collect disciples, money, and sometimes a small measure of power *outside* their circles; but the power they wield within these circles is absolute. They control everything: worship times and places, sexual relations, access to the words of the gods or goddesses, and even matters of life and death. And then the dangers to the outside world reveal themselves . . .

. . . And most recently, rumor swirls around a new sect that may be on the rise on the outskirts of Birmingham, Alabama. Reverend A. J. Davis began his career of spiritual authority as pastor of that city's First Baptist Church, but he shortly went on to found a new group with social views aligning with the Ku Klux Klan and the "True Americans." *(See also "Guardians of Liberty.")*

Something like a Masonic tribe, the True Americans focus largely on asserting political and ethnic dominance over those perceived as weaker or lesser, including all nonwhite persons, Jews, Catholics, and a veritable laundry list of other undesirables—prejudices which they insist can be backed with biblical principles. In the last few years this claim has been further supported by an influx of new members, including Methodist and Presbyterian ministers who have found their way into this hateful flock. Despite its origins as an ostensibly Christian or at the very least peaceful community, this organization openly calls for the subjugation or death of any who would oppose it.

While such groups as these are not wholly uncommon in the South, this one has taken on a freshly sinister element. According to our sources, underpinning much of the rhetoric is a new theology espoused by the Reverend Davis, one that promises the end of the world and the rise of a new age on Earth—one wherein the True Believers, True Americans, or anyone else appropriately affiliated, will find themselves exalted among the new gods.

On the one hand, this is not wildly different from the Adventists, who believe in a Second Coming that will destroy all the infidels in a lake of fire—but elevate the faithful into Heaven, beyond the clouds. On the other hand, the Adventists don't believe there's anything they, personally, can or should do to bring about this result—except to spread their gospel and trust that when it reaches enough ears, then the end shall come (in accordance with Matthew's recollection in the New Testament, chapter 24).

However, through some means yet unclear, Davis's disciples believe in some mechanism that can bring the promised apocalypse to a head, luring their cosmic overlords from somewhere out beyond the stars . . . and they intend to make use of it.

I wonder who their mysterious "sources" are. I wish there were more details. I wish it'd named the Methodist and Presbyterian ministers in question, because I'd bet my life that the Methodist they report is the man who murdered the priest.

I want to sit and think about this, because it's important, somehow.

The article is right: There's only so much difference between believing God is up in heaven, and believing there are gods somewhere out in space. It's a very fine line indeed, and a seductive message at its core: God loves some of us, and is coming for us—and he'll destroy everything and everyone we don't like.

It's a great galactic game of "Just wait until your Father gets home!"

Upon rereading my earlier notes on the subject, maybe that *does* sound like the kind of god a hateful man would pray to. A petty man, anyway. Someone who feels small, and wishes to feel big—someone who is full of fear and uncertainty, and would prefer to be full of power. Oh, there's a dangerous lure there, yes.

Is that what's luring me, too?

No. Something else, though; yes, the idea of a community does appeal to me. I haven't had one in so long, I've forgotten what it feels like. I scarcely remember what it felt like to teach Sunday school to the children in Mrs. Frank's classroom before the sermons. I can't recall the weight of the board-back books in my hands, the smell of the chalk and old paper, the feel of little hands on my arms—petitioning for my attention. I don't recall how warm and ordinary it felt to sit in church and listen to the pastor, or not listen to him, and let my mind wander—but to feel myself surrounded by like minds, in a comfortable place, and hear things I generally agreed with (but didn't think too much about). I must concentrate hard to recall the stiff pews, the thick old Bibles with the worn corners and dog-eared pages, and the jasmine perfume of the ladies who sat behind me in the widow's row.

All of that is gone, and has been gone for decades.

After the Bordens died, I had a smaller version of that community . . . for a precious little while. I had you, Emma, and I had Nance. We had Doctor Seabury, for a time. Maybe that was it, that was all of us, and the things we had in common were terrible, damning things.

But God, at least I wasn't alone.

Ruth Stephenson Gussman

❧

Pedro's place is not very different from my daddy's, except that it's an apartment instead of a house—and it's a whole lot quieter, even though there's people living all around us, and we hear them all the time. I hear people cooking, babies crying, children playing, and it's all music to me—because nobody makes me go to church.

It's a little smaller here, and it's in a different neighborhood where a lot of people speak Spanish . . . but that's not such a big thing. It's been helpful to us so far, actually. Daddy's sent men around looking for us, but our neighbors pretend they don't understand any English and they don't know where we live. Our building locks downstairs, and you've got to have a front-door key to come inside. I like that. It makes me feel safe.

Safer, anyway.

I used to feel safe with you, Father Coyle, at Saint Paul's—and now I don't, and I never will again because you're gone, and I feel like your church is at the center of a storm. But when I do decide to go to church, that's where I go . . . coming in through the back door, and looking over my shoulder the whole time. I go there to remember you, and all you tried to do for me. I go there because it calms me to sit in that chapel, on those pews, and I listen to the new fellow talk real low and quiet in Latin . . . and I don't know Latin any better than I know Spanish (just a few words here and there), but it's a comfort to me, anyhow.

When I sit in that chapel, in the warm and half-dark place lit up by rows of candles and the light that spills inside from the colored glass . . . I can hardly remember the stars, streaking past me like the drag marks of nails on somebody's skin.

When I sit in that chapel, I don't pray because I don't know if anyone's listening or not, and it feels a little like lying. But I don't feel alone there, and that's something.

Daddy's trial starts the day after next. I found out tonight—the inspector from Boston, he told me they've lined up a lawyer for him, a fellow named Hugo Black. I guess the inspector looked it up somehow, or asked around at all the right places to find out. He's got a badge, and that's basically as good as a key, when it comes to opening up doors.

I only just met him this morning, but I think I like him.

He says he was a friend of yours, and that's why he's come here. I don't know if that's true, exactly, but if he wants to help, I'm happy to have him. This inspector, he's a round fellow, a little older than my daddy, I'd wager; and if you were to tell a

Christmas story about him, you might say he was jolly. He dresses nice and he talks fast, and he seems very smart. He wears round black spectacles and shiny shoes. He carries a handkerchief that he uses to pat his face and neck all the time, bless his heart. It's not very hot at all right now, but he's a big man and I guess it's too much for him—after spending so much time in New England.

He says it snows all the time in Boston. I bet it's pretty. I've never seen any snow myself. Just in pictures.

Anyway, I met him down at Saint Paul's when I went looking for Chief Eagan, who isn't the police chief anymore. I invited him to supper because it sounded like the polite thing to do, and because I wanted to talk to him. It's not every day someone shows up and offers any help, and we could use some friends right about now. Inspector Wolf isn't from around here, and if he was friends with you, then he doesn't mind Catholics. I thought maybe he wouldn't mind a Puerto Rican, either, and I was right about that. I guess it's different in the big cities.

(Pedro says it isn't any different, not really. He says there's good and bad in every place, no matter how big or small. I told him we were running low on good folks, as they kept getting murdered by the bad ones; he told me that we still had some left, and look—Boston had one to spare.)

The inspector came over right when I told him to, at the crack of six o'clock. He brought a bouquet of flowers and joked that he'd tried to find a bottle of wine, but Prohibition had thwarted him. I laughed, and told him we'd had prohibition here longer than most anybody; they chased all that stuff out of town back in 1909.

Or they tried to. If anybody really wanted a drink, most everybody knew where to find one.

"That's always the case," he agreed. "In Boston, I can find any spirit in under an hour. We have some of the finest speakeasies in the nation, or so they tell me. Mind you, a friend of mine in San Francisco would argue. He insists they have the market cornered out in California, but I haven't been there lately, so I can't swear to it one way or another."

He hung up his jacket with apologies, and I said he ought to make himself comfortable. I opened a window or two, to let the cooking warmth outside. He took a seat as near to the fresh air as possible, thanked me, and shook Pedro's hand when he appeared.

"Inspector Simon Wolf," he introduced himself like a gentleman.

"Pedro Gussman. Ruthie told me about you. Welcome to our home."

I made fried chicken and rice with gravy, corn bread and okra, and there was banana pudding for dessert. The inspector was very cheerful about the meal, and I could see how he came to such a comfortable size. I took it as a compliment that he finished everything, and cleared out the seconds when he was invited to help himself.

"It's not that we don't have good home cooking back east," he said, ladling the last of the okra onto his plate. "We do, of course. But the flavors are different, the spices and the seasoning. Okra, for heaven's sake—you can't get *okra* in Boston. And it breaks my heart, because I fear I've already developed a deep-seated fondness for it. It simply isn't fair, when earth's bounty of deliciousness can't grow all in one place."

But over the pudding, the talk got more serious.

We needed time to build up to it, I guess. Murder is a hard subject for a getting-to-know-you chat. He started gently, pushing his plate away and placing his napkin on the table.

"You know, it's been ten years since James Coyle and I first met. He was in New York for a conference, and I was there for . . . something else entirely. We were both snowed in, at the same hotel," he said, so softly he might've been talking to himself. Then, a little louder, "We weren't always very good about staying in touch—but we visited whenever the opportunity presented itself."

"When was the last time you saw him?" my husband asked.

He thought about it a moment, and said, "Last October. He was passing through Boston for a few days, and I played tour guide. We ate at some wonderful places, took in some wonderful sights, and had some wonderful conversations. It doesn't feel so long ago as that, but I suppose it must have been." He sighed and removed his glasses, wiping them clean on his shirtsleeve. "For the last few weeks, I've been away from my office on a case . . . and I did not receive his letters until it was too late."

My ears perked up. "Letters?"

"He'd been asking me to visit this fine city, but not on any pleasure tour, I'm afraid. His letters were primarily about the axe murders you've been experiencing . . . but his last one, that was different. He wrote about the Klan, of course, and its affiliate groups—and he mentioned a church as well. You know of it, I believe. You mentioned it this morning."

"Chapelwood." The word squeaked out of my mouth. "He told you about it?"

"Only a little. Now that he's gone, you'll have to tell me the rest."

I cleared my throat and took a sip of water, not knowing how much to say, or how to say it. He might think I was crazy, and then he might not help me. So I had to be careful. I started off slow.

"There used to be a big farm on the outside of town. Most of the land's been sold off now, so these days, the man who owns the old farmhouse and the like . . . his name's Davis. He's a reverend, of some kind. He took the farmhouse and built it up a bunch, and turned it into his own church. And that's what Chapelwood is."

"What denomination does Chapelwood represent?"

I took some more water, and shrugged. "They call themselves the Disciples of Heaven, for whatever that means. There's a bunch of different folks who go out there to worship: Methodists, Baptists, Presbyterians."

"No Catholics, I'd wager." He said that part with a strange gleam in his eyes. Not like he was happy and trying not to laugh, but like he was real interested in the answer.

Pedro said, "No, no Catholics. They're scared to death of Catholics."

"They really *are*," I added. "They have all these pamphlets they pass around, talking about how the pope is the Antichrist, and he's going to end up running America if we let the church get a foothold in the states. A lot of crazy stuff, and none of it true, so far as I know."

"It doesn't have to be true. It only has to fall in line with what people want to believe," the inspector said. "People want to be told that they're afraid of all the right things. It's easier that way. They don't have to go to the trouble of learning anything new."

"You don't think much of people in general," Pedro said. It wasn't really a question.

The inspector shook his head, then did a little shrug. "In general, perhaps. But I've known enough good ones to prevent me from outright misanthropy. Like the good father, for example. May he rest in peace."

My husband crossed himself without even thinking. I copied him, a little slower. I'm still picking up the habits, and I sometimes do the sign in the wrong order. While I was working on getting the motions right, Pedro pressed on. "But you're a policeman, yes? You must see the devil's work every day."

"The devil's work—" He snorted, then stopped himself, almost like he was changing his mind. "There's evil enough in the average human heart . . . we really have no need for a devil. That said, there are terrible things out there. I've seen them myself, and have a hearty respect for them. I shouldn't jest. I didn't *mean* to jest. I apologize."

We all got real quiet, and for a minute, I wanted to tell him everything. Maybe he wouldn't think I was crazy after all. Maybe he'd listen, and believe me—if he'd really seen terrible things that weren't caused by human hands. I opened my mouth, but closed it again. I didn't know how to tell him about the spells, the stars, or the thing in my parents' bedroom. I couldn't find any words that would make it sound like a very bad truth, and not a made-up lie.

The inspector watched me, and I halfway wondered if he was reading my mind. He had that thoughtful look on his face, staring hard without meaning to, I think. Finally he said, "So let's not talk of Chapelwood, if you find it upsetting."

He was being smart and kind, and trying to change the subject for me. But I screwed it up, and blurted out: "I've been to it."

"You've attended services there?"

Pedro put his hand on mine, offering me some of his strength, if I needed it. I let it sit there, and clenched my fist shut. "A handful of times. My daddy's a member. He made me go."

"Do you think the church has anything to do with why your father killed Father Coyle?"

I let go of Pedro's hand and hugged my own arms, thinking maybe it was just the chill of leaving the windows open—but knowing better, deep down. "Maybe, maybe not. It's a weird place, though. Weird and dark, and it stayed with me, every time. I'd smell it on my clothes and in my hair for days after we went. It smelled like . . ." I was hunting for words again, trying to pick them carefully. "Like lightning about to strike. Something like that, and something like the ocean, too. A little bit like the fish and crabs down at the grocer's, when they get a shipment from the Gulf. I'm sorry . . . it's hard to explain."

He nodded anyway, as if I'd told him something useful. "Sometimes a strangely shaped problem requires a strange description, and you're doing a wonderful job of it. I'm having quite a time, though, trying to understand it all. This is quite a scene you've got here in Alabama."

"Axe murders, unnatural churches, and priest-killers," Pedro agreed. "Our newspapers are thick with it."

"Yes, journalists always *do* love a brutal death." He wore a sad-looking smile. His eyes went far away, and he said, "But not just here. Frankly, I'm surprised the rest of the nation isn't lapping up the blood, spreading the story from coast to coast. I've seen a small mention of it here and there, but hardly the circus that comes to surround . . . other stories of this type."

I frowned at him, because I couldn't imagine any other stories like ours having happened before, except maybe that lady who killed her parents with the hatchet . . . and that was a long time ago. "Stories of this type? Axes, and killings? Like Lizzie Borden?"

He looked surprised, then pleased with me. "Her case was a special one, yes. And it happened years before you were born, unless I wildly misjudge your age."

I'm not sure why, but that made me blush. "I've heard the skip-rope song, that's all. About her, and the axe murders."

"Truly, that poor woman shall live on forever on playgrounds and schoolyards."

Pedro's eyebrow went straight up his forehead. "That poor woman? Why would you say that? She *killed* people."

"Not according to the court," the inspector argued. "There was no real evidence against her, so either she didn't do it, or she got away with it cleanly. The world may never know. And yes, I said 'that poor woman' because I meant it. I met her . . ." His voice trailed away.

"You did?" I asked. It was rude to be so interested in something so awful—that's what my momma would've said, but she wasn't there, and I was interested anyway. Besides, it was pretty obvious that the inspector liked to talk. I was just being a good hostess, giving him an excuse.

"Yes, I did. A handful of times, many years ago. Not so long after her trial," he explained. "She lived alone with her sister in a big house, in that same town. It was a beautiful place."

"Were you investigating *her* axe murders?" I pressed.

"Oh, heavens no. And again, Miss Borden remains innocent in the eyes of the law. But no, my trip to Fall River had nothing to do with that case. There were some . . . other crimes. A couple of years after that. Her sister proved a valuable witness."

He was staring off into nowhere again, thinking hard about something. His voice came and went, like a radio tuning in and out. "A man who had been corresponding with her sister . . . well, he'd gone quite mad, you see. He went on a killing spree, murdered . . . oh, I forget how many people, in some of the most gruesome ways. The worst of it was kept out of the papers, of course. We never released the details. No one would've wanted to hear them, believe me. I wish I could forget them myself."

"Did you catch him?" I asked. I sounded too eager, I bet.

"Catch him? That's a hard question to answer," he told me, and now I got the feeling he was the one being careful about how he chose his words. "The murders stopped, and I believe justice was served. But the particulars are classified, you understand."

I didn't understand, but I wasn't about to tell him that. "Sure, sure. But the Bordens . . . Lizzie and her sister . . . they were all right? Nobody murdered them, that's what you mean?"

"Nobody murdered them, that is correct."

Pedro wanted to know, "What was she like, Lizzie Borden? Do you think she killed those people?"

"I think . . . I think that there was much more to the story than any of us will ever know," he answered the second bit first. "As for the rest, it's not for me to speculate. She was a small woman, average in appearance, but with a sturdy look to her— and she was stronger than you'd expect, or so I'd wager. Pleasant, well spoken, well educated. But very, very lonely. I liked what little I knew of her. I believe that she was trying hard . . . to do the right thing."

I thought it was a mighty strange way to sum up an axe murderess, or an *alleged* axe murderess, to borrow one of Chief Eagan's expressions. Maybe he did, too, because he wound up finishing on a different note after all.

"That said, all of this . . . her case, that other case . . . they were years and years ago. I should probably say something else instead: I hope these intervening years have treated her fairly—and she's either found the peace she wished for, or the justice she had coming."

Leonard Kincaid, American Institute of Accountants (Former Member)

BIRMINGHAM, ALABAMA

SEPTEMBER 26, 1921

The rail yard between the stationary boxcars was as dark as Chapelwood. Row by row those cars were lined up, like children's blocks; all along the rails, sometimes eight or ten cars deep they sat. Many of them were packed with freight, stopped at this junction in order to switch engines or find themselves redirected elsewhere, but many of them were empty, too. Hobos knew about them, and they camped inside some of the better ones.

I had to avoid those hobos when I caught wind of them, either by their tin-can cookery and small fires, or their mumbled conversations held upon the couplers, over a bottle of whatever booze was cheapest and easiest to get.

I also had to avoid the rail yard men, though by that hour

there weren't so many of them. They were guards who took their guarding duties only semi-seriously—tired men, most of them, who'd rather be home in bed by midnight than stuck on the graveyard shift.

Mostly they ignored the boxcar men, but sometimes they engaged them, trading cigarettes for news or letters. Rarely, if things got too rowdy or a fight broke out, they'd separate the participants and boot them from the grounds.

Here and there a dog barked . . . at me, or at another dog, or at a man with a can of beans who might be persuaded to share. The dogs were not really guard dogs; they were only part of the background scenery, part of this weird and clandestine community that survived between the cracks.

So too was Lorna Weeks.

The women who'd sell themselves down by the boxcars . . . they weren't there by preference, and there weren't too many of them. It was a last stop of sorts; I could see that when I watched from the shadows. These were the lowest men, and lower still were the women who scavenged there among them. They traded in favors more than cash, and sometimes alcohol or cigarettes. They were sick, or addicted to something they could no longer afford. They were not women with options.

It is true, I pitied them. I pity anyone without options.

It is also true that I found them revolting. Not only the whores, but likewise the filthy men who watched them from the corners with their narrowed, bloodshot eyes. Some may have been merely unlucky, and fallen to a place where, like the women, they'd exhausted all other paths. Since I could not tell from looking who might be virtuous and who might be a criminal, I tried to give them each the benefit of a doubt even as I veered far away from any contact. Still, their odors settled and wafted between the lines—the reek of unwashed bodies and smoke, of illicit gin and rotten food. I felt the fog of it work into my hair and sink into my skin. The virtuous and the criminal all smelled alike to me.

But I had a task.

An unpleasant one, made all the more unpleasant by the surroundings. I tried to take comfort in knowing that Miss Weeks would be an easy capture, and her disappearance would be unlikely to make the news; and for that matter, I was nearly doing her a favor by removing her from this miserable life to which she clung, if barely. But try as I might to wring some good feeling from my excuses, I failed on every front.

I watched for her from behind the station house, a good vantage point for the comings and goings of the folks and creatures who wandered in and out of the rail yard property.

There was very little light. Only a few gas fixtures, and most of those were behind me, or at the edges of the fenced-off zones. Here and there, tiny fires were lit but closely guarded, and they were no help to me. Everything was black, so very black . . . that I looked up in case I might spot the moon or some useful glint of stars, but there was nothing at all up there. It might as well have been a well-washed blackboard.

I thought of this comparison, and when I checked the sky a second time I could almost see my own handwriting inscribed upon it—my own sums, tallies, and figures with tiny notes of script slotted throughout. I watched the numbers wink in and out like the stars should have done, and it unnerved me.

I closed my eyes and shook it all away.

Except that when I opened my eyes again, the sky was still abnormally flat, and I felt like it was pressing down low, a smothering pillow held down upon my face. My scrawling script was gone, but the sense of menace remained.

I wished to shake that away, too, but it wouldn't leave and I couldn't leave—not yet. Not until I'd found and killed and disposed of Lorna Weeks.

I didn't know what she looked like, but that didn't matter. It hadn't mattered in the last four or five killings, either; I could find them whether or not I had any description. This was one of the new skills I'd learned . . . or no, not a skill. More like a *power*, I should say.

No amount of practice could teach a man to spy a coal black aura, the tendrils of something reaching through from someplace else, eager to claim a prize it felt it must be owed.

I theorized that these smokelike edges, these grasping hands that weren't hands—and had no fingers—had appeared and grown stronger around my recent victims because the thing on the other side was growing aggravated with me. I was stealing its spoils, if that's what these people are. Its sacrifices, or its prey . . . I don't know. It wants them, and it feels that it deserves them, and I won't let it have them.

Or else this is all conjecture.

Or else . . . I've begun to hear God speaking after all, and this is what He says, and we Christians have misunderstood a great many things about Our Father, Who Art in Heaven. I hope we have not misunderstood. I hope it is something *else* I'm hearing, and I hope it is no god. I would sooner die than serve it, whatever it is. I would sooner kill.

I spotted her when she came down past the station house, pausing beside an open boxcar. She asked a quiet question of someone inside, but I didn't hear it. She nodded, then turned and limped away. Was she injured, or simply slowed by the coiling tendrils of living shadow that tangled between her feet like an eager cat? I could see them, these things even blacker than this cool, flat night down in the rail yards; I watched them tie themselves around her ankles, crawling up her shins, throttling her thighs beneath the old cotton dress she wore with a shawl to top it off. I saw them better than I saw any details of her appearance—her hair's style or color, her age, the shape of her body.

I saw only that she moved with a measure of difficulty, and that she would be easy to catch.

She vanished into a block of cars parked on the lines. I wasn't worried. She left a trail, not a scent exactly—not like the stink of old boots and stale beer—but more like a humming noise, but not a noise at all. This residue was a physical thing, and I could touch it.

I crouched down in her wake and, yes, there it was: a rivulet of chilly air, fluttering where her feet had passed. I dipped my fingers into it, ran them through it. When I withdrew them, they were cold and a little bit wet.

Wherever the other thing lives, this is what it feels like there. Or maybe it's not a home, exactly. It could be, this creature, this god, this interloper . . . it waits in some intermediary spot between earth and heaven. Or no, not heaven.

The distant reach of space, that would be closer to what I mean.

As of late, I have pondered the great astronomers and their great debates. I have heard the arguments on both sides, and I feel that they wildly miss some larger point—that these are only the same things our ancestors asked, when the church told them to stop asking. The question is no longer, does the sun revolve around the Earth? The question has become, does the universe revolve around our solar system? Or our celestial neighborhood? Or our galaxy?

Stupid, stupid, stupid—this insatiable demand to be at the center of *something*.

Better to stay on the fringes, I say; rest on some outer ring or spiral of some small, insignificant corner of the infinite. And if we are very lucky, and if there is a greater space than infinity to hide us, then perhaps the terrible things on the other side of our universe will never take notice of us at all.

Unless they are summoned by the likes of the idiot reverend, and his idiot followers.

Fine, then. We have their attention. Perhaps I can persuade them to lose interest. It's really all I can hope for.

I followed after Lorna with slow, quiet steps—my pants raised up above my socks so that I could follow her by the chilly vapor that trailed her, without stooping or drawing unwanted attention to myself. I used no light, and I kept my weapon the same simple piece I used at the start of this awful string of missions.

(I did not wear black, but a dark brown that served well enough to conceal me in the shadows. It also did a fine job of hiding any bloodstains or spatters; in the evening, even under the brightest streetlights, no one would know the difference. Black might have been more thorough, but men who wear black are up to something. Or that's the popular assessment.)

The small hairs on my legs prickled and perked, dusted by the slick, icy mist.

It was colder and colder as I grew closer and closer—the very opposite of the children's guessing game. The stuff felt thicker and almost difficult to wade through, and I could see it so vividly (almost a shining black, almost a slick color that glinted, though there was no light at all). I watched it, and I listened for Lorna.

I smelled her cigarette smoke, and only noticed it as an afterthought.

I turned a corner and there she was. Smoking, leaning, her eyes closed as if her head ached and maybe it did. What a happy day, if I could do her the kindness of freeing her from such headaches, such a life. No, not happy. No, I was only lying to myself, and I don't know why. It didn't make the task any more pleasant, and it wasn't the lies that made it easier. It was easier due to simple practice.

She heard me, and then she saw me.

She sniffed a coil of smoke up one nostril, smoke so white compared to the smoke around her legs. It was higher than that, I saw—now that I stood almost near enough to touch her. It had scaled her thighs and it settled around her hips, a pernicious fog that must've made her customers shudder.

I wondered, could they feel it? Could they see it? Or is it only *me*? I had never yet had anyone else to ask, so I had no other experience to compare mine with.

If she felt, or sensed, or was bothered by the weird shadow, she showed no sign of it.

"You're not one of the rail boys," she said. Her voice was rocks and cinders, raked together after a fire.

"No. Not one of them."

"Then what do you want?"

Could she see me, beyond a mere outline of a man? Could she tell that I reached slowly toward my jacket, to get a firm grip on the axe handle? "A moment of your time."

"Can you pay for it?"

"Of course." I nodded. And then, I don't know why, but I blurted it out: "I want to know about the black fog that follows you."

She sucked on the cigarette, a hand-rolled affair that was

sloppily, lumpily created. The tiny burst of light showed her eyes going wide; then they settled back down to suspicious slits. "You're drunk."

"No. And you're lying, I can see that now. You know it's there. You know what's coming." Such conviction I felt, just from that split moment of a reaction, when I asked her. She might not have known what it was, but she knew it was there. I couldn't tell if she was afraid of it or not. I couldn't tell if she was afraid of me.

She dropped the cigarette and it fizzled to extinction upon contact with the pooling wet shadow that surrounded her shoes. We were in darkness again, but I knew that she didn't need the light any more than I did. She made some shifting gesture that I couldn't see, but it was fast.

I made some shifting gesture, and maybe she couldn't see it. But I was fast.

The axe was in my hand and I hoped—and suspected from experience—that she would turn away and run, but that's not what happened. She lunged for me! In her hand she had a weapon, too. It was a blade, the slender, sharp sort the Italians prefer for their violence, if the papers can be believed. (They can't. I know they can't, but I read them anyway.)

She only winged me, catching a slice of my jacket. She struck again and cut across my knuckles, but it wasn't deep, it was only hot and painful—because she caught me on the down stroke of my own fierce swing. Too weak or too slow to deflect me, I'd hit her, but the hit went lower than I liked. It caught her in the neck, somewhere between her collarbone and her throat. Soft tissue. Messy stuff, and gruesome to wound . . . but not enough to stop a determined enough victim.

She slashed and sliced again, grunting and staggering. She nicked my wrist, and that was all.

I grabbed her hand and twisted, and she dropped the knife. I spun her around with a yank. I swung the axe again, and this time, I heard it bang dully against bone. It landed wetly, heavily, behind her ears and above them.

She fell to her knees and the smoke roiled and billowed, as if it wanted to fight me for her.

Too late for that. I struck, and struck, and struck, sending bits of brain and bone flying, I know. I felt the spatter on my face, and heard it land against my collar. I felt my hands growing slick with it. My grip faltered, and I was winded.

The cold fog quivered, and rallied to cover her. Then it drained away, vanishing as if it'd never been present at all—spilled back into the ground or back into the ether or wherever it went, as easily as blood washed down a drain.

Inspector Simon Wolf

~❧~

BIRMINGHAM, ALABAMA
SEPTEMBER 26, 1921

Last night, I had dinner with the Gussmans.

It was delicious, for starters; informative, for latters; and thought-provoking all the while. They are so afraid, bless them. They are lost in their own city, hiding from their own families. And, unsurprisingly, they are not entirely prepared to trust the goodwill of an outsider like me. Ruth (in particular) told me plenty . . . but she probably kept even more to herself. If she had nothing to hide, she wouldn't be so exceedingly careful about what she reveals.

Something is amiss in Alabama, that much is certain. This investigation of mine may prove useful to us yet, and the Quiet Society may well commend me for taking the time to visit.

I ought to say, there's plenty more than *one* something amiss.

Chapelwood, the axe deaths, Father Coyle's murder. Three components, related by proximity and context, and I want to believe there's something else, too, though it's difficult to say. The three come up together in conversation again and again, so closely aligned in the thoughts of everyone who knows anything about any of them.

As I walked back to my hotel room, I pondered what connection might bind them.

Yes, I *walked*. I'd realized how close they lived to my quarters, and the night was cool enough that I didn't feel overburdened by the perambulation. I wanted to know the city better, anyway—I wanted to walk around it, smell it, sense it for myself. Everything I'd gleaned so far was hearsay at best, secondhand gossip at worst. I had much to learn. Much to think about.

Aggravatingly, I kept finding ways to pin two of my three quandaries together, but nothing firm to hang them all upon.

Edwin Stephenson was a member of the Chapelwood congregation, and likewise he was the killer of Father Coyle. The axe murders were committed against Catholics (initially, predominantly), and the Chapelwood congregation harbors an unhealthy hatred toward Catholics. But Father Coyle wasn't subjected to anyone's hatchet, and there's nothing connecting Stephenson to the other murders, either . . . except by distant proxy, via his congregation.

It's a thin string. It would break with the slightest tension.

And, I was forced to conclude, I was only tying Stephenson into the other two because I hated him. It's not a kind or fair thing, to hate a man before ever setting eyes on him—not ordinarily. But this was a man who'd terrorized his own family and murdered a friend of mine.

In all reality, he probably shot the priest because he was

furious about his daughter's impromptu elopement. A gun is a weapon of opportunity, of rashness and anger. It's not the tool of a complicated plot, or a peculiar sect. It's not a thing that requires much forethought or manipulation.

Having come to this assessment, I forced myself to remove that man from the equation. If Coyle's murder was a separate thing, much as I'd prefer it wasn't . . . then the axe murders and Chapelwood still remained.

Were they tethered purely by circumstance? Or was there something more driven and sinister behind them both?

I walked past a newspaper stand. An older fellow was closing it down for the night, clearing away the day's papers and making way for the new ones, which would arrive in another eight hours or so. I bought one off him anyway, for the news was only a little late—and I didn't much care. I'd only made it through half the paper that morning, and now I needed the second half. If I wanted to learn about the local situation, I should start with the local news.

From streetlamp to streetlamp, I scanned the front page.

The big headlines focused mostly on the recent election, and made note of the changes I'd heard about in passing already. George Battey Ward: *Out*. Nathaniel Barrett: *In*. Reorganization of the police structure: Chief Eagan essentially evicted, and Thomas Shirley instated in the role.

I sneered at the blatant descriptor of "Klan favorite," as applied to a man whose job it would be to uphold the law. Sounded like a terrific conflict to me. Not that anyone here cares "how we do it up north." (As I'd already heard, once or twice in my travels below the Mason-Dixon. Fine, then. Duly noted.)

When I reached my hotel room, I settled in with the paper— and with a couple of messages from the Boston office. Those I ignored, until I'd finished reading what passes for journalism down here.

Are all the local papers so biased everywhere across the land? Well, probably. That doesn't make it right, or good. I'm sure it happens in Boston, and I don't really see it. Maybe the people here don't notice it anymore, either. There's plenty we're all prepared to ignore, by virtue of familiarity.

My attention snagged on another mention of the Klan, buried on page four.

It was in reference to a recent parade, and I, for one, could not ignore it. (Yes, the Klan exists elsewhere above and beyond the fabled line, but nowhere else is it so *ubiquitous*. Or I must hope and pray.) Apparently, there were rumors that the early axe killings were perpetrated by black men . . . and someone thought that the solution to this matter would be to invite the Klan to put on a show of strength. Not that they put it that way, but I can read between the lines with the best of them.

I doubt it will work. It was a stupid idea in the first place, and it will serve only to frighten and intimidate perfectly honest men . . . and maybe cause the assault and horrific death of a few, because everyone else will be worked up as well.

I hate to consider it, but the atrocities committed by this group are no great secret; if anything, they go out of their way to advertise their brutality, mounting a campaign of fear against the populace at every available turn. And to think, I'd reflexively felt it best to preserve my hosts from the details of the Massachusetts case of yore—when, apparently, it's common practice to perform comparable acts of terror on negroes with virtually no evidence (or none at all).

I won't record any of it here. It turns my stomach.

And that said . . . though less creative in scope, and more

limited in production . . . these assorted instances of mob justice *do* remind me of those terrible crimes in Massachusetts.

Several things have reminded me of them since I learned of Coyle's death . . . as if a reminder is being suggested by the universe, repeatedly. A gentle hint, growing louder. It's not just the brutality of the Klan attacks, or the repetition of the axe motif. (And it *is* a motif. Everything is, when you stand back far enough and squint.) But just when I was prepared to write it all off to coincidence . . . young Ruth brought up the notorious Miss Borden. Just as the chief did, before I left Boston.

I haven't thought of her in years, and now she's come up twice.

The old Fall River case and these new cases aren't the same, no. Not the same parties or location, not the same *anything*— except for a common weapon and a shared sense of dread that escalates the longer I remain here. But I am listening to these hints from the cosmos all the same, and so I am thinking about what it all means.

I am thinking about the brief time I spent in the company of Lizzie Borden.

No. That wasn't her name, not by then. She was using her father's name, Andrew, or something like that. But a simple change of name is no change at all, not really.

We never did know what happened in the Massachusetts cases. Something was headed for Fall River, barreling toward Emma Borden—we're confident of that much. It wasn't some*one* so much as it was a *thing*, wearing the skin of an upstate biology professor.

That thing killed dozens. (And that's only to count the deaths we confidently know of, and can tie directly to it.)

And then . . . then it reached Fall River. Or it *should* have, according to our calculations. No one from our team was ever able to stop it, at any rate—so either it stopped of its own accord, or someone else stopped it.

My money has always been on Lizzie Borden.

Lizzie Andrew. Whatever.

Her sister (an invalid) was in no position to defend herself, and that old doctor friend of theirs was once in the army, but he lived on the other side of town . . . so there was but one person on the premises at all times with a hypothetical history of violence, and a physical capacity to perform it.

The math supports my conclusion, even if *she* never did.

There's some connection here, between Alabama and New England. I don't know what it is, but I must listen harder, pay attention, and see what the universe is trying to tell me.

Stephenson's trial doesn't begin until Friday, and since he's confessed freely to his involvement in Father Coyle's murder, there wasn't much "solving" to be done on that particular case. He'd either be convicted (unlikely, I fear) or cleared of all charges due to insanity or some other loophole of a justice system with no intent whatsoever to jail him (much more likely, yes). True, I'd collected my stipend and headed south in order to address the priest's murder, but what was there to address? I'd sit in at the courthouse out of respect, if I could. Not that it would make any difference.

Meanwhile, there was always the matter of the axe murders. Coyle thought they were important, and he was no fool—so I decided I might as well take a crack at them while I'm here. I'm still on the fence with regards to their strangeness (or I should say Strangeness), but the Chapelwood business is mighty weird; and if the two are related, I might be right—and this may yet count as a business trip and I might successfully petition you for full reimbursement.

With this in mind, I made a phone call to the police station, to see how their change of leadership was progressing. It sounded like more mayhem over there: plenty of shouting, plenty of questions, plenty of background noise that made it difficult for the young secretary and me to understand each other. Eventually I extracted a bit of useful information from her, which was to say that the axe murder case files were no longer on the premises. They'd been removed to the city commissioner's office a month before, due to concerns about security.

That's how she put it, "concerns about security." From whom or what, she declined to say.

I thanked her for her time, and released her from the call.

A quick check of the local paper reminded me of the name of the outgoing commission president: George Ward. Everyone of any character I've met so far has spoken well of him, and if the ludicrously named True Americans are that desperate to get rid of him, he must have at least a *few* principles stashed about his person . . . or so I told myself as I feathered through the phone book.

I found his listing right away, but when I inquired after him, his wife informed me that he wasn't home. She pointed me toward his old office, where he was cleaning things out and doing his best to ease the transition. I heard a catch in her voice as she said that part; she didn't want the transition eased in the slightest—she wanted to fling a thousand boulders in front of it, and I could certainly understand the sentiment. But as she stressed, Mr. Ward was a consummate professional, and he wanted to fulfill every ounce of his final obligations.

A cab ride brought me to the government center in under fifteen minutes.

The city's administration headquarters were typical of government buildings all the world over, or the Western world, at any rate. Greek inspired, Roman confused. White columns and wide, short steps—oversized entryways, heavy double doors . . . all of it intended to remind the citizen of how small he is, in the scheme of government.

The council wing was off to my right. I found it down a corridor with marbled floors and lots of brass fixtures, everything modernized (very slightly) with the nouveau lines that were popular ten years ago, and already look a bit dated . . . but at least it wasn't more of the humdrum Mediterranean mishmash, so I gave it a pass. Likewise, the plates on all the doors were carved in a current typeface, something with triangle-edged points and doubled lines on the capital letters. It was sharp, and it suggested that someone, somewhere, was interested in bringing Alabama into the modern age.

I watched the nameplates and office designations until I found one reserved for the City Commission president. The door was ajar, for a man with a bucket and a scraper was carefully removing George Ward's name from the frosted-glass window set within it. He gave me a nod, but didn't look at me. I responded in kind, and stepped inside without disturbing the door.

I rapped politely on the frame, in order to announce myself to the fellow who stood behind the desk. He was a lean man, tall and sharp, in a gray linen suit that was cut like it cost a pretty penny. In keeping with the citywide style, he wore a mustache, keenly waxed; his hair was smooth and shiny, parted on the side, as dark as a crow's wing. It was a startling shade of black on a man who must've been in his late forties. Not a speck of salt, nor a hint of pepper marred it. He was holding a phone, but he wasn't using it. He'd either just hung up or hadn't yet dialed.

"Can I help you?" he asked. Smooth voice, and oily like his hair. It was the voice of an educated man, with a higher-class version of the regional accent I'd been hearing on the streets thus far.

"I beg your pardon, but my name is Simon Wolf. I'm an inspector from Boston, visiting your fine city on a bit of business." I produced a badge that identified me as a veteran representative of the police department there. It wasn't true, but no one ever followed up on such a bold claim; and even if anyone did, the police and my home office have a quiet agreement on such matters.

"Boston business? In our fair city?" He set the phone down atop the big oak desk. "I suppose we've had some high-profile crimes over the last year or two . . . but I'm still surprised to see a guest from such a distant corner. Please, pardon my manners: I am the City Commission president, Nathaniel Barrett." He extended a hand, and I took it. We shook, and he continued. "I hope our little town has treated you well so far."

"I find myself enchanted by your cityscapes, your citizens, and most especially your cuisine. And it's a pleasure to meet you." It wasn't, but we were both being pleasant. And I, for one, was being careful. "I've been sent here, that I might look into your recent spate of axe murders. I'm a specialist, you see—and I'm often assigned to strange and violent cases. I have an exceptional record for solving them."

"An interesting specialty indeed," he said, then looked around behind me. "I do apologize—I'd offer you a seat, but as you can see, I'm still getting settled in."

It was true, the office was in a state of disarray. Two chairs were present apart from the one behind the desk, but they were stacked atop one another in a corner. Several boxes of papers, notebooks, files, and other assorted paper goods were overturned and shuffled into madness; two of the desk drawers were lying beside it, their contents scattered across the floor. This did not look like an office changing hands. It looked like the site of a particularly brutal ransacking.

I demurred. "No apologies necessary—I understand completely. In all honesty, my own office rarely looks much tidier, and I don't have an administration change to pin it upon. Speaking of which, congratulations on your new position."

"Thank you, Mr. Wolf. I appreciate your kind words, and I hope I can be of some assistance to you . . . but as I said, I've only just arrived. I'm still learning what archives are kept where, and under what system of organization. My predecessor and I had different ideas about filing."

I almost said, "Among other things, I hear," but I bit my tongue. "Perhaps I could have a word with your predecessor, then . . . ? I understand that Mr. Ward was the commission president during the bulk of the killings."

"That is correct, though you might have better luck at the police station—if it's the case files you're after."

"Ah, but that's not what the station had to say about it. According to my contact there, the files were moved here a few weeks ago. Something about security concerns."

He looked puzzled, but that's easy enough to do. I didn't take it at face value.

"If that's the case, then I must apologize yet again. I really haven't the faintest idea where they might have run off to. I haven't come across them so far, but I assume there's other storage to be found, someplace. Listen, why don't you give me a number or an address where I can reach you, and I'll keep my eyes open. Surely they'll turn up in the next day or two, don't you think?"

"That's a marvelously kind offer, and I can't thank you enough." It might have been a little gushy, but by that point, I think we both knew how much horseshit was being flung about the room. "Here, take my card—and on the back, I'll jot down the hotel where I'm staying. You can reach me there, or leave a message anytime, day or night."

We extricated ourselves with another handshake, just in time for his phone to ring with a jangling clamor that was loud enough to rattle the single office window, which overlooked a rectangular yard. I took my leave, and once again took care to keep from disturbing the man at work on the door.

But as I stepped around him, he discreetly tapped the back of my leg with his scraping tool.

He held a finger to his lips, so I said nothing—I only walked all the way around the door and out of Mr. Barrett's immediate line of sight. From the single side of the conversation in the office, I deduced that he was chatting with his new police chief; and the workman deduced that it was distraction enough to whisper a message: "Basement," he breathed. "Stairs at the end of the hall. Storage Room Six."

Then he returned to the "r" in "Ward," removing it one solitary flake at a time, and studiously avoiding any pretense of having spoken at all.

I would've thanked him, but he gave me the impression he'd rather I didn't call attention to his covert assistance, so I walked away in the direction his head-cocking had indicated.

I collected a few curious stares as I strolled the length of the corridor, but I'd already figured out the easiest way to deflect them—with a nod and a smile, the social currency of the region. It was a simple work-around to my native unfamiliarity; so long as no one heard me speak, and realized how very foreign I was, everyone treated me with cordial acceptance—and although I was not familiar to any of the men or women who worked there, I behaved as if I belonged, and that was sufficient to keep anyone from stopping me when I reached the door to the stairwell.

A sign beside it confirmed what lay beyond it, and furthermore admonished, "Authorized Employees Only," but I ignored that, pulled the handle, and let myself inside—to a narrow vertical space made of concrete from floor to ceiling. I realize that these interstitial places are meant to function, not shine, but it still felt like an oppressive, gloomy nook—all gray, all dark except for the caged lightbulbs positioned at the landings. The steps were stained or shadowed in blotchy patches, and the handrail was covered in glossy black paint that had chipped and peeled in the Southern humidity to reveal a veneer of rust underneath.

I had no intention of touching it.

But in the semidarkness, I reached for it anyway, without meaning to—about halfway down, where the light was weakest between the landings. It felt slick under my fingers, and I jerked them away. I looked for someplace to wipe them, but seeing nothing, I took hold again. I could always wash my hands later, couldn't I? It would be easier than nursing a broken leg.

At the bottom, I gave up and reached for my handkerchief. I rubbed it back and forth across my fingers, turning it faintly red and collecting the flecks of paint as I stared about my new surroundings.

It was brighter there at the bottom, but not much. The floor was still that smooth, drab concrete, but the walls were brick and stone, painted white . . . though I could scarcely see them for the stacks of filing cabinets, boxes, folders, office equipment, and cleaning supplies that formed a maze around me. "Storage Room Six," the man with the scraping tool had told me. I saw no mention anywhere of different rooms or divisions, or any other sign that this repository of Everything Else had ever received any hint of organizational assistance.

Directly before me, a few feet from the final step, a pair of cabinets stood side by side like oversized, threatening sentries. A pair of angels with flaming swords could have scarcely been more intimidating in that close, darkened terrain—but the space between them was approximately the width of a doorway, and a path ran between them as a matter of necessity.

I approached these bureaucratic obelisks and turned sideways, passing through this weird gate and into a veritable tunnel, for the civic detritus towered over me on either side. On my left I saw nameplates and old windows, closet doors and pieces of chairs. On my right, broken lamps and brooms, a cigarette machine that perhaps still worked, a tower of desk drawers stacked one atop another almost to the ceiling.

It may have been my imagination that the way grew more narrow as I progressed, and the storage items more peculiar. But I turned sideways again and now I squeezed past an upended chaise, a bicycle, and the bottom springs of a mattress. I shied away from bookcases covered in dampness and rot, a coffee table that looked like it'd been shattered with a mallet, an umbrella stand shaped like a dead-eyed parrot—and the skeletal remains of half a dozen umbrellas that jutted from its head.

As I explored, farther and farther into this underworld of junk, I detected some noise at the very edge of my hearing: a muttering, grumbling sound, accompanied by the rustle of paper. A swearword or two, and the wadding, crumpling noise of paper being crushed in someone's fist.

It grew louder as I pressed deeper.

I erred on the side of feeling that this was a good thing, that there was some light at the end of this tunnel—or some revelation, some person, some reward for my troubles. I was beginning to wonder how far I could have possibly gone, thinking I must not be beneath the council building anymore, surely . . . when the way widened and the path deposited me into an open space.

It was another hallway, but a proper one with perpendicular angles and nothing to clutter it, save a pair of small desks and an old icebox lying on its side. This landing was marked by a dozen doorways—some open, some closed—that ran its length, and conveniently enough, I was standing immediately before Storage Room Three. To the left I saw Two, and to the right I saw Four, so I made my way to the right until I reached number Six.

Room Six did not have a door. It had hinges from which nothing hung.

Beyond it, there was a man. He had his back to me. He was tearing through file drawers, picking some things out and leaving other things behind, swearing under his breath all the while.

I cleared my throat and said, "I beg your pardon . . ."

He stopped. Stood up straight, and turned around. "Now why would you do *that?*"

Confused, I stammered, "I'm sorry? Why would I . . . do what?"

"Why would you beg my pardon? You don't need it. Nobody needs it," he added with a mumble. "Anybody can do anything he wants around here, especially with regards to me. You can come on in, make yourself at home, put your feet up on the paperwork, pour yourself a drink, and light a match—and there's not a damn thing I can do about it. So why the hell would you bother to beg my pardon?"

"Ah," I said, because I understood, or I thought I might. And because I needed a moment to muster a response.

The man before me was in his early fifties. He was white, though he stopped just shy of appearing swarthy—with dark curly hair and bushy eyebrows to match; and the set of his cheeks made me wonder if there wasn't some Spanish or Italian lurking in his family woodpile. A good-looking man, he was: stout without running to fat like myself, with muscled forearms holding his shirtsleeves rolled up and shoved back.

I cleared my throat again. "George Battey Ward, I assume?"

"Yes, and who wants to know?"

"Simon Wolf. I'm an inspector from Boston, here to investigate your recent axe murders. And likewise the murder of Father Coyle, though that seems essentially solved already—and unlikely to conclude with any real justice."

My response surprised him. That was probably the best I could've hoped for, considering the man was radiating rage like a Franklin stove, and appeared on the very verge of opening fire on anyone who dared to speak with him. From what I knew of his week, I could hardly blame him.

He took a moment, and rested his hands on his hips while he looked me up and down. "Boston?"

"That's right."

"What shit does Boston give?"

"None," I said. "But Coyle was my friend, and he thought the axe murders were worth a closer look. That's why he sent for me," I exaggerated only slightly. He'd *tried* to send for me, hadn't he? It was only a tragedy of timing that found me in his hometown in the wake of his death. "I'm a specialist."

"You're an axe murder specialist?" he asked with something perilously close to a smirk.

"I'm a specialist in violent crime, particularly violent crime of the . . . decidedly strange variety. How well did you know Father

Coyle?" I wanted to know, hoping that a series of pointed questions might calm him down, and reassure him that I meant business.

He didn't answer right away. "I knew him well enough to know he had an interest in . . . the decidedly strange," he borrowed my wording. He sighed then, and wiped at his forehead with the back of his wrist. He closed his eyes, and opened them again. "I ought to tell you I'm sorry."

"I ought to tell you it matters, but I'm willing to skip all that, if you are."

That gave him something more like a smile, but it was not a happy one. It was the social smile of someone trying to convey that I'm not the one he's angry with. "Consider it skipped."

I shook his hand when he offered it, stepping farther into the cramped storage room in order to do so. "This is quite the arrangement you've got. Does Barrett know you're down here?"

"I doubt it. How'd you find me?"

"A fellow scraping your name off the door. He passed your location along like a secret."

He frowned thoughtfully. "That's odd. I came in through the back, and let myself down the service stairs. I didn't think anyone saw me . . . But I've been wrong before."

"Service people always have ways of noticing, without being seen. Regardless, you should be glad he treated the information so quietly. I don't think he wished to expose you to his new boss. But tell me, is this where . . ." I looked around at the mounds of newspapers, magazines, chair legs, pencil stubs, damp-swollen law books, and everything else that made up the jumble of Storage Room Six. ". . . You hid the case files on the axe murders?"

"'Hid' is a mighty strong word."

"The secretary at the police station suggested you'd removed the files for safekeeping a few weeks ago."

"Right, right. Well, *that* was no big secret."

"Why did you take them?"

He shook his head and shoved at one of his shirtsleeves, adjusting the tuck of the cuff so it'd stay aloft. "I didn't. Eagan's the one who brought them to me; I just authorized the transfer. And yes, once I'd heard him out, I put them down here. I thought they'd be safe."

"From what? Or from whom, as the case may be?"

"Barrett. Tom Shirley. The True Americans. Take your pick." He turned around and hauled a heavy-looking box full of folders into the space between us. "Most of the details are here, but a few . . . just . . . *aren't.*"

"Someone found your stash?"

"No, I don't think so," he said, kicking gently at the box. "I set up a few . . . not booby traps, exactly. But I left little tells around, so I'd know if anyone came by. None of it was disturbed. Then again, this basement has a way of eating things."

I offered a polite laugh, but it seemed only to confuse him. "I'm sorry—I liked your phrasing, is all."

"It's not a matter of phrasing. Things disappear down here, and reappear—but different. Like they've been chewed up, digested, and shit back out again. Look around you." He gestured so broadly that he nearly hit me in the chin. "Look at all these things, all of them broken and scattered. Parts missing, never to be recovered. It happens to everything down here eventually. I thought I'd have more time, is all."

I honestly couldn't tell how serious he was, so I amicably hedged my bets. "Basements have a way of surprising us, don't they?"

"Basements, and everything else underground. Look, I'm not a madman," he said with almost too much earnestness. "I'm just a local, and I've just spent enough time in these places, these in-between places . . ." His voice fizzled out.

Gently, I said, "Now I really *must* beg your pardon, for I don't understand your meaning."

His shoulders slumped and he stared down at the box. "What's to understand? Things are decidedly strange, and getting more so all the time. It's the little things at first—and you barely notice. By the time it's staring you in the face, and you finally can't pretend that it's all in your head . . . it's been happening, well, *outside* your head, too. For years."

He dropped to his knees, and urged me to do likewise—but I declined. I have a difficult time getting up and down from the floor, for pity's sake. I was willing to watch from above.

"Here, let me show you," he offered, riffling through the box's contents. "This is the case file for the attack on Joe and Susie Baldone." His fingers flipped past various documents, photos, and notes. "But parts of it are missing. Not just pieces of paper—that's not what I mean; that's too easy to account for—but pieces of text, whole paragraphs that were typed out on my own machine, in my own office. By my own hands." He sighed. "I typed this file myself, and now this page, you see? I might as well have done it up with invisible ink."

He passed me the page. I eyed it closely, holding it up to the solitary bulb that gave me all the light I could expect to use. Whether or not it'd once held much of note, now it held only a partial description of Susie Baldone, mother of one, assaulted in October of last year. A photo was clipped to the page, but it was so faded it told me almost nothing. I saw the shape of a smiling face, a woman's outline in a pale-colored dress.

"They're vanishing, right in front of me." The despair in his words echoed forlornly through the basement, where everything had a soft edge and nothing stayed forever.

I didn't know what to say about that, so I asked another question. "Can you tell me, please—what do Barrett's people care about these files? Would they have destroyed them, or altered them in any way?"

"I couldn't say, but I had a terrible feeling about it all. Barrett asked too many questions, wanted too many liberties with the information."

"You think he's mixed up in it somehow?"

"Him, or the TAs, or somebody in his circle. I want to say it must be the Americans . . . they're so peculiar, and the peculiarness spreads with them. Everything they touch, they leave some stain on it . . . and I can't help but feel like this whole nasty business . . . it's something of theirs. I wish I had a better way to say it, but I don't."

"Far be it from me to disagree with you. What little I've read—"

"What little you've read," he interrupted, though not unkindly, "can't possibly scratch the surface. They are so careful to keep the worst of it quiet, or unprovable at the very least. And like the best of their handiwork, I'll be damned if I can prove any connection of theirs to any of *this*," he said, waving his hand over the box.

Silence filled in the space between us, and around us. The old building settled on its foundations, or maybe some door opened someplace, and that's what explained the soft gust of air I felt tickling the back of my neck. The lightbulb flickered but stayed on. The box of documents on the floor between us performed no dramatic trick when George Ward picked it up and put it back onto its original pile.

"Here's the worst of it," he told me. He wiped his hands on his pants and leaned back, almost sitting on the very things he'd worked so hard to protect. "Even if I *could* prove it—any of it. The least or the worst of it . . . if I had photographic evidence tying them to the recent horrors in Birmingham . . . it wouldn't matter. Just like it doesn't matter that Edwin Stephenson shot Father Coyle to death, and the whole world saw him do it, and he doesn't even deny it. He'll walk away from it clean, and the True Americans will walk away from their crimes, too. They always do," he said with a catch in his throat. "And I'm afraid they always *will*."

I wanted to reassure him, but how? What could I say to a man already so defeated?

Beside him was another box, of the same sort. It held a similarly sad stack of unfiled, unorganized briefs. I reached forward to flip through them, since they were sitting right there—and I'd come looking for such files, after all. "Let's not think that way, George," I said as I sorted through them. "Where there's a will, there's a way. And you're not alone in this. I'm here to help you and . . ."

My platitudes drew up short as my eyes settled on a sketch done in pencil on a rough sheet of newsprint-type paper.

I lifted it out of the box and held it to the light, turned it over, turned it around, and drew it up to my face to give it a more thorough squinting at. I wasn't entirely sure what I was seeing, but the realization was dawning, and I had the very strong feeling that things were about to leap from "decidedly strange" to "markedly weirder than even *that*."

"George . . . what is this?"

"That box? I think it holds the loose file material—bits and pieces that were either scrambled in the transfer or never got stored correctly in the first place. A couple of boxes were dropped, shuffled around—you know how it goes. The stray bits in this one . . . we couldn't find anywhere else to put them, I suppose."

"But they're relevant to the axe murders?"

"They ought to be. Why?"

I showed him the image. It was a woman's face, sketched by a talented hand. Her hair was long and her features were pretty; she was young and lovely, but she wasn't smiling.

He took it from me, and examined it himself. "Oh, yes. *Her.*"

"Who is she?"

He shrugged and handed it back. "We never did find out. One of the axe victims, Gaspera Lorino—he drew it, when we asked him what happened. But you have to understand, he was hurt pretty bad. He'll never recover, not fully. This drawing, it could be anything. Anyone. An image he saw in a theater, or a photo from a newspaper story a dozen years ago. No one recognized her, and no one thought she had anything to do with the attack."

"Why not?"

He shrugged again and leaned back, folding his arms. "We had witnesses: Two shopworkers from the neighborhood said they saw a pair of black men do the attacking. I don't know if they were telling the truth or not, but surely it wasn't some . . . some *girl*, leaping out of the shadows to subdue two grown adults, killing one of them."

"But on the bottom here—is this Mr. Lorino's handwriting?"

"I believe so."

I read aloud, "'The gray lady.'" Then I asked, "He drew this when, precisely? Wait, never mind—here's a date . . ." In the corner, scrawled in another hand: October 4, 1920. "He was attacked in October, I see."

"No, it was the end of September. He spent a while in the hospital before we could talk with him. When they finally let us in, he wasn't any help, not that I blame him. You take a hit to the head like that, and it can really scramble your brains. Why are you so keen on that picture? Do you know her?"

I ran my thumb over the edge of her hair. "Not exactly . . ." But I'd seen those eyes before. I'd seen that jawline, that hair. Not in the flesh, that I could ever recall—though I'd seen a dozen movie posters and at least one photograph where she was embracing another woman. "But I know who she is. Or who she was, I should say . . . because this was thirty years ago. She'd be in her fifties now, if she were alive."

"I'm sorry, come again?"

"She's dead." I didn't know it for a fact. No one did, and for all this time, I'd assumed that no one ever would. "I'm sorry, I don't mean to be obtuse—but this takes me by surprise. It's a new wrinkle in an old case, I'll put it that way. Do you mind if I keep this, just for a few days? I'd like to show it to someone."

"By all means. I bet it's safer with you than down here, waiting to get eaten by the basement."

I folded it, and tucked it neatly into my vest. "Thank you," I said. "And thank you for your time, all of it. Now I must take my leave, if temporarily. I need to send a message."

"What about the case files? I thought you wanted to look at them?"

"Oh, I *do*. Is it all right if I wander down here later this afternoon or evening?"

"Anytime you like. It's never locked. No one comes down here for anything, ever. Not unless they have to."

I laughed nervously, because I certainly understood why no one would choose the basement for a cigarette break or a quick sip of coffee. I tried a light joke: "Everyone's afraid of getting eaten, is that it?"

"Probably," he said, nodding, in all apparent seriousness. "Would you do me a small favor? Whatever you discover in your investigations, kindly keep it between us—and report it to me, rather than the new authorities. I wouldn't ordinarily ask such a thing, I swear to you. I know it's a betrayal of the public trust, and I know it's not standard procedure anywhere, least of all a place like Boston—with better resources than we have, I'm sure."

Before he could continue, I said, "No, I understand perfectly. The new regime has untoward ties to the matter, or there's an excellent chance that it *might*. I'll happily keep the loop small. As small as you like."

"Excellent, thank you. I honestly do believe it's for the best; and if you should learn anything, or have any questions, please come to me—I'll answer what I can, and see if Eagan can't be helpful as well. We know the city, and we've fought for the city, but the city let us down. Or maybe it's the other way around." He sighed.

"You're not finished yet," I promised. "And I'm barely started."

I extricated myself with another handshake and a vow to return, and to keep my findings fairly private. I would've stayed longer and kept him company there, except for two things: one, the basement was beginning to feel oppressive, and I wanted away from it; and two, I had some phone calls to make.

I'd ignored the universe long enough. It'd sent a message loud and clear, and it was my job to respond—both to the patterns at large, and to the Boston office, who'd no doubt want to hear about my pending plans. I needed them, anyway. I needed them because they could find me a phone number for Lizzie Borden with much greater alacrity than I could, since I was stuck in the wilds of Birmingham.

I needed to speak with Miss Borden. I had something in my possession that was bound to be of great interest to her: a portrait of her former companion, the long-gone actress Nance O'Neil.

Lizbeth Andrew (Borden)

⟡

Last year, I had a telephone installed.

Not for any particular reason, really. I like new things, and telephones are new. No one was ever likely to call it, but as I've gotten older, I've become more concerned with the sad eventualities of life, and the sad eventuality is this: I'm growing older, and weaker. I'll never be any stronger than I am right this moment. Next week, imperceptibly, I'll be that much weaker still.

And next year. And the year after that.

So in another ten or twenty years, what would become of me if I should fall? What if I should take some topple down the stairs, or slide across the kitchen floor and shatter my brittle old bones . . . what then? No one ever comes to visit, except the paperboy and the milkman, and the postman, of course—but he never knocks. It might be days before anyone realized anything was wrong.

But (I told myself, in a moment of dire paranoia) if I had a telephone on the premises, and assuming I could reach it, I could summon help. Besides, I had the money . . . and what else was I doing with it? Absolutely nothing, but ordering more books and magazines, and giving the postman more difficulty cramming them all through the mail slot . . . or leaving them on the porch, to be perched upon by the cats.

So I have a telephone, but I usually forget about it.

Today, it scared the living daylights out of me. It *rang*.

For a good twenty seconds I stood there, astounded and confused and wondering what on earth that racket could possibly be. I had literally never heard it ring before. Not once, in the eleven months since it's been hooked up downstairs in the parlor, on the end table beside the davenport. In that time, I've only used it twice: Both times, I placed phone calls to universities to inquire after a library's holdings. It felt strange, speaking to someone I couldn't see. The etiquette was all funny, and we kept stumbling over each other's words—since we lacked the visual cues that would keep us taking turns in an easy fashion.

But the telephone rang, that's what I mean to record here. It rang, and the noise rattled me down to my bones.

Then I felt silly.

Shortly on the heels of feeling silly, I felt alarmed, and then curious (in quick succession). Curiosity won the day. I quit merely staring at the shiny black device, and lifted the receiver like a modern, civilized person.

I wasn't sure what to do next, but the man on the other end

of the chat had more familiarity with the process than I did. He said, "Hello there."

I said hello in return, with the strong hint of a question mark at the end.

"Miss Andrew, it's been quite a long time since last we spoke, and for that I do apologize." He talked quickly, in a clipped city accent. I couldn't decide whether or not he sounded familiar to me, so I let him continue. "But I daresay the last thirty years have been strange for us both; and as for me, they've stayed strange, and gotten stranger—particularly in the last week, which brings me to my reason for calling."

Before he could offer such an explanation, I blurted out, "Thirty years? I'm sorry . . . I'm not sure . . . I don't understand. Who *is* this?"

"Again, I apologize. God, but I seem to be doing a lot of that lately. These blasted Southerners are rubbing off on me." He noted that last bit under his breath, and added, "This is Simon Wolf, and as you may or may not recall, I'm an inspector from Boston. We met in Fall River quite some time ago, and under difficult circumstances."

I was too dumbfounded to speak. My mouth went perfectly dry.

I remembered him, yes. A heavyset, pink-faced man in spectacles, representing some "Boston office" that he was never very clear about. He'd worked alongside Doctor Seabury, before that dear man went mad and passed on. He was helpful to us, at the time: There was a madman coming for my sister, and the inspector had given us what information he had, in order for us to prepare ourselves. He struck me as a competent—if somewhat cryptic—kind of man, the sort who is forgiven all sorts of nosy transgressions by virtue of his manners and his confidence. The sort of man who uses his wit instead of his size to get what he wants. (And I mean that as a compliment, really.)

And now, he'd called me on the telephone. The only person to do so, ever.

I stammered, because that was all I could do. "Inspector Wolf, yes. It was a difficult time indeed, and a long time ago at that."

"I suppose this call surprises you."

"I'd scarcely be human if it didn't."

"It's rather out of the blue, I know. But if the call itself surprises you, you'd better hang on to your hat for the reason I'm making it." He didn't give me time to brace my hat or anything else; he launched forward into his explanation without so much as taking a breath. "I'm working on a murder case, but not in Boston—I'm in Birmingham, Alabama, at present, where a series of axe murders have taken place over the last year. Now, *please*, do not assume that I'm being indelicate, given your own notoriety. Far from it, I assure you. In fact, the simple coincidence of your trial and the hatchet deaths is not *nearly* enough for me to broach such a request as the one I'm about to make: Miss Andrew, could you possibly join me here? I believe our interests may overlap, and we might be of some assistance to each other."

I was so deeply, purely stunned that once again—I couldn't speak.

"Miss Andrew?"

I made some pitiful sound in return. It wasn't a response, but it encouraged him to continue in his rapid-fire way.

"In short, and perhaps I should have opened with this, now

that I think about it . . . in short, I am aware that the fate of your old companion Nance O'Neil has long been something of a mystery." I gasped to hear her name, but he didn't hear me, so he kept on going. "And I regret to inform you that I have no hard evidence in hand to suggest any resolution on that point. *However*, I do have a rough portrait of her—found in a box of evidence relating to the recent axe murders here, drawn by a man with a grievous head injury. He called her the gray lady, and I recognized her. Not immediately, no. It took me a moment of staring, trying to figure out why she appeared so familiar to me; but once I'd made the connection, you can imagine my astonishment. It may sound strange to say this, but I've been thinking of you lately, due to a series of coincidences, if you believe in such things. This portrait I've found . . . this is the most recent one, and I felt that, should I ignore this, I would do both of us a great disservice. I'm sorry, Miss Andrew, but are you still there? Have we become disconnected?"

"No," I whispered. I said it again, louder, in case the word was so small that the line could not carry it. "I mean, yes, we're still . . . I'm still here. I'm sorry, I'm only . . . You've caught me off guard, sir."

"Maybe I should've risked a letter instead, to give you some time to absorb the information; but this is a new age, isn't it? We can speak across the miles—a thousand or more, right this very second—and it's both a virtue and a curse. I'm putting you on the spot, and it's a rudeness, I daresay, this failure to give you time to collect yourself and form a response to what is surely the most ludicrous request you've received in ages."

"No, not rude. Only shocking, and . . . and I want to say thank you, for thinking of me." It was a stupid sentiment, but it was the best I had at my disposal. "You said . . . you're in Birmingham?"

"In the Deep South, rather than the British Isles—though it could scarcely be more foreign if it were."

"You mentioned coincidence . . ."

"I'm always on the lookout for them," he told me. "I like to think of them as hints, or suggestions."

"From God?"

"From whomever."

He said it like an atheist, not that I cared. "I've read about the axe murders recently. I ordered some newspapers, in order to learn more about them. And there's something else going on down there, something that bothers me terribly, but we can discuss it in person."

"So that's a yes? You'll come and join me?"

"I can hardly say *no*, and it's not as if I have any other offers of travel or adventure beating down my door . . . though I'll need to make preparations for the cats."

"The cats?"

"I have some cats. Or they have me, as the case may be."

"Fine animals, cats." I couldn't tell if he was being facetious or not. "So long as they don't prevent you from your earliest possible arrival."

"I'll . . . I'll get a train schedule. I'll hire a car. I'll be there as soon as I can," I told him, and I meant every syllable. "Tomorrow, if I'm lucky. The day after, if I'm not."

"Excellent." He sounded truly relieved, though I couldn't imagine why. *I* was the one too relieved, too baffled, too amazed to do anything at all but accept his invitation.

He concluded by giving me the hotel where he stayed, promising to reserve me a room near his own for the sake of convenience—and then we respectively closed the call.

chapelwood

I stood in the parlor, the phone still in my hand, wondering what had just happened. I was flushed from head to toe; I could feel the pink warming my cheeks, and my hands were shaking. I put the phone back down on the table, lest I drop it and break it; I put my hand over my mouth, and pressed it there to keep from saying Nance's name again, and again, and again.

Ruth Stephenson Gussman

❦

BIRMINGHAM, ALABAMA
SEPTEMBER 28, 1921

My father's trial began today, and all of us are doomed.

Pedro couldn't come with me because he had to work, but George Ward and Chief Eagan showed up. They came partly to support me, and partly to show that they were still paying attention. They want Barrett and his Klan cronies to know that murder—especially murder in the middle of the day, as the sun looks on along with everyone else—isn't all right with everyone.

But it's going to be all right for my father and his friends, and deep down I think we all know it. They're going to get away with it, and it isn't right at all. What kind of world is this, anyway, when a mean old fool murders a man of God before a host of witnesses, and the court just shrugs?

Well, *we're* not shrugging. We're here, and we're watching.

Today we sat in the back row, waiting for the prosecuting lawyer to call me up as a witness. He said he was going to when I talked to him yesterday—and I think he might actually do it. I can't tell if he's good or bad. He was in the Klan before, but says he isn't now . . . and anyway, he doesn't like Hugo Black very much, so that's one thing in his favor.

Hugo Black is Daddy's lawyer. He's the man who's helping him walk free, so as far as I'm concerned, he's the worst man in the room. I said that out loud to Chief Eagan, and he told me not to be so damn optimistic.

So I watched them all from the back row, as they got started with their introductions.

It took forever, I swear—everybody introducing themselves, introducing evidence, introducing all the things they planned to introduce later, except for me. They mentioned me as a witness to be called somewhere down the line, but they didn't mention when that might turn out to be. Mr. Mayhew just told me to make sure I kept myself available, as if I've got somewhere else to be—and as if I don't plan to sit there on that bench and watch every goddamn minute of this trial.

Mr. Mayhew is the prosecutor. I should've mentioned that. I know: I'll introduce him.

Mr. Henry Mayhew is an attorney from Mobile who moved here a couple of years ago. As I said, he once was in the Klan, and says that now he's not. He also said that he wasn't in the True Americans, but he could be lying for all I know. He's a short man, only about my height; but his shoes are always shiny and he dresses like he owns a mirror. His hair is brown, but it's starting to get some gray in it, just above his ears on either side. He's about forty years old, I think. He's not married, or if he *is* married, he doesn't wear a ring. When he talks, he talks slow. I hope he talks slow because he's thinking about his words, and his mouth just drags like that when he's working on a thought. I'll forgive slow, so long as it's careful. But I won't forgive slow if it turns out he's stalling because he's stupid, and he doesn't know what to say.

Anyway, that's Mr. Mayhew. He's the one bringing evidence against my daddy, so I want to say he's the hero in the room, except Chief Eagan says that's optimistic, too.

I'd like to introduce Chief Eagan as a pessimist.

Along the back row with me and the chief, there were a few other folks from Saint Paul's—one of the nuns, her name's Irene; one of the altar boys, and his name's David; two of the older folks, they're Italian and I don't know their last name . . . and they don't speak much English, so I feel strange about asking them. I know them on sight, that's all. They came to support me and the chief, and Father Coyle even though he's surely up in heaven by now, and doesn't much care what becomes of my daddy.

Like the good father used to say, one way or another, we all get what's coming to us in the end.

I know he was trying to say something comforting, but I never felt much comforted by it. Mostly I just felt worried. Sometimes I think I'm a pretty good person, real decent and all; and sometimes I have terrible thoughts that make me wonder if I'm not fooling myself, and I'd better pray as hard as I can that I *don't* get what's coming to me in the end.

(**I** feel bad and angry that way when I look at my daddy. I feel it boiling up hot, when I see him sitting all smug in front of the judge, next to Hugo Black with his slick hair and his smile that shows too many teeth. I feel like if I had a gun, maybe I'd just show them all what it was like—when someone comes walking up to you, and for no reason at all just blows your head clean open. I could do it, too. One by one, until I ran out of bullets. Six bullets, and if I'm a lucky shot that means six heads blown open. I'd start with Daddy's head, then take his lawyer, then take the judge. Maybe I'd stop there, because maybe it'd take more than one bullet on a couple of them. Maybe that'd be enough, and the boiling-hot feeling would be all burned up, and I could sleep at night without seeing blood behind my eyelids, at least until they hanged me for doing all those murders. But then, maybe after that I could dream, without dreaming of murder.

I am an awful woman, and I am probably not going to heaven when I die. But if that's the case, maybe I ought to do something really awful to earn a spot in hell, if it's all the same difference anyway. I could start in that courtroom, and I could leave this world a better place than I found it.)

The courtroom was an uncomfortable place, even when nothing dramatic was happening.

It was cold in there at first, and then it got too warm as the place filled up, and everyone sat thigh to thigh on the wooden pews. (Do they call them pews when they're not in church? Benches, then, if that's better.) I wished I had a fan, but I hadn't put one into my bag because it's been so cool as of late, so I did without.

The chief also looked warm, but he was wearing his wool uniform—the dress uniform that the policemen wear for fancy occasions like funerals. I know he wasn't really a policeman anymore, not with a badge to prove it; but he'd always be a policeman down in his soul, and nobody would've argued his right to wear the uniform. He tugged at his collar once or twice, and I saw a little shine of sweat on his forehead by the time the first hour of introductions was up.

Finally, the prosecutor, Mr. Mayhew, got down to business and started telling the jury what he meant to convict my daddy of.

"The courts will show," he said, leaving his spot behind his desk, "that Mr. Stephenson with malice aforethought arrived at Saint Paul's Church, and with gun in hand, he approached the priest—opening fire on him, and killing him instantly."

Well, no kidding. Everybody knew that part already.

I wished he would say something snappy, make some real accusations, do something to startle the old white men who sat in two rows opposite him. But no, he just paced back and forth, and in that slow, plodding Southern voice of his, he said out loud what everyone already knew. It was old news to us all, and I don't think anyone was moved by it, or gave a damn about it one way or another.

Then Hugo Black got up and said his piece.

He only stood. He didn't pace back and forth, but he leaned forward, his hands on the desk as he spoke.

"It is *true* that Edwin Stephenson shot and killed Father Coyle. He did so in daylight, before a number of witnesses. However, I intend to show that his actions did not represent the behavior of a sane man—that, in fact, he was deranged by a series of events beyond his control, not least of all the elopement of his delinquent, disobedient, ungrateful daughter with a Puerto Rican day laborer . . . an elopement facilitated by the scheming priest, who sought only to add to his own congregation."

I objected to a whole lot of things in that description.

For one thing, I'm no delinquent. I ran away a few times, but that shouldn't mean anything to the judge or jury—and I was never arrested for anything, so the word doesn't seem right. So, yes, I ran away; and, yes, the police brought me back at my daddy's behest until I got married and he couldn't do that no more. All right, if that's all it takes to be a delinquent, then fine. But I don't like the word. It says something about me that isn't true, and it makes me sound like a child.

For another thing I don't like, my daddy has never behaved like a sane man, so it's not like anything he did on that day on the church's front steps was anything out of the ordinary for him. It wasn't some "crime of passion," as I've heard it put. He knew good and well what he was doing, and if he was deranged when he did it, well, he's been deranged his whole life, when he's done everything. Convict him for fifty years of being a jackass, why don't they.

For a last thing I don't like, and the worst thing of all . . . I objected to the way the old men in the jury box looked at me, their eyes all narrow and hateful, like maybe they'd had bad daughters of their own—girls they'd like to beat or lock away, or send the police chasing after. I didn't like the way they shook their heads when Hugo Black talked about me being a disobedient, ungrateful person (and I didn't like those words either). If they had daughters of their own, I'm sure those daughters were never obedient enough, and never grateful enough, either. And I really, *really* didn't like the way they sneered when he called Pedro a Puerto Rican. Who cares if he's from Puerto Rico? Hugo Black said it like an insult, and it's not an insult: It's just a place people come from.

Ah, but not *white* people. Not as far as these men know or care.

It's not like Pedro's even very dark, so I don't see what the big deal is. When I get a suntan on my arms, my skin's browner than his, not like it matters to twelve ignorant Alabamans in a jury box. I guess I'm an ignorant Alabaman, too, but Lord knows I'm not an idiot. I just don't know what's wrong with those men up there.

So I sat there getting mad, thinking about all the things that were wrong with all the things Hugo Black was saying, and it got warmer and warmer in there. My hands started feeling all tingly, and the tingling went up my wrists, past my elbows, up my neck, and into my eyes—where it settled in like silver fireworks, and that's when I realized I was having another spell.

I started to panic, because I'd never had one in front of people before—except for my mother, that one time—and here I was, in a crowded courtroom, and the edges of everything were going black. I had an awful thought: that if I did anything crazy it'd hurt Mr. Mayhew's case when he called me to testify. As it was, nobody was likely to take me too seriously, and if I was some kind of lunatic who had fits and spells, then that just made everything worse.

I reached for Chief Eagan's hand and grabbed it, and squeezed it.

He squeezed it back. I just hoped and prayed that whatever came next wouldn't be too loud, too crazy. I hoped and prayed that the old chief would help keep my feet on the ground, and give me something to hang on to.

There was nothing else I could do. Like it or not, the spell was coming.

It started up at the front of the room, behind the judge. Or maybe it started *with* the judge, I can't say for sure. It poured out from behind him, a cloud of darkness that didn't really move like a cloud, it moved more like fog spilling down a hill, swallowing up tree trunks and hedges, moving almost like water, so very thick, and so very black. It coiled and curled, and billowed sometimes like a giant was blowing on it, fanning it, so it'd fill the whole room.

It *spilled*. Maybe that's a better way to say it. It spilled out from some spot behind the judge and it collected around Hugo Black, and wound between the old men on the jury, snagging up against them. I thought of cotton candy at the fair, gathering itself into fluff around the spool; but this wasn't pink, and it wasn't sweet. It was a shadow spun out of glass and needles, instead of sugar.

I watched it move like it was alive, a living fog shadow, sharp and delicate, too—a frothy thing as sharp as nettles. I wondered if it would prick and sting my skin when it reached me; I wondered if it would stuff itself down my throat and smother me; I wondered if it would touch me at all.

It wasn't touching me.

Or I should say, it hadn't reached me.

But, oh, it was filling the courtroom, drifting about like snow blown into the corners. I've never seen snow for myself, but I've seen pictures in books, the way it's thick and the way it covers everything, piling up against fences and walls like a big blanket shook open and left to drop. This was like that, and it was like water, and it was like smoke. This was like nothing at all, if nothing was evil and it had a shape to it.

The room was almost full, but it still hadn't touched me.

It still kept its distance, only a little. Only a few inches, though it had consumed Chief Eagan by then. He looked straight ahead, not feeling it at all, not noticing it. I could see his shape, all sharp posture and crisp uniform facing forward, and I knew he was looking straight ahead, daring those awful men to call him out. Daring them to let my daddy go. But not seeing the creeping darkness, even as it pushed itself up his nose and around his neck, wrapping there tight like a pair of hands.

He squeezed my fingers, and the darkness pulled away from me, it pulsed like a heartbeat, like it wanted to be up against me. But he squeezed my hand and it wobbled. It gave me another inch.

I couldn't see anything anymore. Just myself: my dress, my lap with my handbag in it, my right arm and hand, the curve of my knees, my feet if I looked down—I could just see the top of my brown button heels, the pointed toes.

Everything else was dark as night, all the lights turned out except for one that was shining on me. Or shining inside of me. Maybe it was the light that pushed it away, and not the squeeze of the chief's hand. I almost felt a tiny swell of hope to think it, but I didn't want to get ahead of myself . . . not when the room was dark, and the whole world was full of spun black glass, of prickly cobwebs and fog.

Then I heard his voice.

Not the chief's. The *father's.*

Not my father, but Coyle, who was dead because my daddy shot him in the face for seeing me married off. The priest was there, and here I was at his funeral. No, not his funeral. His trial. Or, I mean . . . it was my daddy's trial.

Father Coyle sat before me, facing me, in the black cassock with the little white collar tucked inside it—so this time I could talk to him directly instead of writing little confessions to him in my journal. Only that didn't make any sense, because if he was sitting facing me, he'd have to be in the middle of the bench in front of me, straddling the lap of the lady whose hat I'd been staring at this whole time.

That wasn't the only reason it didn't make sense, of course. That was just the first thing that sprang to mind when I saw him, and there was a light inside him so I could see him, even though everything else was dark. (Everything except for me, and except for him.) I don't think we were even inside the courtroom anymore. I don't think we were even on earth. We could've been anywhere.

Father Coyle looked tired, but he smiled at me. That same gentle smile he always wore, the one that said the world was big and full of bad things, bad people, but there were good things, too—and good people could make a difference. Eventually. If they lived long enough.

He said, "Ruthie, there you are. I'm glad to see you're all right." His voice was a million miles away, and I could barely hear it.

"But you're not," I told him like he wasn't aware, and I felt my eyes filling up with tears, and I hoped I wasn't crying back in the real world, back on earth where I squeezed Chief Eagan's hand. "You're supposed to be dead, and in heaven. Am I dead, too?"

I think he said, "No, you're not dead. You're brave, and strong, and alive."

"Can anyone else see you?"

"No. Just you. I'm not in the courtroom, any more than you are."

I was definitely crying, wherever I was. "I don't care, I'm just glad you're here. You're pushing the dark away."

He shook his head. His mouth moved again, and he might've said something like, "That's not what's happening," but I couldn't be sure. I heard the next part more clearly: "Now listen to me, girl: You must stay away from Chapelwood, always and forever. Stay away from anyone who wants to bring you there, anyone who tries to talk you into visiting. They want you, Ruthie. They will feed you to the night."

"I don't understand . . ." I strained to listen, but it felt weird. It looked like he was right in front of me, but it sounded like he was hollering through a tin can on the other side of the city.

"You understand they mean to harm you. I know you understand that much. You should stay away from the courthouse, too. The Americans have contaminated this place, you can see it for yourself."

"I can't see anything at all, except for you."

"That's what I mean. You and Chief Eagan and everyone else with a droppa good left in you: Leave this place. Leave it, and don't return."

"But I'm a *witness*," I insisted. "I'm going to help them convict my daddy, for what he did to you."

He told me, in that stretched-thin voice that faded in and faded out, "No, you won't. And it doesn't matter anyway. What's done is done, and what comes next is set in stone. You'll be a drop in the ocean, Ruthie Gussman. I appreciate your faith, your determination. More than you know, dear girl. But it can only hurt you now, and it can't help *me*."

"Are we in purgatory? Is that what this is right now?" I asked suddenly. I remembered him telling me stories about purgatory.

"No. This is only a place, Ruthie," he said sternly, and the light flickered and came back, but not quite as strong. "Ruthie, there is darkness coming. I want you to leave before it gets here. Leave Birmingham, leave Alabama."

My cheeks were wet, and my voice hardly worked at all. I wondered if he could hear me, any better than I could hear him. "How can I stop them if I leave?"

"You can't stop them anyway."

"It can't end like that," I argued. "Not like this, without any justice, not without a *fight*. I can't do much, but I can fight."

He sighed, or his ghost sighed—if ghosts even breathe at all. "Justice is for the living, dear girl. Don't stay for me. Find some other old spirits to comfort you, but find them somewhere else."

I wanted to argue some more, but there came a sound that wasn't a sound—it was something I *felt*, not something I heard. My ears popped so hard that it hurt, and my hand hurt, too, and the darkness was unspooling away from me . . . back to the judge, or behind him, or underneath him. Father Coyle was gone and the darkness was leaving, and Chief Eagan was holding my hand, and I was crying like a baby.

Someone handed me a handkerchief and I took it. I blew my nose and wiped my eyes and wondered what I was supposed to do, because I thought I was supposed to stay here and fight—but what if I was wrong? I didn't want to be wrong. I didn't want to believe Father Coyle, or his whispering ghost, because it was easy . . . when all I had to do was show up for court and answer the lawyer, and say my piece even if it didn't mean anything in the long run.

I second-guessed everything.

The devil reads the Bible too, and that old serpent is everywhere, under every rock and up every tree.

Through my tears I wondered if that *wasn't* Father Coyle, or his ghost, or his not-purgatory . . . and maybe the advice to leave is just what something, somewhere, wants me to think is the good priest's friendly direction, helping me find my way along this crooked path. Maybe that ghost was just a piece of the darkness, just a trick of the spell that ate my vision and flooded the room with nothing at all, a night sky without any stars, brought down from heaven and dropped inside the courthouse.

I couldn't trust anything, anyone. Not even myself, and the spells are mine alone. They come from my own damn head, as far as I know—nobody else can see them, nobody else can feel them, or knows what they sound like, what they say, what they mean. Nobody else knows why I run from them, and nobody else saw Father Coyle's ghost in the pitch-black room that wasn't in the courthouse.

Nobody can see this but me.

And just like Hugo Black will tell you, and just like the old men in the jury box believe without even wondering . . . you can't trust me for *shit*.

Just ask them.

Lizbeth Andrew (Borden)

~❦~

From the time I hung up the phone, concluding my conversation with Inspector Wolf, I had three hours to make my preparations before I would be compelled to leave for the train station.

I had no idea how long I'd be gone, no idea what weather I'd find, and on a whimsically morbid note, no idea if I'd ever return. I didn't much care, until I considered the cats—but it wasn't quite the dilemma it might've been. Strange as it felt to me, I used the phone; I tried several numbers and several addresses, and eventually I reached Miranda Closely at the Boston Humane Society— who assured me that one of their Fall River affiliates would be happy to keep watch over the colony of felines in my absence. It was a great relief to hear it, especially since the little tin-bucket kitten was growing stronger. I thought he had an honest chance of making his way in the world, if someone would just feed him and make sure he came in from the cold.

I am very glad for the Humane Society. It makes me feel less like I watch over these small things alone.

(The Fall River office had no phone, thus my roundabout dealings, and lest you wonder, I cemented Mrs. Closely's assurances with a sizable grant. I did not mention to that fine woman that, should I fail to return, what remains of my fortune is entirely theirs. You're no longer in need of care, Emma—indeed, you're well beyond it. I have no one else to leave it to, and at least it can do some good in the Humane Society's hands.)

After my phone calls, I packed up my trunk and waited for the car to collect me. It was a nice car, not so rattling and loud as some others I'd ridden in, and the young man who drove it made minimal polite conversation—in the fashion of a professional who speaks only enough to earn his tip, and not bother his passenger.

I tipped him well, not least of all because he honestly seemed to have no idea who I was. He must have been new in town, or new to the car service at least. Either way, it was a refreshing change of pace, and it set a good tone for the journey to follow.

I left Fall River, and I became anonymous.

I was no longer the round-faced girl of thirty years ago, wearing high-necked dresses and nervous smiles. I was not the defendant, the axe murderess exonerated by the courts—but not her fellow citizens. Outside the city limits, no one recognized or thought twice about me: sixty-something years of age, my hair gone nearly white.

(It went that way suddenly, not long after Nance disappeared. It went white long before you died, Emma, but you know that already. For a long time, I thought it was almost funny; I thought I looked too young to have such hair. These days, my face is catching up to it.)

No one knew me as anything but Miss Lizbeth Andrew, lone spinster riding the rails on spinster business. Heading for warmer climes, I hinted to the few fellow passengers who chitchatted enough to require an answer. Needed to heat up these old bones, lest the arthritis make me slow and infirm.

I've gotten bad at chitchatting. I feel stilted and rude, but I try. And I have money, so I'm usually forgiven the lapse in etiquette. Thank heaven for grandmother's jewelry, and for silk. I was rich and anonymous, and the farther I traveled from Fall River, the more powerful I felt.

I cannot remember the last time I felt powerful.

I want to say that it was uncomfortable, but it was not. It was only normal, or how normal should have looked . . . how normal *might* have looked for me, if I'd left thirty years ago and found some other place to haunt.

I could not catch the very first train out of Fall River, so I had to catch the next one, later that evening. It ran through the evening to Providence, and then I took another train to Boston. A roundabout journey, yes, but Boston was the closest place from whence I could get a more or less direct rail line to Birmingham, Alabama.

I say more or less because I had to change trains twice, and the journey took a full day and a half, but it was *only* a day and a half. Due to the arcane rituals of train schedules, it would've been two days or more before I arrived, if I'd tried to be more direct about it.

A day and a half was plenty, though. A day and a half of trying to get comfortable in a single seat that scarcely reclines, subsisting on galley food, enduring awkward conversations with strangers . . . I'm not looking forward to the return trip, I'll say that much. If I make it at all.

But as mentioned above, I shouldn't really have thought of it as some kind of odious burden to interact with my fellow passengers. I ought to have considered it *practice*. It's been years since I've had any regular social interaction, but you'd think it'd be the kind of thing that's difficult to forget—that the patterns of speech and behavior should come naturally, and be easily remembered. Not for me. Unless I'm being too hard on myself, and I've been guilty of such personal unkindness before. For all I know, I'm doing quite well. I have nothing to compare my progress to, so I must assume that any and all progress is to be lauded.

That's how I'll come at the matter: with optimism, rather than self-flagellation. I'm too old to beat up on myself like that anymore.

I'm also too old to travel comfortably for more than a few hours at a time. It was hell on my back and shoulders, trying to sleep with a little pillow—my head leaned against the space between the seatback and the window, rattling in that rumbling rhythm of the tracks. By the time I arrived in Birmingham, Alabama, I had a headache of immense proportions . . . combined with an intense desire to bathe and change clothes.

First, I needed to find my hotel.

No, *first* I needed to retrieve my trunk and find transportation, *then* the hotel. And then, to locate the Boston inspector who had so suddenly roused me from my isolation.

No, that wasn't true, either—as it turned out. The inspector found *me* first, and thereby upended my half-formed plans.

The porter took my trunk down from the steps and I followed behind him, squinting against the midday sun. After the overcast dimness of the train cars, it was perfectly awful—and rather hot, once I stood outside, at the mercy of its full brilliance. The air wasn't so bad; it wasn't the muggy wonderland of outermost hell I'd heard about, but instead it was almost cool and dry. The sun, though . . . it was relentless up there, and it cooked me inside the navy blue travel dress I'd chosen for the trip.

"Can I find you a car, ma'am?" the porter offered, and I almost told him yes, that I'd appreciate it greatly—but someone else answered for me.

"There's no need for that. I've gotten us a car. It's waiting just outside the station."

I held my hand over my eyes to shade them, and behold, there stood Simon Wolf.

His appearance was not so different from our previous meeting. He was older, of course, but so am I. He was still a big man, all pink-faced and light-haired, in well-tailored clothes and shiny spectacles that caught the sun and threw it around his cheeks. He smiled broadly and stepped forward, removing his hat. "Miss Andrew," he said, as cavalier as could be.

"Inspector Wolf, it's a pleasure to see you again." See? My social niceties were recovering. I tipped the porter and thanked him for his assistance as the inspector helped himself to my trunk.

"Likewise, I can assure you. The meeting may be a strange one, but I'm happy to have the company all the same. Here." He held a door open for me. It was tricky for him as he navigated the oversized trunk, but he pulled it off with flair. "The car is waiting across the lot."

"I must say, I'm surprised to see you. I thought I'd find you at the hotel, perhaps."

"Surprised? But I'm a detective!" he noted happily, wrangling the trunk into the road. I let him lead the way, for all the cars looked the same to me—some marked as public taxis, some not. All black and shiny, the same model of Ford you're starting to see everywhere.

"That's true, and it's not that I'd forgotten . . ." I stepped down off a curb, sticking closely in his wake. "I'd only thought you'd be out . . . detecting."

"Nonsense. It took ten minutes with a schedule to see which engine would likely bring you to town. There were only four arriving through New York or Boston before the end of the week, and I had a feeling you wouldn't have time to catch two of them—and wouldn't wait around for a third. That left this one, and here you are. Easy as pie!"

"Your detecting skills are as sharp as ever."

"You sounded eager, so I chose your most likely departure, charted a most likely course, and took my chances. Detecting, *indeed* . . . And here we are." He stopped beside a big black car, somewhat larger than the average Model T. It wasn't a coupe or a roadster, but some kind of touring car. The driver climbed out and assisted him with my trunk, and then we climbed inside. "I thought we would visit the hotel first, so you could leave your trunk behind and refresh yourself, if you like. Then a bite to eat, and then . . ." He glanced up at the driver, who stared straight ahead—but I understood. He didn't wish to say too much. "Then we have a lot to talk about."

"I'm looking forward to it."

It was true, despite my aching head and travel weariness. This man had a portrait of my Nance, and this city had strange things prowling its streets at night. Fall River once had strange things prowling its streets, too, and I didn't like the symmetry of it.

So we had work to do, and despite the circumstances, I was glad for it. It'd been ages since I had any real work in front of me. Once

upon a time, I would've looked forward to such tedium as my life
has lately become; it appeared infinitely preferable to the mayhem
of thirty years ago—and only a fool would reject the comfort of rou-
tine for weeks of murder and monsters.

And yet . . . there I was.

Again.

The hotel was quiet and pleasant: not too fancy, but no flophouse, either. Wolf said he chose it for its discretion and proximity to downtown, but I think he might've also had his eye on the
meal schedule. I don't say this to tease him for his size; I say this
because he brought it up twice on the ride over there, and once
again upon our arrival—praising the offerings, and recom-
mending them highly.

Once I was checked in, I asked for twenty minutes for
myself. He offered an hour, but I can dress more quickly than
that, and I was hungry, and I wanted to see this portrait of
Nance so badly that I hadn't been able to ask about it yet. The
anticipation had positively paralyzed me.

I changed into a fresher dress, a cream-colored tea-length
affair with yellow roses and sleeves that were only three-quarters
long, but the outfit worked nicely with a wrap, in case the tem-
perature were to plummet when the sun went down. I chose a
round-brimmed hat and button-shut sandals for comfort, and
hoped I struck a dignified silhouette that wasn't too much "mut-
ton dressed as a lamb," as they say. I was covered, at any rate, and
I would not be too warm. I wasn't sure how different the fashions
might be, from New England to the Old South, but surely we all
receive the same catalogs, don't we? Everyone must have a Macy's
or a Nordstrom, I should think. A Sears Roebuck, if nothing else.

I felt silly dedicating so much thinking time to making

myself presentable. I usually didn't bother. So few people ever saw me outside of the house, it just wasn't something that I counted a priority.

But when I was finished at the mirror, and I was satisfied that I'd achieved this presentable state, I rejoined Simon Wolf downstairs in the banquet hall.

It wasn't so much a hall as a large room with several tables, all impeccably set, with pitchers of iced tea and lemon slices chilling on plates with ice. Wolf held out a chair for me, and I took it; then he explained that it was a bit late for lunch, around these parts . . . but the hotel mistress had not yet closed the kitchen, so we were in luck.

Lunch was divine, and the talk was small until we were into our second glass of sweetened tea (a new thing for me, and one I rather liked) and the dessert plates had been taken away. (I'd never known there was any such thing as key lime pie, but I now consider myself a great fan thereof.) But after the plates were effectively licked clean, the napkins were folded beside our silverware, and the table was cleared between us . . . Wolf reached into a satchel he'd left sitting beside his chair.

"I know what's brought you here, and I can't flatter myself by pretending it was the promise of my company. To keep you waiting any longer would be unkind."

He produced a thin sheet of sketch paper, folded in half. He let me do the honors.

With trembling hands, I straightened it.

"The likeness isn't perfect." He sounded almost apologetic. "But it's clear enough that I knew it, and I thought of you. The connection with the axes notwithstanding."

I ran my thumb along the edge, careful to keep from rubbing the pencil marks that made up the halo of her hair. And it *was* her hair. It was her face, her eyes, her jawline. Her mouth, full and wide, ready to turn up at the edges for a bawdy joke or a sip of scotch. It wasn't a caricature, or a loose sketch; it was indeed a portrait, and a good one—if not from a hand with formal training.

I would've known her anywhere, even after all this time. Even though she didn't haunt me, for all that I wished she would.

My heart squeezed tight, and I tried to keep from squeezing the paper, too. I swallowed hard, and blinked back the dampness that welled up in my eyes. "Where did you find this?"

"In a basement, beneath the big government building downtown. It was in a box with other evidence, regarding the city's recent spate of axe murders. But I think I mentioned most of that over the telephone."

"Yes, I'm sure you did." I couldn't remember. I looked up from the image, though it almost hurt me to do so. "What does this . . . what does *she* have to do with the local axe murders?"

"This picture was drawn by one of the attack survivors, a man named Gaspera Lorino. He was badly injured, and his recovery has been incomplete—or so I'm led to understand—but that's the way it sometimes goes with a bad head wound. He called her the gray lady, but if he offered any further explanation, it wasn't passed along to me."

I stared at the drawing again. *The gray lady* . . .

I remembered Nance, her body as gray and pale as a fish's belly. Alive, but changed, or changing. The image I held in my hands—it wasn't an image of my beloved as she'd appeared toward the end, no. This was before the darkness took her, when her eyes were still bright and she still smiled at me when I said her name. This was before the water, and before Doctor Zollicoffer. Or whatever he was, by the time he reached us.

"I haven't yet spoken to Mr. Lorino," Wolf said gently. "I

was waiting for you. I thought you might want a word with him, and for that matter, I think his sister might prefer a woman's inquiry to mine. I chatted with her briefly on the phone, through the sanatorium offices; she did not sound wildly enthused about the idea of a detective interviewing her brother, so I might've mentioned that Lorino's artwork depicted a woman from a missing persons case, unsolved all these years. I said that you were coming into town, at my request . . . and I may have implied that Nance was your sister. As a matter of narrative convenience, you understand."

"You didn't mention my name?"

"Not your old one. To the best of everyone's knowledge, you are Miss Lizbeth Andrew, and far be it from me to correct anyone's assumption. Yours is a veritable reincarnation!" he said, but his smile looked almost forced. "I hope this arrangement meets with your approval, and my caution has not proved . . . insulting? For that surely was not my intent."

"You've played the situation admirably," I assured him. "And don't look so bashful about suggesting my rebirth; it's a fascinating belief that I've studied more than a bit. So I'll be Nance's sister, and play upon the sympathies of Mr. Lorino's sibling in turn. It's the best cover I could hope for in a thousand years."

"The plan sounds mercenary, when you put it like that."

"How else should I put it?"

"No, no. I didn't mean it was a bad thing." His smile was easier now. "I'm glad that we agree in intent and execution, that's all. So! The sanatorium's hours extend through five o'clock and it's only one thirty now. We have plenty of time—but I *did* tell the sister and the staff that we'd come by after lunch."

"You've constructed all sorts of plans ahead of my arrival."

Without even being certain of it, I did not add. His confidence amused me.

"Time may be of the essence. It would not do to dally."

We found another car—or rather, Wolf had one arranged for us already. Quite an architect of the calendar, this man. One step ahead of everything. I liked it, even though I found it intimidating (if I was honest with myself). Why did he need *me,* after all, if he was already so prepared? What role did he expect me to play in this weird drama?

If he had anything particular in mind—apart from "pretend to be Nance's sister, for interrogation purposes"—he did not disclose it on the ride to St. Vincent's Hospital.

The hospital itself was situated on a great lawn, green with lush grass and manicured hedges, and shady trees that hadn't lost any of their foliage yet to fall. Despite its exterior elegance, as we pulled up a driveway and parked in the shadow of the place, the word which sprang to mind was "hulking." The main structure was enormous and made of brick, with stone details lovingly applied in the last century's style. Grand, stately, and *hulking,* yes. Four and a half stories, with a steeplelike appendage on top, pointing toward the sky, plus a secondary wing with white porch rails running the length of each level.

The place was only thirty years old, and it already looked dated. But all in all, there were surely worse places to be sick.

"Reminds me of a sanatorium I know in Providence," I murmured, craning my neck to look out the window. I meant the one where Emma had gone, at the very end. (The one where you died without me beside you, because that's what you had chosen, and I chose to respect it. Even though I didn't want to.)

He opened his door and climbed out. "There's a certain style to these things, all across the land. At least, there's a certain

style to those built in the last century. Cut from a template, each
and every one of them."

"It's a nice template, though."

"Nice enough on the outside." He paused to pay the driver,
and then to dart around the car's hood in order to open my door.
"They're more progressive within, but not so much as a modern
inmate might prefer, I think."

(He's really quite the gentleman, Emma. It's a pity you never
gave him a chance. I think you could've been friends.)

Up the walkway we went, and through the main door. Beyond it,
there was a desk with a nun behind it. Obviously, I could've
guessed that it was a Catholic hospital, given the name, but for
some reason it still surprised me to see a woman in a habit working up front like that. I'd heard such awful things about how
Catholics were treated in the region; and when I looked around,
I saw that certain measures were being taken to ensure the safety
of the patients, and the security of the grounds.

An armed guard sat in a corner reading a newspaper. He
glanced up at Wolf and me as we entered the lobby—then
quickly judged us harmless, and went back to reading. An alarm
was established behind the main intake desk . . . I assumed
there was some kind of trigger or lever hidden beneath it somewhere, to be pulled in case of emergency. I wondered if they
treated this space like a saloon, and kept a shotgun behind the
counter.

Has it come to that, do you think? Emma, it's unreal. This
really is another country, I fear.

Several stacks of forms were presented on clipboards, and I
was compelled to fill them out—though Wolf merely signed

himself in. "I did all my paperwork yesterday," he explained. "Now they have me on file."

I obliged St. Vincent's with my new name (it was legal, after all, and therefore true), my address, and even filled in my phone number—since there was a place to put one, should the visitor have one to offer. I could've lied about any of it, but there was no point. I had nothing to hide, not really. Not anymore, and certainly not anything relevant to my visit.

When all was sorted and accepted, I signed my name on a different sheet, and noted the time of my arrival.

The nun gestured toward an orderly. He was an enormous man, half a head taller than the inspector and nearly as wide; but he wore a pleasant expression to go with his uniform, and I assumed that this was just one more form of security—something more subtle and versatile than a hidden firearm.

"This is Jeremiah. He'll bring you to Mr. Lorino's room. Please stay with him at all times, and obey any instructions he may feel compelled to give you. Most of our patients are peaceful and content, but a few are prone to outbursts. Should you see such an outburst, please resist any urge to intervene. Our staff is comprised of trained professionals. Please leave matters in our hands."

We agreed to these terms, and followed silently behind the big man.

Down one long corridor we tagged along, past rows of rooms with doors closed, their small windows lit from within (though we couldn't see what was inside). On the other side of the hall were larger rooms, common areas where patients gathered to play checkers or read pulp magazines drawn from well-thumbed stacks. I saw a piano in one such area, with sheet music open and ready—though no one was playing it at that time. The floors scrolled by in checkered linoleum, a modern amenity that kept the place quieter than tiles or stone, so that all the voices, the ringing phone at the desk, the squeaky wheeled carts, and even our own footsteps were too muffled to echo very much.

Finally we reached our destination, a door with a small square window crisscrossed with tiny bars threaded through the glass.

Jeremiah said, "Mr. Lorino is usually a calm man, and happy for company—but he doesn't always understand as much as he pretends to. The blow to his head, the blade . . ." He hesitated, as if uncertain how much he should say. He settled for, "There was bleeding in his brain. He sometimes gets confused, and there are subjects that agitate him."

"Is he ever violent?" Wolf asked.

"Not deliberately. His coordination isn't what it used to be, and there are times he struggles to control his limbs. I don't think he would harm you on purpose, but be aware—patients like him may prove full of surprises."

He knocked gently upon the door before opening it; I noticed that it wasn't locked, or else it only locked from the outside. "Mr. Lorino? You have visitors." He looked back at us, and said, "His sister was called away on a personal errand, but she will return shortly. Her name is Camille, and she knows that she might find you here when she's finished."

With that, he opened the door to reveal a man seated in a corner rocking chair, beneath a large window set well out of his reach. Sunlight streamed down on his head, making his very dark hair appear as if streaked with rust, and giving his pale blue hospital uniform an almost translucent appearance at the sleeve cuffs and the loosened collar.

In his hand he held a Bible, opened to what passage I could not tell.

He closed the book and left it lying across his knees.

He wore glasses, thin-framed ones, like the inspector's—but with lenses that were markedly thicker. They looked to be roughly the density of a good serving platter, so I shuddered to consider how poor his vision must be without them. They left an indentation across his nose and the top of his cheeks.

"Good afternoon, Mr. Lorino," I told him with a smile.

He smiled back, but said nothing.

Simon Wolf stepped forward to introduce himself. "I'm Inspector Wolf, from Boston—and this is Miss Andrew. Your sister told you we were coming, did she not?"

He nodded.

"Do you mind if we take a seat?" I asked, and when he did not object, I went to the edge of his bed and perched there, facing him. Wolf declined to join me on the quilt, but he stood beside me all the same.

I wasn't sure where to begin, but that was all right—the inspector had a plan, as usual. Not that it did him a great deal of good. He launched into his explanations: "Mr. Lorino, we're here about—"

The man in the rocker interrupted quickly. "You were sent by the stars, I know. It's about the church in the trees, and a blade on a stick, and the men in white—except when they're in black. You're here, and I knew to expect you. They told me you'd come." He spoke far faster than I'd expected he might, the words rattling out of his mouth one atop the other in a rapid rush.

"Your *sister* told you we'd come," Wolf insisted calmly.

"She doesn't know anything. She thinks you're here because of the gray lady, but that was only the cause, not the reason. It was only a piece, only a note. A telegram from the solar system, and from the cosmos beyond it."

I realized I'd have to dive right into the fray if I wanted to get a word (let alone a question) in edgewise. "But I *am* here because of the gray lady. That's what you called her, the woman in the picture you drew." I fished it out of my bag and, while I unfolded it, I continued. "I'm missing her. I've been missing her for years."

I held it up and showed it to him, but he stared right past it, at me instead. "And you'll miss her for all the years you have left. I'm sorry, but that's what the patterns tell me. Her image was only a lure. Through her and through the old doctor you touched the in-between place; you engaged it, you *battled* it—yet you returned with your life, and your sanity. You are the middle point between then, and now. Between that, and this. The patterns request your assistance. They have recalled you from the middle distance to do battle again."

My throat tightened. "The . . . the patterns?"

"In the stars. Good ones and bad ones, I'd say . . . but *they* say that's not true. They say there are only patterns that align with our interests, and those which do not. I do not know how much the will of humanity can sway them, or adjust them, or deflect them. That's the great question of the age, not the small ones—not the small patterns, small wars waged by Shapley and Curtis. Theirs is only a war of semantics, in the grand scheme— an argument between big and bigger with no idea how much bigger the biggest has biggened."

"I'm sorry . . . I don't understand. I only wished to ask you about this drawing." I still held it aloft, but it was drooping toward my lap.

"Ask whatever you like. I don't know her, and never did."

"Is she alive?" Wolf broached suddenly. It's the question I would've presented, had I gotten the chance.

"She is gone from this world."

"That's not what I asked."

Mr. Lorino frowned, and the left edge of his mouth twitched. "But I can't answer the question you asked. She is gone, that's the best I can tell you. She's gone, and she won't be back."

"Have you ever seen her before? In person?" I tried. Maybe the right arrangement of words would make the question better, or tease more information from him—since semantics seemed to matter.

"Only in the bladed night, in my dreams after the axe." He sighed. "Never in life, Miss Andrew. The drawing was only a little bait, a little candle in the darkness. They wanted you here. Or something wants you here, someone does. Someone wishes to fight blades with blades, to confront esoteric knowledge with esoteric experience—yours, and his." He nodded at the inspector. "Someone. Something."

Wolf said, "*I* am the one who invited her."

"No," he insisted stubbornly. "*They* did. They want you, too," he added with a nod. "They want all the help they can get, because a pattern has been . . . bent."

"Bent?" The conversation was getting away from me. It had been steered well away from Nance, at least, and it looked like it was going to stay aimed in some other direction. I let the paper lie in my lap, but I held it almost for comfort, as if it could ground me while the strange tide of this man's words worked to sweep me off my feet.

"Bent. Manipulated. Forced out of balance. That's a better way to put it," he muttered to himself. "*Balance*, that's a more correct term. There is balance in the universe—it was left in the wake of the old things. They left it behind, not that they meant to. It was only a happenstance, an unintended consequence of their leaving. Their upheaval was so great, so unprecedented, that everything they left behind, everything they failed to consume . . . it all aligned in favor of entropy, as a matter of self-preservation, you might say."

Inspector Wolf was stunned into silence, and I was right there with him.

Our confusion agitated our host; he fidgeted with his Bible, and then tossed it aside. It hit the floor with a thud, its pages fluttering and then settling, open to some chapter in Daniel.

It irked him, the way we did not grasp the universal truths he was doing his best to share with us—but what did we know about universal truths? Nothing. And what did we know of this man in the rocking chair? Very little, except that the dented place in the back of his head was where an axe blade had struck him, and although it had healed, it had left him a man who drew portraits of missing women—a man who chattered about entropy and the stars.

(I remembered, in the back of my mind, a tidbit about the Adventists—or rather, the woman who founded their church: She was a schoolgirl when she was hit on the head by a carelessly thrown rock. When she awoke, she could hear the voice of God. Or so it is said.)

"You will understand," he told us, but I think he was trying to convince himself. "Someone else must understand—someone who can bend the pattern back, while there's time to reshape it. Right now." He leaned forward, and his tone took a turn for the conspiratorial. "Right now, the only men who understand the pattern wish to use that understanding for evil. Or, no. Not evil. Unbalance, yes. I'll stick with that word. Balance. There is balance and unbalance, that is all."

I thought at first that this was his conclusion, his great final proclamation—so I took the pause to try one last time: "Please, Mr. Lorino. You're the only one who can answer this for me . . . If the gray lady is gone, and she isn't coming back, then where *is* she?"

He didn't exactly sneer, because he wasn't exactly being cruel. The twist of his lips was more like a dismissive thing, like once *again* I was on the wrong track, asking the wrong questions. But if he wanted me to ask the right ones, he could damn well give me some hint about what they were!

"No one can answer you. Not me, not anyone else." Then his eyes went almost cunning, and it worried me. For a moment, I could not be certain if he was balanced, or unbalanced. "However, there are others you can ask. They will lie to you, of course; but the lies might tell you something all the same. Ask at the church," he said, looking sideways over to Inspector Wolf. "*He* knows the one."

"Chapelwood?" he asked, but it wasn't really a question—I could see the certainty on his face, and the set of his jaw suggested resignation, too.

"The unmakers of balance. The benders of patterns. It's their magic, after all. They're the ones who shouted the invitation out into the galaxy, the ones who have raised their trumpets to the great Milky Way—whether or not it's the center of anything, or merely a small tendril in a greater picture, but the Great Debate is nothing, it means nothing. It's not about the balance. It's meaningless. The men at Chapelwood . . ." His attention wandered upward, to the small window over his head, and when he spoke again, his voice slipped from one thing to another. It dropped an octave. Syllable by syllable, it lost its manic warmth. "Ask them, but be careful about it. They've lost their offerings one by one by two by three, and they seek more to replace them. They'll tell you anything, if it might keep you there—and you have a glaring weak spot, my lady."

For a tense, awful minute his voice rang in my ears, and it wasn't his voice. Not the quick, nattering prattle of a madman who might not be mad, but the lower, richer, slower tones of a professor from upstate. His was the voice of a man who would've killed us all thirty years ago; and besides the sound of his words, there was a flash of the flat, terrible emptiness behind his eyes. I saw it, for all that it moved quickly—it darted across his face, fast and cold as a shark.

My heart stopped. I felt it, I swear—it went cold and heavy, and I couldn't breathe.

Wolf put a hand upon my shoulder. "Miss Andrew?"

I tried to swallow, but my mouth was so very dry.

"Miss Andrew?" Mr. Lorino said my name now, and when he said it, he sounded like himself again. The memory of an old shark was gone, and only this little man in his little room remained. "Are you all right?"

I would've answered, but a knock on the door spared me. A woman's voice announced, "Gaspera, it's me."

The woman who entered was younger than Mr. Lorino by perhaps as much as ten years. She was modestly dressed, with flat shoes and her hair in a tidy bun—but she wore a hint of rouge. Her eyes were tired but kind, and pretty in a doelike way.

Inspector Wolf smiled broadly. "Miss Lorino, I'm so glad you could join us. Miss Lizbeth Andrew, this is Miss Camille Lorino."

"It's a pleasure," I whispered. My heart was moving again, but feebly; my eyes were not watering, but I felt some lightness in my head and saw a faint smattering of sparks. I wasn't going to faint, was I? *No,* I told myself repeatedly. *I will not faint.*

I did not faint.

I said, "Your brother has been telling me about this drawing he made."

"It's a picture of your sister—isn't that right?" She closed the door behind her and came to sit beside me on the bed.

"That's correct. She . . ." I swallowed, desperate for the moisture. I would've given anything for a glass of water. "She disappeared thirty years ago. There's been no sign of her since. No sign but this one."

"I'm sorry to hear that," she said, softly and with sympathy. "Gaspera, what did you tell her? Could you help?"

"Not at all. Her Nance is lost, but," he said to me rather than to Camille, "you should keep the drawing if you like it."

"Technically, it's evidence," Wolf said. It wasn't quite an objection; he was only trying to move the conversation back to someplace more manageable. "In the axe murders, you know. That's where I found it, in a box with other evidence."

"Evidence," Mr. Lorino mumbled. "There's evidence, and then there's *evidence.* The attacker won't be caught, not by the likes of you. Maybe he shouldn't be."

"Gaspera, don't say such things."

"I'll say what I like," he snapped at his sister. "If that's the one privilege I gained by the bend in my skull, I'll take it. The man who attacked us is misguided, but not so misguided as he seems. His heart is in the right place."

Camille Lorino looked at me with apology in her eyes. "I'm sorry, but you see how he is. Talking in circles, and I never know what it means."

He leaned forward and patted her knee. "It's just as well. You have no part in this play, and I'm glad for that. It's a small mercy. Maybe those are all the mercies we have left. But you don't need to understand. *They* do." He bobbed his head toward me, then Wolf. "They will unbend the pattern. Maybe they'll even straighten the wrinkle—though if they don't, he'll straighten himself soon enough. Or someone else will do it for him . . . one of the robed men."

"Mr. Lorino, are you saying that you know who attacked you? Who murdered all those people?" Wolf asked. He was not quite incredulous, I think because he didn't know how much to believe. You could believe as little or as much as you liked when Mr. Lorino spoke . . . but good luck understanding any portion of it.

He shook his head, and the change in angle showed me quite clearly where the dent behind his left ear was deep and long, though it'd healed enough that his hair was growing back around its deeply cleft scar. "Do I know his name? No. I only know his shape, and his motive. He wants to unbend the pattern, too— but he's making a mess of it. I wouldn't worry about him."

"You wouldn't worry about an axe murderer?" I asked, trying to keep my eyebrows from lifting too high, or my voice from carrying too much insult.

"Not this one. He'll stop before long, or they'll stop him. Another two or three victims at best. There are bigger things at stake," he said with great and sudden earnestness. "More lives, *exponentially* more lives. Look at you, both of you—you're worried for the solar system, when the whole universe writhes in peril!"

His sister noticed the Bible on the floor, and bent to retrieve it—but he slapped it out of her hand, and rose from his seat. "It's useless, and I want you to take it away! Worse than useless, because it makes promises but offers no answers!"

"Gaspera, calm down," she told him firmly, and then retrieved the Bible. She held it to her chest, and did not offer to return it. "I'll take it away, if that's what you want—but you're the one who asked me for it in the first place."

"Take it away! Bring me something else, something with answers, not promises! I don't need a prophet!" he all but shouted at her. "I need an astronomer!"

The situation had tipped, or as Mr. Lorino would've put it, it had become unbalanced.

It was time for us to leave, so we excused ourselves before we could rile him any further . . . and before Jeremiah could return and compel our exit. Camille apologized and apologized, and we reassured her again and again that we understood and took no offense.

We left her holding the book against her bosom, staring with patience and sadness at her brother, waiting for something like sanity—or, at the very least, reasonableness—to return to him.

Back down the linoleum halls we retreated, walking side by side, not touching or speaking until we'd made it outside. When the big doors closed in our wake and we stood in the sunshine, beside the trim green lawns and rows of meticulous flowers, I retrieved enough of my senses to say, "Chapelwood."

"It's an estate outside of town. I've been looking into it."

"Coincidentally, so have I."

He gave me a crooked eyebrow and a pursed lip. "You don't say . . . ?"

I looked up at the bright blue sky, and blinked against the light. "Not Chapelwood exclusively, mind you. It's more an interest in alternative forms of worship, and Chapelwood has attracted the attention of people who"—I cleared my throat, still so very dry—"people who watch such things."

"Church-watchers? How funny," he said, but it didn't sound like he thought it was funny or even odd. "I didn't realize you were that sort of enthusiast."

"There is truth in the faith that raised me, but that's not the only truth to be found. It's not the only path . . . and some of the older, stranger paths . . . intrigue me."

"I know the feeling," he told me with a grin. "Well, let's find our driver. Ah, there he is—parked over there. I told him to give us an hour, but we've scarcely spent two-thirds of that."

"And where shall we go next? To Chapelwood?"

"Not directly. First I want another word with Ruth, and I think you'll want a word with her, too. Her father's the man who murdered the priest, and conveniently enough for us, he's on trial for the crime. Right this very moment."

"But what does the trial have to do with the church? Or his daughter?"

He strolled off toward the car, and I went with him.

"Edwin Stephenson had recently been drawn into the Chapelwood congregation, and he dragged his family along with him. Ruth did not appreciate or approve of the place at all, which speaks well of her intuition, I'm sure. At any rate, there's something knocking around in the back of my mind . . . something Lorino said, about Chapelwood having lost its offering. I think I know what that offering was, and I think Ruth may have more to tell us."

Leonard Kincaid, American Institute of Accountants (Former Member)

SEPTEMBER 29, 1921

The math is broken. Or I am broken, and haven't figured it out yet—I can't tell which. It's not that things aren't adding up, because they are; it's just that they're adding up to things that don't make sense. I'm not finding the numbers of Chapelwood's next targets . . . instead, I think the equations are trying to tell me something else this time.

If algebra is the language of God, or the universe, or of space and time for all I know, then I wish I understood its syntax better. The grammar baffles me, and the sentence structure pulls me in circles.

I ran out of blackboard space.

Rather, I woke up and found my blackboard covered in

numbers so small, handwriting so very tight, that at first I thought I'd simply fallen asleep and—in another dreamy daze—I'd laid the chalk on its side and scraped it across the slate. Upon closer inspection, I saw that I was mistaken. Tiny, tiny numbers, all over the place. Tiny columns and tables, only some of them running left to right, top to bottom. Some of them crossed on the diagonal, and some even overwrote the blackboard's wooden frame. In those weird little places, the text was not sharp enough for me to read it.

I knew that I had written it. Even if I didn't know my own script so well, there's nobody else who comes or goes from this flophouse room, and I've paid it far enough in advance that even the proprietor can't be bothered to check on me, unless I should cause trouble somehow. I never cause trouble, for him or anyone else. I never give anyone a reason to come inside, and I keep the door locked when I'm "home," and when I'm not.

So the numbers were mine, drawn from my own brain when I was unaware. I wasn't surprised by that simple fact—after all, I'd been pulling these numbers from thin air for over a year, using them to populate the equations I devised for the Chapelwood monsters. Some mornings I'd awaken to find them scrawled on notepaper left beside my bed, and some mornings I'd find them on the blackboard, or left upon my desk directly in pencil (on one odd occasion).

No, I was surprised by the sheer volume of it all, and likewise, I was surprised to see the pattern changed. These weren't the neatly slotted digits that lined up nicely with my graphs; these were systems that swirled and dipped, broke apart and reassembled.

I traced them with my eyes, trying to determine what I was meant to see. I can read a formula like other men read Shakespeare—teasing out the truths and particulars from the empty spaces, and divining meaning from scant hints and puns.

(Yes, numbers can twist themselves into puns. Any crackpot numerologist could tell you as much.)

What do I see? What does this tell me?

I think it means interference. I see new chess pieces coming into play, two of them at least—and always that uncertain variable of Ruth Stephenson (or whatever her name is now), who escaped before they could take her, and before I had to kill her. She got away, and the thing that waits on the other side of the wall is none too pleased about it; it would send them after her again, and maybe it will in time . . . but for now, she's too visible, too much in the public eye. After her father's trial, I think. They might well settle upon her again, and then I'll have to reassess her importance and safety in the scheme of the universal good.

Does that sound strange? Of course it does. Everything is, though, isn't it?

Upon the blackboard, in the soup of numbers I left there in my sleep, I saw poetry . . . but it wasn't the straightforward kind that makes cheap rhymes about the beauty of a woman or the freshness of spring. This poem is talking its way around something else. "Interference," I said. Maybe "resistance" is a better way to put it.

But resistance to whom? To me? To Chapelwood?

I made myself a pot of coffee and pulled up a chair. I retrieved a pair of reading glasses I don't often need from the top drawer, and I leaned forward with my face so close to the board that my breath left brief puffs of fog upon it.

I took it all in, and I let myself detach away from it . . . I closed my eyes and let my attention distance itself, in a faint approximation (or a reaching toward) of that mesmerized state which prompted me to produce the numbers in the first place. I retreated, trying to see the bigger picture instead of just the individual numbers, statistics, and symbols.

When I blinked myself back to alertness, I felt only a sense that I was no longer alone in my fight . . . but that it might not be a good thing, and I couldn't understand why. The thought of an ally thrilled and delighted me! But it neither thrilled nor delighted the universe, so far as I could tell.

I could not conclude that I was the one in danger, because the numbers cared nothing about me, personally. The numbers were only a guide to a greater good, whether or not that was their original intent. This unexplainable cosmology sought to explain itself, and I struggled to understand why a powerful friend could do anything but help my world-saving enterprise. I would be overjoyed to find my load lightened, after all.

Unless . . .

. . . I squinted at the chalk, and with the tip of my finger I tapped one corner of the message—collecting a bit of white dust that smelled like school. Unless the dark thing (which surely is not God) is interested in the powerful, more than it is interested in me (for I am powerless, except for my axe). Unless the dark thing will prey upon it, before it can assist me.

Should the darkness consume me, what would it gain? Nothing, really. One lone mortal who bends his brain around the exponential zeroes of the galaxy in order to hear a voice from the other end of it. But what if some more useful party should topple into its hunting gaze?

What then?

I stood from my chair and finished the last of my coffee. It was bitter and lukewarm, but it sharpened my brain. I pushed the chair aside and pushed the reading glasses up onto my forehead. I was still missing something. (Missing quite a lot, no doubt, but that was always the way of things.)

I carried my cup to the sink and deposited it there, washing it with a little soap and setting it aside to dry.

Over my shoulder I glanced again at the blackboard, its lure impossible to ignore.

It was still trying to tell me something. It was drawn from my own hand, unspooled from my own mind, and still it could not make itself understood.

Or could it?

I turned around, leaning backward against the sink. I was as far away from the blackboard as I could get without opening a door and letting myself into the hallway. And maybe, if I relaxed my eyes . . . if I let them unfocus until the numbers were so much chalk dust, smeared across the slate . . . I saw something other than the mutilated web of formulas.

I could swear I almost saw the face of a woman. A face I almost knew—for I'd seen a sketch of it once before, in the city newspaper.

Last year there was an Italian man, and I almost killed him with my axe . . . only because he fought to protect his wife, not because he was of any interest to Chapelwood or its gods. He survived, because I had no real interest in killing him, only removing him as an obstacle; and when he awoke he spoke of the stars, and of miracles and Milky Ways.

And he drew a picture of a woman no one knew.

Lorino, that was his name. (I don't remember the names of all of them. There are too many now—but he was an unfortunate bystander, so his name is lodged in my head.) He's at the hospital downtown, I think. Or he was, anyway, and I never heard that he left it.

If I were to visit him, would he know me?

We met in the dark, and our meeting was swift and violent.

I don't know if he ever saw my face, but then, I don't know if he ever saw that woman's face, either. It wasn't his wife or his sister, and no one ever stepped forward to identify her. Who was she? Would he tell me?

It was a preposterous thing to wonder, and to halfway plan . . . a dangerous thing, more dangerous than the murders themselves. But as I stared at the blackboard and, yes, the face I could now see quite plainly that had formed upon it, at a distance . . . I was wondering and halfway planning how I might go about visiting Mr. Lorino, so that we might exchange a word or two.

I might need to. It might matter.

Ruth Stephenson Gussman

They finally called my name.

I don't know why I jumped; I knew they were going to ask for me, and I knew good and well what I had to do. I don't know why my whole body acted like it was a big shock when they said, "The prosecution calls Ruth Stephenson Gussman to the stand." I'd rehearsed it a million times, over supper and in my dreams. I'm sure Pedro was sick of hearing about it, but that was fine, because I was sick of thinking about it. It was time to talk about it.

My face got real hot, and my hands started to shake. I was half afraid I was about to have one of those spells, because what a god-awful time for it, you know? But this was only the ordinary kind of scared, and I could still see fine. Nothing was crawling around my ankles, and no darkness descended, bringing ghosts down with it.

I rose to my feet, gripping the back of the bench in front of me.

Chief Eagan stayed seated beside me. He patted the back of my hand and whispered, "Go on, girl. Say your piece, and don't let them rattle you."

I nodded, swallowed, adjusted my hat and my sweater, and stepped out into the aisle—thinking of you, Father Coyle. And I'm telling you this because I haven't found any other spirits to chat with, and I miss you, and I trust you. Maybe if I keep talking, you'll answer me again.

It felt more than a little like going to church at Chapelwood, its pews lined up just like these benches with an aisle in the middle.

(Is that on purpose, do you think? Are courtrooms supposed to look like churches, with the judge up front just like a preacher, and the lawyers and everybody on either side like deacons? What's that supposed to tell us, exactly? The more I think about it, the less I like it.)

On either side of me, people watched me go up there. It was like being a bride, or going down front to kneel for an altar call, or something like that—except a million times worse. I was afraid I was going to trip and fall; I was afraid I was going to pass out cold. The aisle felt way too long, or maybe I was walking way too slow. My footsteps were the only sound at all, and they were cheap little secondhand heels echoing on the floor—but I couldn't hear anything else, not even anybody breathing, or sneezing, or waving paper fans against how warm it was getting indoors. It sounded like I was walking down a tunnel, all alone, and at the end of the tunnel, God only knew what I'd find.

All I found was a witness stand. I don't know why they call it that, since you sit down once you get there.

Mr. Henry Mayhew was waiting for me to get myself situated. I raised my hand when the bailiff brought the Bible and I said my name for the record, and all that nonsense, then fiddled with my sweater and shuffled my feet around—but as soon as I realized I was doing that, I forced myself to stop. I couldn't sit up there and fidget like a little girl. I had to hold my head straight like a woman.

Mr. Mayhew, in his voice as slow as molasses, asked me if I knew you, and I know it was just for the record but that was real dumb, because everyone knew I knew you. I spent the first few minutes on that stand answering a whole bunch of questions like that—easy ones, and maybe that was Mr. Mayhew being kind and letting me warm up. Mr. Black didn't object to any of the questions or anything I said, but then again, I was only saying facts.

Then he got around to the day you died, and I hadn't been there when it happened, so I couldn't say much about Daddy killing him.

"But you'd seen him earlier that day?"

"Yes," I said. "First thing that morning, I went out to Saint Paul's and Father Coyle married me and Pedro."

Over in the jury box, the sour-faced old men were shaking their heads and clicking their tongues. Oh, well. I already knew what they thought of me before I climbed up into the box in the first place. I wouldn't give a damn, except their opinion mattered. Just this once. And it mattered big—but God, I wished it didn't.

"Was your father aware of your betrothal?"

"No."

"You didn't tell him?"

I shook my head. "No. He didn't want me to get married, and he didn't like Pedro."

"Why is that?"

"Pedro's a good bit older than me, and he's Puerto Rican, and he's a day laborer . . . take your pick. That's probably what he'll tell you. But the real truth is, he just didn't want me out of his house, because then he couldn't tell me what to do anymore."

"Objection," called Hugo Black from his seat at the defense's table. He said it like this was all very dull, and a total waste of his time. "Calls for speculation."

"Withdrawn," Mr. Mayhew said obligingly. "But you are a grown woman, over the age of sixteen, and able to marry as you like."

"Damn straight I am."

"Language, Mrs. Gussman."

"Sorry," I mumbled. I felt my face getting hot again, but I took a deep breath and kept my head up. "But it was none of my daddy's business who I married. Like you said, I'm a grown woman. And we didn't have a wedding, so he wasn't paying for anything—and he didn't get any say in it."

I was real glad he wasn't in the courtroom just then. He'd taken a fall in his cell, that's what I heard through Chief Eagan. They had him under a doctor's care, but it didn't sound like he was too bad off. I wouldn't have been worried about him even if they'd said he was beat up something awful. I was glad he was gone, and glad he wasn't down there glaring at me while I talked.

But I couldn't help looking at his empty chair every once in a while anyway.

The rest of it was pretty straightforward and Mr. Black didn't object to anything else, and when Mr. Mayhew said he had no further questions for me, I wanted to die of relief. But then Hugo Black stood up for cross-examination and then I just wanted to die.

"Tell me, Mrs. Gussman," he began, "how many times have you run away from your father's home over the years?"

"What's that got to do with anything?"

"Just answer the question, or I'll treat you like a hostile witness."

I didn't know what that meant, but it didn't sound good. I had a feeling that he was going to treat me hard enough without it being called "hostile." So I said, "Off the top of my head, I don't know. Maybe five or six."

"Five or six times," he repeated, just for show—and not in case the jury hadn't heard me. "You fled the home of the man who'd raised you, cared for you your whole life."

"I fled the home of a man who beat me and my momma like a dog when it suited him."

He gave me the ugliest smile I ever did see. "But the Good Book tells us to spare the rod and spoil the child, and you are truly spoiled enough. Every child who's ever reprimanded finds the sentence too harsh."

"The Good Book says a lot of things nobody listens to anymore, too."

"Mrs. Gussman," he said, pretending to be gentle but mostly being cruel. "This is not a conversation. You'll answer the questions I ask, and leave any editorializing out of it. Do you know what 'editorializing' means?"

"Of course I do," I snapped. Then I remembered how he wanted it phrased, so I said, "Yes. I know."

"Good, good. So answer me this, if you please: How many times were you caught alone with boys after school?"

"Twice, and once it was my cousin Albert—and everybody knew damn good and well there was nothing going on."

"Editorializing . . . ," he warned me. "And language, too. I'll let it slide, because I want to know about the other time."

"The other time I was lonesome, and he was nice. He didn't pull anything funny. We just sat on a swing and talked, then Daddy found us and—"

"And he was upset, I expect."

"I couldn't leave the house for a month." I added real quick, before he could shoot me down, "Because he gave me a broken leg."

To the judge, Hugo Black said something about striking that last bit from the record, because it wasn't relevant. I wondered how on earth he could claim such a thing, but I'd already been told that the courtroom doesn't work like real life, and there are strange rules you've got to play by. Chief Eagan had told me, and so had Mr. Ward, when everyone was getting ready for the trial.

Mr. Mayhew objected to Hugo Black's objection, so the two men approached the judge to chat about it.

I looked back at Chief Eagan and he gave me an encouraging nod. I appreciated it, but it didn't do much to make me feel better. I wished Pedro could've been there, but he had to work. I wished Mr. Ward had been there, but I didn't know where he was— and come to think of it, I hadn't seen him for a couple of days. I wished I wasn't quite so alone, and maybe I wished it so hard it turned into a little prayer . . . because just then the doors opened at the back of the courtroom and two more people slipped inside.

One of them was Inspector Wolf, and the other was a woman about his age—but I didn't know who she was. She was not too tall and was rather ordinary-looking, except that she was dressed more nicely than the rest of us. I don't mean she was wearing anything flashy; it was just a nice cream-colored dress that suited a lady of a certain age, and it probably came with a nice price tag, too.

When she first walked in, she looked uncertain. The place was packed, so I thought at first she was just wondering where to sit, or if she should bother trying. But we locked eyes while the men beside me argued with each other and with the judge . . . and I swear, I think she understood. She felt sorry for me, and she wanted to say something to that effect—I could see it all over her face. Under ordinary circumstances, I might've been put off by that because I don't need anybody's pity. But right about then, I was feeling pretty sorry for myself, and that lady was welcome to join the party.

Inspector Wolf and the mystery lady stepped over to the side so they didn't block the door. They stood at the rear of the room, just behind Chief Eagan—but he didn't see them, because he didn't turn around. If he had, he probably would've said hello to the inspector, because I know they've met before.

Anyway, the lawyers and the judge quit arguing and they went back to their respective corners, like a couple of boxers in a ring. Hugo Black checked some paperwork he'd left there, then returned his attention to me. He didn't bother to come up to me again; he just half leaned, half sat on the edge of his table, facing me while he talked.

"So you felt that your father's household rules and punishments were excessive, is that right?"

"They *were* excessive," I told him. "And that wasn't just my opinion, either."

"You're the one on the stand. Other opinions need not be considered at this time—there's already plenty of hearsay to go around. Let us stick to verifiable facts: You've run away before, by your own admission."

"That's right."

"Because your father treated you poorly, most recently by making you attend church against your will."

"That's right, too."

The men in the jury box got even more lemon-faced. Hugo Black said to them, and to the rest of the room, "Let the record reflect, Mrs. Gussman found the very idea of Sunday school so odious that she was compelled to seek a less virtuous arrangement."

"That's not fair!" I blurted, which was the wrong thing to do, and I knew it. But I kept talking anyway, even though the lawyer tried to talk over me at the end. "I ought to be able to pick whichever church I want! I didn't want to go to Chapelwood, that's all. I was happy to go someplace else, almost *anyplace* else!"

Fast on the heels of me saying that, he said, "Anyplace like Saint Paul's?"

I could tell it was supposed to be all dramatic, and it was supposed to make me embarrassed because just about everyone in the room thought Catholics were so bad, but I wasn't embarrassed and I didn't feel bad. "Yes, like Saint Paul's. They were kind to me there. Kinder than my daddy's ever been, since the day I was born."

"But their teachings are false, and they follow the Antichrist— or so some people would say," Hugo Black was quick to add—I don't know why. It's not like anybody in a position to judge me disagreed with him any.

So I told him, "I didn't believe everything they taught me, any more than I ever believed anything the Methodists told me, either. And I believed even less of what they were saying at Reverend Davis's church. That place is crazy, and I didn't want to go back. That's partly why I ran."

A murmur ran through the jury box and went around the

room. I knew the reverend was a popular man, but I might've underestimated how popular, exactly. Tough luck, because I'd already said my piece. My neck was burning hot, and my head was starting to hurt. All right, maybe I was a *little* embarrassed and feeling bad—but it wasn't due to anything Hugo Black thought was appropriately shameful.

The lawyer lifted his butt off the edge of the table and slowly walked toward me, shaking his head like I'd done something awful. "You shouldn't say such things," he said, talking to me as if I were some naughty schoolchild who'd copied off someone else's slate. "That's very offensive to the Reverend Davis, and to the church's members—some of whom are in this very courtroom."

"They . . . they are?" I didn't like how nervous I sounded when I said it. But like everything else, it was too late for me to go back and fix it.

"Why, I've attended services there once or twice myself—and I can assure the fine gentlemen of the jury that nothing strange or untoward ever takes place. Chapelwood welcomes worshippers of many faiths into the fold. It's not at all like the vipers of the Vatican, who would make each man, woman, and child stand upon elaborate ceremonies before they enter the sanctuary."

"That's not true," I argued. "None of it's true—not about Chapelwood, and not about Saint Paul's. Father Coyle didn't make me do anything in exchange for his help, he—"

Faster than you could blink, Hugo Black snapped, "So he was helping you? You admit to this?"

"Everybody knew he helped me. I already told you, he's the one who married me and Pedro."

"Had he helped you before?"

I hesitated. Of course he'd helped me before; he'd given me a place to go when I felt like I couldn't go home, on more than one afternoon. He hid me from Tom Shirley once, after my daddy called him around to collect me. But if I'd said any of that out loud, they'd use it to make me sound bad and Father Coyle sound worse. So even though I'd put my hand on the Bible and made my swears, I shook my head. "He was somebody to talk to. A nice man who didn't treat me like dirt—and when I asked if he'd marry me and Pedro, he said he'd do it." That was another lie. It wasn't my idea to get married, but it wouldn't go over too well if I put that part on the record.

"Was Father Coyle aware that your father disapproved of the union?"

"It wouldn't have surprised him any."

"Answer the question directly, Mrs. Gussman."

"Fine." I crossed my arms. I didn't know what to do with my hands. "He knew my daddy wouldn't like it."

"But he performed the marriage anyway?"

"Obviously."

I glared at him, just daring him to tell me to answer directly again, or properly, or in the manner of his preference. I was getting fed up with this whole courtroom-language business. It was starting to feel like a trick, like a big old game and nobody whose life depends on it knows the goddamn rules.

I think they do it that way on purpose.

Finally someone made a call for "recess," and they let me get down off the stand. I could hardly get away from it fast enough . . . I even had to stop myself from running down the aisle toward Chief Eagan. I took a real deep breath and mostly held it, putting one foot in front of the other until I reached that back row.

He stood up and smiled real big, and he said, "I'm proud of you, girl. They didn't take it easy on you, did they? But you said your piece all the same."

Then Inspector Wolf leaned over the bench and said, "Unfortunately, I doubt they're finished with you yet."

The chief turned around, surprised to see him—but he didn't look unhappy about it. "Inspector, what brings you here?"

"A combination of things, but mostly I wished to support Mrs. Gussman, and to see what steps toward justice were under way, with regards to Father Coyle's murder."

"Feeble ones," Chief Eagan muttered.

We all got real quiet then. The courtroom was emptying out, and Hugo Black was coming down the aisle. I didn't mean to stare at him. I think he likes it when people stare at him, and I wouldn't give him that satisfaction on purpose. He looked right at me as he went on by, and spared a glance for those who stood around me. He gave Chief Eagan a bob of his head that was supposed to be polite, but I think it only meant that he'd seen him, and that he was glad the chief was getting to watch him work.

That man is truly a bastard, in the nastiest, coldest sense.

The chief wouldn't give him a smile or a nod in return any sooner than I would; but those of us at the back row were the only ones who weren't grinning at him and trying to shake his hand as he left, swarming him and telling him how good he was and what a great job he was doing. He was eating it up, and his appetite was strong.

I looked around and watched the jury men whisper back and forth to themselves as they either stayed in place or wandered off in clusters, sneaking peeks at me when they thought I wouldn't notice—like I had no idea who or what they were talking about. Jesus, but Hugo Black only told them I was a delinquent. He didn't tell them I was an idiot.

Inspector Wolf had been exchanging pleasantries with Chief Eagan but I hadn't heard them, until he said, "But I am terribly sorry—where are my manners? Chief Eagan, Mrs. Ruth Gussman . . . this is an old friend and colleague of mine, Miss Lizbeth Andrew. She's joined me from Massachusetts, to assist with my investigation."

"Like Father Coyle used to?" I asked, since he'd mentioned they'd sometimes worked together.

"Very much like that, yes."

I shook Miss Andrew's hand and said it was nice to meet her. She said, "Likewise, Mrs. Gussman, I'm sure. And I know it is terribly difficult, but you handled yourself admirably up there. It's very brave of you to stand up to them."

"Everyone keeps saying that." I didn't mean to sound fussy, but I probably did. "It's not brave, though. It's just what Father Coyle deserves, after all he did for me. So Miss Andrew, are you some kind of inspector, too? Do they let ladies do that in Boston?"

She blushed, and I hoped I hadn't said something rude without meaning to. "Please, call me Lizbeth, dear."

"Only if you'll settle for Ruth in return," I said back, and that seemed to please her.

"As you like, Ruth. But to answer your question, no, I'm not a proper investigator. I'm more like a . . . consultant."

She was leaving something out, but that was fine. We were all leaving something out.

"I've never heard of a lady being a consultant before," I said, and maybe I shouldn't have, but I was distracted. The last of the jury men were filing by, and the recess was only supposed to last for thirty minutes. I wanted some air, so I said, "Let's get out of here, if you don't mind. It's all stuffy, and I feel like I'm surrounded."

Outside the courtroom, I didn't feel any less surrounded by the folks who were milling about in the lobby. I tried to keep from looking at them, face by face, to figure out who I might've seen at Chapelwood and who I hadn't . . . and it didn't matter much. Even if I hadn't seen these men and women at church before (and there were a handful of women, too—but it was mostly men) . . . I knew some of them from the newspapers.

Over here in this corner, a bunch of Klansmen chattered; over there along that wall, a cluster of shifty-eyed True Americans lurked; and the more I thought about it, the more I felt smothered by the lot of them. The judge was a wizard, once—and maybe he still was. My own representative, Mr. Mayhew, told me he didn't participate in that group no more, but he could've been saying that to make me feel better, if he was so inclined to bother. Hugo Black—everybody knew about him and the True Americans. And all those grouchy old men in the jury box were peers of my daddy's indeed.

I spotted the jury foreman chatting with Hugo Black. The foreman had a button on his lapel. It had the letters "TA" with a red, white, and blue background behind them, and it was disgusting. Not just because it was a signal, a reminder that all these men were in the same club and they all ought to hang together—but because they gave themselves that name: True Americans. That's horseshit of the highest order, and I can't stand it. There's nothing *true* about them, and American? Sixty years ago they were willing to fight a war to keep from being Americans. Besides, *American* ought to be a good thing, the kind of thing that brings everybody together instead of deciding who's good enough to be one and who isn't. I've read in my history books, I've seen pictures of the statue in New York, the lady who greets all the people coming in from other countries. She doesn't pick and choose; she takes everybody. And that's how it ought to be.

This "True American" business—it's nonsense, plain and

simple. No, it's worse than nonsense, because I think they actually believe it.

I might've started swearing about it, or even crying out of pure frustration with it all, but then the front doors opened and in strolled the Reverend Davis, just as easy as you please. He walked in like he owned the place, and I guess, in a sense, he *did*. He looked around the room and settled on me, and gave me this nasty little half smile that made my stomach drop. But there he was . . . dressed in ordinary clothes, no spooky robes or funny gloves. He still looked strange to me, though . . . like his arms were a bit too long, or maybe his hands had too many joints. When he moved, it didn't look natural—maybe that's what I'm trying to say. It looked like someone had built a person-shaped puppet and had done a real good job, but not quite perfect. Even in a gray cotton suit and with a politician's grin, and even with his hair slicked back just as shiny as his shoes, he didn't quite look ordinary.

I fought the urge to retreat; I wanted to back up against the wall, or hide behind the big, sturdy shape of the inspector. No, that's not true at all. I wanted to run screaming from the building, just like I always wanted to run screaming from Chapelwood every single time I went there.

"Dear, are you all right?" Miss Andrew asked me. I mean, *Lizbeth* did. She put her hand on my shoulder and stepped closer, all protective-like. She smelled like fancy rosewater cologne and powder makeup. She smelled like money, and someplace else— and that's how she sounded, too.

"Yes, ma'am, I'm all right," I lied.

Then I noticed that she was looking right at the reverend— she just picked him out of the crowd, like she knew without even asking. Her eyes settled on him, but he didn't look our way again. Once he'd finished trying to scare me, he'd lost interest in me—or anyone I was talking to. But she looked at him hard, so hard he must've felt it.

He frowned, and glanced up over his shoulder. He probably would've looked away in a flash, but her gaze hooked him hard.

Chief Eagan growled to them both, "That's the dread reverend, it is. He's the man who owns and operates the church at Chapelwood."

"Reverend Davis," Lizbeth murmured, still holding his stare, blink for blink.

He couldn't have heard her over the ruckus of the courthouse visitors, but he saw that she mouthed his name. He nodded, but he didn't give her that same condescending sneer he always saves for me. He didn't give her any look at all . . . all he did was give up and look away.

I was shocked. It was a little thing, I know, but it gave me great joy to see him back down from someone—from this lady I'd only just met, this tiny thing, really—an inch or two shorter than me, and she was wearing square little heels that gave her a smidge of lift.

She was the one who made a condescending sneer, and she sent it in his general direction. He wasn't looking anymore, but she didn't do it for show; she did it because that was how she felt about him. She sniffed and said, "I've tangled with worse."

The inspector shook his head. "You don't know that yet."

For a second, she seemed uncertain. Then she straightened up, set her jaw, and said, "Well, I've tangled with just as bad. Don't worry, Ruth. If he picks a fight with you, he picks a fight with us; and I promise, that's more trouble than he's prepared for."

"Thank you, ma'am, I appreciate it," I said, and I truly did.

But standing there beside her, and the inspector, and the old police chief, and nobody else . . . I felt well and truly surrounded, regardless. I'd seen the awful red, white, and blue button on the reverend's lapel, and I knew where he stood. I knew where all of them stood—they all wore it on their collar, on their sleeve, wherever.

Someone was passing out the damn buttons—yes, there she was. A tall woman with a box of them, standing by the front door. I only just then saw her. She was smiling real big and greeting everyone who came and went, offering a button and a pamphlet. Most everyone declined the pamphlet, because most everyone already knew what they were all about. But everyone took a button.

The thirty-minute recess was almost over, and people started filing back into the courtroom. One by one, two by two, animals into the ark—each of them wearing one of those TA buttons, putting on a united front against the four of us, and it wasn't hardly fair.

The woman at the door shook her box as if to see how many buttons she had left, then looked up when another man came inside. With a bright "Good afternoon!" and a huge smile, she held one out to him.

He pushed her hand away and told her to go to hell.

Inspector Simon Wolf

❦

SEPTEMBER 29, 1921

Over by the front door, someone told the button-pushing blonde with the awkward hat that she ought to go to hell, and I thought, "I know that voice . . ." Indeed I did: It was George Battey Ward. He shoved past her into the lobby, or foyer, or whatever you call that space between the front door and the courtroom; he scanned the place, spotted Ruth and myself, and made a beeline for us.

He took her by the arms as if he meant to shake her—or convey something very, very important and he wanted her full attention. "Ruth, are you all right?"

The poor girl was somewhat rattled by this weird how-do-you-do, so she stammered, "Yes . . . yes, sir, I am. Are . . . are *you*? All right, I mean?"

"Me? I'm fine. I only . . . I'd heard . . . It's just . . ." He paused to collect himself. "I wanted to make sure you weren't alone." He released his grip on her, which caused Lizbeth to relax. For a moment there, I thought she was going to produce an axe and smack him away from the girl. It might've been a sight to behold, but I'm glad she restrained herself.

George looked like a maniac, and I say that with all the casual affection of someone who was actually quite pleased to see him. His hair was mussed, his shirt rumpled, and there were smudges of dust at the top of his thighs—presumably where he'd wiped his hands after foraging in that bizarre basement downtown. Storage Room Six had not been kind to him. I had a feeling that it wasn't kind to anybody.

"I'm not alone," Ruth said bravely. "The chief's been here all along, and I can't remember if you've met the inspector or not—"

"I did, the other day," he cut her off. He shook my hand and said, "I'm glad you've come to lend your support."

I told him I was happy to oblige, and then said, "I'd like you to meet an old friend of mine, a consultant from the Boston area. Miss Lizbeth Andrew, this is George Ward, former city commissioner and friend of Father Coyle's."

He took Lizbeth's hand and gave it a genteel kiss. "Charmed, I'm sure." Then, to Ruth, he added, "I'm sorry I haven't been here, girl. I've been studying, researching. Trying to find some foothold, you understand? It's distracted me, and again, I'm very sorry. But I'm here now, for I thought you might need me."

"I'm happy to see you, sir," she told him. "But why now, in particular?"

"Because . . ." The courthouse door opened with a creaking swing, and a bailiff darkened its threshold with another man in tow. Quickly, George told her before she could see it for herself: "They're bringing in your father. He wasn't hurt in the jail cell, he was drunk on a gift from the reverend. Now he's up and about, and he's deigned to appear for the second half of the day's testimony."

The girl went pale, but her mouth was fixed in a firm, straight line. "How'd you know?"

"It was all the gossip at the police station. I still have a few friends there, at least until Tom Shirley figures out who they are and sends them packing."

The bailiff accepted one of those damnable "TA" buttons, and so did the man he escorted—a smallish fellow, wiry and faintly sinister. He was wearing a suit that didn't fit him very well, and the way his hair oil struggled against the salt-and-pepper fluff suggested he didn't often keep it so tidily coiffed.

Call it prejudice if you will, but he looked like the kind of man who'd beat his wife and shoot a priest. Which is to say, I loathed him on sight even more than I'd loathed him before looking at him. I might've loathed him even if I hadn't known who he was, or what he'd done—there's a certain stink on a certain kind of soul, a foul scent of hateful smallness too often thwarted . . . then given an ounce of power. There must be a word for it, but I'll confess to not having one immediately on hand.

He had a false smile plastered across that craggy, tiny-eyed face, but it turned to an ugly glower when he spied his daughter standing beside me. The hateful little gnome didn't even put the scowl away when Reverend Davis strolled up to shake his hand, though he bowed and scraped sufficiently to demonstrate that his displeasure was *surely* not aimed at the clergy.

I do not think it was my imagination that the room became quiet.

True, some of the crowd had already dispersed for other places—back into the courtroom, or to other appointments elsewhere; but plenty of men remained, and now that I looked around, every last one of them was wearing one of those stupid buttons.

It felt childish to me, this need to wear your team's colors. It felt like showing off, or more precisely, a deliberate and ham-fisted attempt to intimidate our little band of sane folks in this wretched sea of madness. I, for one, was not intimidated. Neither was Lizbeth, who took it all in almost dispassionately. I'm confident she was thinking along the same lines as I was.

But George and the old chief felt the need to respond, for whatever reason. They closed ranks, Eagan taking hold of Ruth's elbow as if to direct her gently to her seat in a theater—and George folding his arms, planting his feet in front of her, staring down the reverend and murderer.

In all fairness, this is *their* troubled city, not ours. They know the stakes and the players better than we do; perhaps we should take our cues from these good souls who struggle against the tide . . . but it's as Lizbeth said: We've tangled with worse, or just as bad.

And we are still standing.

Lizbeth Andrew (Borden)

September 29, 1921

We all filed back into the courtroom, and they put poor Ruth back upon the witness stand. My heart went out to her, it really did. I remember it all too well myself—even after all these years. Was Ruth on trial? Technically, no. But any fool could see she was being tried all the same.

She sat up straight and said her piece, again and again, even as that lawyer did his best to trip her up . . . and her own representative (of sorts) did very little to intervene. I don't know if he was merely a bad lawyer, or if he actively sought to undermine her appearance on the stand. Either way, the result was the same: The girl was effectively on her own up there.

No, not the girl. The *woman.*

She certainly carried herself like a woman, despite the nearly uniform opposition to her stalwart presence. She's twenty-one, I think—or thereabouts. Someone mentioned it to me at some point, perhaps it was Wolf. He whispered a great many things into my ear as the dull, infuriating drama unfolded. We were in the back row, and discreet enough that no one hushed us, or asked us to leave.

This is what I learned.

Hugo Black is the defense attorney for Edwin Stephenson, who in broad daylight assassinated the priest James Coyle. Black is somewhat notorious for his activity with the True Americans, a group that scarcely distinguishes itself from the Ku Klux Klan—except that it opposes a broader variety of people, and perhaps it dislikes them more deeply. If there's one positive thing that must be said about the group, it *does* seem to be relatively local. You don't really hear about it outside Birmingham, so there's one small blessing to be tallied.

Mr. Black is very likely in the pocket of the Reverend Davis, a man who operates a "church" out at Chapelwood. Edwin Stephenson has also attended this church, and there you see the connection between his costly defense and the house of worship. All three are likewise intimately bound to the True Americans; indeed, the overlap might as well be one hundred percent, from where I'm sitting—in this veritable ocean of revolting little buttons with their awful little initials stamped thereupon.

Henry Mayhew is the prosecuting attorney, in title if not much in action. He's doing his duty as an officer of the court, by which I mean to say that he's shown up to present the case against Edwin Stephenson. His enthusiasm for the proceedings is difficult to gauge. He's a slow-talking sort, and he's from out of town. He may or may not be affiliated with the True Americans or the Chapelwood church, but he certainly isn't a firebrand for justice in this matter.

The presiding judge is Harold Holt, about whom precious little is known. He was appointed by the new City Commission president, Nathaniel Barrett—the man who defeated George Ward, who sat at the end of our bench. I've only just met Mr. Ward, but he strikes me as a sturdy, intelligent man who did his best to defend and protect the citizens of this city regardless of their race or religion. Sadly, that didn't work out so well for him—or for Martin Eagan, the former chief of police (who also stands with Ruth, or rather sat in the audience to support her).

Our small row, in the back of the room, is the last line of defense against something awful, or that's how it feels to me. It also feels precariously empty, given the circumstances. The room is packed, mostly with angry-looking white men and their smug-looking wives, happy to gaze scornfully upon Ruth for every decision she's ever made—including the decision to testify against her father.

If Ward were still president and Eagan were still chief, then the situation might appear less dire, even with the numbers stacked against us. We would have some rightfully elected or appointed authority on our side; we would have some shields to protect us, for isn't that what their badges are made to symbolize?

We would have someone left in power who wished something better for the city, for justice, for Ruth.

Instead we sat there, our allies stripped of their official assets. And the inspector and I, we were strangers, interlopers. Our appearance did not hurt Ruth's credibility because it could not have been any lower than it already stood. Still, we added little to her store of resources, so far as the court of opinion was concerned.

That was another small silver lining, I suppose: No one

knew who we were, or why we were there. No one had any reason to consider us a threat, or to treat us accordingly.

Of course, why would anyone bother? Our foes had an
entire city's worth of bureaucracy, manpower, and friendly sentiment at their behest. We were a band of five civilians, as I
sighed to Wolf. He almost argued with me, ready to flash his
own badge, I'm certain; but Eagan beat him to the punch.

Having overheard the inspector's breathy summing up of
the matters at hand, he offered his own whispered contribution:
"It's not so dire as that, but you can see it from there."

"Are there others?" I asked him quietly. "Any other allies we
might call upon?"

"Not in this courtroom, but yes."

I liked his vestigial brogue, and found it reassuring—but
not so reassuring that I did not argue with him. "If you mean the
colored folks, the Catholics, the Jews . . . I meant the kind of
allies who might prove peers to the reverend or the commission
president, you understand."

He gave me a sidelong look that I no doubt deserved, but I
was only trying to be realistic. "Aye, we have all those folks in our
corner, and you'd be ill-advised to count them out. Their numbers alone might aid us in time; but yes, there are still good men in
positions of service. We might find a few, and call upon them."

"I think we *must*," I said anxiously. "For as it stands, I'm not
sure our merry little band is enough to protect Ruth, or your
city, or anyplace else from whatever weird threat presents itself."

At the end of the row, George Ward made a harrumphing
sound. Under his breath he added, "Weird threat . . . Madam,
you have no idea."

I leaned forward, around the old chief's chest, so that I could whisper my answer more directly. "Oh, but I might surprise you, sir."

"You surprised me by coming at all, but there's more to this . . . there's more to Chapelwood . . . ," he muttered, not speaking to me anymore. Speaking to himself, I believe. He did that quite a lot—the mumbling under his breath. It worried me, I confess. It reminded me too much of dear Doctor Seabury in his later days . . . that rumbling grumble that threaded through his every conversation, editorializing everything he meant to say aloud.

Wolf saw my frown, and gave me a nudge with his elbow. "We should chat, when this is finished."

Finally, at what surely seemed to be long last, a fellow seated in front of us turned around and said, "You've been chatting for the last twenty minutes. Save it for the close of day, would you? Some of us are trying to listen."

He was right, of course. It was rude of us to natter on, even in our most precious whispers. This was not the place to con-spire, whether it felt like the thing to do or not.

Regardless, I appreciated Wolf's loose sketch of the players on this chessboard . . . for all that it made me feel ill to consider our perilous position in this game. Or it isn't a game, but you know what I mean, don't you, Emma?

I'm sure you would, if you were here. I'm sure you *do*, if in fact you haunt me.

We spent the remainder of the day's testimony in silence, and again I was struck by the strength of Ruth Gussman. She was getting tired and impatient, something I recall all too well about my own time on the stand; she was hounded and harangued by the lawyers, who asked her the same questions again and again, phrased differently by a word or two—just in case she'd trip over herself and say something incriminating.

No, not incriminating. She wasn't the one on trial.

But you know what I mean. You once sat where I'm sitting, Emma. You've seen it yourself.

I observed her struggle and was pleased to see her remain steadfast, and I thought about how they treated her just as badly as they'd once treated me, when I'd sat vulnerable and afraid with everyone watching. It's an awful thing, if you aren't accustomed to being watched. For someone who'd spent time on the stage, or now in the "movies" as they call them . . . for someone like Nance, I don't know. She might have seen it as an opportunity for performance, and taken some grim glee in the proceedings. Or then again, she might not have. I wish she were here. I wish I could ask her.

But back then, I was not accustomed to having so many eyes upon me, and I know that Ruth wasn't, either. She was sweating, but we all were sweating a little by the end. She tried not to look at the defendant's desk, where her father glared, nearly unblinking. I could see his profile, just barely—I was at just the right angle to glimpse his hateful scowl fixed upon her like a lamp.

She refused to look at him, and good for her. He didn't deserve her regard, not in any meaning of the word, and she knew it—that's what she was doing up there, telling the world that the murdered priest was a thousand times better in every way than the man who'd raised her. Her old father was broken, so she'd gone out and found herself a new one, even though he was a Catholic, God forbid, and a virtual pariah to everyone she'd ever known.

Still, she held her own, and answered their questions, lobbed at her like cannonballs.

When they finally let her go, she climbed down the two

short steps and faltered, holding the rail. Her father barked
something—I couldn't hear it, but she finally glanced his way.

I thought for a moment that his eyes were like Medusa's, and
the dear young thing had been turned to stone; but no, she was
stronger than that, stronger than him by far. Whatever he'd said,
she didn't answer it. She only stood up taller, straightened her
shoulders, and tossed her hair before exiting down that aisle.

When she passed us, we all rose together in order to see
her out.

George Ward opened the door for her, and let her onto the
courthouse steps—where she sat down and put her face in her
hands, and cried like a child.

I crouched beside her and took her by the arm. As gently as
I could, I said, "Not yet, dear. Soon, but not here. Don't let them
see it—if they see it, they'll think they've broken you. And you
and I both know they *haven't*."

Leonard Kincaid, American Institute of Accountants (Former Member)

OCTOBER 1, 1921

It was only a small delay, only a small problem with the numbers. The woman's face, if I squint at the slate board sideways, is long gone—replaced with the usual digits I've come to expect, upon awaking from sleep or from a daze (whichever is most convenient).

I used to work the math myself, and it was a laborious undertaking, if not unpleasant. Now the math does its own work while I'm not paying attention, and I wait for it to announce its results. It's faster this way. It's cleaner this way, though I wake up with chalk dust on my hands—or ink smudges, if I've run out of slate and resorted to paper notations. I wake up with an ache in my skull, and a sense of confusion that I can't seem to shake—almost a motion sickness, except that it seems prompted by my very dreams.

Coffee helps, except when it doesn't. Cigarettes help, too,

{225}

though I've never cared for the taste of those. Whiskey doesn't help at all, which is fine; it's no longer as easy to acquire as it once was, and since it's technically illegal, there's no sense in drawing attention to myself by breaking the law—however minor and common the infraction.

So I stick to coffee and the occasional puff of tobacco, even if it's not my favorite combination of stimulants. It looks ordinary enough, anyway. No one watches me sip or smoke and thinks it's cause to alert the police.

I worry about that a great deal, these days; I worry about what will happen when the numbers outpace my ability to intercept them. What will happen if I am caught or captured? There's no one standing by to take up this mantle of mine, and no one I'm likely to convince of its virtue. Any friends I once had have been gently ushered out of my life. What family I have left has scarcely noticed the irregularity of my contact—but then, I've never stayed close with any of the cousins or uncles who remained loosely in touch after the death of my parents, over a decade ago.

I could use a protégé. An assistant. I'd settle for a confidant, but my wishes amount to nothing.

I am a sentinel, standing between the fiends of Chapelwood and the world at large. Or does that lend me too much credit?

More likely I'm a minor inconvenience to them. Nuisance and vermin, idly tolerated (instead of exterminated) because their plans and methods are slow, and I do little to interfere with the long-term goal of their proceedings.

I hope that's not the case. I hope these men and women I've killed have served some larger purpose in the baffling scheme . . . but in the end, do any of us? I'm sure I cannot say, and it's a thought that keeps me awake more consistently than the coffee ever does.

And so the numbers come, and the numbers go. They don't always send me out on the town with my axe, but that failing might be my own. I don't always understand what's being asked of me. I don't always detect whatever the math of the universe attempts to convey. But I sleep and wake, I read the papers and watch for patterns. And the numbers come, and the numbers go.

It might be my imagination, but in the last few days I've wondered if I wasn't losing some thread . . . if my grasp on the messages wasn't slipping in some specific and concrete way. It's possible, I know. I am only one man, an ordinary and mortal one at that; what mere human brain can possibly be expected to process these mysteries? But regardless of my lack of suitability, *I'm* the one who's been assigned the task.

So yes, it might be that my faculties are failing me. It *must* be my faculties, for the numbers wouldn't fail me, would they?

No, I don't think they could. Sums and figures do not deteriorate with time; they remain as true as they ever were, when they were first inscribed on clay tablets, poked into that willing substance by deliberately shaped sticks, however many millennia ago.

Any deterioration is mine. I'd rather believe that I'm the weak link than believe whatever guidance I receive has begun to falter. If that's the case, then all this toil really has been for nothing.

I won't accept that. The ghosts of those who've died at my hands . . . they won't accept it, either.

I came to a realization this morning, when I struggled with the little lines on the slate, and on a table—they'd spilled over to the other surface, but I'd not shifted my writing implement. So whatever I'd written on the polished wood was lost to me. Not with all the squinting in the world could I force it to appear.

I needed help. A protégé. An assistant. A confidant.

And I remembered Gaspera Lorino, waiting out his days at the hospital downtown—not even two miles from where I sat despairing at my desk. My hands so dry and pale, my knuckles outlined in white chalk dust.

I'd heard about him before. His sister had spoken to the papers, after I'd hit him with my axe and nearly killed him. He wasn't my primary mission, but he stood in its way. That was all. I bore him no ill will, no more than I ever bore anyone I was charged with killing. It was only a happenstance of timing and location.

His sister told the newspaper that he was alert and conscious, but changed. She said he had frenzied thoughts and wild outbursts, that his mind was not what it once was—that although he still seemed like himself in most of the usual ways, his interests had changed, and his reading habits had changed. He'd taken up an interest in astronomy.

Something had connected with him.

Not merely the blade of the axe, but it must have been the tendril of darkness that clung to his wife's ankles when she walked. It might have found its way inside the wound. Or something else did, I don't know.

It occurred to me that he might actually be the closest thing I had on earth to a kindred spirit.

I looked to the slate again, and saw only the soup of numbers, bubbling as if they floated in a cauldron. I didn't know what they meant. I didn't understand what they were trying to say, not today. Maybe not anymore, at all. It was hard to guess, just like everything else.

But given all this uncertainty, perhaps Mr. Lorino could

grant me some kind of direction or guidance. Does that sound awful? Trite? I guess it might. That's what they do in the old stories, isn't it—they seek out someone who's crippled or maimed, as if some weird magic has found its way in through the cracks in their bodies or their souls. Nonsense, of course . . . except in this case, perhaps not. His was no ordinary injury, after all. It's one I created. *I* cracked him open, and something came inside him. I am responsible for him, whether I like it or not.

I thought about calling for a ride, but decided instead that the air was fresh, the day was warm, and the fewer witnesses to my visit, the better. The distance to the hospital wasn't great, and I was in the mood to think. Walking aids thinking. Doesn't it?

Sometimes yes, sometimes no.

Mostly the thoughts I had were dark, unpleasant ones, regarding the likelihood that this was a terrible idea, a terrible mistake in the making. A thin sheen of guilt covered everything. I wondered if that wasn't a mistake, too—if this was only some quest for forgiveness, and a selfish one at that.

But it was only a small amount of guilt, overshadowed easily by my curiosity and sense of desperate aimlessness. If this was a selfish quest, it was a selfish quest of an entirely other sort.

3 reached the hospital and strolled inside.

I gave no thought as to how I might gain entry to Mr. Lorino's quarters, and it may sound strange to relate, but no one asked me any questions. No one stopped me when I approached the nurse's desk where the nun kept her paperwork and answered the solitary telephone. No one intervened when I reached for the sheet that logged visitors, and no one questioned my actions when I ran my finger down the columns, hoping to spy his name—yes, there it was, Gaspera Lorino, room 14B, and he'd received two visitors as of late. No one so much as blinked when I placed the clipboard back onto its proper spot, and left it there.

I turned to regard the room, and no one in the room regarded me back.

One large orderly exited a set of double doors, removing his smock at the end of his shift—replacing it with a gray sweater. He bade the nun a good morning and left the lobby. Another orderly arrived, signed himself in, and disappeared down the corridor through those same doors. Three young women sat in the waiting area, waiting for God knew what. A doctor came and went, his gleaming brown shoes *tap-tap-tapping* on the bright white and shiny black squares of the linoleum floor; the seats were seafoam green with bright metal armrests and the windows were frosted glass, threaded through with chicken wire to make them strong against thrown bricks or other forms of escape.

This was a hospital, wasn't it? Certainly, but it was a prison, too, with doors that locked and windows with bars both big and small.

This was a destination.

This was a lobby. This was a man, standing in the midst of it, and no one saw him. Me. No one saw me, and I stood in the midst of it, right before everyone, and I might as well have been made of the low black fog that no one ever spotted except for me.

I took it as a sign. Not from God, because I didn't really think God was speaking anymore (or not to me, probably not to anyone), but a sign from whatever pattern had sustained me this far, this long. Something was still working with me, coaching me forward, urging me to continue this awful path—and assisting me when necessary.

I think?

Or else . . . or else it's something odder yet. There's always the possibility (there's always a possibility, another one, another two, another thousand) that this is a force of my own creation. This invisibility, for that's what it is . . . it might be a skill I've acquired—like my ability to see the carnivorous black smoke. But if that's the case, then how did I acquire it? And from whom?

It hardly seemed wise to stand there philosophizing, when I'd been handed all the information I needed in order to find Lorino. The very ease of it all suggested I was on the right path, or so I chose to assume.

(I choose many assumptions these days. I choose to believe in my own valor, in the righteousness of my acts, in my sanity, in the successfulness of my campaigns against the reverend. And I might be wrong about any of them.)

I pushed the swinging door and it gave way easily. I entered the chilly corridor of the hospital, and I walked along it—checking the doors for numbers, checking the faces of those I passed for some sign that I'd been seen. None of the doctors, nurses, nuns, or any other official person gave me a second glance.

One or two of the patients did, but none of them called any attention to me. More small blessings, or small gifts from the Patterns That Be.

Room 14B was halfway down and on the left.

It was unlocked, from the outside. Or rather I should say, when I put my hand on the latch, it unfastened and it let me come in. I do not know if it would've opened for anyone else who might wander up without a key.

Mr. Lorino was seated on his bed, his feet dangling over the side. His toes dragged upon the floor when he waved them back and forth—his cotton socks sagging low, and leaving small streaks of sweat that vanished as soon as they appeared.

He did not look up at me, but he knew I'd arrived. "Was it a good idea, do you think? Did the stars suggest it, or did the numbers?"

"I'm not sure." I let the door slip shut behind me.

There was a chair positioned under a window, across from his bed. I took it, drawing it forward so that I could face him.

He looked up at me then. He was older than I recalled, but then again, I'd only seen him by the light of a streetlamp, the sort of light that's kind to everyone. He observed, "You're running out of good ideas."

"I never had many to begin with."

"That isn't what I mean," he said. He didn't exactly frown, but his forehead wrinkled with concentration. "The good ideas you've been given . . . they're drying up. Is that why you've come?"

"It must be." I sighed, and leaned back into the chair. "Drying up, you said . . . that's one way to put it."

"You have a better one?"

"No. But to hear you say it . . . I'm all the more worried. I'd hoped it was my imagination."

He nodded slowly, but at the same time, he spoke quickly. "Almost nothing is imagined. The numbers came, and you did your best. Now the messages come fewer and farther between, and you want to know what it means. You come here, you slip inside the fortress like a ghost, like the true ghost you are. Or no, that's not what I mean. *I* am the ghost, summoned by the witch at Endor— and *you*, you are Saul upon the battlefield, casting about for some hint that all is unfolding according to plan. Some plan. *Any* plan. You want to believe that there's a plan. I suppose you need to, given the task you've been assigned, and subsequently accepted."

"Do you mind being my Samuel?" I asked him frankly. My voice cracked, a very little bit, when I added, "I have no one, you see."

"I do not mind. You and I, we are bound these days."

"I wish it were not so."

"Wishes . . . well, I know. What's the point of them? They can't help, and might hurt. It's done, that's the sum of it. And *you're* almost done, that's the answer."

I felt a warmth behind my ears. It crept down my throat, and blushed my chest beneath my shirt. "Do you mean . . . I'm almost done with the axe? I hope that's what you mean. I'm sorry, but I'm not sure. I don't understand."

"Sorry, sorry, sorry. Of course you're sorry—you're human still, not like some of the others who've killed because the stars and the sea had conspired against them. And that's why—" He sat forward, locking me down with those earnest eyes. "That's why it's not so bad, what happens next. Too much longer, and you would change too much. You'd lose yourself to the other side, or to the middle state. You're losing yourself already, aren't you? The first deaths were hard, and the last ones were easy."

"Easi*er*," I corrected him, sounding more defensive than I'd intended.

"The next ones would be easiest of all, and on the other side of easiness is pleasure at a job well done. Beyond that lies anticipation for a task yet to be accomplished. Do you see what I mean?"

I did see, and that was the horror of it. He wasn't wrong.

"I must stop what I'm doing before I enjoy what I'm doing. Is that somehow part of the pattern? That only a reluctant knight can perform the duty?" I was flailing about, and I believe we both knew it. "Will the numbers stop coming to me altogether? Or is it worse than that?" I had the . . . nerve? fortitude? courage? . . . to ask him the only question that mattered in the end.

"Worse, better." He shrugged, as if these things were all the same. On some greater balance than my own life, perhaps they are.

But this was no greater balance; this was only my time upon the earth, and I pushed him for more. Even though I didn't really want to hear more, because I already suspected where the conversation was leading. "So the numbers, the instructions . . . they will dry up. And what becomes of me then?"

He gave me a long, hard look. Then his gaze softened. "The numbers will not abandon you," he assured me. "They have changed in nature, that is all. They will accompany you for all the rest of your days."

I let out a deep breath. It almost whistled as it left me. "Are you certain?"

"Quite certain. Your place in this story, your role . . . it will change, that is all." He patted me on the knee, a reassuring gesture that did its job, albeit somewhat weakly.

"That's a relief to hear. I was afraid, you know . . . afraid that I would be compelled to kill forever."

He lifted an eyebrow. "Are you sure?"

"Of course I'm sure! What are you suggesting?"

"That all is right with the universe, and nothing more. I am *glad* you will not be compelled to kill forever. I am *glad* you will never take pleasure in that task, or any greater pleasure—no, *satisfaction*, and I beg your pardon—than you've come to feel already. I am glad your task will change, and I wish you well on your new path, when you find it."

I wasn't sure I believed him. Something about that eyebrow lift, and something about that softened look . . . it was a gaze of pity. He pitied me, and I did not like that—because I didn't know *why*.

Maybe it was only the obvious. That's what I tried to think.

I thanked him for his time then, and stood in order to take my leave.

He stopped me with a hand on my arm. In a whisper, but at that same nearly frenetic pace of speech, he told me, "I've never held it against you, you know. The pain, the loss. I could see, when I awakened . . . I could see how you did what you were forced to do, and I saw that it was for the good of us all. I saw the things that wait on the other side, or in the middle distance—that's a more appropriate way to put it. I know why you do what you do, and I admire you for the courage it's taken to bring you to your task, and to this room, and to where you will proceed next."

"Thank you . . . ?" I said. I must've made it a question. I wasn't sure.

"No, it is my thanks—*mine*—that I extend. As well as my apologies, for I cannot be of any help to you, not really."

"No one can."

"You're right." His grip loosened, and his fingers slid down to my wrist, then my hand. He held it lightly, like a child who needs no real direction but wishes for the parent to feel safe. "But that's fine, or it will *be* fine. I wished to say that others will come and take over your duties . . . but that isn't the case, not quite. Your numbers dwindle, they dwindle, they do. It is either very good, or very bad, now that I consider it."

I drew my hand away, for his gentle stroking felt strange. "Now that you consider it?"

"Now that I've had more time to consider it, I should say, for I consider everything. Your numbers dwindle, perhaps, because there are fewer left who need to die. So the threat, you see . . . the threat will either be vanquished very soon—or it will find victory. Either way, either way . . ." He mumbled the rest: "Either way, there are fewer left who need to die ahead of the cosmic schedule. Fewer keys to be tried in that terrible lock."

I was half afraid to extricate myself, but he did not take hold of me again—and did not bear me so much as a formal farewell as I left his room. I don't think he even looked at me again. It was as if he'd fallen asleep upright, seated on the bed as he was.

Back into the corridor I moved like a phantom. I felt like a phantom, like smoke. I stepped out of the way of gurneys rolling to and fro. I dodged the nurses and the nuns with their trays of pills and their folders full of paperwork.

I veritably danced, as this was veritably a ballet of ghosts.

Back outside, and back into the sun I stepped. I shielded my eyes, for it seemed very bright—I don't know why, for the interior of the hospital was bright as well. I can't imagine why it pained me for those thick, muddy seconds while my eyes adjusted. But pain me it did, along with many other things. Poor Mr. Lorino. Poor me. Poor everyone, if the Chapelwood men have their way, and their god is allowed inside our world.

I began the return walk to my flophouse room, deep in thought. I didn't realize how late it had become; that harsh, angled light was a result of afternoon toppling toward evening—and the air cooled as the hours stretched. I would be home before dark, certainly. I was not afraid. I was the thing other people were afraid of.

$\mathfrak{I}$'m not sure when I first noticed that my feet were cold.

The rest of me wasn't cold. My face was flushed with exertion and the low sun's blush, and even my hands—which often do run toward chill—were just fine, buried within my jacket pockets. If anything, I was almost a little warm. That's why it surprised me. That's why it snuck up on me, I assume.

My feet were cold, so I looked down at them, and I think there's a chance, for a shattered fraction of a second, that my heart stopped.

My feet were cold, and they were hard to see. A dim gray haze laced with black filled the space between the sidewalk and my knees—a roiling, fluffy mass that moved thick as fog around my ankles.

If my heart stopped, it did so briefly enough that nothing else noticed, and my bodily processes continued at their usual rounds . . . but given a jolt of speed. My surprise and fear were shocking things, tandem things that set upon me like electricity.

I wanted to run, but could scarcely move. I wanted to scream, but could not open my mouth.

Yet I was not paralyzed, or held hostage by any weird mesmerism. I was only confused and frightened, or no . . . not confused. I knew precisely what the dark smoke meant: It meant I was marked.

But hadn't I been marked already? Lo these many months?

No. Not like this. I had touched something on the other side, or in the middle distance, as Lorino put it. Yes, you touch these things and they touch you back—that's the nature of everything, everywhere, I know. But *this* kind of mark?

I looked around the street and saw no one to consult, even with such a ridiculous question as, "Tell me, good sir, is there anything peculiar about my feet?" If anyone *had* been present, and if I *had* posed the query, it wouldn't have mattered in the slightest—for I already knew the answer. I had known for ages that no one apart from myself could spy the sinister smoke.

I wondered if Lorino saw it.

Then, fast on the heels of that wondering, I wondered if Lorino had somehow *caused* the smoke—if this wasn't his fault, in some regard. But no, that was a stupid thing to ask myself. Even if, in some roundabout way, the injured and hospitalized Italian had cast some spell upon me, pointing me out to the things on the other side of the veil . . . the blame came back around to me, anyway. Didn't it?

But yes . . . yes, I think he saw it. Or he sensed it somehow, even before I was aware of it. His pity . . . that terrible pity in his eyes . . .

Oh, indeed—my task was drawing to a close. And indeed, it was better for me to cease my hacking ways now, before I came to enjoy them too much.

I felt a sharp stab of anger, and it must've come from the same place that provided my wicked, unconscionable pleasure at a job well done. It wasn't fair. Not in the slightest. I was only doing what I was asked. I was only trying to save the world. And this would be my repayment? Death by some other instrument of the pattern, bringing balance around in his own way, driven by his own numbers—delivered in whatever fashion was particular to him.

Again I let my eyes dart around on the street. Again I saw nothing and no one to rouse any suspicion. There was no one to confront, no one to defend myself against. No one to attack, should that be called for.

It was the very opposite of being inside the hospital, where no one could see me.

I could feel my neck flushing, and my heart pounded loudly in my ears. How far was I from the safety of the flophouse room? Not a mile, I didn't think. I looked at my feet again, and could scarcely see them; the smoke grew thicker, coiled tighter . . . or was it only in my mind? Were my legs any colder than when I'd first noticed the foul stuff's presence? I started to run.

I took the back ways and the alleys when I could, for when people reappeared on the landscape I realized that I didn't want their attention at all, and I very much preferred being invisible.

I must have been quite a sight, in my pale blue cotton suit and everyday shoes—out for a dash around the streets of Birmingham. It must have been a thing to behold, this middle-aged man huffing and puffing, then finally running up the stairs and over to the door that signified safety.

I fumbled for my keys, found them, inserted the right one into the slot.

It turned. I twisted the knob. I pushed the door with my shoulder and flung myself inside—then leaned back against the door to shut it again, and to hold it closed against everything out there that might wish to do me harm.

But it was no good. The smoke had followed me, for one thing. And Reverend Davis was waiting for me, for another.

GRUESOME MURDER AT FIFTH STREET FLOPHOUSE

Birmingham Post
October 1, 1921

Last night around ten p.m. at the Fifth Street flophouse sometimes known as Little Neil's, a maintenance man discovered the body of a resident, Leonard Kincaid. Foul play is all but certain, as the corpse was discovered affixed to the wall in a mock crucifixion, his hands and feet nailed to the building's studs. His death was actually brought about by blood loss, for he suffered significant head wounds and a gash at his side, in what was clearly some sacrilegious effort at a Christ-style pose. The coroner supposed that he'd been dead several hours by the time he was discovered, for his body was nearly cold and there'd been time enough for the neighbor downstairs to detect a spreading, dark stain upon his ceiling.

No motive has been proposed, for it would seem that Mr. Kincaid had neither friends nor family, nor foes to speak of, either. He had scarcely spoken to any of the other residents at the flophouse, and was orphaned some time ago. According to the building's manager, no one knew him well enough to have an opinion of him.

No suspects have been named at this time, and if the police have any suspicions, they haven't made them public. The new police chief, Thomas Shirley, has likewise declined to answer any questions as to whether this new and ghastly murder bears any relation to the hatchet killings of recent months. It would seem that little is known at this time, except that room 209 will not be rented out again anytime soon—and the police have yet another appalling death on their hands, likely produced by yet another creative killer.

What kind of unholy fiend would draw a cross upon a wall and crucify a man upon it? Some suggest that it's the handiwork of a mentally unbalanced person or persons, while others propose that it might represent some weird retaliation from the papist community, given the recent restrictions upon them. But why would they single out Kincaid? For that matter, why would anyone?

Mr. Kincaid, formerly an accountant working for the city of Birmingham, had quit his job and all but vanished sixteen months ago. It would seem he'd been living at Little Neil's ever since, though his friends and former coworkers seemed unaware of whatever circumstances must have brought him to such a place in life. He was a lifelong Baptist with no ties to any known Catholic or anti-Catholic group, though his former employer suggested that he may have once attended the church of Reverend A. J. Davis out at the old Chapelwood Estate, and the beliefs espoused there are somewhat shrouded in mystery.

When contacted for comment, the reverend admitted that Mr. Kincaid had once attended services there, but denied that he'd been in attendance in the prior year. He also denied that any mystery surrounds his church, which he describes as a "strictly Christian service for those who seek to follow the Good Book to the very best of their understanding."

Police continue to seek information on Mr. Kincaid and his activities, associates, and habits. If you or someone in your household can contribute to the investigation, please approach the downtown station and inquire after Chief Shirley, as he would very much like to hear from you.

Inspector Simon Wolf

❦

OCTOBER 1, 1921

The newspaper rested beside my plate; I hit it with the back of my hand, which still held my forkful of carefully speared sausage. "Can you believe this? Crucified to the wall, and the reporter still feels compelled to note the likelihood of foul play. I'm reasonably confident that it's impossible to crucify one's own self."

Lizbeth sat across the table from me, slowly chewing her breakfast while scanning her copy of the daily rag of note. She did not look up when she asked, "How would you get the last nail in?"

I nearly choked, but only laughed with a full mouth instead. "You're wonderful, you know," I informed her, and I meant it.

She smiled demurely, and took another bite of scrambled egg. She swallowed, and said, "You're not so bad yourself, Inspector."

"Thank you, madam." I squinted again down at the newspaper

article, focusing on that second-to-last paragraph. "And you noted the bit about Chapelwood, I trust. What do you make of it? He wasn't hacked to death, except perhaps in the very broadest sense."

"How do you figure that? Even in the very broadest sense?"

"He was stabbed, apparently. Not such a far stretch from hacking to stabbing. Big metal blade at work, and so forth."

"It's still a stretch," she said, but I didn't feel like she was really arguing with me. She wasn't wrong, anyway. "But at this point, I wouldn't put anything at all past the Chapelwood gang. It's hard to see precisely what they're up to, no matter how hard you look at them. Axe murders, religious coercion, and . . . and what else, do you think? Whatever they're up to, it's enormous and oddly shaped. If there's a pattern to it . . ." She sighed, and retrieved her napkin from her lap. She left it on the table. "I'll be damned if I can see it, and I surely don't understand what Nance or I have to do with it."

Mrs. Becker chose that moment to appear, and I thought she was only present to clear the plates and see us off—but she came to me with a strange look on her face. "Inspector?"

"Yes, ma'am?" I replied, for I was picking up on the local linguistic quirks.

"There's a phone call for you. At the desk, you know—that's the only phone we've got, anyway. It's George Ward."

"You don't say?" It was my turn to deposit my napkin. I stood and pushed my chair back into place. Lizbeth rose, too, wearing a worried expression. "Is it Ruth, do you think? I hope she's all right."

She accompanied me to the phone, then hovered at the other end of the hotel desk.

I accepted the receiver from Mrs. Becker, who then discreetly retreated to the office . . . where she was out of sight, but surely not out of hearing range.

"Hello, George?" I asked.

He didn't offer any similar preamble. "The jury's reached a verdict. They're going to read it in an hour."

"You can't be serious. They only closed the arguments yesterday."

"They're reading it in an hour, with only a few hours of deliberation—if that much. Yes, I'm serious." George sounded worse than serious, in my opinion, but it wouldn't have made anything better to point it out. "They're going to turn him loose, Inspector."

I'm not sure why, but I told him, "Stay calm, George." He already sounded calm. Resigned, anyway. Maybe I wasn't saying it to him, but to myself—because God knew I could feel a hot, angry flush rising up in my belly. "They might surprise us. It's not settled yet."

"It's settled. It's been settled since before it got started. We always knew they were going to turn him loose."

"Don't borrow trouble, George."

"Don't get your hopes up, Inspector."

My hopes weren't up at all, and they were sinking by the second. "We're on our way, as soon as I can summon a car." I hung up, and said to Lizbeth, "The jury's coming back in. They've reached a verdict."

"Since *when?*" she demanded. "They only had yesterday afternoon, and . . . and . . ." She glanced at a clock on the wall. "The past hour, perhaps? Oh dear, oh no. That can't be good."

"We don't know anything for certain, not yet."

"Yes, we do, and false hope won't help anything—we both know that."

"False hope, false justice, false sense of security," I muttered as I dialed for the car service that had worked so well for me thus far. "James deserved better."

"So does Ruth," she said.

I was told the car would be around in twenty minutes, and it turned out the dispatcher was underselling their speed by fully four minutes. Not that either Lizbeth or I was complaining. We fidgeted outside on the front porch, waiting without speaking much. I think we were both anxious to get this over with, whatever it was.

We both knew that Edwin Stephenson was going to walk free. It was only a matter of time, a matter of forty-five minutes—once we were both seated in the sedan, and Lizbeth was holding on to her hat, lest the wind make off with it.

Maybe that was what spurred our sense of urgency: the thought that these were the last safe minutes Ruth was likely to have. Once her father was free, would he come for her next with his gun? Would he come for anyone else? I had no way of knowing how deep his resentment ran, or how likely he was to pursue vengeance. A normal fellow might take the break of having gotten away with murder, and consider himself blessed. Stephenson wasn't a normal fellow, though. He was a Chapelwood fellow, and a True American, and probably a Klansman, if one delved deeply enough into his past activities. He was definitely a killer of priests and a beater of women, a charlatan of the clergy who preyed on starry-eyed young couples outside the courthouse. I knew absolutely nothing to recommend him.

We pulled up to that same courthouse where he'd performed his phony wedding ceremonies, and stepped onto the very same sidewalk where he'd presented himself as a man of God and a friend to marriage's bureaucratic processes. We stepped across it quickly and went to the stairs; at the top, George Ward was waiting for us, with Ruth standing beside him as if she wished to hide behind him, or cling to him like a kitten—but had just enough dignity to restrain herself from all the silly things that outright terror might prompt her to do otherwise.

Lizbeth trotted up the steps, and I was close on her heels. She rushed to the girl and took her hands. "Everything will be fine," she assured her, but it was too earnest and her eyes were too serious to convince anyone, even herself. "Everything will be just fine," she repeated, then addressed George Ward. "We're in time, aren't we?"

"In time to hear that monster go free? You've got another ten minutes, at least."

"What will happen?" Ruth asked. "Once they let him go?"

My heart nearly broke for her, but I couldn't lie. "Not much, I expect. He'll go home to your mother; you'll go home to your husband. And Father Coyle will stay right where he is, but there's nothing to be done about that."

"It isn't fair," she whispered, her voice choked with tears. "They're going to let him go, like he didn't do anything at all."

"That's not set in stone, not yet," Lizbeth argued determinedly. She released the young woman's hands and gave her a quick, motherly hug. "We must have a little faith."

George Ward said drolly, "Oh, I've got faith as far as the eye can see. Faith that they'll cut the jackass loose with a pat on the back and a hearty handshake."

"That isn't what I meant," she griped.

"I know. And I want to say, I appreciate the effort and the indignation . . . but around here, these days, all the good intentions in the world won't amount to *shit*."

We heard the call of a bailiff, so we rallied ourselves to head inside.

As we entered the foyer, I scanned the scene for some sign of Chief Eagan, but spotted none. When I asked after him, George said he'd tried to reach him, but it was such short notice that he'd failed to do so. The chief didn't have a telephone, he told me. George had sent a messenger after him, and that was all he could do.

Everyone filed into the courtroom, and again, we took up our positions at the rear of the chamber. It was only then that I spied Edwin Stephenson, looking smug and impatient beside Hugo Black. Reverend Davis was there, too—right behind the defense, seated on the front row as if it were his rightful due. Maybe it was. He was the man who bought and paid for the verdict, wasn't he?

Or was it the True Americans? I don't know—the money trail became so convoluted the closer you looked. Come to think of it, even at a distance it really just appeared to be one big pot of money, shared among bigots and fools, doled out to bolster their terrible causes.

At any rate, he was instrumental in the proceedings, and his position behind the defendant all but announced as much.

I realized, as I sat back there—staring across the room at the back of the reverend's head—that I was doing it too: I was assuming that James's killer would go free, like it was a given. But I'd tried to be positive, hadn't I? I'd tried to assume the best, and not conclude that this small-city, backwater judicial system could be so useless and corrupt?

I wanted to give Birmingham credit, if only because James Coyle loved the place and believed it was worth serving; I wanted to hope for the best because of men like George Ward and Chief Eagan, and fierce young women like Ruth Gussman. I wanted to put my faith in the court system Massachusetts shared with Alabama, even after all this time—and even after these damn idiots had fought a war to extricate themselves from the binds that tie the states together in unity.

I wanted to think better of those men than I did.

They did not make it easy for me.

The jury foreman stood, and the judge asked him if they'd reached a verdict, and the bailiff took the little piece of paper over to the judge for him to read.

The judge wore a pair of spectacles pushed up on his head. He drew them down to sit on his nose, adjusted their fit, and read the verdict to himself, and then aloud: "We the jury find the defendant, Edwin Stephenson, not guilty by reason of temporary insanity."

As if this weren't bad enough, the audience broke into applause.

Lizbeth took Ruth's hand and squeezed it; Ruth squeezed back. George Ward said, "Goddamn," very softly, under his breath. It wouldn't have mattered if he'd shouted it, for no one would've heard it over the consensus of delight.

"Well"—Lizbeth sighed—"at least we aren't surprised."

"Let's get out of here," Ruth suggested. She rose to her feet, and we rose with her, exiting the courtroom with ease. Everyone else had already flooded forward to congratulate Stephenson, so there was no one left to block us there at the rear.

We hadn't gotten far, though, when the tide shifted and everyone spilled out behind us. A reporter had joined the fray, and there—a woman in a blue dress with the same nose as Ruth. Her mother? I guessed correctly, for she was immediately pushed beside Edwin and asked her opinion by the fellow with a notepad.

"How do you feel, now that your husband has been exonerated?"

"I . . ." She looked frightened, but generally pleased. I suppose she wasn't accustomed to having anyone ask her what she thought about anything. "I . . . I thank the Lord, of course. I'll be glad to have him home again."

"And you, sir?" the newspaperman asked, pointing his pencil at Edwin. "Have you anything you'd like to say? To your daughter, perhaps?"

Ruth cringed.

Stephenson smiled, and it was the ugliest thing I'd ever seen on any man's face. "First of all, I'm happy to be free, and I thank God that the men of the jury were able to see the truth of the situation. And second, to my wayward daughter Ruth . . ." He paused and searched the crowd for her. When he found her, that grin of his got even more gruesome. "I'd tell her she's forgiven, for all her transgressions—against her parents, and against her Lord and Savior."

I wondered if such a sentiment might make Ruth cry or turn away, but no. Ruth looked like *murder*. No, she really did—and I thought all the better of her for it. I felt like murder, too, and it wasn't even *my* miserable father who'd done the deed.

The notebook-toting man followed Edwin's gaze straight to Ruth, and turned his attention to her. "Mrs. Gussman!" he called, for he was ten yards away and there were twenty people between us all. "Would you care to respond?"

"Not in the slightest," she snapped. She turned on her heel, pushed open the front door, and walked right out.

Lizbeth and George went after her, but I lingered behind as the reporter shrugged and returned his attention to the Stephensons.

"And what will you do now?" he asked. "Go home, have a hot meal?"

Edwin shook his head. "No, I think it's time for a change.

All this trouble, it's made me want something more, something better for myself and my wife—since my daughter won't keep our company no more."

The reverend came to join them then. He put one hand on Edwin's shoulder, and answered the rest. "Mr. Stephenson is on the verge of being ordained as a minister in our church out at Chapelwood. As such, he and his family are welcome to reside there, on the grounds of the old estate. There's plenty of room, and we have a handful of other ministers living on site already."

"So you can tell Ruthie—" Edwin leaned forward and tapped the reporter's notes with his index finger. "You tell her she can have the house if she wants it. We won't need it no more, and she can take it as a sign that all's forgiven, and I guess . . . if she wants . . . I might be just a little sorry about how things happened between us. I hope she's happy."

Pretty words, but I didn't believe a single one of them.

(Except that perhaps I believed he was leaving for the company of his own foul kind.)

I left, too, back outside to follow after Ruth and Lizbeth, and George Ward. They were clustered together, slipping away as a group before anyone else with a notebook or an opinion could bother Ruth. I joined them shortly.

"My mother was with him. Did you see her?"

"Yes, I saw her. Did you want to talk to her?" I asked. By the time the words were out of my mouth, I already knew the answer.

"What would I say? Should I tell her to leave and come with me? Should I . . ." She sighed heavily and shook her head. "Should I tell her I'm afraid for her, and that she should stay away from Chapelwood, and Daddy, and the reverend, too? She knows all that already. I've said it a thousand times, and either she doesn't hear me, she doesn't believe me, or . . . or she doesn't care."

Lizbeth wrapped an arm around her shoulder and gave her a short hug. "I understand."

"You do?"

"Yes, I do. It's easier to hope that she's only being manipulated, and not that she's given up or that she doesn't love you." Lizbeth's earnestness was back on display, and she reconsidered it immediately. "I mean, I'm sorry. That didn't come out quite right."

"Sure it did," Ruth said. "You said it exactly right, and that's exactly how it is. I just . . . I want to go home, all right? I just want to go home."

I stuffed my hands into my jacket pockets. "You know, your father says you can have his house. He and your mother are moving into Chapelwood, and leaving it vacant. He alleges that it's some sort of apology."

"If he really wants to give it to me, that's fine," she said with a sniff. She tugged at George's arm, and began walking toward his car. "I've got a box of matches in my purse."

Reverend Adam James Davis, Minister, the Disciples of Heaven

CHAPELWOOD ESTATE, ALABAMA

OCTOBER 3, 1921

The order is righted. I knew it would be, but the specifics eluded me—in part because of young Mr. Kincaid's treachery, though I'm loath to admit it. I preferred to think that he was a gnat in the air, something annoying but ultimately harmless . . . something bound to be squashed in a very short time, by virtue of its own ridiculous behavior.

Or does that carry it too far? I'm not sure. The sentiment remains, regardless.

It doesn't matter anyway, not anymore. It might not've mattered in the first place at all—who can say? Not Leonard. He only read the messages. He did not manage them, or deploy them. He barely even transcribed them, and when he did, he was not always correct or successful.

I know that now. His methods were good, but not perfect.

In time, if he'd been more patient, he might have led us to perfection.

But I put too much pressure on him, and assigned him too much importance. I entrusted him with too much—that's one more mistake I made—but ultimately, I must be fair to myself: It was right to bring him into the fold. It's a pity he did not stay. Had he remained with us all this time, we might be closer yet to our goal.

I say that . . . but.

Here, where I am being true, and fair, and right—to myself, and everyone else . . . I must confess that I cannot be certain.

Some things are certain, yes: We receive the messages, we hear the voices, we see the smoke. We close our eyes, and we touch the nearest edge of that damnable wall that separates us from divinity. We reach out, with our inefficient chisels and our small hammers, and we chip, chip, chip away, knowing that heaven awaits us on the other side.

It awaits us, and us alone.

Leonard Kincaid brought us closer than we'd ever been. He refined the language we used to communicate with Our Lord, I will give him that. I will grant that he showed uncanny intelligence, and a natural propensity toward the tasks we required of him. I admit freely that he was useful to us, and that he might have been great among us.

That's especially easy for me to say, now that I've seen his handiwork. He always behaved like such a benign, nervous man, afraid to blow his own nose. Who knew he had murder in him?

I should've known it. I know good and well that everyone has murder inside, given the right stimulus.

Now . . . now I would like to think that he may join us yet. Not in any full capacity—not with the glory of a disciple whose faith stayed strong and never wavered, no. But his help was such a blessing, I honestly hope that there is some room for him in the Land of Glory beyond that aggravating wall between life and death, God and man.

Because Satan was wrong, you know. It is better by far to serve in heaven than to reign in hell.

As Leonard should have known already.

He's gone now, I've seen to that—in what might be described (if I flatter myself) as an artful fashion. I was pleased with my handiwork, at any rate. I feel confident that, likewise, heaven approves. And if he's waiting for us on the other side, so much the better—but I'm thinking too hard about things yet to come. I mustn't let it distract me from the present, where great things are happening.

We are finally thirteen, in accordance with the pattern. Twelve disciples and one prophet leading the way. I will do my best to prove worthy of this leadership role. I will do my best to serve the Lord.

Edwin Stephenson was the final piece, which I frankly did not expect.

I appreciated his zeal, of course, and I was pleased by his dedication to the cause, but I did not imagine that he was really "disciple" material. For in all reality, the man is a little thug. With time, penitence, and prayer, I thought he might rise through the ranks to "deacon," but he's certainly proved himself more useful than that. I'm well aware that it was not mere rage that sent him after the priest; yes, he was furious about his daughter—but he'd been furious about his daughter since the day she was born, and she was not a son. But no, that wasn't what sent him to Saint Paul's. Coyle's murder was *officially* an act of rage, as the courts concluded, but it was also an act of *devotion*—and an act of very fine timing for Chapelwood.

Stephenson told me in confidence how he saw that the time was right, that the pattern had revealed itself to him in a divine and sudden fashion. He *knew*, he told me, that this was his destiny—that the wheel had turned to align events in his favor. And it was that choice of words, "the wheel has turned," that made me consider that he might be correct.

I've seen the phrase myself, in the scriptures the mad Arab left behind.

It stands to reason. A wheel is a pattern of another kind, each spoke rising and falling again and again to the same point, in the same path. Everything comes around again, in some form . . . until the wheel is broken and reassembled into something greater, and rolled onward to someplace better.

So I gave Edwin's behavior a blessing after the fact. He'd operated independently, but he was guided by the same hand as the rest of us. If I was wrong, then fine: I was wrong—but I still had an inconvenient figure removed from the equation, at no reputational cost to myself or Chapelwood. There is room in the world for little thugs. Like everything and everyone else, they serve a purpose, and that purpose might as well be higher than rage or chaos.

Since the trial is done, and since Edwin is free, he has come here to join the fold in a formal manner. It only seemed fitting, after our last service in the underground hall, where I received the expected revelation.

As every piece slots into position, a new edict appears.

Much as Edwin Stephenson is the final member of our coterie, his daughter is the final sacrifice after all.

She was taken from us by the priest, and now she's been given back. Or she *will* be given back, that much is assured and I am much relieved to hear it. Though Leonard hacked his way through our lists of worthy subjects, and though he inconvenienced us and delayed us, he has not *prevented* us from anything. His success has turned out to be our success, for he adjusted the timing in a fortuitous manner.

This was how it was intended all along. We all serve our purposes. There is a place in the world—and beyond it—for all of us.

I asked the Lord how we should collect Ruth Stephenson, and I was told to wait. I was told that she would bring herself to Chapelwood in time, and then our setting would be complete. She will be the lynchpin, the keystone. We will unlock the door, and she will hold it open.

I am assured, and I am trying to have faith . . . that she will come to us.

I hope it is soon. The wait has been so long already, and so fraught with delay and confusion. I want her here, *now*, at our disposal and at our mercy.

If only she knew. I can't help but think that if she really understood, she would march directly to the estate, climb the steps with confidence and pride, and offer herself up in service to the greater plan.

She will hold the door ajar. She will save the world. Her blood will be the solvent that wrecks the walls between heaven and earth, and then . . . then we will all be whole, and home with our Creator.

I tried to make her understand, but I could not. That particular failing is mine, but as another book says, "All things work together for good." This, too, this failing of mine, this stretching of the timeline . . . Oh, how we have trudged through the calendar, and our trudge was all the more disheartening for not knowing whether we yet progressed, or only treaded water.

I am impatient, and this is another failing. We have all fallen short of the glory of God, but it is upon us all to do our best to correct ourselves. This is part of that effort—this record I leave behind: It makes me feel like I'm accomplishing something, like my time is being used productively, rather than simply *passed*. It's all I can really do, while I wait for the young woman to find her own path back to the fold.

The pattern is a promise. It brings us all home, in time.

George Ward, Birmingham City Commission President (Former)

OCTOBER 3, 1921

Here we are, then, on the other side of the trial.

Here we are, on the other side of the election.

Here we are, at the end.

It took so little time for them to undo so much. We spent years upon years trying to heal the grievous wound left by the war; and for a moment there, during the one that engulfed the whole world so recently, I wondered whether a *different* war wasn't the answer we'd all been seeking. We rallied together again, North and South. One country, joining other countries—fighting a good fight, for the benefit of the whole world. All of us, rallied together for a greater cause.

It was not a perfect solution, no. But is there one? Could there ever *be* one?

Sixty years ago, the Confederacy tore itself loose . . . only to be conquered and stitched back onto the Union. Might as well try to reattach an unwilling arm or a leg, and expect everything to work just fine again in a fortnight. Some things are only impossible.

And when the Great War began in earnest, when the United States of America threw its hat into that ring of fire, I had the horrible thought that, *yes*, one war might mend the damage of another. Someone *else's* war, this time. Let someone else's land be the battlefield, and let us ride together, blue and gray beneath the red, white, and blue.

It worked, didn't it? In some places, yes, I must believe that it did.

But not here. Not for the long haul. Oh, it's true—we had a wave of unlikely immigrants, Jews and Italians and Bohemians, and it looked like we might all live alongside one another in peace, didn't it? We even had the sanity to take strides toward equality for all our citizens, and to beautify our city, and to bring it into the twentieth century with pride. Electrical lights and traffic direction, telephones, paved walkways, and more . . . we are a modern city, for Christ's sake! How can we behave like this, and expect the rest of the world to judge us as civilized and progressive?

We can't. It shouldn't.

We should be judged for precisely what we are, and nothing more: a city full of villains and victims, and the hopeless men who failed to change it.

I'␣e gone back to Storage Room Six, Ruthie. That's why I'm writing this, to tell you that much—so you'll understand to go looking there, in the event I do not return from my errand. I'm not sure how much help the storage room will be to you; I'm not sure how much will even be left by the time you find it. It's as I told the inspector: The place eats things—evidence, relics, time, and memories alike.

Piece by piece, shred by shred, all the evidence with which we ever even *tried* to serve justice and goodwill is eroded, right out from under us. This is a cliff we stand upon, Ruthie. A cliff that will fail in time, and we'll all fall into the ocean unless we walk away, leave this place, find bedrock somewhere else.

You should walk away. You've done literally all you can, and more than was asked. There's nothing left for you here. Take your husband and go, make a home in another town. Anywhere else. Leave while you can. Leave before they force you to stay.

I sat in the storage room and I listened hard, closing my eyes and opening my ears, breathing as quietly as I could. When I do this, when I slow down the world, muffle out the distractions, sometimes I can hear little voices when I'm in that weird basement.

No, not voices. That lends the wrong impression. It's more as if . . . I can feel the currents of some conversation taking place around me, regardless of me. It's a soft thing, tendrils almost. Think of the softest silk you've ever touched, and imagine it stripped down to its very threads. Imagine those threads drawn across your skin by an invisible hand, or imagine (better still) that you sit inside a cauldron full of the things, being stirred by an unseen spoon.

That's almost what I mean.

And when it's very quiet, when I sit inside the damp, musty silence of Storage Room Six, I feel those threads. I feel them and I can almost see them, hear them. Believe them, when they move around my ears like whispers.

I only catch stray words, here and there. The occasional phrase. Sometimes it's helpful, sometimes it's nonsense—or taken so far out of context that it might as well be. But there's a rhythm to it all the same. A tidal fluctuation, a coming and going. A *beat*.

I have sat there, in Storage Room Six, for hours upon hours. I have pored over boxes full of files, wishing for the pieces to assemble themselves in my mind—demanding that the evidence lend me some hint of a killer, or a motive. Anything, really.

I've wondered at that motive time and time again. What would make a man (or men, or woman, or women) hunt down fellow citizens on the streets? What would make him (or them, or her) relentlessly murder, all across the cityscape?

And beyond it, too. There's rumor of a new death, this one outside the usual parameters. This one, they found in a set of run-off tunnels that dump into a creek. Usually these tunnels (and they're not tunnels, really—they're concrete chutes, as much as anything) . . . usually they carry detritus from the rail yards—they sluice off all the wet things. All the things that are easier to dump down a drain than to bury or burn.

I don't think the body was flushed down the drain; I don't think there's a drain big enough to hold it. I think the body was carried to the creek's edge, and jammed up inside that cold concrete casket, and left there to rot. I think that the killer assumed, and correctly, that by the time the corpse was found, there'd be little left to identify it. There'd be nothing present but bones, and strips of fabric, and muddy damp flakes of peeled skin.

I'm not sure if it's the same man.

Not "Harry the Hacker," for he never existed. But the same fellow who committed (most of) the other killings. I'm not sure if it's him—or if it *is*, then we may have something awful on our hands. More awful than a spree killer with an axe, that is.

(Dear God, would you look at how far my standards for *awful* have fallen? It's as if they never existed in the first place.)

But here, this is what I mean: The killer never tried to hide the bodies before, no further than a cursory dragging to haul them out of a main thoroughfare. If this is the same killer, then he's learning. He's improving. He intends to continue unabated, and with greater efficiency. If it's not the same killer, then it's some other one—hoping to ride the first maniac's coattails.

Either way, it spells bad things for Birmingham.

All the more reason, Ruth. All the more reason for you to leave, while the leaving is good.

The room tells me little, and it tells me lots. It gives me hints and signs, and it takes everything else away. Pages of evidence fade until they are clean white sheets, or unfilled forms never typed upon, never signed. Envelopes vanish into the air. Paper clips collect at the bottom of boxes, freed from whatever documents they once held in meticulous place. Pencils shorten themselves, reduce to nubs, and are gone altogether without having ever been sharpened. Pens run dry. Photographs lighten and lighten and lighten until they may as well be pictures of sheets strung out on a line.

All the signs are there, and all the portents have evaporated.

Whatever has happened, whatever is coming, it won't fall in our favor. We have few allies, no legal standing. No knowledge of what we're even fighting, though it wears a man's face and speaks with a man's voice, for all that it's unreal and untrue.

Whatever that reverend is, whatever he claims to be, whatever he once was. Whatever his connection, you can bet he's the monster behind this. Somehow. Whatever. There are no words true enough to describe him. I know that now. I know that he will destroy the world with his books, formulas, and figures. He thinks of them as scriptures, that's one thing I've gathered from the silk that drapes itself in currents and waves throughout the room. He has scriptures, and they're no scriptures for the likes of us. Setting eyes on them would be a horror. Reading them would be madness.

𝕳𝖊𝖗𝖊 is what I think, Ruthie.

Read this note, and don't bring it down to the room, lest the room eat it up and then no one will ever see it except for you—and that's a burden I won't wish upon you, not for any reward. You should share this with those you trust. (Hell, you can share it with the world, for all I care.) But here is what I think. I need to convey it somehow, before I'm absorbed into the room as well, as surely as the notes and the pictures and the scraps of evidence, unraveled in front of my eyes.

Here is what I think.

It's one part police work of the old-fashioned sort, one part conjecture, and one part the whispered voices made of silk, spinning a web in that room. (And nothing escapes the web. Nothing ever has, and nothing ever will except for you, if you go. You are the lynchpin, dear. The keystone.)

I think the axe killer is one of the Chapelwood men, either by will or by compulsion. I think he hunts at the reverend's behest, or command, or direction—I don't know which. But he is one of theirs, I'd bet my life on it.

And why would Chapelwood seek to kill so many of our citizens, in such a specific and strange manner? I don't know, but there is strange geometry involved in their efforts—they view the world through maps made of numbers, and via instructions relayed through formulas and sums. I'm not sure how, and I don't know exactly *why*, but the fellow whose death made the papers last week, Leonard Kincaid, he had something to do with it.

I spoke with his former employers, at an accountant's firm here in town. Kincaid was a good worker and a sane man, helping balance the city's budget and manage its tax rolls until about eighteen months ago. His secretary (a Miss Josephine Engle, for the record) informed me that he'd attended some kind of religious camp meeting outside the city—she didn't know which one, and she didn't know what they were preaching that piqued his interest so strongly; but afterward, he'd become preoccupied with the prospect of communicating with God through math.

I told her that sounded unlikely, and she agreed with me—but she also said that Kincaid was quite insistent on the point, and he'd always struck her as an eminently sane man. He'd declared that numbers were the language of the universe, and if God created the universe, then that's how He would speak.

As Miss Engle noted, the idea is so insidious because it tiptoes so close to logic.

Shortly after catching a case of religion, as the young secretary put it, Kincaid quit the firm and vanished. Miss Engle attempted to visit him at home, in order to return some of the personal effects he'd left at the office . . . but she found the house empty, and for sale. She was never able to procure a forwarding address, and never able to return his belongings.

I have those belongings now. I'm adding them to Storage Room Six, though I can't say why. I ought to know better. I ought to bury them in a hole in the ground, for that would be more secure, wouldn't it? Undoubtedly. But something compels me to stash them there, and so I carry the strange box with its strange contents and I deliver it to the basement, to the strange and hungry room.

At this point, I feel like I'm feeding the place.

Does that make sense? No, I'm sure it doesn't. But, Ruthie, have you ever by any chance fed a stray cat? Some scraggly thing that roams around the block, darting in and out of yards, dodging dogs and horses and (these days) cars . . . if you have ever spotted such a thing, and offered it a scrap of supper, then you might know how I feel about the storage room.

You only have to feed it once, and it will never leave you alone again. It will beg and beg and beg, and you will give and give and give, because it seems like there isn't any choice. You know the thing now, and it needs you, and you can't let it starve.

(𝔇𝔞𝔯𝔢 I pen something even crazier? I might as well. I tried "feeding" the storage room useless things, like old phone books, out-of-date newspapers, and Sears catalogs from a decade ago. Do you want to know what happened to them? *Nothing*, that's what happened. They held no interest for Storage Room Six. It only wants material that *matters*. Specifically, it wants material that matters to the axe murders and to what Chapelwood members we've been able to identify. It positively *hungers* for it.)

𝔖𝔬𝔪𝔢𝔥𝔬𝔴, Leonard Kincaid, crucified to the flophouse wall, was part of Chapelwood and part of the axe killings, too. You can see it in the box, in the things he left behind. You can see it in the stars, if you look hard enough. You can hear it in Storage Room Six, when you close your eyes and open your ears and hold very still, and are willing to listen to voices that come from nowhere, everywhere, and all around you at once.

I'm not strictly suggesting that you *should*.

Or maybe I *am*. No doubt, I could use a measure of context or perspective on the matter. Some ordinary soul might step inside the storage room and conclude that it's an ordinary place, stuffed with the ordinary detritus of civic workings, abandoned after a regime change. That inspector fellow, Wolf, he came down there—he saw the place. I don't know precisely what he thought of it. Maybe he heard the whispers, maybe he did not. I should've asked.

I might actually be going insane.

I don't want you to go insane, Ruthie. You deserve better than that. Of course, James Coyle deserved justice, and Birmingham deserved better leaders, and the mutilated dead deserved life or (at the very least) dignity after the fact.

Didn't they? Don't we all?

I don't understand what is happening, I'll be the first to admit it.

But something is coming, and it's coming with purpose. It's coming closer. Faster. Homing in on us, or that's not quite it. It might be better to say that it's focusing on us, adjusting its attention the way an astronomer tweaks the lenses on a telescope, all the better to bring the distance into sharp relief.

Whatever it is, we shouldn't call out for its attention. We should hide from it, and pray that it passes us by, oblivious to us and all our efforts upon this anthill called Earth.

Look at these pieces, Ruthie. Puzzle pieces, and without a helpful box lid to show us what we're meant to assemble. Chapelwood. Axe murders. The True Americans. Your father. Leonard Kincaid.

You.

And me, too, I assume.

See if your new friends can be of some help. The inspector and his consultant, that woman Lizbeth Andrew . . . there's something odd about them, if only because they behave like civilized, sane individuals who yet retain some shred of decency. They don't belong here, but they're only visiting. They'll leave, one day—soon, I should expect.

See if they can be persuaded to take you with them.

Lizbeth Andrew (Borden)

❦

OCTOBER 4, 1921

I was flattered and frankly touched that Ruth showed me the letter George left her.

He'd slipped it into her mailbox slot overnight, it would seem. Upon finding it first thing this morning, Ruth was alarmed by the rattled tone, the rambling connections . . . It didn't sound like him, she said. She insisted that something must be wrong.

So she ran to the post office down the street from her flat and used the phone there to call him—to no avail. No one answered at the Ward residence, and when she finally navigated the street-cars and residential blocks to reach his home in person, no one answered the door, either.

Eventually, Chief Eagan was able to rouse Mrs. Ward, who was uncommonly groggy for ten o'clock in the morning. It was the chief's estimation that Mrs. Ward had been drugged the night before . . . probably by George himself, though he hated to suggest it—but the dose had been a gentle one that hadn't harmed her. She'd gotten a most excellent night's sleep out of it, and had no idea where her husband could have gotten off to.

"Which was probably the point," I said to Ruth.

I was still holding the note, reading bits and pieces of it again and again. It reminded me all too much of another note, one I'd held and read in a similar fashion, years ago. It did indeed sound like a man who was slipping into madness.

"You think he drugged her so he could sneak out of the house without her knowing?" Ruth asked. She was not quite incredulous, but she clearly did not want to believe it.

Inspector Wolf was seated beside her on a long chaise in our hotel's lobby. "Yes, I think that's probably the case. He did it for her own good, I bet. If she didn't know where he'd gone, then she couldn't possibly tell anyone about it—even if she wanted to."

"He's obviously . . ." I didn't say the rest, because I didn't want to say it in front of Ruth. Instead I declared, "He's obviously performing his own investigations, even though he's no longer on the city payroll. If Nathaniel Barrett thought he was still poking his nose into the axe murders, you can bet he'd have Tom Shirley put a stop to it."

Wolf shot me a glance that said he knew I must be fibbing. He was right, of course.

If anything was obvious (in my opinion), George was headed for Chapelwood. But to what end? To force some confession out of the reverend? To deliver his own brand of justice to Edwin Stephenson?

(Well, Wolf was right, yes. But he didn't want to say anything about Chapelwood in front of Ruth any more than I did, otherwise she might feel like storming the place. Perhaps the place *needed* storming, but it did not need storming by *her*—or even by the bunch of us, not yet. We didn't know what we'd find there: what resistance, what coercion, what crimes. What unholy, unhealthy conspiracy.

After all, when it all came down to it, we knew virtually nothing about that place except for its wealth, its secrecy, and its bigoted leanings that encompassed almost every human being except those masculine, Protestant, and white. We knew that it was ostensibly a church, occupying a large estate on the out-skirts of town. Ruth was the only one of us who'd been there, and she'd already told us how little she'd seen of it.)

Ruth wasn't sure how she felt about my fib, but ultimately she granted the chance that I might be correct. "I guess that's . . . possible. He called it his 'unfinished business' after the election. But this room he's talking about in the note . . . do you know what he means? Storage Room Six? Inspector, he says you met him there."

Wolf nodded. "It's in the basement of the civic building, and that's where we met for the first time—the day after he lost the election, I think. For what it's worth, I *did* notice a strange air about the place and an unsettling sense of being watched; but poor George, I must say—he struck me as positively *cracked* upon that first encounter. Or I should say instead . . . he sounded like the man who wrote this note, and less like the upstanding, normal sort of man who kept us company through your father's trial."

Ruth sighed. "His wife said he wasn't sleeping well, and he was drinking more than he ought to. More than anyone's *sup-posed* to, since our prohibition. But that's not peculiar, is it? Considering the circumstances?"

"Not at all, dear. Not at all." I handed the letter back to her.

"What should we do?" she asked.

Wolf and I exchanged a look again.

I let him answer. "First, Lizbeth and I will see you home. Your husband might want to know that you're all right, since you left him in such haste this morning and haven't yet returned. Then you'll have a little rest, perhaps a tipple of your own, if there's anything on hand. It's been a difficult week for you, too, and you mustn't jump to conclusions or leap into premature action."

"But—"

"And *meanwhile*," he asserted, "Lizbeth and I will see if we can track down George. Something's sent him off the rails, and we should probably find out *what*—before he gets himself into trouble."

"What about the box? The one with the dead man's things in it? It's in that storage room, and I want to see it."

He patted her hand and said, "Yes, that's where we'll begin. George might have left some other hint or clue behind, and if that's the case, we'll let you know."

Ruth gave us both a pointed frown. "But I want to go, *too*. I want to see for myself."

I didn't think it was a good idea, and I told her so. "No, dear—not while you're still so very *interesting* to the newspapers. Everyone knows you now, Ruth; you're famous here, most especially with the new commissioner and his regime. Barrett will be there, and perhaps Tom Shirley, and maybe even the reverend . . . there's really no telling, but any given one of them might make trouble for you, if they see you."

"So? They'll make trouble for you, too. Everybody saw you keeping me company at the courthouse."

She had a point, but Wolf waved it away with a flap of his

wrist. "Oh, we were only in your background. No one has the slightest bit of interest in us. I'd be stunned if we were to be recognized."

"*I* wouldn't," she sulked. "You're out-of-towners, and you're friends of mine and George's. Somebody's noticed, I can promise you that. People around here, they notice *everything*—they're always suspicious of everything and everyone they don't know, and they gossip like hens."

But Wolf was unswayed. "That's true everyplace, I assure you. It's not a trait special to Alabama. We'll be fine, and we'll be happiest knowing that you're safe at home while we brave the corridors of injustice on your behalf."

"That's a funny way to put it, and I don't like people doing things on my behalf. I want to do things on my *own* behalf."

"But surely you understand," he pressed, less cavalier and more kindly, "that we're less likely to be stopped, or detained on some trumped-up charge, or harassed out of the building . . . if we proceed without you. I'm an inspector, Ruth. Let me inspect, and let me do so while being confident of your security."

Finally, she gave up. I suppose she figured she might as well, as Wolf's impenetrable wall of fatherly firmness stood in the way of any argument.

Wolf had a car at the ready, so we dropped her off and promised to report back by dinnertime, a promise which she reluctantly accepted—and vowed to hold us to. Once we'd seen her safely inside, we climbed back into the sedan.

"Where to now, sir?" asked the driver.

Wolf hesitated, giving me an uncertain look. "I suppose you want to see the mysterious storage room, too, don't you?"

"The sooner, the better—and you said it yourself: Right

now, that's our best hope for finding George, or finding out what he's up to."

He nodded, and to the driver he said, "Kindly deposit us at the civic building downtown, if you please." Then he leaned back into the padded seat, and said more quietly, just to me, "But it's a worrisome place, he was right about that. The one time I visited . . ."

"How bad can it possibly be?"

"The one time I visited," he repeated, still letting the thought dangle for a moment, "I left it hoping it was indeed the *only* time I would ever visit."

"That's a sinister thing to say."

"It's a sinister place. I didn't want to oversell it too much in front of Ruth, but George has a point about it being unwelcoming and hungry. I can't explain it with any precision . . . there's a miasma down there, the whole basement, even—not just that particular storage room, though I do believe that's where it's concentrated most."

"And George had been spending so much time there. More time than anyone knew, it would appear—since he offered that little aside about trying to feed it like a stray cat." I thought of my own strays, and I hoped they were well without me. I was certain they must be, for cats always have that competent way about them. They don't need people in the slightest, so when they choose our company, it's such a pleasant surprise.

"It can't have been good for his mental state—and it won't be good for ours, either. You should be advised of that before we arrive."

We rode on in silence for a bit, until it occurred to me to ask, "This storage room . . . it's where you found the drawing of Nance, isn't that what you said?"

"Yes, that's right."

"Was there any other sign of her? Anything else you might have noticed?" Because hope could not fail to spring eternal, even when it damn well knew better.

"Not that I saw at the time, but I wasn't there for very long. I didn't spend long with the boxes and files; there's plenty yet to be explored."

"Or maybe not, if George is to be believed. I've never heard of such a thing, have you? A room that consumes anything it holds, given time enough to do so?"

He shook his head, but I could tell he was racking his brain trying to think of some corollary. "No, nothing springs to mind. George tried to explain it when I first found him there, and I wrote it up in my notes—then sent the packet back to Boston, in case anyone there might have any ideas. I do that every couple of days—mail off my findings, that is. I like to record my progress and report it, for the sake of posterity and the sake of my own safety, too. Should my investigations suddenly cease, along with any communication, the office there would know to send someone after me."

"A wise plan," I agreed. I liked the idea of it: a paper trail to stand witness.

(𝔍'𝔳𝔢 left plenty of paper trails myself, but I've never had anyone to direct them toward—no one except for you, Emma, and that's wholly an act of sentiment, since you're gone. You're beyond reading these things, and you might not have been interested in them anyway.

Probably, I bring up Nance too much.

Probably, you're sick of hearing about her.)

"𝔍𝔱'𝔰 a safety measure more than a plan," he continued. "Besides, once the case is finished—or as finished as some of them ever get—it's helpful to see the whole thing laid out from beginning to end. Sometimes I can see patterns after the fact . . . details that seemed insignificant may add up or line up to spell something important."

"How many cases have you solved?" I asked, afraid that it might verge on impoliteness—since it might imply his efforts were not uniformly successful. But I was too curious to restrain myself.

"More than I've abandoned due to lack of evidence," he answered quickly, without sounding insulted in the slightest. Then, more slowly, more thoughtfully, he added, "But solving a case . . . it doesn't always mean that an answer to a riddle has been found, or that a great truth has been revealed. As often as not, a solution is little more than a conclusion—the ability to say, 'This is what happened.' Or even, 'I don't know what happened, but here is the mechanism by which it operated.' It's rarely quite so simple as the detective stories would lead you to think."

"Maybe not, but the prospect charms me. The idea of a community like yours . . . an organization that at least *attempts* to address the things others may dismiss." Suddenly I sat up straighter, and with a gasp. Two ideas had collided in my brain with such velocity that I was stunned they hadn't met before.

"Lizbeth? Was it something I said?"

"That's what you were doing in Fall River," I noted. "You were there about Zollicoffer."

He was puzzled; you could see it in the zigzag lines of his forehead. "You knew that already. You knew it at the time."

"No, that's not what I mean. You investigated that case, those deaths, that man . . . because none of it was natural, not in the traditional sense."

"You are correct." He nodded, still uncertain as to why this had unnerved me so. He must have assumed I'd figured it out already . . . and to some extent I *had*. But given all the excitement, I hadn't really stopped to consider . . . so I asked him, "The Zollicoffer case. Do you consider that one . . . solved?"

"It's as I told you, 'solved' is a slippery term at best. I believe I called that one 'concluded.' After my last visit to Fall River . . . shortly thereafter, that is, if you'll excuse me . . . erm . . ."

"Go on," I prompted. I *wanted* him to ask about it. I'm not sure why.

Likewise, I'm not sure why he was so reluctant.

He arched an eyebrow toward the back of our driver's head, as if to remind me that we weren't alone. Cautiously, he said, "We'd suspected that Zollicoffer's course of action would lead him to Fall River—but we did not have anything firm to base it upon until it was . . . to be frank . . . entirely too late to do anything about it. I had some grand ideas about rushing into your town, lending a hand, saving the day, and so on . . . but there wasn't time. Certainty came to us in increments, you see. And"—he shifted in his seat so he could better face me, and lend the impression of earnestness—"that was one of my great complaints, with the way the case was handled. Everyone was so afraid that we'd predict the wrong path and miss the monstrous fellow altogether . . . that no one wanted to make a decision on the matter. No investigator would stand up and say, 'I believe the professor will next strike *here*,' because what if he turned out to be wrong? It was a coward's handling of the matter, from top to bottom."

"What about *you*?"

"Me?" He sighed and settled back, leaning halfway against the seat and halfway against the door. There was quite a lot of him to lean, after all. "I was one of the cowards. I had my hunches, but not much more—not until the very end, you know. I was younger then, and the professor's case was unprecedented . . . the kind of thing that comes along once in a hundred years. I was only allowed to participate on a provisionary basis; I could scarcely talk my superiors into a per diem and travel allowance, not even after the Hamilton murders. Too many people in the bureaucracy were too willing to write it off to coincidence."

I shook my head in disbelief. "What a world, where such deaths are common enough to call coincidence."

"I couldn't agree with you more. And that said, I feel this is as good a time as any to apologize."

"To me?"

"To you," he affirmed. "I left you alone, to face whatever would come. It's something that still bothers me in the wee hours of the morning sometimes. Even after all these years."

"Really?" I wasn't sure I believed him, but some petty, dark corner of my soul liked the idea of it.

"Really. You and your sister, and the doctor—Seabury, that's right, that was his name—you had no idea what you were up against. Our office might have been able to help . . . but it chose not to, not until our help was no longer required. Or so we were forced to assume."

He was finally on the verge of asking me what had become of Zollicoffer, I could see it then: the hesitation after the admission, a sidelong glance to check his apology's reception. A gleam of curiosity, regarding a case never solved so much as concluded, as he'd so carefully put it. But he was too much of a gentleman, or there was still some cowardly residue left over from thirty years ago, I don't know. But I wanted to tell him, because I'd never told anyone. Seabury and Emma had known, but both of them clutched that secret in their coffins.

So I gave Inspector Wolf the chance to hear it. I gave myself the chance to say it out loud, for the first time ever. "You want to know what happened that night, when Zollicoffer came around."

He perked right up, but not so much as to be unseemly. "I'd very much like to know, yes. The folders are sealed and covered with dust in the farthest corners of our Boston storage facility, but for my own satisfaction, yes. I'd very much like to know."

But drat the timing of it all—we had just pulled up to the civic building downtown, and our driver cleared his throat to attract our attention. "Sir, madam. We've arrived."

It was just as well, and we both knew it. A good driver was as fine a vault for secrets as a good bartender, but we didn't know this man, and at any rate . . . he'd heard enough already.

"Inside," I told Wolf. "If the storage room is hungry for secrets, it can eat this one, too."

He left instructions and money with the driver, telling the man how long to wait before leaving us to our own devices; and together we climbed the wide white stairs that led up to the civic building. It wasn't so different in design from the courthouse, and indeed it gave me the same anxious feeling as we scaled the expanse between the street and the front doors.

"It's bustling in here," Wolf said. "And Ruth wasn't wrong—there's always the chance we'll be recognized as allies of hers and George. I haven't had any trouble so far, but then again, I haven't been back to the civic center here since before the trial." He left his fingers briefly on the oversized door handle and said, "Walk briskly, smile and make small talk with me, and behave as if you belong here as much as anyone else. No one's likely to bother us."

I nodded and said, "Of course," with more confidence than I felt. In the back of my mind, I was always a little worried about being recognized for something worse than being a friend of Ruth's; there was always the chance that some old fool might recognize my face from a newspaper picture or a magazine story. Was it likely? No. But neither was a storage room that ate evidence and drove men mad.

He took my elbow, smiled brightly, and ushered me inside.

Offices lined every hall, broken up by conference rooms and other brightly lit meeting spaces; and everywhere we saw men wearing suits and doing business, or carrying on arguments— while older men in nicer suits talked loudly on phones or to their underlings in the corridors, making sure everyone knew that they were busy, and they were in charge. Sharply dressed young women toted folders and coffee, and office boxes, and oversized purses, and clipboards from room to room, their button-toed shoes making a chatter of scuffs and scrapes on the brightly shining floor.

We passed an office with "Nathaniel Barrett" stenciled on the window, but I only glimpsed it as we hurried past—Wolf's nattering about the weather leaving a dull hum in my left ear.

"This way," he said, guiding me around a turn, and to a stairwell door marked "Exit Only." Before I could protest, he'd opened it anyway and darted inside—drawing me behind him. The door shut, closing us inside a concrete space with a single fizzing lightbulb, and absolutely none of the hectic charm on display outside. "And now we go downstairs—where it's going to get strange. Don't let it bother you; I know where we're headed."

"Are we likely to run into anyone else?"

"No," he said, leading the way. "Unless we feel like hoping and praying that George has been stuck there, and we won't have to go looking for him after all."

"There must be a more *direct* route to the basement," I observed. I dodged a lone strand of cobweb that dangled from the lightbulb cage at the next landing, and tried to ignore the dirty light and the dusty smell.

"An elevator, shared by the whole building."

"For three stories and a basement?"

"Modern technology," his voice echoed up in his wake. "Any excuse for it, I suspect. But if we took the elevator, we might be called upon to explain ourselves to other passengers— or to the fellow who operates it. I don't know about you, but I would just as soon skip that social nicety."

He stopped at the bottom, partly to let me catch up and partly because he didn't want to go any farther. His whole posture shouted his reluctance to proceed: His face had gone red and tight, his breathing shallow, his shoulders squared against whatever awaited us. But he was being brave for me, the dear man. He needn't have bothered. I'd been in more frightening places, and more frightening positions than this one— standing before a half-dark labyrinth of office furniture, crates, and bookcases.

We took in the scene together, until he felt he'd hesitated long enough and to do so any longer would make him look less manly. "There's a pathway," he promised. "Straight back, through here."

Once again he played tour guide, leading me between tall hedgerows of unneeded items that no one wished to throw away. In some places the passage became tight, and Wolf had to shimmy himself sideways to fit. In other spots, we both were compelled to duck when mop handles and lawn-care tools formed a menacing canopy overhead.

The air felt different down there. It was musty, yes—but that wasn't the core source of the weirdness. It was dark except for the sparse electric lights, and the place never saw sunlight or felt ventilation, so the smell of old paper and damp was no surprise; but there was something else to it, something cold and almost slimy in its feel . . . like the air left a sheen upon my skin, as if it were fog or a seaside mist.

"Almost there," he pledged.

"It's all right. I'm keeping up just fine."

"Are you . . . do you sense anything . . . unusual?"

I wasn't sure how to answer, so I was honest. "Yes, but I couldn't describe it if you held a gun to my head."

"Fair enough," he muttered. "I couldn't, either."

Eventually the path widened, and we were deposited at a cleared area—a juncture where a series of rooms branched off from the main space, all in a row. They were each numbered, and at least two of them had contents that spilled outside their doorless entryways. Another one appeared empty, and I couldn't see the rest.

"Six is over here," directed Wolf. "It looks like George left a light on for us."

Down on the right, there it was—and yes, there was a pale orange glow that expanded from the doorway. "Are you sure there's no one else inside . . . ?" I asked, but it was a dumb question. He didn't know any better than I did, so I called out softly instead: "Hello? Is anybody there?"

No one replied, so we approached the ugly light. I rapped on the doorframe for good measure, and again I asked, "Hello?"

Wolf poked his head around the side. "We're alone, more or less."

"Well, it doesn't *feel* that way."

"Yes, I know. Welcome to Storage Room Six."

I didn't feel too mightily welcomed, I don't mind telling you, Emma. That room didn't welcome; it trapped. I could sense it all the way down to my toes that I was standing in a spider's parlor. Or no, nothing so nice as a parlor—even one that lures on behalf of an arachnid. This was more like a cell.

It lacked the typical prison trappings of a bucket and a sink, but there was a cot laid out along one wall. The cot had linens upon it that were not folded, but were not dirty, either; and the attendant pillow bore the impression of a man's head.

(I'll say it was a man's head, because there were smudges of hair oil still left upon it.)

"Was George sleeping here?" I wondered aloud.

"His wife didn't mention that he'd been missing any evenings at home, but then again, she didn't notice she'd been drugged and abandoned this morning, either. She might have missed a great deal, from not paying attention—or from writing off his more unusual behavior to the stress of the election, and then the Stephenson trial."

Wolf approached a desk that was covered in cardboard boxes, and I roamed the rest of the smallish space, dragging my fingertips across items small and large, leaving trails in the dust. Boxes were piled as far as the ceiling, and one even leaned a corner against the lightbulb's cage—giving the whole ceiling an askew appearance. The floor was poured cement, and it was scattered with paper clips and wadded-up balls of paper and little black dots that I was forced to conclude must be mouse droppings. The walls were painted that bland taupe color you used to see on hats; its glossy paint felt damp to the touch.

Standing there, staring at my fingertip—wondering if it was wet or merely cool—I had the most terrible flash of memory: I was

standing in my basement at Maplecroft. I was not basking in
the glow of a dull caged light, but the brighter gaslamps I'd
installed . . . and I was not imagining or wondering at the damp.
I knew it like I knew my own breath, my own skin. The walls
had always wept down there, too. They were always collecting
small rivulets of dew, puddling on the floor.

But I shook it off. I did not have a basement anymore, not at
Maplecroft. I had sealed it off, closed it up, and put a new kitchen
wall across the place where its entry used to be. There was no
basement. I was not home. The wall was not really wet, it was
only cool, and it was only a trick my mind played upon itself.

"Lizbeth? Lizbeth, are you all right?"

He sounded worried, so I snapped my head up and said,
"Yes, don't be silly. I thought I smelled something odd, that's
all," I lied outright. "I was trying to place it—don't mind me. So
this is Storage Room Six, and these are the boxes over here—
aren't they? The ones with the axe murder files? The ones where
you found Nance's picture?"

The look on his face said he didn't believe me, but I didn't
care. I wasn't enthralled by the sinister forces of old memories,
and that was the important thing. "These are the boxes, yes.
George brought them here for safekeeping, for all the good it did
him. You know, I hate to say it, but I think he might have been
right about the room eating his evidence." He pushed his spectacles up the bridge of his nose. "There was more than this, I'd
swear to it."

I joined him at the desk. The boxes held old folders, yes . . .
but the cases weren't so old, were they? "These look like they've
been here a hundred years, rather than . . ." I checked the date

on the nearest one. "Eleven months. Look at the foxing, here and there—just like an old book, or an old lithograph. Look at how faded the ink is on this page."

"Perhaps George was coming at it from the wrong angle, and something about this place ages things prematurely," he suggested. Then he shrugged. "Though the result is the same anyway. Things vanish. Information is lost."

"Only the useful information, according to him." I indicated a stack of phone directories and last month's newspapers—undoubtedly the ones he mentioned in his note to Ruth. "Those look just fine. There's not even a coat of dust upon them."

"One way or another, it's all as weird as can be. Look," he said, abruptly adjusting the conversation, "here's Gaspera Lorino's file—or the file related to his attack, at least."

He handed it to me. I strained to read the fuzzy light gray type. "His wife was killed, and he was maimed. Last word here says he was still unconscious. No one saw the need to update the files to reflect his recovery, then." But then I flipped to the next page, and was less confident. "Or . . . or else those are some of the details taken by the room."

The next sheet was almost blank, but not quite. The corners had gone brown, and the lines of type were almost inkless, nearly absent except for the indentations where the typewriter keys had pressed against the paper.

"Maybe it was on that page." Wolf sighed, then brightened. "Wait, this box is new—these must be the personal effects he collected from the crucified accountant."

"What a shame, that the poor man will be remembered that way."

"It could be worse. He could be remembered as . . ."

"Yes?"

He didn't respond immediately. He was pushing things around in the box. "He could always be remembered as an axe murderer."

"I'm sorry, come again?"

"No, I didn't mean . . . not like *you*," he corrected awkwardly.

Before we could trip over each other any further, I said, "That's not what I was suggesting. What do you mean—you think Mr. Kincaid killed all those people?"

"Here's his desk calendar," he said, relieved to be off the hook, I imagine. "Over here, look—the names are fading, but what do you see?"

I squinted down at the chicken-scratch handwriting. "I see . . . Bes . . . Besley? Is that what it says? Kincaid's penmanship was *terrible*."

"Besler, I'd bet you a small fortune. And the next one, what do you think that other name says, there—under the June 22 listing?"

"It's another 'B' I think . . . Baldone? Is that right?"

"Do those names ring a bell?" he asked, clearly thinking they ought to.

But I didn't recognize either one. "I'm afraid they don't."

"Besler and Baldone were the first two victims—or the first two universally agreed-upon victims, as there were undoubtedly others—of Harry the Hacker."

"What a stupid name." I put my own hand into the box and pushed the items around to see them better. I found a desk clock that folded into a travel case, a nameplate still in its holder, three pens, a copy of *Vern and Hightower's Legal Guide to Civic Accounting in the Modern Era*, two old issues of *Life* magazine, three or four bus tokens, a white coffee mug, and a pair of reading glasses in a silk sleeve.

"It looks like you've located the only useful thing in the bin," I noted.

"George didn't say it'd *all* be helpful; he just said we'd find what we needed." He flipped the calendar's pages, looking for any other items that might be important—and by luck or by design, a small bulletin slipped out.

I caught it before it could hit the floor.

It was printed on light blue paper, and the front read, "Give Me That Old-Time Religion!" I held it up for Wolf to see. "Get a gander at this, would you? 'The Reverend A. J. Davis hosts three days of song, sermons, and celebration at the old county fairgrounds, starting March 5, 1919! Come one, come all— bring the family, and share the Glory of God with kids and grandparents alike!' Well—" I paused. "The author surely has a flair for exclamation points."

"Never mind the flair, take note of the fact: This is our first tangible connection between the axe murders and Chapelwood."

"*If*, in fact, Mr. Kincaid—"

"Oh, come now," he interrupted me in his excitement. "Why else would his box have wound up here? Why else would the record already be fading?" He held up the calendar again, with its ghostly script surely growing more ghostly by the hour. "And the names of the first two victims, right alongside what looks like some sort of equation, doesn't it?" he asked, but he didn't hand it back to me. He didn't really want or require a second opinion. "I think it looks like an equation," he assured himself. "And remember what George's letter said, about the secretary? She said he was going on about talking to God with numbers. Oh, it fits together so *nicely*, doesn't it?"

"You must be right. There's too much here to write it all off as a coincidence."

He bounced on his heels while he scrutinized the calendar. "I can't figure out why God would tell him to kill people, but then again, I've never been able to figure out God at all, so that goes to show you what I know."

"There's no telling who . . . or *what* . . . was talking to him with those numbers. We have no idea where he got them, or how he went about interpreting them."

He lowered the calendar and settled back into his shoes. His eyes grew suddenly serious. "You're absolutely right. The simplest explanation is that he went mad, but that's only somewhat likely. A man can be both mad and correct."

"He can be driven mad by being correct, too—or so I'd wager. Maybe the truth didn't set him free, but it drove him insane."

Wolf gave me that intent, thoughtful stare that I'd come to recognize. "I've seen it happen before. But it's not a given, is it? That's not what happened to you when you brushed up against something this huge, this strange."

Ah. So it was time.

I hope you won't think less of me, Emma. But I had to tell someone, you understand? Please understand. I hope you understand.

Nance would.

I sighed and leaned back against the dust-covered desk, halfway sitting upon it. "No, that's not what happened to me. I think? I assume? I'll tell you the truth," I added, before he could respond with some polite demurral. "Sometimes I'm not entirely certain."

"But that's a good sign, isn't it? If you were well and truly daft, you'd never wonder about it."

"Seabury never wondered," I said softly. "He spiraled and spiraled and spiraled, gently at first and then swiftly, like a paper boat headed down a drain. But he never quite went completely mad . . . and I think that was the worst of it. He'd spend an hour telling you about the starfish and moon, and the tides, and the monsters with their cunning plans . . . but then he'd brighten up, and ask after the basement renovations or my volunteering at the Humane Society. He never quite left me entirely. He only wandered far enough away that he . . . he couldn't find his way back in the dark."

"You miss him."

"Yes, I miss him. Even after all these years. I've had so few close friends, and he shared two of the greatest secrets of my whole life."

"Two?" he asked, one eyebrow perking with curiosity.

I looked down at the boxes, at the decaying details of other people's lives and deaths; I gazed around the damp, musty room that smelled of mildew and sorrow, and hunger. If any room ever ate secrets, then yes. It was this one.

All right, then I would speak it aloud here, and nowhere else. Not ever again.

"Two," I confirmed. "He knew what happened to Zollicoffer . . . and he knew what became of my father and stepmother, as well. He knew everything, and he took it all to his grave. My sister did, too, of course, but that was different. That was blood, and we needed each other."

I gave him a sidelong look, watching his face to see what it might tell me. It said that he was thinking, but I did not see any indication that he was judging. "I won't ask after your parents, for it's no business of mine, except for this: Were their deaths . . . somehow connected to Zollicoffer and the havoc he wrought?"

I nodded. I had to. My neck felt loose and my head was so heavy with the weight of it all.

"I don't know how it began, exactly. I don't know whose fault it was, or what brought it about. There were these stones . . . ," I said, then realized that we'd be there all afternoon and all night, too, if I tried to tell him everything. "It's a long story. But they came from the ocean, and they were somehow kin to the sample my sister found on the beach, on that one clear day all those years ago . . . when she still felt well enough to stroll if the air was nice. She sent it to him, and it changed him. I think it changed her, too. She was never the same after she picked it up. Her health failed faster, and more precipitously. But it did the opposite to the professor, didn't it?"

"I beg your pardon?"

"It didn't make him weak," I explained myself. "It made him strong."

"No, it made him *different*. I think . . . and mind you, this is only my theory of the most feeble conjecture . . . I think it killed him, and replaced him with something else. By the end, he wasn't human anymore. I doubt he even noticed."

Emma, do you think he was right?

"I . . . I'm not sure how I feel about that. I hope you're right, I suppose. I hope that no human being is capable of the things he did." I stared at the floor, not saying the rest of what I meant.

But Wolf drew it out of me anyway. "By the end, let us say . . . by the end, he must not have been human. Does that make it easier?"

"Yes? No?" I shrugged. "Surely, given his activities, he deserved worse than any mortal hand could deal him."

"Worse than what you did to him?" He broached the question carefully, almost whispering it.

I took a deep breath, and with it I said, "What I did to him was necessary, and barely even possible. I couldn't have done it without Emma and Seabury, so we're all three guilty—no matter how you divvy up the blame." I took another deep breath, and it felt clean, almost. "I had a device in the basement: It was an industrial piece of equipment, mostly used on farms to dispose of carcasses that can't be eaten or otherwise processed—a steam-pressure machine, full of hot lye and so forth. We trapped him inside it. There was nothing left of him in the end, nothing but a scream and some black-colored sludge."

The confession hung in the air between us, lifted up on the currents of our breathing, the disturbances we made as we walked and moved and talked. It settled on the desk, the boxes, the floor, the papers. It coated the room like so much dust.

He cleared his throat, maybe due to the cloudy air, or maybe due to me—and what I'd said. "I always assumed you'd done . . . something. Creatures like Zollicoffer don't just quit killing, once they've started. Someone has to stop them, and I'm glad you were able to."

"As am I, though I wish . . ."

"Yes?" he prompted gently. I couldn't bring myself to say it, so he filled in the rest with his impeccable intuition. "You . . . you wish it hadn't cost you Nance O'Neil?"

I nodded, unable to muster any other response. I almost dug her sketched-out portrait from my bag—I almost held it up so I could stare at it, and grieve more concretely, or feed my guilt with stronger memories, for the years had sometimes left my recollections threadbare. I knew the upturn of her mouth, her eyebrows, her every crinkle of eyelids . . . or I believed I did, until I tried to summon them. I knew the sound of her voice, each note and each sigh, each laugh, every whisper. Until they were all whispers, and the rest was hardly more than a hum in my brain.

Why couldn't *she* have haunted me, Emma? Why did it have to be you instead?

You, I knew for all my life; I could no sooner forget the details of your presence than forget my own face. But Nance . . . I did not have her for so long, and I am old now, you see? If only she had haunted me, I'd have something left—her ghost as a souvenir, or is that obscene? I can't tell. I honestly can't tell.

"*Lizbeth?*"

I shook my head, and dabbed at the corner of my eye. It was only a little tear, but I didn't want it anyway. "I'm sorry, but I think it's this place. It's eating more than secrets and old paperwork. Maybe it's eating my memories, too."

"Then we should either leave immediately or stay long enough to ease your sorrow."

"No," I said quickly. "No, we should go. Those old memories are all I have of my Nance, and should they fade . . . there's nothing left of the joy we knew. I'll keep them, as many as I can, for as long as I can—even for all the sorrow they cause me—as payment for holding them close. Staying here . . . good heavens, I'm not sure why you'd suggest it."

Flatly, he told me, "Because your protests sound like remorse, as opposed to nostalgia. It is a privilege to remember those we loved and lost; but what you're doing is self-flagellation, my friend."

Was he my friend? Would a friend suggest forgetting another friend?

Maybe he was only trying to be kind, if misguided. "Either way, I find some comfort in what remains. Or some . . . some reassurance? The universe is unfolding as it ought to, so long as I feel terrible for what became of her. I *deserve* to feel terrible. I deserve everything that happens to me, for all the rest of my years."

He hesitated, on the verge of saying one thing, I think—but letting his curiosity drive him in another direction. "What *did* become of her, then? If you don't mind my asking. I've always wondered. It's always been an unfinished note in my files. She never reappeared, never acted in another play, never went home. Did she meet her end in the basement, too?"

"What a vulgar thing to ask."

"Why? You've offered up more vulgar and sensitive information quite freely. If it's a sensitive subject, I'll let it go. As I've said before, it's no business of mine, after all."

"Indeed it isn't," I snapped, but it was already rolling through my head—that night, out on the water, after she'd escaped the basement . . . but into the arms of what? And where? I was half afraid that I couldn't keep it all inside, and half afraid that everything I tried to recall was being devoured by that uncanny room. At least if I said it aloud, there'd be someone else to remind me later. Would voicing the truth lend it some kind of insurance?

Perhaps.

So I told him, "But in all honesty, I don't know where she is.

I don't know what happened to her. She had been . . . changing, as if preparing to abandon the land in favor of the ocean, and whatever weird 'mother' awaited her there. And then she disappeared, shortly before Zollicoffer arrived—so I can't say that he took her, or killed her, or that he stole her away from me. If it were as simple as that, surely she would've returned upon his passing."

"One would think. Then I apologize, from the bottom of my belly—which is infinitely larger than my heart. I did not mean to . . . it's . . . well, such a painful subject. I should've let it lie."

I sighed heavily, both at his apology and his attempt at endearing levity. This wasn't the time or place, but he was making an effort to placate me. "It's all right, Simon. Consider yourself forgiven, if perhaps . . . when all this is finished, you and your organization might lend your expertise to the matter."

"I volunteer every spare moment of my own, and my office," he said gallantly. "I don't know if we can help you solve that mystery or not, but by heaven and math alike, we will try."

"Thank you, and now let's leave this place. Take the box with you, if you think it might tell us more—but nothing is safe when stored here, not in containers, and not in the skulls of little old women like myself."

"Very good, yes. Absolutely," the inspector said decisively. "We really must see about finding George, anyway, and keep him out of whatever trouble he's courting."

"Do you think he's gone to Chapelwood?" I asked. It was only the most logical of questions, but it left a bad taste in my mouth.

"I think that's as good a guess as any, but we can't charge headlong over there demanding his return. We might be wrong, for one thing. For another, he's a grown man—free, white, and twenty-one, isn't that the expression?—and he can come and go as he likes, even into peril."

"Just like us," I observed dully. I gave one last glance to the revival tent flyer, the accounting books, the sad and dusty place where George must have come to sleep, to research, and perhaps to forget. "But there are still souls left to save, and I've failed so many in my time."

He put a hand on my shoulder, an awkward little pat of reassurance. Then he picked up the box of fading evidence. "Don't talk that way. No one's finished yet except for James Coyle. The rest of us still have a fighting chance—and we must make the most of it."

Inspector Simon Wolf

❧

I strongly doubt I will ever solve the mystery of Nance O'Neil, but I do not regret promising Lizbeth the effort. You never know. The Quiet Society might learn something new.

Or it might only waste a great deal of time and money. What of it? We waste time and money all the time. We may as well waste it toward a good cause—toward easing the suffering of a lonely old woman, and exploring the possibilities beyond Zollicoffer, beyond the ocean.

I've always known there was something beyond him. But what?

I may well need to learn to live with never knowing. I don't like the idea. I don't know how my friend has done it all these years.

After leaving the basement together, Lizbeth and I retreated upstairs to try our luck at the civic offices, in case there were further records we might get our hands upon. But Nathaniel Barrett was not present, and I couldn't decide if I was glad or not, so I ended up erring on the side of "pleased that I didn't have to shake his hand again." Mostly we were ignored, apart from a few curious stares, but in the background we heard whispers. Word was getting around: The two fancy out-of-towners were friends of the Stephenson girl (no, the Gussman woman) and therefore enemies of the True Americans, and so forth, and so on.

We left before the balance shifted from idle chatter to threat. There probably wasn't anything useful left to be found there anyway. If the storage room hadn't eaten it, it was no doubt hoarded by men who'd never let us touch it . . . or otherwise it had surely been destroyed.

So, that luck tried, and found to be lacking . . . I suggested the police.

"What might we find there?" Lizbeth asked.

"I'm very curious about the death of Mr. Kincaid. Perhaps my badge can get us a peek at whatever evidence they collected in the wake of his 'suspicious' death by crucifixion."

But by the time we arrived at the station, some tipping point had been reached—some critical mass of gossip and group information had found us out—and it was made entirely clear that we could expect no further assistance from any authorities. I suppose word might have spread by phone, except that no one else knew our next stop—so instead, the chilly reception we received at the station must have been the result of one *truly* outstanding grapevine. The receptionist could scarcely be persuaded to acknowledge our presence, much less the badge. She only repeated, "I'm sorry, but it's a local investigation—and no outside assistance is required. Or preferred, either. I can't help you, and neither can anyone else."

We gave up and planned to retreat to the hotel, but on our way to the car a young man in a patrolman's uniform came trotting up to us.

"Ma'am." He tipped his hat at Lizbeth. "Sir." He bobbed his head at me.

"Can we help you?" she asked him. It was a silly question, but a sociable one, and I suppose she felt the need to say something.

He checked over his shoulder, saw no one, and whispered, "This is for Chief Eagan." He slipped me a folded note.

"You'd like me to . . . deliver this to him? Is that what you mean?"

He shook his head. "No. I'm giving it to you because you've stood with him. Excuse me, and good afternoon to you both." With that, he ducked back into the station.

I glanced at the note and tucked it into my vest pocket, and strolled away with Lizbeth at my side—as if our departure had not been interrupted.

"What is it?"

"An address," I replied.

"Whose?"

"Let's find out, shall we?"

Twenty minutes later we found ourselves at a flophouse on the south side of town. The district was seedy, but I'd seen far worse; and if Lizbeth was put off by it, she hid her revulsion quite admirably. The front face of the building was flat and made of wood siding, covered in peeling gray paint that might once have been the color of custard. Its windows were intact, if swollen with damp, and all of them were open.

No one greeted us or stopped us at the door, and the room number we'd been given was upstairs on the second level—so that's where we went.

Lizbeth, being somewhat more nimble than I, scaled the steps more swiftly than I did. She reached the door first and stood before it, pausing to wait. Finally I joined her, and stood beside her— catching my breath. We listened to the sounds of men coughing, a couple fighting, a dog barking, and a badly maintained automobile chugging by . . . but that grew tedious in only a few seconds, so my companion reached for the knob and turned it.

The knob swiveled easily, and the catch released. Lizbeth lifted an eyebrow at me, then used her free hand to knock—loud enough to announce us, but not so loudly that anyone down the hall might ask us what we were doing.

"Hello?" she called. I did not join her, or offer to go first in any pseudo-chivalrous fashion. A woman knocking and saying hello was surely less threatening than a man of my size doing likewise, so let her take the lead.

No one answered. We looked both ways and saw no one to interfere, so we let ourselves inside with a slow creep forward . . . punctuated intermittently by Lizbeth's continued efforts to make our presence known in a discreet, pleasant fashion.

Within moments, we stopped bothering with the civilized charade.

"Oh God," she said. "This is Leonard Kincaid's room."

I swallowed hard, gazing at the smudged and dripped shape upon the wall, outlined in the rough shape of a hand-drawn cross. A day or so ago, it was red. Now it was rusty brown, and drawing flies. The room smelled exactly like it looked: dirty, and as if something had died there. "Well, we were asking after him, weren't we? That nice patrolman must've overheard us."

She withdrew a lavender handkerchief from a pocket and held it up over her nose. "How . . . thoughtful of him to send us here."

"He was only trying to help, I'm sure."

"I know, but . . . but . . . isn't there someone who cleans this sort of thing? The landlord, if no one else. Wouldn't you think?"

"But it only happened last night, or yesterday . . . I forget what the newspaper said. Perhaps the police forbade it, until their investigation was concluded. Besides, I can't imagine anyone is beating down the door, hoping to land the living space for himself."

"You say that as if the landlord has any intention of telling prospective tenants what occurred here."

"Good point, madam. He'll probably empty the place and throw a fresh coat of paint on the walls. It'll hide both the blood and the odor. Well, while we're here . . ." I returned to the front door and shut it quietly. I turned the dead bolt, not to prevent interruption, really—but to buy us time, in case of it. "Let's not dally, but let's be thorough. You never know what the police might have missed or ignored entirely."

She went to his bed, which was made up as neat as anything you'd find in a hospital, and sat upon the edge while she went through his nightstand drawers.

As for me, I went to the desk pushed up against a wall, with a large slate board mounted above it. The board itself had been wiped clean. Resting on the tray at the bottom, I spied a large gray eraser chock-full of white dust, but whether the police had cleared away the chalk marks, or the killer himself . . . I couldn't say. The desk's top two drawers were empty, but the middle one on the left held a roll of old newspapers wrapped in a rubber band. Upon inspection, they were not entire periodicals—but clippings that were slapped together.

"Did you find something?" Lizbeth asked.

"For a moment, I thought so." But the excerpts didn't relate to the axe murders, for that would've been easy, wouldn't it? "I appear to have been mistaken. It's just a loose assortment of stories and advertisements, and if they're related to one another in some way, I don't see it offhand. There's also . . . a small flask and two little glasses, another tome or two relevant to accounting, and half a pack of the office stationery he once used at work. How about you?"

"Mr. Kincaid occasionally enjoyed a pipe of tobacco and a sip of bathtub gin. He also sharpened his pencils to a very fine point, and wore them down to nubs."

"That says plenty about him," I murmured, returning my attention to the desk. I found a box of unused chalk, a very nice pen, and some lined paper with an assortment of numbers and formulas jotted across the top sheet. (The rest were blank.)

I looked up and saw an empty box in the corner. It resembled the sort a postman or an office secretary might use, and indeed might have been either one of those things. It would hold the dregs of evidence well enough, I decided—so I tossed in the newspaper clippings, stray sheets of lined paper, and everything else, and suggested that Lizbeth do the same should she find anything promising.

She sighed in my general direction. "I'm beginning to fear that George, or the investigators, beat us to the punch. At least we had a chance to see the highlights, before the storage room gets around to eating everything for good."

"Check under the bed and in his drawers," I suggested. "I'll poke my head inside the icebox and the cupboards."

She grinned at that, and agreed. Between us, I didn't think we'd need another ten minutes to scour the place in earnest. The modest flat was not large at all, barely two rooms—a bedroom with a washroom, and a combination kitchen/living area/everything else so cramped that I could have packed the whole thing into my own office back in Boston. With room to spare.

We'd be best served to hurry, anyway.

The cupboards were lined with cans of vegetables and jars full of rice, beans, and pasta. I found a variety of sauces and tins of crackers, peanut butter, and the like—all of it organized with an architect's precision. Or an accountant's, as the case may be. "A precise fellow, this Kincaid. Everything so organized and tidy."

"He even folded his socks," Lizbeth informed me.

I wasn't surprised.

The icebox handle stuck, but I wrestled it open anyway. The door popped ajar, and a cool, damp gasp of air escaped when the seal was broken. Inside it was wet, for the ice had melted (as ice is wont to do), but it still held a bottle of milk, and a box of something else, too. It looked like the kind of thing you'd take home from a restaurant—made of stiff waxed paper. I opened it up, expecting to find leftovers, but instead I retrieved a stack of photos tied up in twine.

The whole batch was soggy and unpleasant to the touch, but the images weren't yet lost. "I've found something. Maybe." Or so I announced to my companion, who'd finished her examination of Leonard Kincaid's worldly personal belongings.

"Oh, good, because I didn't find a thing. I was afraid this was all for naught."

"It might be still. These photos are decidedly waterlogged."

"Why would he keep them in the icebox?"

I shrugged, and looked back into its dark, dank depths. "It's a safe, insulated place. In case of fire, not much else would be likely to survive. I suppose he thought he was protecting them—and he surely didn't plan to be murdered before the ice block melted."

"No doubt. But tell me," she urged, coming closer to look inside for herself. "It's lined with . . . what? Lead, do you think?"

"Lead, asbestos. Anything to insulate it. This is a cheap model," I noted. It was built into the kitchen cabinetry, a permanent part of the flophouse structure. It ought to be considered a feature, no doubt—despite the poor construction and a latch already falling to rust. "It might have sawdust in between its walls, for all I know."

"I bet it's lead," she said firmly. "Vintage lore says lead can protect almost anything."

"From what?"

"From almost anything else. Let's take those back to the hotel and hang them up to dry. There's . . . look." She indicated one of the slippery scraps. "He wrote something on the back."

I turned it over. "Not in pen, I hope." But there was already a smudge of black ink on my fingertips to suggest I wouldn't be so lucky as that.

"Some of it's in pencil. Here, don't try to pull them all apart just yet; let's take them back to the hotel, and take our time with them. We've seen all there is to see here. We should go before someone throws us out."

She was right, and we withdrew to sequester ourselves in my room—indecency be damned. We ran a line of string between the foot-end posts of my bed, and with the help of a few stray paper clips, soon all fourteen photos were strung up to dry. They grew brittle as the moisture left them, and their images were washed out to varying degrees, but the progression was clear enough.

"I daresay we gaze upon the visage of Mr. Kincaid himself," I declared.

"Over a span of . . . how long, do you think? These might be dates, written on the back . . . but it's hard to tell. Well, no—here's one, clear enough: January 18, 1921." She crawled up onto my bed and dangled her feet over the side so she could see the back of the photos more intimately.

"What else does it say? I think your eyes might be better than mine. I'm a tad farsighted in these spectacles, but wildly nearsighted without them. Everything in life involves a trade-off, after all."

She drew it closer with the very edges of her fingernails, careful not to touch or damage anything further. "Something about . . . a shadow, I think. But I'm not sure I see any kind of shadow in the image, just some water staining . . . ? Where did he take these, anyway? Did you see a camera in his flat?"

Upon reflection, I did not. "No, but the police might have retrieved it and sent it off to be examined by a technician. If he did keep one on hand, there might have been film inside it. Ah, over here, yes, look at this one—it's quite clear: These were taken inside the flat, in front of the blackboard. He used it for a background."

"Did he have help, do you think? Can one take one's own photo so easily?"

"There's a simple switch on a cable with a button," I said, now peering as intently as possible at the other portraits—all the same, just a shot of Leonard from the waist up, standing in front of that blackboard. "If you could see his hands, I'm sure you could see him holding it, and snapping the picture that way. This was not a man with friends or coconspirators; that much is obvious from his home—if nothing else of use was gleaned there. You know, I'm not entirely sure this is all . . ." I ran my finger thoughtfully along the bottom of each photo, scarcely touching them at all. "This isn't water damage. Not all of it."

"On the back of this one I can make out some of the writing. 'I can't be the only one who sees it.' That's what it says."

"*Which* one?"

"Here." She tapped one of the first in the series. I say it was a series, but really I only hung up the photos in the order they were stacked. Lizbeth continued. "And I think I see the word 'shadow' again. Do you see a shadow?"

"I might see a shadow disguised as water damage. Here, around his waist, at the very edge. I expect he would've loved to take a full-length shot, but lacked the room to set one up in that tiny hole of a place. I thought it was only the water at first, but it doesn't crest the white border at all. It must be part of the image."

She scooted off the bed. It was quite tall, and she landed with a short hop. "Let me see . . ."

"I think if we scan these from left to right . . . I think we got the chronology correct after all. There's something around him."

"Yes . . . There it is," she muttered. "You can barely see it here at first . . . but by the end it's quite clear. Or quite hazy, depending on how you think of it. He wondered if anyone else could see this dark fog, or if it was even real—so he took these photographs, trying to find out. Oh, that poor man . . ."

"That poor man? This fellow who apparently axe-murdered heaven knows how many people?"

"*That poor man,*" she asserted, "who feared he was going mad, and fought against delusion with science—with a camera, trying to find evidence that might counter his confusion and terror. That poor man who was crucified to the wall of that dark little flat, by parties unknown."

"Your well of sympathy goes deeper than mine."

"My intuition, too, perhaps. I'm a woman, after all. Supposedly, ours is exceptionally keen."

"And what else does your intuition tell you about this man, these photos? That he was some kind of victim?"

She nodded. "Yes. Whatever terrible person or thing may have driven him, it claimed him in the end, didn't it? And no one had any ill to speak of him, if George can be believed. There's more to this, that's what my intuition says. Rather, it *screams*. This man and his numbers, his theories . . ."

That offhanded remark of hers reminded me of the papers, with their penciled notes. "His numbers and theories, yes. Are you any good at mathematics?"

"Average or better. It wasn't a favorite school subject, but I performed well enough."

"Then you've outstripped me. I've never had a head for it myself." By then, I was sorting through the box with its meager offerings. "So tell me, do these equations mean anything to you?"

She took the lined paper from me and gave it a cursory examination. "No, I'm afraid not. This is well above my skill level. I don't even recognize half these symbols . . . but the numbers are enormous, I can see that much. He's jotting down figures to the thirtieth or fortieth power—digits with hundreds of zeroes at the end. Whatever this refers to, it must have been positively *cosmic* in scale."

"Cosmic . . . ," I echoed, because the word sounded correct when I wrapped my tongue around it. "There *is* something cosmic about it all, isn't there? All these churches, every last one of them is looking up to the sky. It's not like the good old days, when you dug temples out of the earth and talked to snakes. Wait. I actually know of churches where snake handling is practiced . . . hmm . . ."

"I don't believe churches typically think of prayer as space exploration, but I'd agree with the sentiment," she granted.

"It's an absolute fact, and I'll not settle for hearing it called 'sentiment.' If there's any God out there, He's someplace we can't reach Him. Otherwise, all this nonsense would be put to rest with a quick interview and a sip of holy wine."

"You're tragically blasphemous, dear Inspector."

"Says the woman who studies the dark arts in her spare time."

"Hardly," she said, but it was half for laughs, and half to defuse the awkwardness I sensed was brewing within her. "An interest is scarcely the same thing as a devoted study, though one day I do hope to perform a proper séance."

"As opposed to an improper one?"

"I . . . I might have asked for Emma, but I didn't do it in the usual prescribed fashion. I was one part afraid of failing, and one part afraid of succeeding. Besides, such an appointment with the dead is probably best left to the professionals."

"Speaking of, have you ever been to Lily Dale?" I asked her quickly, for the question sprang to mind and flew out of my mouth in an instant. Lily Dale probably wasn't the *nearest* spiritualist community to Fall River, but it was near enough—and quite famous.

"I haven't yet had the pleasure. Perhaps after this little adventure of ours."

"As a tourist, I hope—and not as a drop-in at a séance."

She laughed then, and I think it was genuine. I adored her sense of humor, which was almost as awful as mine. "From your lips to God's ears, as they say. Though if I ever do meet some untimely end, I hope you go looking for me."

"Why is that?"

"The obvious, is all," she said, giving one last look at the line of photographs drying on the string at the foot of my bed. "In case there's another side, and no heaven or hell to be found there. Should that prove the case, I'd enjoy having a friend to chat with."

"Then it's a deal," I vowed. "But you must promise me the

same: Should you eventually learn of my untimely passing, I want you to try to reach me. Go to Lily Dale and seek me out for that incorporeal chat, and I'll gladly get the conversation rolling. Let's say this, shall we? We'll need a secret phrase between us, something a charlatan couldn't manufacture by way of guesswork or research. What should we use as a signal—if one of us is dead and reaching out for contact?"

"Nance," she said quickly. Then she changed her mind, just as fast. "No, wait. Not Nance. That's too obvious, and someone might guess it through patience or research. How about, instead . . ." Something unhappy and unpleasant crossed her face . . . perhaps a memory that caused her pain. It wasn't painful enough to stop her, though. "Let us speak of the ocean . . . Let's talk about starfish, shall we?"

"Starfish? That's random enough."

"No. It's not random. It's something between us, in a way. Doctor Seabury chattered about them quite a lot toward the end of his life. 'Starfish hands,' he would tell me. In his dreams, the creatures who waited there . . . they had starfish-shaped hands."

"Very good, then. 'Starfish' it is."

"Somewhere down the line, I hope. A very long time from now."

I nodded. "Years and years. And not a moment sooner."

Ruth Stephenson Gussman

◈

Maybe they aren't spells at all. Maybe they're something else, or maybe there's more than one kind. I feel like a window is opening every time—and I'm seeing into some other place, only it's not heaven and it's not hell; it's just where dead people go in the end. Some of the dead people, I guess. Not all of them, I hope.

These spells (or whatever they are) confuse me, and they scare me. Today's was the worst one yet, but that's only fitting, right? Because this time, the spell warned me of the worst thing yet, and I was still too dumb to do anything about it in time.

Unless the timing was wrong. Or the message was wrong. *Everything* might be wrong, but I couldn't say one way or another. Not anymore. Not considering.

I left the house. I wasn't supposed to, but I left the house— even though it isn't a house, but that's what I'm used to calling my home, no matter where I live. So I left the apartment, if that's more correct, even though they all told me not to: Chief Eagan, the inspector, Lizbeth. Everybody said not to leave except for George, and he told me to get as far the hell away as I could. More or less.

Everybody else seemed to think it was too soon to take such drastic measures, and I ought to stay put, inside my own place where my daddy couldn't find me and the reverend couldn't reach me without going to a lot of trouble—and we've got good neighbors, as I think I've mentioned before. Someone would come and warn me, if he started asking around.

But I got that letter from George, and I took it over to that hotel—to give it to Lizbeth and the inspector. They didn't chide me too bad about it, since I'd brought them something useful; but they didn't want me coming with them, either.

I know it's true that I'd only make trouble for them, and they're trying hard to find out what George has gotten up to and what the reverend is getting up to . . . but I'm not a little girl and I don't have to stay indoors just because they said I should. So what happened was, I didn't go home after they left for the storage room at the civic building, even though I was supposed to. Pedro was at work, so he didn't know the difference, and I was tired of being cooped up in the house all alone, or cooped up in the court-house with everybody staring at me.

Instead, I went down to Five Points and visited a drugstore there—a little place where I used to get sweets and maybe a lemonade, if I had an extra nickel in my purse. I hadn't been there since before I got married, and since you got killed.

And I had a nickel to spare.

It was strange, walking down the street and realizing that not every single person was looking at me hard. Not every soul in the whole city knew who I was, or what I looked like, and most of the ones who *did* know likely didn't care. I'd just been at the middle of the storm for so long that it felt like I'd been in a fishbowl, or on a stage with the whole world watching, except it wasn't the whole world at all. It was only a handful of people in a theater.

I liked that thought. It felt good between my ears, and made me think that maybe everyone on earth wasn't against me.

(Of course it isn't everyone on earth, and it never *has* been. There's the inspector, and Lizbeth, and Pedro, and Chief Eagan, and all the people who care about any of them, I expect. That's more than a few good souls right there. But they were in the fishbowl with me, so that wasn't quite the same.)

I took the trolley, and then I walked. The whole time I was out there, wandering around in the sunshine, I felt downright normal—wearing a sundress and a shawl, with my button heels on. The weather was nice, and I was on my way to get some chocolates and a drink right out of the icebox Mr. Cowan keeps beside the front door.

Really, I should've known better.

I guess I'm not allowed to be normal anymore, at least not in Birmingham. Like as not, it doesn't matter if I'm in Birmingham or Boston, because there's no place far enough to run when you don't even know what you're trying to get away from—and all you know is that it can find you if it wants to. And whatever it is, it's probably dead. So it's not like you can kill it and be finished.

I had just lifted the lid on the icebox and stuck my hand inside for a chilly bottle of something I don't get to drink every day. The coldness inside the box startled me, and it chased me, sort of like the awful black shadow does when it creeps up around my ankles and starts climbing.

I was mad and I was confused, because this wasn't that, not

at all. Was it? No, this was just a whisper of ice, fogging inside the big metal bin with the sodas and lemonades clinking together—that's what I told myself. That's what it felt like, and that's what it must be.

But I'm a liar, to myself and the rest of God's green earth. I've even lied to you.

I knew better than that when it wrapped itself around my wrist—and that was a first, because usually it started at the ground and worked its way up. This one began at my hand instead, and when I tried to draw it back and slam the icebox lid shut, the cold grip wouldn't let me. It held me fast, and kept on crawling, and this time it wasn't just a fog—it was fingers, strong and long, clenching and squeezing; and around the edge of my vision, I could see the darkness slipping in.

I think I fell to my knees, but I'm not sure. I don't remember that part. It only took a few seconds for the blackness of the spell to fall over me like a blanket, like that starless sky I've seen once or twice and been so afraid I couldn't breathe. This particular spell was like the one in the courtroom. It came upon me and I was a million, billion miles away—moving past the stars, running past the planets and moons and a thousand suns until I was so far away that I'd never find my way home, not this time.

I didn't stop until there was no light left at all, no stars, no suns, no comets.

There was nothing except for me, sitting in an empty room with all the lights turned out. All alone except for a shuddering blob of light that eventually, given another half minute to make up its mind, took the shape of a man.

He wore a white shirt with a vest, and nice gray pants with shiny shoes, and his hair was combed and oiled so not a single strand was out of place. He was clean-shaved, and his nails were clean and filed, and his clothes were pressed, and even his eyebrows looked like someone had taken a pair of trimming scissors to them. I wondered if he ever really looked like that at all, or if this was just how he thought of himself, whoever he was.

Once he was all there, so solid-looking I might've been able to touch him, and maybe hit him upside the head for doing this to me . . . he lit up with delight, but his smile faded off to fear real fast.

"*There* you are," he said. His voice was higher than I would've expected, and it didn't sound far away like yours did, when you visited me like this. We might've been in the same room, sitting across a table from each other.

"Who are you?" I asked this man, only halfway wondering what I looked like to the real world, a million billion miles (or years?) behind me. Was I collapsed on the ground? My eyes rolled back in my head, while people hovered around me, trying to get my attention. Were they calling for an ambulance? Had I swallowed my tongue? Did I look dead?

"My name is Leonard, and I must speak with you. I've gone to great trouble, so please . . . a moment of your time?"

Like there was anything I could do to chase him off. Or if there *was*, I didn't know about it. "All right, say your piece."

"I killed those people with an axe, and I would've killed you, too. Not because I wanted to, but because I was trying to help."

I was so stunned I could hardly pretend I wasn't, but I did a decent job of staying calm when I asked, "So why would you want to kill me? Hell, why *didn't* you—if that's what this is about?"

"I didn't *want* to kill you. I never wanted to kill anyone, and I didn't kill *you* because it wouldn't have helped. Your marriage and subsequent departure changed the equation," he said, like that just explained everything. "Or I thought it did, but now the numbers have shifted again—they're slippery, they are. You aren't the victim Chapelwood expected, but you're the one it wants after all."

"I'm nobody's victim!"

"That isn't true. Or it's only temporarily true, if you don't listen to me."

I threw my hands up, or I thought I did. Again, heaven knows what I was really doing, with my real body, back in the real world. Maybe it looked like I was having some sort of fit. Maybe that's what they were saying about me, on the sidewalk outside the drugstore. I tried to push it all out of my head. I asked him, "Why should I do that? Why should I listen to some murderer?"

"Because I mean to *help*."

"Help who? Me?"

"*Everyone*. The world is at stake, Ruth Gussman, and maybe more than that."

"Well, I've got to be real honest with you, Leonard: I don't much care about what happens to anything outside of this world."

"But you *should*. There are worse things beyond the stars and under the oceans than you could ever imagine, and there are worse men on earth than you could ever believe—because they want to bring the terrible things home to us, to mate our world with theirs. These men are wrong, oh, you have to believe me," he insisted, and those nicely groomed eyebrows were all wrinkled up with worry. "They'll destroy everything you've ever known and loved—everything you might ever know, everyone you might ever love—and they'll use your blood to do it."

"Why me?" I demanded.

"Why anyone? They used my formulas—my own research!— and chose stepping-stones, human breadcrumbs . . . they would have killed them all anyway, and each death would've pried the door between our worlds open that much farther. I stalled them, that's all I could do," he protested, and it looked like he might cry, if he were alive. And I knew, I understood from the bottom of my soul, that just like Father Coyle . . . he *wasn't*. "But this is all my fault, you understand? I gave them the means to decode the words of God, and when they did, when they chose their sacrifices . . . I was forced to choose them, too. It's as if I damned them all twice over."

"So are you dead? Are you in hell? Is that where we are?"

"Hell isn't a place." He said it offhandedly, as if this were the least important question I could possibly ask. But this was too much, too confusing. I was drowning, and I didn't know the right word for "rope."

"Then where are you?"

"I'm gone, that's all that matters. I'm gone, and you're not— so there's still a chance. You can see and hear the dead, and maybe the dead can help. But you have to get away from Chapelwood and the Reverend Davis, and you have to stay away from them both, forever. They will never stop looking for you, and if they catch you, you must end yourself on the spot."

"You're telling me to go spend the rest of my life in exile, and be prepared to slit my own wrists at the drop of a hat. Is that the gist?"

"It sounds awful when you put it that way."

"It sounds awful no matter how anybody puts it. If you're trying to reassure me, or . . . or encourage me . . . you're doing a shit job of it, Leonard."

He shook his head, and looked both weary and annoyed. "I'm not trying to encourage you. I'm trying to motivate you to run or die before they can catch you and kill you. I know, it's not the most reassuring or optimistic of motives, but you're on borrowed time anyway. Everyone is, when you think about it—but you? You might have died months ago, but I didn't kill you then—and I can't kill you now. You have nothing to fear from me, not anymore."

"What do you want from me?"

"I couldn't stop the reverend, but you can. I want you to stop him."

"How?" I asked, and it probably came out sadder and more desperate than I wanted. "I can't stop anyone from anything, not even when I try, and I know what I'm doing."

"You have to evade them, in life or death. They can't open the final lock without you, that's what the numbers tell me."

"Numbers? What numbers?"

He didn't answer my question. "The old chairman, he told you the truth—you should go, and go far. As far away as you can. Know that, and know this: If you fall into their hands, they'll use you to destroy the world." His face tightened in a frown, and his wrinkly eyebrows went even more crooked. His eyes had gone all vacant . . . he stared off into nothing. "Oh dear . . . I'm too late. I haven't helped at all. That's one thing we have in common, then—neither one of us could ever save anyone . . ."

I was losing him.

"Would you stop running your mouth about nonsense, and tell me what to do?" I tried to get his attention, tried to make some demands—anything to bring him back around—but he wouldn't look at me anymore. He was looking through me, or past me, at something else.

"Get up. Get up and fight," he said, and it was easy enough to understand, but his voice was starting to sound all far away like yours did just before you left me. "Fight them, and run. Run and die. Or *everyone* will."

The last word was hardly a whisper. I started to say something back, but it was too late for that already, I could tell. I could feel that old tug, the sense of falling through absolute darkness, at a terrible speed, toward something I couldn't see. The tug became a yank, and then a hard draw—all the tension and strength of a heavy weight being spun around and around and then let go.

I couldn't see Leonard anymore. I couldn't see anything, not the stars and comets and moons. I was falling headfirst, down and backward, down and backward, all the way back to earth, to Birmingham, to my body.

I didn't hit the sidewalk, not like I'd expected. I didn't feel some bone-breaking collision, or even some squeezing sense of forcing myself back inside my own skin. It was as simple as opening my eyes and staring up at the clear blue sky, and seeing only a few clouds, and a few people chattering worriedly because I was lying there on my back outside the drugstore, not saying anything and not answering anybody.

But there was another voice—a voice that cut through everything else. It made my stomach cramp up, to hear it so close. It was right beside me, right above me. It was touching me, if a voice can do that.

It was my daddy's voice, at its scariest: It was being calm, and reassuring. So that meant it was lying.

Not lying to *me*, because Daddy never cared about calming or reassuring *me*. No, he was talking to the people who wanted to help me, and he was saying that I was just fine; don't worry—he was my father, and I had little fits like this sometimes, but he'd take me home and take care of me.

I tried to sit up, but I was already sitting up, already being lifted up under my armpits. (He isn't a big man, but he's wiry and much stronger than he looks.) He was apologizing for any disturbance I might have caused, but promising that everything would be all right once he got me home and safe. He'd just put me to bed, and when I woke up, all would be well.

I was stumbling, not really at home again in my body, not yet. I couldn't walk, and my eyes wouldn't focus like they ought to. I'd seen the sky and all its cotton white clouds clear enough, but looking around all I could see were blurry faces and the shifting shapes of the storefronts as I staggered past them, my head dropping and lifting, my daddy pulling me along.

"No." I said it like a command, but it came out just a funny-shaped breath too soft to call a whisper. "No." I tried again, but it wasn't any stronger.

Daddy had a car waiting nearby; I guess it was parked on the street outside the store, because we didn't go any farther than thirty or forty feet, I wouldn't think. It confused me. Daddy never had a car of his own. He said we couldn't afford one, and that was probably true, but he had one now—some kind of touring car, something shiny and dark, and I knew he definitely couldn't afford that one, so he'd borrowed it from someone, or maybe he even stole it. It gleamed in the sun, some scrap of reflection hitting me in the face and blinding me all over again, just as I was starting to get my vision back.

It wasn't fair.

It wasn't fair that he wrestled me inside, and someone was already sitting there waiting for me. An extra set of hands pulled me up by the shoulders and Daddy folded up my legs like a fresh-pressed shirtsleeve and stuffed me inside so he could shut the door. I blinked, and almost felt better—because the other person in the car was my momma. But that was no good, and I knew it. I knew it even before she brought the cloth down over my face and pressed it there, and I breathed something wet and sweet, and the last thing I saw was her face, wearing the same weak smile as always before. The last sound I heard was her voice, lying to me about how everything was going to be all right, and just fine. She couldn't even make up something new. She just ran with whatever Daddy'd told her to say.

Just like always before. Just like forever.

Lizbeth Andrew (Borden)

∾

By dinnertime, Leonard Kincaid's self-portraits were dry and
much easier to inspect. Our initial impressions held true—there
was something hovering at his waist, or just below it . . . and this
fuzzy black mass rose up higher and higher in each subsequent
image. In the final frame, it had reached his neck; and though
Simon insisted he could detect a swirling pattern of fingers, or
tentacles, or some similar shape, I was not so confident. The lines
were too grainy. I refused to see things that weren't there, purely
because they fit the shape of a pattern I liked.

(If that isn't too ungenerous of me to think.)

We left them all in a row on the inspector's chest of drawers
and headed down to the dining hall for the afternoon meal. The
proprietress served it up a bit earlier than I'm accustomed to taking
it, and she called it "supper" instead of "dinner," but the spread

was outstanding. Simon positively beamed at the offerings, and if he'd been wearing a belt, he would've loosened it upon sight of the veritable bucket of mashed potatoes, accompanied by corn bread, biscuits, beans with bacon fat, buttered corn on the cob, rice with sugar or gravy, baked apples, plus two pitchers of sweet tea and the three different pies on the sideboard.

But our feast was interrupted before we reached that sideboard, when Pedro Gussman arrived—as breathless and frantic as ever I saw a man. (I had not yet laid eyes upon Mr. Gussman, though I'd heard about him and assumed the best of him, courtesy of his wife and Simon—who spoke well of him. But his identity was confirmed almost immediately.)

He burst into the hall in his work clothes, still splattered with paint. He launched immediately into his plea: "Inspector, you have to help me! It's Ruth—she's gone!"

Simon whisked his napkin from his lap and flung it onto the table. "Missing? We only just saw her a few hours ago. I believe she was headed home."

"She never came home." He pulled his hat off his head and wrung it like a rag. "Or if she did, she turned around and left again."

"Any sign of a burglary?"

"No, everything was in its place. Nothing was broken. No one had forced a way inside—but that's not where she was taken. She went to Cowan's down in Five Points, the drugstore where she used to get soda pop and sweets. She told me about it one night. I remember . . . ," he said faintly. And then, as if also remembering that we were there, he added, "She didn't often talk about good things, good times. So I thought . . . maybe I thought I'd go down there and see. It's been a hard month, and a hard week for her especially. Maybe she wanted to take a walk, treat herself a tiny bit. That's where she always went."

I removed my own napkin and stood. "Mr. Gussman, my name is Lizbeth Andrew. I'm a friend of your wife's."

He nodded vigorously, and then apologetically. "Yes, yes. She told me . . . I'm so sorry. I don't mean to be rude, but she's gone, you understand?"

"Gone where?"

"To Chapelwood," he said, like the word was sick in his mouth. "*He* was there—her father. He took her right off the street. She had some kind of fit, that's what the shopgirl said. She fainted outside by the icebox, and when people saw her, they tried to help. Then her father came. He put her in a car, and drove away with her!"

Simon adjusted his glasses and rubbed at his eyes. "Oh God . . ."

"We have to go to Chapelwood. We have to get her back!"

"But you don't know for certain that's where she's gone," he protested. "Let's take a moment and be calm about this."

I hated to do it, but I had to point it out. "But, Simon, her parents went to live there, after he was acquitted. It's the only logical destination."

Pedro held out one hand, gesturing toward me. "She's right— Ruth would not go anywhere with her father, not willingly . . . and she'd *never* go to Chapelwood again, not if her life or soul depended on it. I came here because I did not want to go there alone, because I think they'd shoot me, too, just like Father Coyle. I do not have a gun, but I thought *you* might. And you're a big man, with a badge from a big city. They'll listen to you . . . or . . . at least they'll listen to you before they'll listen to me."

He wasn't wrong, but I shook my head anyway, and I told him, "You can't go there. Stephenson would take any flimsy excuse to murder you on sight, and if he does it out there, no one will ever find your body." He began to protest, but I cut him off. "It's true, and you know it as well as we do."

"But she is my wife, whether they like it or not! I can't stand here and let them *have* her."

"And you won't," I promised him. "But if you insist upon visiting that enclave, then let the inspector and me go first. We'll drive out to Chapelwood immediately, and you will go to Chief Eagan's home and tell him what's happened. He's a good man, and though he's no longer the chief in a proper sense, there are other good men who will answer his call. If you must storm the place, storm it with them. Please? Will you promise me that? Don't leave us at the reverend's mercy, but follow us with reinforcements."

He was warming to the idea, but not committed to it yet. He wanted to rush in where angels fear to tread—but that was *our* job. Even if it was his job, too, from a certain angle, we were better equipped to handle whatever we might find there . . . or that's what I told myself. I'd faced worse before. Simon had faced worse before.

We'd surely faced its equal, at any rate.

Pedro had never met anything of the kind—not directly, I supposed, and though he was stout of heart and pure of spirit, those fine traits and a sense of fair play might only hinder him in the battle to come.

I was already thinking about it that way, Emma. Can you imagine? What ought, under any sane circumstances, amount to a knock on a church door and a request to speak with a young woman . . . already I knew, and believed, and feared, that we were in for something terrible.

I'd certainly had enough warning. So far, everyone we'd met who was worth a damn in Alabama had told us to stay away from

chapelwood

Chapelwood. Bad as things had become in town, somehow it was so much worse out there at the reverend's compound, worse than anyone could know. Worse than bigots, and worse than robes or maybe even axe murders—of which the congregation played some terrible part. Oh yes, I knew that now. So did Simon. I saw it in his eyes, when he made his promises to Pedro, and gave his instructions, and jotted down a message for Chief Eagan on a piece of the hotel's stationery.

The chief would come. That's one more thing I was sure of.

But was that a good thing or a bad thing? Good for us, I believed. Bad for him, I feared.

There's always the chance that it won't matter anyway. We're miles and miles from the ocean here, my sister, but I can hear it calling all the same—ringing in my ears, calling like it once did, all those years and years ago. Years and years, miles and miles. A different way of saying the same thing: that I am so far away from you, farther than I've ever been in my whole life. I'm now a whole generation away from our nights reading in your room, and from my nights not-reading-at-all in my own room, with Nance.

I know, I know. You don't want to hear about that. You don't want to hear about *her*. Well, too bad. You were the two people I loved most in all the world, and in that way, you are stuck with each other. Like it or not. Even if you're only dead, and she's only lost.

Simon asked me, "Do you have a gun?"

"No, I'm afraid I don't. My father's old service revolver is all I ever kept—and I left it at home, like a fool."

"How about an axe?"

"I didn't think to pack that, either. But between a gun and an axe, I'm more comfortable with the latter than the former.

My aim is nothing to praise, but my swing is a thing to behold, or so I was told once or twice."

It was Seabury who told me that, after the battle. He said I looked like Joan of Arc headed off to war, with a more useful tool than a sword. More graceful, anyway. He said I looked like Joan if she had been a dancer. I don't know if she ever danced. I wonder.

"Then again . . ." I changed my mind, because that's a woman's prerogative. "I'm older now. I might destroy my shoulders if I tried to strike anything, or even swing something so heavy as an axe. A gun would be better, if you have a spare . . . and for that matter, were you being funny? When you asked if I'd like an axe?" He'd never known, had he? He'd never seen me swinging that weapon at the creatures, spinning and cutting like Joan of Arc dancing across the lawn.

"It was a joke in poor taste, but you seized on it so happily . . . I admit, I'm confused."

"Don't be confused, and I don't mind the poor taste." I picked up my purse and tucked it under my arm. "I must change clothes, though—and you should probably do likewise. The sun will set in an hour or less, and we may find ourselves wanting to hide."

"You're sure I haven't caused offense?" he asked, trailing behind me as I led the way down the corridor to the stairs and then up to our rooms, which faced each other across a hall.

I was a little charmed that he was so concerned, but I was likewise well beyond such delicate worries. By way of explanation, I said, over my shoulder, "Zollicoffer didn't come alone to Maplecroft, and before he arrived, there were . . . minions. Monstrous things, smaller than a man but stronger, and more dangerous. I couldn't very well let them inside, now could I? No," I answered my own question, and shook my head as I climbed the steps. "They would have killed me, and killed Emma . . . or worse. So I killed them all first, and disposed of them in the very machine that eventually claimed the mad professor. In fact, I bought it for *them*—and not for him."

"You did?"

"Of course. We knew about the creatures long before we knew of the unfortunate doctor, or his impending visit. That's why—" I stopped in front of my room and held my key before the lock. I faced him as I finished: "That's why I went to the trouble. We knew something awful was happening, but there was no one we could approach for help. Who would have believed us—much less sent us aid?"

"*I* would have," he insisted. "The Boston office would have . . ."

I believed the first part, but not the second. He didn't, either, if the waver in his voice was any indication. I reminded him, "But we knew nothing of you until you arrived. Even then, we didn't know enough to trust you with the truth. And even when this fabled Boston office of yours was aware of the horror, you told me yourself: It sent no one. It did nothing."

He paused, his own key in hand. He gave me the look of a kicked puppy. "I cannot apologize enough. I can try—I can apologize until the end of days, and I will happily do just that, if you'll let me."

"Don't be ridiculous—I don't need your apologies. Whether or not your office might have been some service to us . . . no one will ever know, and it scarcely matters now. *Now*, I need your assistance to retrieve Ruth Gussman from the hands of murderers, who will surely add us to their tally of corpses and mayhem without a second thought, if they are given the opportunity. So we must be subtle, insofar as we are able. I have a navy blue travel dress, which is close enough to black—and if you have anything more funereal than the cream-colored linen you've preferred thus far, you'd be well advised to try it out."

"You want me to attempt stealth?" He looked well and truly astonished at the thought.

"In the dark, all men look the same," I reminded him. "Don't sell yourself short."

"I've never been accused of any such thing."

"Excellent." I unlocked my door and said, in parting, "Give me five minutes, and I'll meet you downstairs. Bring an extra gun if you have one, or don't, if that's not an option."

"But I have no other gun. So what will you carry when we storm this bastille?"

"My wits, and my experience. And we'll see what else the Good Lord sees fit to provide."

Reverend Adam James Davis,
Minister, the Disciples of Heaven

❧

CHAPELWOOD ESTATE, ALABAMA

OCTOBER 4, 1921

I might have spoken too soon, with regards to Edwin Stephenson.

On the one hand, he did us a service by removing James Coyle from the equation. On the other, I was told to wait, and that Ruth would come to us, of her own free will—and now this is simply not an option. No amount of faith or patience could ever bring the young woman back here again, as it's only pure brute force that's brought her around today. Even if we set her loose, and wished her well, and reimbursed her for her time and trouble . . . she'd only take the opportunity to flee us for good.

This is entirely the fault of her father. *He's* the idiot who dragged her here. Not kicking and screaming, but unconscious in the back of a car he'd "borrowed" for the purpose.

The car belonged to Ned Wilson, who would not have loaned it to Edwin in a thousand years. Ned says it was stolen. Edwin took a different view, for the vehicle has since been returned undamaged, and besides, he was doing Heaven's work. Or so he claims, though I wonder if he honestly believes it.

I mediated the dispute, and all is resolved between them to my satisfaction, if not (entirely) theirs.

The woman, though . . . she's not here of her own accord, and that was part of the bargain as I understood it. I thought I'd made this clear to her father, the aforementioned idiot, but there's always the chance I failed in that regard.

For the sake of peace, I resolve to assume that the failing is mine. I am content to be the recipient of my own anger. Edwin wouldn't survive it.

(So we make these deals, with ourselves and with others. Lies we agree to. Compromises we pretend are victories. But so long as they serve the greater purpose, I'll make no apologies for my concessions, my behavior, or my bargains.)

The question now, of course, is what do we do with Ruth? Is she still the preferred key for our cosmic lock? The patterns are precise, and they are happiest when they're followed to the letter, as if they were instructions for the assembly of a great machine. So what will it matter if we have slipped and improvised with regards to one small directive? Doesn't everyone, when a thousand nuts and bolts must be accounted for? Surely there is room to adjust, in a universe so chaotic as this one.

I hope. I pray. I ponder, consider, and fret.

This isn't how I wanted it to be.

I wanted to open my arms and wait, and see the young

fledgling approach tentatively, but earnestly, into the arms of love—into the arms of infinity, the likes of which she never would have considered in that bizarre papist compound she frequented . . . long ago, in another life.

But now the situation has been forced to a crisis. There is no going back, no hope to reinstate the conditions of a week ago. There is only this woman, unhappily caged (and groggy, and confused, and angry), and there is only the plan, set into motion a billion years ago, or more.

When I think of it that way, I am reassured. For in a billion years, or more than that—how many small variables might slip, slide, or adjust themselves outside of the plan's original scope? Surely not the deviation of a single number, in a single table, can upend the universe?

Leonard Kincaid would have argued with me.

But if Leonard knew everything, he'd still be alive. He'd still be here, at Chapelwood. A brother, instead of a martyr.

I'm the one who made him a martyr. Not when I killed him, though that was simple enough—but by virtue of the story I fed the congregation. Some of the members here knew him. A few of them respected him, even after his fall from grace. And when I told them about his demise, I reminded them that this was the man who had given us the keys to the kingdom. Even if it's true that he'd fallen in his final days, it was still his work that brought us to the place where we are today: the very threshold of God's Kingdom. We stand at the door and wait, because he was able to bring us here.

He is a saint, of a kind. I'll hear nothing to the contrary.

Edwin Stephenson, on the other hand . . .

. . . I'm not so sure. I am reminded of the Catholic saint Peter, a rough-hewn man who lied (thrice, as I recall, before the cock would crow), was blunt, and was not entirely personable to those he sought to teach . . . and I wonder if there isn't some lesson here to be retrieved from the old and false doctrine.

Then again, I rather hate the little Stephenson fellow, and I wish I'd never met him.

𝕴 should erase that. It isn't fair. I dislike him, I do not *hate* him— and my preferences are no fault of his. It's not his fault that he's uneducated and brash, or that he's thick-skulled and thin-skinned—an unfortunate combination in anyone, anywhere, however common it may be. It isn't his fault that I find him abrasive.

Yet it can't be entirely random, given that no one else particularly cares for him, either. We can't *all* be mad or delusional. There must actually be something intensely and innately unlikable about him, something universally perceived and abhorred.

But he is true to the cause, even in his errors. There is a place for him here, I must remember that, even if I must drill it into my own damn head a dozen times a day. If nothing else, he might one day prove a fine scapegoat—should one be required, for something. Should our plans be delayed yet again, and yet more steps need to be taken before we can bring ourselves home.

But I don't think it will come to that.

𝕴𝖙'𝖘 too bad the police are closing in on Leonard as the axe murderer. If they haven't figured it out yet, they will soon. They can't possibly be stupid enough to miss the clues he left behind in his home, and Tom Shirley ought to know already, because I took a chance and told him of my "suspicions." Though I *do* wish I'd had more time to comb through Leonard's belongings before the landlady came knocking. I would be more comfortable if I were absolutely confident there was nothing to tie him to Chapelwood; but I'm only *somewhat* confident, and Shirley says that a portion of the evidence he collected has gone missing—an entire box, vanished into the ether.

Nothing really vanishes. It's gone someplace, at the hands of someone.

Honestly, I'm not *that* worried. But it's a loose end, something unfinished that lingers in the back of my mind. This should have been tidier. This should have been entirely cut-and-dried, but . . . and here is the confession that I hate the most to make, and would not whisper aloud if my life depended upon it: *I do not know the numbers like Leonard did.*

They don't speak to me the way they spoke to him, and they never have—it's always been a terrible difficulty for me, though I hate with all my soul to admit it (even here, where no one sees it). In school, my hands were routinely rapped with rulers, and I was often sent to the corner in a dunce cap for some error or another. At least once per week through my entire education, a teacher was likely to bemoan the fact that for someone with such apparent intelligence, I was nonetheless *dreadfully* stupid.

All because I couldn't divide or multiply, either in my head or on the blackboard. I could add well enough, but scarcely subtract, and even though rationally I knew that the larger number must go on top, in a subtraction formula, somehow I kept reversing it with the smaller one . . . leading to tears and trouble, and constant recriminations.

Even now, I must use my fingers when I count, though I don't do it in front of others. It would not do to appear weak before my flock.

Mind you, I'd argue it's no weakness at all. My expertise lies elsewhere, that's all, and a solid understanding of my own limitations is no failing. Instead, I surround myself with men who have the expertise I lack—and the end result is a stronger team all around. Woe to us all, if I were the sort of figurehead who must shoulder the whole weight of an operation.

Woe enough that I've done the bulk of it since Leonard fled us.

So I've done my best with the equations the little accountant left behind, but my best has never been very good when it comes to this sort of thing, and that's only an acknowledgment of fact—not flaw. I *did* attempt to find another accountant, but had no luck; all potential candidates were either inferior or not entirely trustworthy with information so delicate and powerful in nature.

For those first few months, I was furious with Leonard. If I could have found him, I would have murdered him on the spot—or hauled him back here, chained him securely, and compelled him to continue his work by force. But then, as my wrath burned low, I began to feel something more akin to sorrow at his leaving us.

He could have been so *great*. He could've stood at my right hand, but he abandoned us instead. He abandoned *me*, and I found no substitute for his numerical proficiency.

I thought he was my friend.

I often wondered if I should ask someone else in the congregation . . . we have no other mathematicians, but there are engineers and architects among us. Surely their training and know-how exceeds my own when it comes to sums and figures . . . ? But to do that, to invite someone into these sacred formulas, these holy rituals of columns and tables and graphs . . . it would have revealed me as lacking some necessary skill, for one thing. And for another, we couldn't afford to create another infidel, should a new fellow prove turncoat.

So I did it all myself.

I watched Leonard perform the calculations a thousand times, and although it's not my favorite task or my greatest talent, I am muddling through all the same. I have gotten results that have proven correct—not least of all Leonard's location, that awful flophouse where he lived under a new name, spelled out in a code so simple even *I* could understand it. It also gave me reassurance that Ruth would return to us, and reminded me of her importance in this process.

If I am to be generous, I could say it's one more way that Edwin was useful: He produced this daughter upon whom hangs so much promise and potential. Yet he's also the impetuous dolt who brought her here against her will, when I specifically told him *not* to.

He only wants to further our agenda, he says. He only wanted to help, he swears. He felt in his heart that the time was now, he confesses, and that much may well prove correct. But a man who will go against orders for his own satisfaction will lie just as easily, and I do not trust him. And if I can't control him, I will not be held responsible for his behavior.

None of this changes anything about the present problem, which is named Ruth, and is sequestered in one of the basement worship rooms—where she sleeps off the chloroform that rendered her easy to transport.

I hate doing things by force. I'd much rather do them by conversion, but here we are, and if my math can be trusted (can it be trusted?) there's truly no time like the present. Even if I've missed a little something, somewhere, the numbers—which once gave us months, or even a full year's worth of calendar to work with—now stop at dawn tomorrow. I've run them all a dozen times, and occasionally I get a slightly different result with the minor bits of revelation, but that major one remains consistent: We make our move tonight, or we never make it at all.

Ruth is here, and the numbers know it. *God* knows it. And as far as I can tell, the woman's unapproved arrival does nothing except shorten our time on this earth.

Very well, then. Even if my math cannot be wholly trusted (and it can't), Our Lord and Savior has seen fit to guide us, regardless. He says that the time is nigh, and I believe Him. He says to prepare ourselves, and so we shall.

I've sent out word to the congregation. We assemble in the true sanctuary in an hour.

And may God have mercy on our souls.

(He will, I know. He does.)

Lizbeth Andrew (Borden)

❧

OCTOBER 4, 1921

Simon and I scared up directions to Chapelwood, courtesy of
the hotel proprietress and a local map she kept in the office. Mrs.
Becker (I believe that's her name) tapped the little atlas with her
index finger.

"Are you *sure* you want to visit that place?" she asked,
frowning down at the unfolded paper, now marked with arrows
and a big red circle.

"Not tonight, of course," I lied through my teeth. "Tomorrow morning, I think."

The inspector added, "We'd like a chat with Reverend
Davis, and it wouldn't be polite to pay him a call so late."

Mrs. Becker shuddered. "That one gives me the willies,
though I shouldn't say such things about a man of the cloth."

I might have muttered, "On the contrary, I couldn't agree with you more." And Simon might have gently elbowed my arm.

Then, as if to cover for my breach in decorum, he said, "A friend of ours has gone missing, and we believe he might know what's become of her."

"Ruth?"

We both blinked at her in surprise.

"Oh, don't look so shocked," she said, with a wave of her hand. "Word gets around."

"At speeds that would shame the telephone company, it would seem." Simon took the map, folded it into its original pamphlet form, and placed it in his vest pocket. He was wearing a charcoal gray suit now. It was a little formal for a nighttime raid, but it was the darkest thing he'd thought to pack. "Dare I ask what you made of the trial? Since you've been kind enough to help us, despite our allegiances."

"I don't know that I'm helping you, and I fear for your soul if Chapelwood's where you mean to go. But . . ." She shook her head. "But I'll tell you this, because I want you to know it: There's more to Birmingham than men in sheets and murdering hillfolk."

Then she did the most astonishing thing—she reached to her throat, and tugged a little necklace out of her cleavage. For one brief moment, it glimmered in the shimmering lights of the lobby, and then she stuffed it right back between her breasts for safekeeping.

She wore a tiny gold Star of David.

"You see?" she said with a shaky smile. "My parents came to this land fifty years ago, and changed their name to keep the secret. Some are more open about it, but . . . not them. They suffered too much in Europe, I think. It seemed safer to start again, in a new place, with new names for their children. Of course, in

days like these—the men who'd run us out of town are too busy
trying to run the colored folks and the Catholics out on a rail. It's
an awful shield in front of us."

"That's tragic, but true," I agreed. I put my hand on top of
hers, and she squeezed it, then let it go.

"You know the maids here? The Malone girls?"

Simon nodded. "I've seen them."

"And the man who does maintenance when it's needed, Mr.
Cooney? And MacGrath, who keeps the bushes trimmed? Catholics. You're not supposed to hire them," she whispered. "Not
anymore, not since Nathaniel Barrett passed that legislation as
soon as he got in the door. But a man's got to work if he wants to
eat, and my own family saw enough of that injustice back in the
old country. So we give them work, if we're able. And we wait for
the True Americans to come, and we worry. But . . . we do what
we can."

I didn't want to ask, but couldn't stop myself. "What if they
do come?"

She shrugged. Not like she hadn't thought about it, but like
she knew there was not much to be done, regardless. "Then they
come. We'll see what happens, but I think . . ." She fiddled with
the chain, but didn't reveal the pendant again. "I think they'll find
our numbers are greater than they know. These days, there are as
many outcasts as in-casts. We own businesses, banks, and homes.
We pay taxes like everyone else, and when we have to, we'll stand
together. The rest of us, I expect. Well," she said, releasing the
chain and flipping her hands up, "you know what I mean."

We left with the map and with Mrs. Becker's blessings, and Simon
took the wheel of a car he'd arranged, sans driver this time. We
didn't talk much, as we were both paying attention to the road

signs—and the lack thereof—but he did say, with less optimism than I wanted to hear, "They didn't stand together. They didn't stand with Ruth when they came for her. No one did but us."

"No one came for Ruth. She went to that trial of her own accord."

He didn't reply, but I knew he was thinking about it, and deciding how true that was. As for myself, I didn't know. I've been an outcast longer than I ever was part of society, and I will say this much: When you're left out of things, you don't know who else is left out, too. Most people assume they're alone, because it's safer that way. To confide is to risk exposure, after all. I think most of us would rather be pleasantly surprised to find like-minded or equally reviled others to ally ourselves with.

So I know he's right about Ruth, because I sat there, too, and watched her all alone except for the small handful of us—and Simon and I weren't local to the place, so we had precious little to lose. But I also know how punishing fear can be, and how hard it is to break the patterns that have frightened you into silence.

I don't know, Emma. It's all both better and worse than it appears on the surface.

Night fell as we drove; the faster we pushed the touring car on the inconstant, half-kept roads, the faster the darkness descended. I half imagined that the moon raced us, creeping across the sky as we struggled toward the compound at Chapelwood, but then we lost even that celestial sign—when a low blanket of clouds cut off the day entirely. As the way grew thinner and rougher on the outskirts of the city, we truly felt as if we were disappearing into the woods like Hansel and Gretel.

There were no civic lanterns to encourage us along, only the automobile's headlamps—which shook and rattled in their sockets. The light they cast did the same, spilling jerky yellow beams across the path in front of us. It dizzied me, and my head hurt from squinting, trying to hold my focus steady against the workings of the road, the automobile, and the dismal, dark scenery we penetrated more deeply with every passing mile.

Simon had given me the map, so that I might play navigator. I held it up to the windshield, trying to siphon off an ounce or two of that front-gazing light, and seeing very little to encourage me. Not all the streets were marked, this far out into nowhere; not all the roads had even a smattering of gravel to set them apart from the wagon ruts or footpaths that one might otherwise call them.

I nearly despaired.

There were no helpful gas stops to pull over and ask, no friendly hitchhikers whose local expertise we might exploit, though when I bemoaned this fact, Simon laughed nervously.

"You wouldn't want to offer anyone a lift, not out here. We're as likely to grab a Chapelwood man as a farmer or student hoping for a ride to the city."

"If someone is trying to escape Chapelwood, I say that's all the more reason we ought to lend a hand," I said stubbornly.

"You've got me there, but unless that person is Ruth . . . or perhaps George, if that's where he's gone off to . . . we ought to restrain ourselves. Discretion being the better part of valor, and so forth."

I wanted to give up on the map, but it promised a turnoff within the next two miles, so I clung to it like a saint's medallion—though I'd never owned one, and had only the vaguest idea of how to pray with one. "What should we do when we get there? Do we make some covert effort to get inside?"

"That was the original idea, wasn't it? You were the one who proposed the darker wardrobe."

"But is it the right thing to do?" I pressed, increasingly uncertain.

"Rescuing Ruth *is* the right thing to do. We can be entirely certain she's being held against her will, and that's reason enough to try our hand at subterfuge. We must reconnoiter first, I suppose. Since we don't know where she's kept."

I sighed, and set the map down onto my lap. "God, we know almost nothing about this place."

"Which sets us apart from only a chosen few. They've kept it a secret on purpose. There's no one we could have approached for information . . . except for the dearly departed Leonard Kincaid, in the event you'd like to host a spontaneous séance out in the trees."

"It's not the worst idea I've heard this week."

"And what would the worst of those be?"

I almost said, "Mounting a rescue mission blind, at night, and alone except for a cavalry we only hope and pray will follow in our wake." I thought again of how fear can paralyze and stun, and how even the bravest of men and women might freeze in the face of it. And I did not say the first thing that sprang to mind. Instead, I changed the subject. He was probably thinking the same thing, anyway, and now was not the time to air our discouraging thoughts. "Never mind. Let's look forward, and do our best to plan with what information we have. Now . . . we're looking for New Hollow Road, and I'm crossing my fingers that we haven't passed it."

"I fear the description of 'road' might lead to some disappointment, when we do eventually stumble across it. This is scarcely a road upon which we presently ride, so a side street into the wilderness isn't likely to be an improvement."

"Ever the optimist, you are. Wait—there it is."

He leaned his foot on the brake hard, for we'd almost zipped past before I'd had a chance to speak. He reversed, backed the car up a few feet, and turned off onto a dirt road that ran between the trees at just barely enough width to accommodate us. And once we were firmly off the main path, positioned in this narrow channel between woods and more woods, we stared ahead at the lean black shadows cut sharply on the glare of the car's unblinking lamps.

Simon let the engine idle and the lights point the way forward, but he did not give it any gas and I did not press him to do so. I think we were both almost too frightened, too full of awful thoughts and uncertainties.

"How far is it from the turnoff?" he asked me.

I retrieved the map and again held it up to the windscreen, which gave me just enough light to read it by. "If this can be believed, we're within a mile. Under different circumstances, I might suggest that we turn down the lights and approach the place quietly."

"Under different circumstances I'd agree, but we'd run headlong into a tree trunk in no time, and leave ourselves unconscious, at the mercy of . . . of wolves, or mountain lions, or whatever predator is most common out here. I'm a more ample treat than you, my dear, so forgive me if I'm none too eager to proceed the rest of the way in the dark. I haven't bullets enough for all the forest's carnivores and Chapelwood, too. For that matter, we still aren't sure where we're going, or what to expect when we get there. With luck, they'll be too occupied doing whatever it is ridiculous cultists do on a Friday night—and they won't notice our arrival. Maybe they'll even mistake us for one of their own, at first."

He adjusted his posture to suggest that he was about to urge the car forward, but I put a hand on his shoulder to stop him. "Wait. I . . . well, it's a silly idea, maybe. But I have one all the same. You're the one who gave it to me, so if it's awful, it's entirely your fault."

"All right. Go on . . ."

I swallowed hard, but my mouth still felt very dry. "Let's do it: Let's have a little séance. Right here, in the woods, before anyone at Chapelwood is likely to spot us. It isn't a fine parlor full of professionals at Lily Dale, and we might not reach anyone of use . . . but we could do it in front of the car, by light of the lamps—just leave the engine running—and we might have a word with Leonard Kincaid. He might be willing to help, if you don't think that's completely mad of me to suggest."

Simon stared straight through the windscreen, either at his own reflection or the ribbon of dirt in front of us.

"You don't think that's insane, do you? I told you, I've done a great deal of reading about alternative religious practices—and you're a man who investigates the preternatural. Between us, we must have the skills, even if neither one of us is half so gifted at speaking to the dead as poor Ruth has become."

"It's dangerous." He turned to me, his face more serious than I'd ever seen it. "The dead can lie as easily as the living, you know—and although they might know more than we do, they don't know everything. We could scrounge up an improvised talking board easily enough, but there's no telling who—or what—might answer our summons."

"But we're doing this *blind*, Simon. Even the wrong information could tell us something useful. Have you ever performed a séance before? I've only read about them. Do you know how it's done?"

"I've watched several of them, and I've done some reading myself—but never participated. It feels . . . not dirty, exactly, but suspect. Too many questions, too many variables, too little certainty for my taste."

"But we have all those things in abundance already, don't we? What's a little more thrown into the mix?"

"Ruth is waiting for us," he said uncertainly.

"She'll be waiting in another ten minutes, and we'll be better prepared to help her." I hadn't convinced him, and I probably wouldn't, not all the way. But there was always the chance I could wear him down. "We're dithering, regardless. We could at least dither more productively."

He sighed, threw the car into park, and left it running. "Fine. Let's give it a try, though we might be better off asking for Father Coyle than Leonard. Leonard may have firsthand knowledge of the place, but James is more likely to tell us the truth. Of course, there's always the chance that something will *claim* to be James, and we'd have no way of knowing . . ."

"Good heavens, have a little faith."

"I should pull some out of thin air, you mean?" He opened his door and climbed out, and I did likewise, rather than wait for him to come around. These were not polite, civilized conditions, and we did not have all night, for all that I spoke of productive dithering. I was all too aware that we needed to keep this quick.

𝕴 could feel it, Emma. The weight of a cosmic clock, ticking, ticking, ticking . . . down to some awful resolution. It's nonsense, isn't it? Or I thought so at the time. Now, I guess . . . I don't know. But I felt a desperate need to hear from someone, somewhere, that we were on the right path, and that we could help, and that we definitely weren't too late. Because if we were too late, then it wasn't just Ruth we'd failed—it was the whole world.

Insane, that's what it was. But not untrue.

𝕿ogether, we stood in the headlights. I held my hand up to shield my eyes, and peered around the trees. "Now, I've never done this before, and I've never even seen one," I confessed. "But I know how it works in theory. We don't really need a board, but we'll need letters. I'll just grab a stick or something . . ." I found one of a good length and size, and I used it to stand before the car and write out the alphabet, splitting the letters into three rows and adding the numbers zero through nine.

"Put down a 'yes' and a 'no,'" he directed. "And that ought to be sufficient. If it's going to work at all, that is."

"Really, if you're going to be so glum about the whole thing—"

"Really, you should be a tad less giddy about it, I think."

I frowned, and pointed my stick at him like a wand. "Who's giddy? I'm fascinated, but keenly aware that time is short. Your glumness does nothing to hurry things along, now does it?"

"Very well." Defeated, or willing to pretend as much, he sat down cross-legged with his back to the car, and the makeshift board between us.

"We need a planchette," I noted.

"It doesn't matter what actual object we use; it's the intent behind it. The stick will suffice. All right now, come sit down."

I tried not to be too fussy about my dress and the dirt, and cross-legged isn't a common position in which I find myself—but I managed to lower myself down with modesty, if not grace. I held the stick out to him, and he took it, then broke it into pieces until he had one about as long as my hand from wrist to fingertips.

"Hold the end," he instructed. I did. He held the other end, took a deep breath, and began without further preamble. "If there's anyone listening who might have cause to help Ruth Gussman, or anyone who bears a grudge against the Chapelwood Estate, then I would ask you: Spirit, show me your sign."

At first, nothing happened. We sat there in the dirt, the auto's headlamps glaring at us, and its engine rumbling smoothly in the background, almost drowning out the bugs and the frogs that clicked and squawked somewhere out of sight. The trees loomed tall overhead, so tall I couldn't see their tops; and they seemed so thick around us that they might have been solid walls of stagecraft scenery.

Something like a fluttering mist appeared before my eyes, and I was momentarily encouraged. Then it tried to sting me, and I realized that I was merely an object of interest for a small cloud of mosquitos. I waved them away, telling them to shoo.

If the insects bothered Simon, he didn't let it interfere with the business at hand. Again he tried, "Spirit, show me your sign. And, Lizbeth, both hands on the stick, please."

I gave up defending myself, and did as he asked. The tiny winged things sparkled like fairies in the strong, straight light of the car.

This time, I felt a tug on the stick. It wasn't a little tug, but it stopped short of being a yank—drawing the pseudo-planchette away from me, toward Simon. Then it pulled to the left, and toward me, and to the right . . . in a pattern like a large oval, drawn over and over again.

My breath caught in my throat. I looked hard at Simon's hands, but he held the stick as lightly as I did, and the grim concentration on his face suggested he wasn't out to test the limits of my gullibility. On and on, the stick swirled—a spoon stirring a pot, a toy train running around a track. It thrilled me, and gave me a wash of chills despite the sticky warmth of the Alabama evening.

"Spirit," I said in a whisper that could scarcely be heard above the idling engine, the hoots of owls, the drone of stinging things that fluttered between the trees. "Give us your name."

The pattern slowed, but didn't quite stop. It changed shape

and it changed rhythm long enough to draw our small stub of wood over to the letter "R," then "U," then "T" . . .

"Stop that! Leave us, trickster," he commanded, and forcibly drew the stick over to the place where I'd scrawled "no."

I was panting now, gasping as I breathed and watched, and felt the draw of the makeshift planchette ebb and then leave altogether. "That *wasn't* Ruth. I don't care what it said. It *couldn't* have been Ruth."

"It almost certainly wasn't. I told you, the things that like to speak when a board is presented . . . as often as not, they're liars and fiends. This kind of contact only works if the spirits of our friends are stronger than the little pests that hover about, drawn like moths to a flame—or those gnats to your nose. Let us try again."

My hands shook, but I nodded.

This time, the pattern that emerged was more of a figure eight. When asked its name, it spelled out "George," but Simon didn't believe that was George Ward. By way of explanation, he told me that, as far as he knew, the newly dead can't muster the strength for communication like that; for some reason, it takes time. Days or weeks, at least, and we knew that both Ruth and George had been alive much more recently.

I believed him because I had to, for the sake of my own sanity; but still I shook like the hood ornament on the car behind me, my bones knocking together in time to the fire and clang of the motor's combustion.

"Stay strong, Lizbeth. This was your idea, remember?"

"No, it was yours—but you were only joking. Don't worry about me: I'm strong. I'm ready. One more time, and then . . . then we admit that this was a silly stunt after all."

"Let the third time be the charm, eh? Spirit," he said, directing his attention to the stick, and to the letters I'd scratched into the earth, "show me your sign."

Slowly, jerkily, the sign began to form. This one had angles, or so it became apparent when it found its stride. It swooped up toward Simon, down toward me, then to his left, and off to my right. Once it'd created that jagged groove, worn in the fabric of whatever separated us, the gesture became smoother as it repeated itself again, and again, and again.

It looked familiar. It looked like what a priest does, or what a Catholic does, when he bows his head to pray.

"James." Simon breathed. "Please, be James."

The stick dragged us gently to the "yes."

I jumped right in, afraid that my friend would banish this one, too—though the look on his face and the moisture in his eyes told me that, this time, maybe he wouldn't. I began with a simple hello, like we were at tea and required a formal introduction. "Hello, Father Coyle? We haven't met, and you don't know me—but I'm Lizbeth Andrew, and we have some friends in common."

The stick swung out of its pattern, and began to spell.

Borden.

"Yes . . . yes, that's . . . that's right," I stammered. I don't know why it surprised me. But then again, I had no idea how much the dead may know, or why they know it. "My name was Borden."

Help her.

"We're *trying*," I told him with all my heart.

"But we don't know what awaits us at Chapelwood. We don't know how to save her." He paused, and then with something like sorrow asked, "James, what do we *do*?"

Rush in.

My eyebrows aloft, I added, "Where angels fear to tread?" It'd come up once already.

Front door.

"Is that wise?" Simon frowned at the message, then said to me, "It might be some other fiend. Our third try may not be charming in the slightest."

Front door, the spirit insisted. *Facade.*

The extra word stopped him from banishing the speaker, at least. "The front is all for show? Then where do they worship?"

Downstairs. Below.

I jumped in. "Is that where we'll find Ruth?"

Find them all. Save her. Go.

The stick went slack between our hands. The car's engine coughed and revved, and the headlamps flared—then went dark. The whole world was silent, and so were all the living things that crawled across it. Even us.

Ruth Stephenson Gussman

꧁ꕥ꧂

OCTOBER 4, 1921

I woke up in a room that was mostly dark, except for a handful of candles lit and dripping. One sat on a nightstand beside me, its base resting in a chipped saucer; one was stuck in a shot glass, sitting on a chest of drawers across the room; and one was on a windowsill, high above me. I'm not sure I could have reached that one, even with a stepladder—and *that* told me I was probably underground, because where else do you see windows set up so high? There was something about the way the place smelled, too, like a basement with a leak someplace.

The bed I was lying on had a summer quilt, but I was on top of it. It was hot in there, and muggy as hell even though it was night already.

I was pretty sure it was night. It was always possible someone had covered up that window to make it dark, but I was tired, as if

I'd been asleep for hours anyway. The room was dark and bleak, and the candles didn't help it because there were all these shadows, all these black corners that the flame light didn't touch at all.

I sat up and swung my legs over the side of the bed. I was wobbly, and my head was stuffed with cotton, but I was getting clearer and stronger by the minute.

I stood up. My vision went all runny, so I reached out for the bedpost to see if it would steady me. "Stay calm," I told myself. There was nobody else to do it. "Wake up."

At least, I thought there was no one else. I'd been wrong before.

In one of those very dark corners, there was a chair with a pile of clothes on it, and the clothes shifted, rearranged themselves, and took the shape of a woman. And then it wasn't a pile of clothes. It was my mother. Or it wasn't her, exactly.

She leaned forward, so the edge of her face caught what little light the nearest candle offered. It outlined her: just the shape of her forehead, the curve of her nose, the divot above her lip. She didn't blink, and her eyes were much, much darker than the muddy green they've always been. She was wearing a black robe, so that's why I hadn't seen her at first, or I'd mistaken her for part of the furnishings. Even her hands were gloved, I saw when she scooted to the edge of the seat. Her skin was so much whiter than I ever remembered, and her hair was bound back under the hood; you couldn't see it at all. She was a face floating toward me, and the dim light made her look unreal, or maybe she looked unreal already—and she didn't need any help from the candles.

"Ruth." She said my name like a spell, but she's never been that kind of witch.

I didn't say anything back. I just stood there, holding the bedpost.

"They're coming for you, real soon. You've got to do what they tell you."

"I don't got to do *shit*."

She didn't frown at me, or smile, either. She was unearthly—and I don't mean she was like a ghost, not precisely. She made me think of something from much farther away than just the "other side." She didn't move like a person anymore. She moved like something born with different joints, different muscles, different habits and patterns of motion.

Even if she *had* been my momma, same as always, it wouldn't have been any help to me. She never could protest anything or anyone, much less Daddy or anything he had in mind. She wouldn't have let me out of that room or said anything to comfort me. She was just as bad as he was, and maybe worse—because she let him do whatever he wanted, to me and to everyone else. And she did it with her mouth clamped shut, and a smile, while she looked the other way on purpose.

Funny thing was, I couldn't even get too mad about it. It'd be stupid to expect anything different from her after all these years.

She said, "I left out a dress for you. Put it on."

"No."

"Put it on, or they'll put it on you. There's no sense in resisting. You'll make it harder on yourself than it needs to be."

"Harder than getting stolen off the street? Getting drugged up, and locked in a dark room?" I didn't know for a fact that it was locked, but I would've bet a bunch of money on it.

"Only if you fight it." She sighed, at me or the world in general. "You've always done this, haven't you? Got to fight everything, all the time."

"Somebody has to." I squeezed the bedpost. It felt good and solid between my hands. It reminded me that I was alive, and in a bedroom, and it was weird—but I wasn't dead, and nothing too bad had happened yet. I was alive. I was standing.

They hadn't killed me yet.

Were they *going* to kill me, or did they have something worse in mind? I knew there were worse things than dying, and whatever they'd done to Momma . . . I didn't want them doing that to me. I wasn't even sure what it was.

The word "unearthly" popped into my head again. But I don't mean she was from heaven, that was for damn sure. Not an angel, not a saint. Nothing holy. Nothing sacred moves so smoothly, so silently, and without breathing or blinking. And when the candle-light hit her eyes just the right way, they looked black all around, not just in the center, where the color used to be.

She had changed, God, yes. But how? And into *what*?

"Leave me alone," I told her, partly because I wanted time to wake up on my own, and maybe look around for a way to escape—and partly because I didn't want her to touch me, and she looked like she was thinking about it.

"That's not what you want."

"Yes, it is. You're not my mother anymore, and I don't want you here."

"Don't say such things." She didn't say it like a command, or even a suggestion. It was just a preference on her part. I didn't give a damn, and she didn't expect me to—and that almost made the whole thing sadder, how she'd transformed into something else, and wasn't even any stronger for it.

There's more than one kind of strong, if you know what I'm talking about. There's strong in mind, strong in body, and strong in spirit. She was never any one of those three, and no matter what became of her body, the other two lagged behind.

She was a monster, and I still wasn't afraid of her. I was

afraid of everything else, sure. But not this phantom, this weird haint that used to be a woman I knew and tried to love. "Get out of here. You're not here to help, you're just here to watch. Just like your whole damn life."

I turned my back on her, deliberate-like, to show I wasn't scared.

I looked down at the dress, folded at the foot of the bed. Even in the mostly dark, I recognized it from her hope chest: It was the one she'd got married in, a pretty yellow thing that Grandma had made for her. It'd probably fit. We were about the same size, but I wouldn't put it on, not if my life depended on it. Same size or not, we weren't the same otherwise.

Behind me, she said, "I wish you thought better of me."

"I wish you'd give me a reason."

She didn't say anything back, and when I looked up, she was gone.

I jumped when I realized it, that she'd up and vanished like a puff of smoke—my first thought was that she'd left through the door, but I hadn't heard it open or close. She couldn't have reached the window any easier than I could, and if she'd tried I would have seen her. I ducked down and looked under the bed, shoving the dust ruffle aside and seeing nothing but darkness, but nothing to suggest that awful white face or weird gloved hands. I swept my own hand back and forth under there, not worrying about rats or dust. I found nothing.

She wasn't in the chair. I know because I grabbed a candle and looked in that dark corner—and I checked the other dark corners, too. It didn't take me long. The room wasn't very big. The little light shuddered in my hand, the flame doing its damnedest to show me every cobweb under every piece of furniture without setting the place on fire.

But it was a fact. I was alone. *Really* alone this time.

I still wasn't afraid of her, but I was surprised and a little impressed. Disappearing was the only interesting thing I'd ever seen her do. Now I wondered how she did it, and I wanted to think I could do it, too—just close my eyes and wish real hard, and evaporate to someplace else.

I knew better, though. I knew I wouldn't be able to walk through walls like that unless I let the Chapelwood folks get hold of me, and I didn't plan to let that happen.

I tried to keep from thinking about my vanishing momma, and wondering if she was still there—only now I couldn't see her. I tried not to worry about being watched by unseen eyes, black like hers, through some peephole or crystal ball or whatever men like the Reverend Davis were inclined to use.

If they were watching, fine. Let 'em watch.

I put the candle back where I'd found it, on the dresser. My head had cleared out from pure surprise, and now I needed to free up my hands.

I climbed onto the bed, stood there, and kicked the dress onto the floor. I was wearing what they'd captured me in—just a brown cotton number I liked because it fit me nice but didn't squeeze me anyplace. I still had my shoes. Nobody'd thought to take them off me, which was stupid on somebody's part. The heels dug into the quilt and made it hard to stand, but I didn't care. They gave me another inch or two of height anyway, and I needed every bit of it.

But even standing on the bed, on tippy-toes, I couldn't reach the windowsill. It made me wonder how anybody'd gotten a candle up there in the first place, but there are taller people than me out there in the world, so it must've been one of them.

I put my hands on my hips and looked around. What had

they left me, besides a dress I wouldn't wear, and some old furniture I didn't like?

Actually, the old dresser might be useful after all.

I hopped down off the bed and went to the dresser, thinking
maybe I'd push it up under the window to get me closer to it, but I
was wrong about that. The dresser was nailed to the floor, just like
they do in hotels, or so I've heard before. The reverend hadn't left
me a hammer lying around, so I couldn't pry the nails out and
move things around—I know, because I checked all the drawers
and looked under and around everything in the room. Nothing
moved, no matter how hard I pushed it, shoved it, or kicked it.

So I was out of luck.

Unless . . .

. . . I tried something else. I pulled out the dresser drawers
and looked at them good. They were sturdy, too cheap to be oak,
but maybe poplar or pine. If I'd stacked them all up together, it
wouldn't have given me a boost bigger than the bed, but if I
stacked them *on* the bed, maybe I'd get somewhere.

Only three of the four drawers were willing to come out, but
that was all right. I wasn't sure I could get even those three to
stack up well enough to use, but it was worth a shot.

In a minute or two, I had a rickety setup that might let me
reach the window, or might slip out from underneath me and
send me crashing to the ground. I'd already gotten knocked out
once today and I wasn't looking forward to the prospect of doing
it again, but it was either take that chance or wait around to see
what the reverend wanted with me.

So I did my best to steady the stack of drawers, and I adjusted
them so that two were on the bottom and one was on the top—and
that didn't give me as much lift, but it was a whole lot steadier.

One, two, three.

The windowsill was in my hands.

I pushed the candle over to the side, so I still had the light, but it was out of my way. I felt around for the latch, and found it. It stuck, because I think it'd been painted over; and the window frame stuck when I gave it a good shove, but that was probably because of the damp air inside and out. And I can hardly explain how happy I was—how I almost laughed, and almost jumped for joy—when the thing skidded open an inch or two, and then another one, and then all the way open.

I wasn't sure it was open enough to make room for me, but I was going to try it anyway; and if I had to, I could always break up one of the drawers by stomping on it or something, and then use that to smash the glass out. It wouldn't be quiet, but it might work. I put that idea on the back burner, though. I'd gotten the window open, and that was a start. Now I just had to pull myself up and shove myself out—which was harder than it sounded.

I'd never tried to pull myself up by my hands before, and there wasn't much to hang on to up there. My fingers slipped around, and my nails cracked when I scrambled along the wood, trying to get a better grip. Once I got a decent handhold, I pulled—I tried to use my knees and my toes to help push me up, and it didn't work too well at first. So I took off my shoes and stuck my hand through the straps so they could hang on my arm, and I tried again, barefoot this time. With naked toes, I had better luck. I tried again another couple of times and finally I was up! I had my waist on the windowsill, and my elbows were shaking, I swear to God, and my arms were about to fall off, they were so tired from holding my own weight.

I knocked my head against that window, which wasn't really open enough to let me slither outside, or that's what it looked like—now that I could see it up close.

I refused to settle for that. I held my position, even though it hurt like hell. I held it and I didn't move, because outside my door I could hear footsteps.

Maybe I'd made too much noise. Or maybe my time had come.

Something was coming, anyway. I didn't even want to think it was "someone," since I'd seen Momma; but then again, when she moved . . . she hadn't made any footsteps or any other sound. But I didn't care if this was somebody more ordinary. Whoever it was, it was somebody who believed in Chapelwood and wanted to put me in a yellow dress and force me to take part in something awful.

Or so I assumed. Nobody forces anybody to do anything nice by kidnapping them and locking them in a dark room with monsters.

The footsteps rang louder and louder, with a funny edge to them—almost the kind of echo you hear when you open your eyes underwater, and everything wobbles back and forth, and nothing is clear. It reminded me of how Father Coyle had sounded when he appeared to me in the courthouse, so far away. He might have been on the moon, or at the bottom of the ocean.

Now I was scared.

Before, I was trying to solve a problem, and that kept me distracted from how much danger I was in. Now, I was out of plans, the window looked too small, and someone was coming for me.

I struggled, kicked, and dragged and hauled my body up until I got one knee on the windowsill with my hands. I'm sure it looked ridiculous, but I was leaving that place one way or another—and I wanted to do it alive, so I went ahead and looked ridiculous. Having a knee to help hold my weight made it easier, and gave my arms a rest.

With one elbow, I knocked at the window to see if I could

push it out any farther. It only creaked and made a pitiful splintering noise, but it didn't go anywhere.

How long did I have before the footsteps reached my door? Thirty seconds? Ten?

My mouth was dry as a desert and my arms were aching, and my knee was starting to slip—but I thought, if I could just get one leg outside through the opening . . . maybe I could slide out on my belly, and that would work, even if I went backward out into the yard.

So that's what I tried, and at first, I didn't think it was working.

The window's edge dug into the back of my thigh and tore my dress, but I wrangled my other leg up and over, once I had enough weight up there to balance it. Feetfirst and on my belly, I writhed and wrangled myself through that sliver of an opening, hardly any higher than a loaf of bread. My skirt scrunched up around my thighs, then up over my behind so God and everybody could see my underpants and I didn't care a bit. Thank God I've never been a big woman—which is not something I say every day, because there've been plenty of times I wished I was tall and stout and burly enough to defend myself. But not today.

Today I praised Jesus and His Mother, too, for making me a hundred and twenty pounds, according to the grocery store scale, and that's if I was soaking wet with rocks in my pockets.

I scooted out onto the grass just as I heard the doorknob start to turn.

I was out. But the window was open and the candle stub was still lit, sitting right there. I could take it with me and have some light, except light might not be my friend right now. I had a better idea. I reached inside and knocked it over, right onto the bed.

I didn't stick around to see if it started a fire. I didn't even stick around to shut the window; it's not like they wouldn't figure out that's how I'd left, given the drawers and the bed and everything. I crawled out of view and tried to put my shoes back on, but my arms were all wobbly and I could tell they'd hurt in the morning. Too bad. I still had some escaping left to do.

Finally I jammed the shoes onto my feet and yanked the straps where they ought to be. Then I stood up, wiped my hands on my skirt, and looked for some direction to run.

Inspector Simon Wolf

❧

OCTOBER 4, 1921

I'd never seen anything like that before—when the car shut down and left us in the dark so violently, so suddenly. I confess I indulged a brief panic about it, and the glaring orange filaments in the bulbs that were simmering down to nothing; but there wasn't any time for panic now, was there? We only had time for *action*.

I ran to the driver's door, whipped it open, and hopped inside with less than my usual grace. I pumped the pedals and turned the key, all the while muttering some pointless prayers under my breath, but I don't even remember what they were or who I directed them toward. I only know how badly my hands were shaking as I commanded the engine to *turn over*, goddammit. But then Lizbeth was there, at the passenger door—having felt her way there, for there was no further light to be of any aid.

She opened it and leaned inside. "What happened?"

"Your guess is as good as mine. There are . . . in the back, in the . . . in the boot," I stammered. "There's a lantern and some matches. We may be forced to resort to them if—"

But with a gurgled complaint, the motor interrupted me. It grumbled to life!

The headlamps flared whiter than a stage's spot lamp, bleaching the trees and the road before us. Both Lizbeth and I shielded our eyes against the beams, far too bright, far too much like the swords of angels at the gates of Eden—except we both knew there weren't any angels here to guide us . . . or waiting for us at Chapelwood, either.

"They'll see us coming a mile away," I complained.

"If that's true, then they know we're here already. As I said, if the map can be believed, we're only that far from the main compound. Of course, if they're all hiding underground, they might not detect our approach."

"Surely they have lookouts, or some form of warning system. Dogs, at least . . . ?"

"Put the car in gear, Simon," she commanded me. "It's time we go find out."

I did as she ordered, though my heart was thick as lead about it. I wanted to save Ruth, yes, obviously. I wanted to bring James's killer to justice, absolutely. But we had only confusion and the word of ghosts on the former, and the ship may have sailed on the latter. Besides, it was increasingly apparent that Edwin Stephenson was only the smallest of nasty little fish when it came to the strange machinations at this unlikely church in the woods. The Reverend Davis was the puppet master, and Stephenson but an underling acting on his orders.

The more I thought about it, driving down that bleak, unpaved corridor, the less certain I became. I honestly believed that Stephenson had killed Coyle out of white-hot anger, not on the orders of some divine directive; so it was always possible that he'd kidnapped his daughter apart from religious sanctions, too.

But Chapelwood wanted her, didn't it? And one way or another, it had her now.

All Lizbeth and I had was my gun, some extra bullets, a lantern and some matches, our advanced ages, and respective wits. It wasn't nothing, but it was hardly a formidable arsenal, either. Still, here we were, driving slowly along a pair of loose-cut ruts that were more sand than gravel, the car's lights guiding the way and yet showing us almost nothing beyond the front bumper— for there was nothing to see but more trees, and the cavernous black maw of a path that ran between them.

This was the hand we were dealt, and we were duty-bound to play it.

Lizbeth rode with her eyes closed, and I wondered if she was praying, but it wasn't my business to ask. When she opened them, she blinked at the headlights on the other side of the glass, took a deep breath, and said, "This must be it."

The road widened ahead, and the lights cut a broader path— for just beyond the edge of our lamps, there were no more trees to contain the glow. We were arriving at a clearing, and I couldn't decide if I was relieved or appalled that we'd come so far so fast. It felt like only a minute or two since the car had returned to life and we'd piled back inside it. Surely not, though. Surely it'd been closer to five or ten minutes burned from the clock as we'd crawled forward on narrow tires that protested the terrain every foot of the way.

But yes, here we were—and there was nowhere left to go.

The road deposited us into a wide space, a half-moon the size of a baseball field. All was dark except for what the car showed us, so we could see no farther than the jiggling head-lamps allowed.

Chapelwood. It's hard to explain.

In the middle of a cleared semicircle stood a large building, the centerpiece, if you will. It was one part cathedral, one part courthouse, one part antebellum gothic mansion. Not a single light burned in a single window, and a row of four white columns held up a large portico. It looked like a grinning skull with a row of long, wide stairs spilling forth from its mouth, or maybe that was only my imagination—combined with the stark, sudden light from the automobile in the otherwise pitch-black woods. This light showed everything in hard relief, exaggerating corners and crevices that would go unseen in the daylight, and I *knew* that—I believed it and understood it—yet I could not escape the sordid terror of the chimneys, three or four of them, jutting from the gabled and turreted roof like so many blocky, twisted horns.

It was a massive structure, though how massive I couldn't gauge; and on either side it was flanked by smaller outbuildings: a garage, I think, and some storage sheds, and what looked like it once was a barn.

The air was dark, thick, and miserably humid around us. It pressed against the windows and doors, as if forbidding us to exit the vehicle . . . or else we only didn't want to, and we found it hard to muster the courage to do so. A bit of both, I'd like to believe. Otherwise, I'm entirely a coward, and like all men (surely women as well), I'd prefer to think otherwise.

"It's nearly Halloween," Lizbeth said so softly I scarcely heard her. "Only a few more weeks until that dreadful night, but I've never been anyplace so warm, so late in the year."

"Nor have I. Not in recent recollection, at any rate."

"I don't see anyone, do you? I don't hear any dogs. The spirit said they're all underground . . . Could that be true? Do you think? Surely the reverend has left someone to stand guard."

I shrugged, and kept my hands on the wheel, my foot on the brake. "If they're all in this together, and if they honestly believe they've nothing to fear . . . they could feel perfectly safe down below. Who in their right mind would storm this place, anyway?"

"No one. But we must screw our courage to the sticking place."

I sulked, though it was no doubt unbecoming. "I've never really understood that turn of phrase. I don't care if it was Shakespeare who coined it, it's not terribly elegant."

She reached for her door latch, and pulled it. "No, it isn't. But the time has come." The fastener uncoupled, and she swung one leg outside—quickly, a hasty gesture undertaken before she had time to think about what she was doing.

I put the car in park and dithered another short moment. "Get the lanterns from the trunk," I suggested before killing the engine, and with it, our only source of light.

The lid creaked when she lifted it. Every sound was a gunshot, a cannonball, a Fourth of July fireworks display—even though the rough hum of the motor did its best to provide a muffling blanket of neutral noise.

Surely we'd be heard or spotted at any second. Surely our time was limited. Surely they'd come for us, bursting from the doors and windows like so many rats.

The lid came down again with a firm but restrained clack, and behind me, a small pop of light said that Lizbeth had lit a match. Otherwise, Chapelwood was dark and quiet. So dark, so quiet—except for the flare of one little match lighting one little lantern, and the fizzle and snap of the flame as it caught, warmed, and grew.

I pushed the keys into my pocket, and shoved them down deep. They were warm and hard against my thigh, but I liked the pressure, even the discomfort of it. They reminded me that there was a way out of here after all, when we eventually retrieve Ruth and must flee with the Reverend Davis upon our tail.

Who was I fooling? No one. My keys were a rabbit's foot, a four-leafed clover—wielded vainly and impotently against the danger to come.

Lizbeth held the light aloft, a talisman of another, more practical kind. "Shall we?"

"The front door?"

"Let's see what it gets us."

I'd say that she led the way, but in truth I walked beside her. She held the light, and that felt like leading—since I couldn't go anywhere without her, or without that small totem of hope. I looked back at the car, sitting forlorn in that clearing at the foot of the big old house, or church, or whatever it'd been originally intended as. The engine popped and cooled beneath the hood, but otherwise there was no sound but our footsteps, crunching through the dirt, leaves, and grassy spots on the way to those stretched-out steps.

Even the insects had left us by then. So had the moon, the stars, and everything else we might have found reassuring. When I gazed up to the firmament, I saw only the blank black surface of a slate washed down with a wet rag—but without any of the polish or texture. It was nothingness, that's all. It wasn't even empty.

We took the steps one at a time. They were filthy, each and every one—no one had swept them in heaven knew how long, so I took some comfort from that. However these men came and went on a regular basis, this wasn't it. We weren't likely to encounter any resistance.

We hadn't exactly arrived with the utmost stealth, and our little handheld light may as well have been a chandelier in an outhouse, for it easily stood out that much.

When we reached the double doors, we paused at that threshold and examined them—Lizbeth running the lantern up and down, giving us all the details. These doors were carved with scenes . . . no, not scenes. Maps, more like. Or closer still to what I'm attempting to explain: They were illustrated with astrological diagrams. Over here, I saw a series of dots that once connected, indicated the constellation Capricorn. Over there, the circle and tail of the great lion. Across the front, the vaguely sinister mark of the scorpion.

"Scorpio," Lizbeth correctly identified. "And Cassiopeia, isn't it? That one, right there."

"I believe so."

"But it's not a map—these aren't in proper alignment. They're a series of decorations, that's all," she concluded. "They're nicely done, I'll grant, but they're no proper zodiac. And look at this knocker. Have you ever seen its equal?"

I shook my head, and held out my hand to merely touch it— not use it, I assure you.

It was brass, and oxidized, but otherwise rarely used; there were no telltale places where the patina had rubbed away under a visitor's regular summons. At first I thought it was created in the form of an elaborate octopus, but when Lizbeth adjusted the light again, I reevaluated. "It's not an octopus or squid, but . . ."

"Some kind of cephalopod, surely? Not one I'd recognize. My sister, she would've known." My hand reached out, and she stopped me. "Don't touch that."

"I wasn't going to strike it."

"I know, but—" She frowned, and I think her eyes were wet.

CHERIE PRIEST

Perhaps that was my fault. Perhaps it wasn't anything but the atmosphere. "It looks unholy. Unhealthy. It has—look, Simon— spines, and teeth. You'll prick your finger upon them, and sleep for a hundred years."

"What a terrible fairy tale."

"I was never any good at stories like that." She pressed her shoulder against the wood and set her ear against it, too. "But never mind. Listen . . . I don't hear anything, so let's keeping moving."

Before I could stop her, she tried the door's latch.

(Would I have stopped her, given the time? No, I don't think so. It was only the jerk of a knee, the nervous impulse to stay outside—and leave this place, run as far away from it as my fat old legs could carry me.)

The latch released. The door retreated one slim inch, at Lizbeth's slight pushing. That inch scraped and squealed, but not as badly as I might have expected—but as I'd absolutely anticipated, not a shred of light or sound exited Chapelwood through that tiny gap. Only a small gust of mildewed air puffed to greet us, smelling of dust, mold, and old death. And something else, but I couldn't put my finger on it. I didn't even try.

"It sounds like no one's home."

"Not here—upstairs." She sniffed, one nostril crinkling and rising while the other one flared. "Do you smell that?"

"I smell something. Whatever it is, it's unpleasant."

"Reminds me of the ocean. The shore, in the sun—after the tide goes out."

I nodded. "But worse. No, it makes me think . . ." I hated to say it, but she was forcing me to make the connection—though I'm sure that wasn't her intent. "The bodies in the morgue, in Fall River. All those years ago, when I visited those strange brothers at their funeral home. This smells like that, almost."

She pushed the door farther, adding her thigh to the lever-age. "Then I'm glad I didn't accompany you on that errand."

"No good would have come of it."

She stepped inside.

"You are fearless, madam."

"Hardly. But I'm confident that we've not yet reached what-ever terrors lurk below. Or above . . . ," she added in a weird murmur.

"The sky *is* strange tonight." I said it as some mild, anxious form of agreement.

"Everything is strange tonight. Right now, we're as safe as we're likely to get—neither underground, nor under that naked sky. Help me, Simon," she pleaded. "Look for a way downstairs. Or look for any sign of how these people might come and go, or where they gather."

"Of course. But turn up the light, if you don't mind. My eyes aren't as strong as they once were—and they were never very sharp in the first place."

She obliged, and soon the lantern was as bright as we could expect it to become. It showed us the whole great space—not a foyer and a sanctuary, but one huge open area full of pews in disarray. They weren't lined up in tidy rows; they were pushed aside and stacked, as if this was someplace they were stored—rather than used for their traditional purpose.

Above, we saw rows of stained-glass windows mounted so high against the ceiling that I couldn't make out any of their details. Perhaps on a sunny day I could've seen something more distinct than "black, blue, and green shapes," but that was the best I could surmise by the light of our little lantern. Up front, where a pulpit should hypothetically go, there was a large piece of furniture better suited to an altar. I would've been more alarmed if it hadn't been knocked onto its side, suggesting that, like everything else, it was rarely (if ever) touched.

"This is the strangest church I've ever seen . . . ," I observed.

Lizbeth agreed with me. She walked down the center aisle, such as it was—holding the lantern over here, over there, trying to tease out more information from this bizarre and unlovely chamber. "It looks less like a church than a place where churches store old fixtures. It reminds me of Storage Room Six."

"Indeed. I wonder if it likewise eats paperwork."

"It consumes worse things than paperwork, if anything. Health, reason—sanity . . ."

I couldn't argue, and I had no intention of trying. "Then let's be swiftly on our way. There's nothing for us here."

She didn't turn around, and didn't really seem to hear me. "If everything happens underground, there must be an entrance *somewhere.* More likely, there are entrances in a number of places—secret ones, for the sake of safety and access. We must keep our eyes and ears peeled for trapdoors, stairs, or any spot where the floor sounds hollow."

"You make these men sound like groundhogs, or chipmunks."

"Evil ones." She made a small grunt, like she'd prefer to giggle—but not here, and not now. She cleared her throat instead. "It's only logical, wouldn't you say? They *must* come and go. They *must* have taken Ruth someplace. Don't believe in the ghosts, if that's your preference; but believe your own eyes. This place is abandoned. She's someplace else, and my money says it's somewhere below us."

The smell was wafting up my nose, into my mouth, and back against my throat as I breathed. I could taste the dank, putrid air, and it made me want to lose my supper. (Terrible waste though that would have been.) I coughed a little and said, "Over there, that's a choir loft, of a sort."

"We want to go down, not up."

"I know, but do you see the staircase?" A corkscrew spiral against the wall, partially hidden by a heavy curtain of indeterminate color. "It might go down to parts unseen, as well as up."

She ushered herself toward it, and I followed along behind her; there was no way to walk side by side anymore, not in this maze of lengthy and discarded benches and books. I kicked one of those books, and it was nothing more thrilling than a Holy Bible. Even when I opened it with my toe, no hollowed-out space revealed treasure or trap. Another book nearby turned out to be a tome about the True Americans, and yet a third was an ordinary hymnal. All were kept around for the sake of appearances, I guessed—but it was clear that no one cared about those appearances anymore.

That fact worried me almost as much as the awful, familiar odor. The congregation was finished with the pretense, which meant these deranged, villainous people were very, very near to their end goal. Whatever that might be.

"Good God, Simon! That was one hell of a guess—"

"Was it?" I joined her at the staircase. It did indeed vanish into a slot in the ceiling, but it likewise disappeared down into the floor, where a circle had been cut to accommodate it. "No, I don't think so. You're the one who suggested keeping an eye out for stairs."

"This wasn't what I had in mind, but"—she knelt beside the hole and cautiously lowered the lantern—"it might be what we're looking for, regardless. See, over here." Lizbeth pointed with her free hand. "No footsteps, no dust recently disturbed on the upward steps—but heading down, there are plenty of shoe prints. They're coming from . . ." She looked over her shoulder, and brought the lantern around to help her see. "Coming from *that* way. If we had nothing but time, I'd say we should back-track and see what we can find; but given the circumstances, we'd better skip that side path of an investigation and head directly down."

She rose to her feet and dusted her knees.

I held out my hand, gesturing for the light she held. "This time, I'll take the lantern. And the lead."

"Oh, will you, now?"

"Yes, I will. I'm much larger, and these stairs don't look particularly sturdy. But if they'll hold me, they'll hold you. Besides, I'm a consummate gentleman with a gun. In case you were unaware."

She smiled at me, and it made me sad for reasons I'd be hard-pressed to explain. It wasn't a happy smile, but it was a fond and polite one. "Very well, as you prefer. Take the light, and lead the way. You're the one with a gun, after all."

"Right. I'm the one with a gun." Chapelwood had me rattled, that's all I can say to excuse myself. The whole place was off-kilter in every way, and it was giving me a headache—like staring too long in a fun-house mirror and trying to make sense of your reflection. The smell, the angles, the silence, the darkness. Neither church nor temple, nor shrine nor memorial. Neither human, nor divine. It was something in the middle, and the middle was a horror.

What an awful place for Ruth to be, alone and afraid, captured by the very men she feared the most.

I took the lantern in my left hand. I retrieved my gun and brandished it with my right—though this left me with no stray hands to hold the rail for balance. It would have to suffice. I was descending into hades ahead of my time, but I would do it on no man's terms except my own . . . even if those terms were ridiculous, and I was a ridiculous coward, even with a gun and a light. Well, show me the man who does not cower in that place—and I'll show you a monster who has found his way home.

I steeled myself. I paid close attention to the spiral of wood-plank steps below me. One foot at a time . . . down . . . down . . . down . . .

With an unarmed woman behind me, and horror ahead of me. So help me God.

Or whoever.

Lizbeth Andrew (Borden)

❧

I crept down the stairs behind Simon, treading carefully out of atmospheric suggestion rather than necessity. He was more graceful than one would expect a big man to be, but the steps creaked and shook beneath our feet, loudly enough to announce us to anyone near enough to spy us.

We weren't sneaking up on anyone, that was for damn sure.

But at the bottom, we still found ourselves alone. He turned up the lantern as high as it would go, for the ceiling was low and there were no windows; when he lifted it aloft, his knuckles grazed the damp, peeling plaster above us.

I hunkered as we looked around. I wasn't tall enough to strike my head upon any low-hanging light fixtures, but then again, there weren't any. It was only the air of the place, so cramped and tight—despite the fact that the room was long and virtually empty.

"It's too tall to call a crawl space, and too wide to call a corridor. What a peculiar space . . . just like everything else here, neither one thing nor another," Simon observed. "No windows up there. No lights. I don't even see any candles, do you?"

A quick sweep of the place proved him correct. "I suppose they carry a light around, like us."

He jiggled the lantern in response, and the room swayed back and forth. None of the angles felt right, and nothing felt level, even when the light was perfectly still. "Maybe. Or else they don't need it."

"That's an ominous thought."

"Which only means it's appropriate. Now which way, do you think? I suppose back over here . . ." He held the light forth, and indeed, there appeared only one direction we might travel for more than a few yards. Besides, when he dropped the light again we could see pathways worn in the filth that covered the floor—solidly indicating that, yes, we should proceed toward the left, to the edge of the light, where there was only a blackness as flat as the sky.

He started walking, and I joined him.

I was almost relieved to be free of the lantern, for without it I could concentrate on my surroundings—rather than on the simple necessity of showing the way forward. Now I could take note of the crusty patches of brown-stained walls and oozing bubbles of mold that sagged from the ceiling above. Here and there, tree roots and rocks and clumps of dirt poked through cracks (below us, beside us, above us), and small spills of pebbles crunched under our feet.

𝔈𝔪𝔪𝔞, we were walking through a grave.

I fancied myself a little thing—a beetle or a mouse—exploring the collapsed ground where a coffin has rotted through and the body has long since been eaten by the worms, the ants, and the wandering rats. Even the smell was not so different, though it was much wetter down there than I'd hope to think of any grave. The air was so moist, so thick, it clotted in my lungs like old cream in a cup of tea.

The quietude was gravelike, too, broken only by our own feet, feeling about on the floor—and in time, by something else: a susurrous hum that wasn't quite a hum, and wasn't quite a rumble. I heard it only barely, at the very edge of what my ears could detect—strain though I might to bring it into sharper relief. I thought maybe it was singing or chanting; it was alive, at any rate, and not the mechanical clanks or grinds of gears and pulleys.

On second thought, it might have been the sound of something breathing.

So this was a grave, Emma, and I looked around for ghosts. I looked for you. I listened for you, as hard as I ever listened at home when I smelled the spirit of your perfume. But you weren't there, and neither was Nance, and nor was the minister James Coyle, who may (or may not) have spoken to us through the board we'd made out of sticks and wishes. If this unique place of worship was a monument to the middle distance, and if I'd ever touched it, I still had no idea what it looked like, what it felt like, or why it'd called me—and no other.

$Simon$ paused, his head cocked to the side. He could hear it, too—I knew it, even before he asked me, "What's that? Do you hear it?"

"Barely, but it's getting a bit louder. We must be getting closer . . . I'm not sure if that's good or bad."

"Nothing's good down here. Let's think instead in terms of helpful or not helpful. And is it my imagination, or is the ceiling getting even lower?"

I reached up and drew my fingertips along the flat, dirty space above us. "I can't tell. But the smell is getting worse, and the noise is getting louder. And the floor . . ." I squinted down at the tracks we more or less followed.

(There was only one way to go, so everyone went this way. We weren't following them, or tracking them. We were only flowing in the same direction as others had before us.)

I said, "There's something funny about these marks. Some of them aren't footprints."

He nodded at them, and then at me. "I thought that might be my imagination, too—but no. Some of them look like drag marks, where a person's heels have scraped along the dirt. Ruth, do you think? Or other, previous unwilling visitors?"

"I'd rather not consider either of those possibilities. We might be wrong, anyway," I said, but I did not specify that I didn't think they were drag marks. They weren't straight, and they didn't come in pairs—but in random patterns. To me, they looked more like the paths of enormous snakes, the boas or pythons one reads about in *National Geographic*, when one would rather not sleep at night for fear of finding one in the washroom.

I did not want to say that out loud. I locked it down in my mind, pulled the shutters down, and refused to look at it. I refused to look down anymore, except in furtive glimpses to keep from falling over the detritus of a basement that was slowly being crushed by the weight of the church above it.

Before long, we arrived at what could best be described as a clearing—and in this clearing we were confronted with three options: two hallways that had been dug out of the dirt like mine shafts, or a single reinforced place that offered a rough-hewn set of steps going down into yet more darkness.

We hesitated and investigated each one, neither one of us mentioning what we both knew all too well: that we were no longer in any kind of basement or cellar, that somewhere we had passed the point of subterranean civilization and now there were only walls of mud to separate us from whatever lay beyond the dank, miserable corridors we traversed together.

The light wasn't great enough to show us anything down any of the three passages. But the weird singing—yes, I think it was singing, very low, very deep—was coming from down those awful, uneven stairs.

We knew what to do.

"Take my hand," Simon suggested.

I very nearly did, but was startled by a sudden shout rising up from below.

The singing stopped abruptly, disintegrating into a jumble of voices, each one carrying a question we couldn't hear—and might not have understood, regardless. Another shout, another cry, and the sound of footsteps at the bottom of those stairs—which must have gone very deep below.

Our light would give us away.

Simon took my hand and yanked it, pulling me down into one of the rounded, earthy openings that passed for a doorway, I guess. He pressed his back against it and shuttered the lantern until only a tiny white seam declared it—and although it must have been quite hot, he concealed it behind his jacket. I prayed he wouldn't burn himself, and prayed that he wouldn't set fire to himself, either, and likewise I prayed that we had chosen wisely in our hiding place.

Not that it mattered, really. We had but two choices, and it all amounted to the toss of a coin.

Up the stairs they came, as many as a dozen of them, I gauged by the sound of their hustling, frantic feet . . . but I couldn't see them. They traveled without light, and I wondered how they could see anything at all—but I didn't wonder hard, or long. It was one more thing to toss in that locked-up room in my head. One more thing to walk away from, without looking back.

"She went out through the window."

"And you're certain?"

"She went *out*, that's all I'm certain of. We checked the room, top to bottom. Her mother swears she was there not five minutes before."

"But the window? She could have never reached it."

"She piled things on the bed, and climbed them."

My heart surged to hear it. Ruth? Surely they were speaking of Ruth!

Simon was thinking it, too; he squeezed my hand with joy, then let it go. He shuffled nearer to the opening, in order to hear better, I suppose.

I retreated farther, not to be contrary—but because I thought I felt something against my hip. It was wood, and squared off. A railroad tie? Perhaps. I'd seen some down there below, holding up shafts and generally littering the landscape. Yes, I was more sure of it as I ran my hands over the grain, over the shape of the end. It was piled atop others, left behind for future projects or merely abandoned. I felt a knob of metal jutting from one end. The head of a spike? Probably. I was dying for some light, desperate to take the lantern and give myself just a few drops of illumination—it wouldn't take much more! Not when my eyes were so accustomed to the gloom. But I knew better, and so I "saw" only with my fingers while I listened to the chatter just beyond us.

"She can't have gotten far. Not on foot, in the dark."

"There were candles in the room. She might have taken one."

"She won't get far with it if she did. Can't run and keep one lit at the same time, now can she?"

"Get her parents. I'll get the lens and see if I can find her. We only have tonight, you understand? Catch her, and bring her back down to the Holiest of Holies."

"What if we're too late?"

"The Great One's heart won't beat again for a thousand years. If that brat costs us this opportunity, I'll have her dead myself—rather than simply transitioned. Go on. Find Shirley, and have him meet me at the lens. And get that girl—do you understand? Bring her to me, or spend the rest of your life running from me. Do I make myself clear?"

"Perfectly."

The lens? Well, it was just one more question, added to the pile of them. I turned around and felt with both hands now, running them over the pile of beams and wondering what else I might find. The planks were too heavy to use as weapons, but there could be something else left among them—a hammer, a pry bar, *anything.*

The footsteps faded, back the way we'd come; but another minute's pause allowed another three or four of Chapelwood's residents to clamber up from the depths and dash out in the wake of whoever'd been given those awful instructions.

Meanwhile, I proceeded with my tactile investigations. I found what was, yes, certainly, a railroad spike—heavy and pointed, but dull. A weapon of last resort.

"What are you doing?" Simon whispered.

I realized then that I'd gotten away from him. "Is it safe to use the light?" I whispered back.

"I don't know."

I might have asked him for a small dab, just a dribble of that precious stuff to warm my eyes and show the way . . . but at that very instant I set hands upon something familiar. It was lodged in a slab of wood and I had to rock it back and forth to extract it. I did my best to do this in silence, and my companion did not shush me—so I must have done a reasonable job of it.

"What are you doing over there?" he asked again.

I didn't answer him until I had the tool free, and in my grip. I knew the weight of it, and I felt reassured to have it. What a random thing, really—or else the universe is fond of patterns after all, as my dear departed Doctor Seabury had always insisted.

I insisted it, too, didn't I, Emma? I said there was a pattern to the mayhem, though I was seated too near the action to see it for myself. I always believed that if I could just extract myself enough—if I could remove myself to a distant place, with a wider perspective—it would all become so clear that I'd feel silly for having ever missed it.

Who was it who said . . . I don't know, was it some dead Greek or Roman? I can't recall. But it was something along the lines of, "Show me a place to set a fulcrum, and I will move the world." Is that right? Probably not. But it was something like that. We spoke of it before, you and I. Back in the old days.

That's what I mean. Does that make sense? I bet it doesn't. Or maybe it does to you, wherever you are, and whatever you can see. Maybe, being dead and long gone from this world, you have the perspective I've longed for. All I'm trying to say is, I am certain that the universe, or God, or whatever you want to call it . . . it has an inordinate fondness for patterns.

Because, God help me, Emma. I was holding an axe.

Somehow, I believe, I retrieved it from that fabled middle

distance . . . where Nance disappeared to and where Storage Room Six serves as a portal. I understand that now. I brushed against it, and escaped with my soul. With such a near miss, I suppose, there come privileges.

𝕰𝖎𝖙𝖍𝖊𝖗 Simon decided that the way was clear or his curiosity overwhelmed his sense of self-preservation—because he unshuttered one sliver of the lantern so he could see me better. I hope he saw me as I saw myself: armed, fierce, and invigorated.

If he didn't, he was kind enough to keep it to himself. "Would you look at that! Well played, Lizbeth. The look suits you."

"It's familiar and versatile, and I can hide it behind a skirt if I need to—even these slimmer silhouettes that are all the rage these days." I tested it in my hands, turning it over, getting a feel for the balance of it. It would be an exaggeration to say that power flowed through me; it would not be an exaggeration to say that I felt more confident, and on firmer footing than the loose, damp dirt that made up the floor beneath me. The axe was something I understood, in a world full of things I didn't—and I would cling to it, brandish it, and swing it if I needed to.

"If you're happy, I'm happy," he assured me. "But what next? Ruth has escaped to the great outdoors. God, if she's found the car . . . I should have left the keys in it."

"Does she know how to drive?"

"I haven't the faintest."

"And if she took it, how would we flee when the time arrives?" I asked, though, in truth, I would trade our safe path out of Chapelwood for her to escape safely.

"I know, but still." I think he was considering the same. "But here we are, and the cards have already been dealt. With that in mind—and I do hate to suggest it—perhaps we should part ways. Whatever lies below must be attended to, but likewise we must make every effort to save poor Ruth."

He wasn't wrong, but I wasn't happy. "Ruth has escaped of her own volition; are you sure she needs our help?" God, I hated myself for saying it. I sounded like a coward, but it was true—I didn't want to flee the only company I had for certain.

"No. Yes. I . . . Lizbeth, I have no better idea than you do."

"I'm sorry, I'm sorry. Then . . . then I'll go after Ruth, and help her return to the main road. We might get lucky and catch Chief Eagan as he arrives. He *will* arrive, don't you think?"

"I know he will. He might not get all the way to Chapelwood proper, but if you and Ruth can meet him at the edge of the road, he'll be happy enough. And your plan is solid, madam. I'll go below and see what lurks in this 'Holiest of Holies,' if ever there were a worse sacrilege. Here, take the lantern."

I almost argued with him. I almost wanted to see it for myself—whatever it was—and I was almost jealous of him, but that's nonsense, isn't it? He was better suited to that task, for he had more experience than I did. I only had articles, ordered from libraries and read in the sunroom at Maplecroft. He had been in the field for thirty years or more, and we hadn't discussed it much, but I knew he'd seen terrible, strange, even horrible things in his time behind the badge.

Instead I said, "But you have no light!"

"Neither do they. Or rather . . . *they* do, I think. Can't you see it—down there, a little glow?"

Hardly, but maybe. I squinted down the stairs and he might have been right; there might have been a faint gray lurking somewhere near the bottom, rather than the wholesale black that blanketed everything else.

"Simon . . ."

"No." He shook his head. "Don't worry about me. Give me a few of those matches, in case of absolute emergency—and we must wish each other well, and part ways for now. Let me give you the car keys."

But I refused them. "I don't know how to drive," I admitted. "They won't do me a bit of good—and if you hand them off, then you may deprive us all of a ride to freedom. I'll see if I can find Ruth, and I'll take her back to the car. We'll try to meet you there, but if we don't . . . if we can't find you . . . then . . . I suppose we'll head down the side road, and hope to meet Chief Eagan somewhere along the way. I won't leave you behind—you know that, yes?"

"And I won't leave you, either. That's a promise, Lizbeth. This great adventure of ours, it isn't over yet!"

He tried to sound chipper, but the smile that stretched across his round, kind face was forced—and I couldn't shake the feeling that this was a terrible good-bye. We had to deny it, and pretend otherwise. For the sake of our sanity, and our mission. For the sake of Ruth, who was on the run, in the dark, pursued by monsters.

Because weren't we all?

Impetuously, almost girlishly, I leaned forward and planted a large, heartfelt kiss upon his cheek. I had to stand on tiptoes to do it. I think he was surprised, but not displeased; after all, he hugged me tight, then let me go.

I gave him the matches. He gave me the lamp.

"I'll try to be quick, but stairs have never been my greatest joy. Wait for me at the car if you can. Run if you can't. Get Ruth to safety either way. I know you can, and I know you will. Now go," he urged.

Before I could change my mind, I turned on my heel—the lantern in my left hand, and the axe gripped firmly in my right. Without stopping to consider if I was alone, or likely to be confronted . . . without hesitating and second-guessing my directions, I dashed back the way we'd come. The sound of my heart banged between my ears. The sway of the light as I ran made the whole place dance some cruel tarantella, the walls bending and breaking and falling away, or rising up to stop me.

But I ran. And I did not stop, not even when I heard voices call out behind me.

Ruth Stephenson Gussman

❧

OCTOBER 4, 1921

The sky was a low, black, flat canopy like I'd seen it before—no moon, no stars, nothing to give me a friendly hint of light to let me know where I was going; so when I ran, I was running blind.

I used my hands and my feet, feeling my way around the building and trying not to make too much noise while I was at it. I dragged my fingertips along the brick—but the brick didn't last, and soon it was wood paneling again, so it must've been a chimney or something. I touched something slick and smooth like glass, and I guessed it was a window. I knocked my knuckles against the window frame when I reached the end, and I kept going.

The whole time, I struggled to remember anything at all about the way Chapelwood was put together, or how to get out of it. I recalled it was set up in kind of a half-moon shape, with the big church house in the middle, and some littler buildings on either side—but I didn't know where I was, and that made it even harder to tell where I was going.

I wished I was wearing more comfortable shoes, but at least they weren't the highest heels I owned. I wished I had some matches, or better yet, a lantern—but if I had one, I'd be easier to spot myself.

I was trying to look on the bright side. In case there was a bright side.

Every move I made sounded too loud, even my own breathing, and the banging of my heart around in my chest—I could hear it between every gasp for air, and every slap of my hands along whatever building I was following. I didn't have any other path to guide me, so this was it until I could find that stupid little road that ran into the compound. It couldn't have been more than two ruts leading off the two-lane strip of asphalt someone calls an automobile highway—and I think it must've been some kind of joke, because we probably didn't have enough cars in the whole county to make use of it.

But if I could make it to that highway, such as it was . . . there was a chance I might flag somebody down—somebody who wasn't part of Chapelwood, and wouldn't drag me back to whatever fate the reverend had in mind.

Getting to the main road wasn't much of a plan, considering I didn't even know what direction I was facing, but it gave me something to look for. If I could make it to the tree line, I could feel around, and hope to find a cleared spot where the cars and carts came through on the way to church—back when anyone was still pretending Chapelwood was a church, and not . . . not whatever it really is.

Over the sound of my own body making a ruckus, I heard

voices. They were coming from behind me, mostly, and off to my right. I thought about sitting down, curling up into a ball, and praying nobody would see me; but I had the awful suspicion that they could all see better than I could. I was only human, you know? These people out here, worshipping at the feet of the reverend . . . they were something else now. And if I stopped running, if I just held still and waited for them to catch up, I would just be making it easier for them.

Maybe they'd catch me anyway, and drag me back. But I wouldn't go easy, and I wouldn't go quiet. If they wanted me, I'd make them *fight* for me. So I took another step and ran out of the building's shadow.

My hands flew off into space, and my feet tripped over themselves, now that there was nothing handy to direct them. I turned back in a panic and grabbed the building's corner again, needing some kind of anchor to hold me down to earth. (Or that's how it felt, when I'd let go and lost touch with everything except the dirt under my feet. It felt like flying, and I didn't want to fly. Not at all, not especially in the dark so thick I might as well have had a bag over my head.)

I clung to that corner so hard my fingernails probably started to bleed, but I didn't care. Forward I went, in this new direction—and now the voices all were behind me, which was encouraging . . . but that other noise wasn't.

I don't know how to explain the other noise, except to say it was the sound of something growling or groaning, a long way away. It was almost like the tone you hear when you're trying to make a phone call, but choppier and thicker, and more alive.

Whatever it was, it was hungry. And sometimes, between those little bursts of humming, moaning, and throbbing, I would swear to God that I heard it call my name. Just a whisper, threading through the song, over and over again like it was part of the beat of a drum—lurking behind the notes.

Was it a song? I'm not sure. It might've been a song.

It was a *cry*, at any rate. And I wasn't getting away from it, because it was coming from everyplace at once. Where could I go if I wanted to escape it? I could have heard that cry at the bottom of the earth, or on the moon. It would've found me anywhere.

But that didn't mean I shouldn't run.

I kept up what I was doing, hugging the building I couldn't see, because it was something to feel, at least, and that was all I had—but the cry wouldn't leave me alone, and it drowned out everything else, even the way I panted from getting tired and being scared.

That's why I didn't hear it when someone came up and grabbed me.

It took me by the arm with a snarl and a hiss like a big cat would make, but it had hands like a person—and it probably *was* a person, once. Now its skin was so white I could actually see it in spite of the starless night. I couldn't see it real clear, but there was a pale oval for a face, and white spiders for fingers, gripping me hard and trying to throw me to the ground.

I kicked for all I was worth, and twisted my body to wrench free from the white thing's grip, and it worked—but it also threw me free from the wall, and then I was floating again, a balloon cut loose from the string. I scrambled away, backward, then on all fours, and then up on two feet because it was faster. And that thing was coming, and it was yelling at me. I heard the yelling despite the booming sound, louder than thunder, because the thing behind me wasn't alone.

I heard more of them—this time, I heard them before I saw

them, swooping around the building I'd used for shelter, coming from at least one other direction, too. They homed in on me, and all I could see were those bobbing white spots where their faces ought to be. Were they wearing robes? I remembered the sea of dark robes and gloves the times I'd been forced to visit before, but I couldn't tell—I was so confused, so turned around.

All I could do was dodge them, one at a time, and soon I wouldn't be able to do that anymore. They were herding me the way a dog herds sheep. They were chasing me back toward the main building, I could sense it—or I could fear it. That meant I needed to go the other way, but it was blocked by more bobbing, weaving shadows hissing like somebody'd done let the air out of them.

I shoved one in the face, and elbowed another in the belly. I wondered if I knew them. I wondered if I was hitting my mother, or my father—no, probably not him. I'd feel more satisfaction than terror if I'd cracked him in the nose. Even if I couldn't see his face and didn't know for certain who it was—my gut would tell me.

I spun around, waiting for the next one, trying to stay light on my feet and keep moving so they couldn't grab me; I squinted into the bleak, flat nothing and, lo and behold, I saw the trees. Just outlines, barely sketches . . . like chalk marks that hadn't been erased all the way. But they got brighter as I watched, and I wondered what I was seeing.

Then I realized there was light coming up behind me.

I turned to look and saw a ball of glowing yellow headed my way. At first I thought it was a ghost—something like Father Coyle. But then I thought it might be something bad—like Reverend Davis. Then I realized I was wrong both ways, because it was a woman holding a lantern.

And something else.

It was Miss Andrew. I mean, Lizbeth. I was so surprised I stopped moving, and that meant something grabbed me right away. I went to shake it off, but this one held on tight and I couldn't wriggle loose. The thing got its hand all tangled up in my hair and it hurt like hell, so I started screaming. Why not? They already knew where I was, didn't they? There was no more sense in playing quiet and waiting to get killed.

Round and round I went, so I only saw Lizbeth in flashes. She dropped the lantern she was carrying and then two-fisted whatever she'd been holding in the other hand—and that's when I saw it better: She was holding an axe.

Weird. Where would she get an axe? And why would she know how to use it like that? These were the thoughts going through my mind—in between screaming and wondering how I was going to get loose of this creature that had such a hold on me.

Another thing took me by the foot and swept me off my feet.

I dropped to the ground on my back, knocking the wind out of me—but the pain on my head kept me from giving up yet. I kicked like a madwoman, and my hair started to rip, tear, and break. It stung like crazy, but I kept on struggling because I only had to hold them off another minute or two. Lizbeth was coming. Sure, she was old enough to be my momma (even my grandma, I think), but she was coming—armed with an axe, no less—and I felt good about that. It was the first hint of hope I'd had all day, and I held on to it as firmly as I'd held on to the building while I ran in the dark.

Lizbeth moved a whole lot faster than anyone expected. She swung that axe harder than any lumberjack I ever heard of, and she caught one of the shadowed figures square in the chest. I gasped in surprise—that was murder, right there. Wasn't it? No, never mind—I don't think so, because, like I said, they weren't human anymore, no how. You can't murder something that's not a person.

Another one ran up close to her—not even slowing down, just flinging itself at her, to knock her flat, I guess—but she wasn't having it. She clocked it upside the head with the dull end of the axe head as she swung it back around from clipping another one.

The axe snared on a piece of fabric, one of those robes (if they were robes, and yes, I think they were). She yanked it free in time to catch a man's face, right up under the chin. It shocked me to see such violence, but I don't know why. I'd seen enough in my time, blood from myself and other people, broken noses and broken bones; and I didn't know exactly what the Chapelwood men and women were capable of, but I wouldn't have put anything past them.

They were definitely trying to kill me, one way or another.

They were definitely trying to kill Lizbeth, one way or another.

Neither one of us was having it. I wrenched a leg free and used it to kick somebody hard in the jaw—I'm not even sure how I did it, but I felt the heel of my shoe hit against bone, and the grip on my other leg slipped. I got my feet up underneath me, and even though it hurt—oh God, it hurt where the bastard had hold of my hair—I turned around and swung my leg up to where the fork of somebody's crotch ought to be. And that's how I found out they were still a little human, maybe. The creature grunted and let go—thank heaven I'd found the right off switch.

I was free for a second or two, but more creatures were coming—so I ran toward Lizbeth, and I think I was crying the whole time, just from plain old relief. She screamed at me, "Get down!" and I didn't question it at all, I just dropped like a stone as she came forward and swung that axe over my head. It hit something hard but wet, and one of those things called out in pain.

Lizbeth took my hand and ran back to the lantern, still sitting on the ground. I couldn't believe nothing had thought to take it and put it out, but these things were pretty single-minded, you might say. They had a goal, and that goal was me. Everything else was just part of the background.

"Where are we going?" I gasped. Until I gasped, I hadn't realized how tired I was. My scalp was pulsing under my hair, and my legs ached from being pulled or from kicking anything within reach, and the tips of my fingers were starting to ache where I'd squeezed the building so hard.

"First, to the car."

"There's a car?"

"Yes," she confirmed. "Just over there. Simon might be there—he's supposed to meet us, if he can."

"Where did he go?"

"Downstairs, without me. To the . . . Holiest of Holies—that's what the reverend called it."

My stomach twisted itself up into a ball and I almost stumbled, but caught myself at the last second. I was trying to keep up with Lizbeth, but she was so much faster than she looked. I tripped behind her, recovered, and tripped some more. I was doing more tripping than running.

She was right. There was a car—and I was so thrilled I could've thrown up right then and there.

Lizbeth stopped dragging me along behind her. She held the lantern up, looked around, and said the only swearword I ever heard her utter: "Well, god*damn*. Where is he?"

She looked at me, then back at Chapelwood. She looked at the courtyard, and saw it littered with lumps of black fabric with snow-white hands and faces, like piles of laundry. How many had she hit with that axe? How many of them were dead? How many were only hurt? I just couldn't make myself care, not even when I thought about the police, and a trial, and prison for either one of us. To hell with all that. None of that mattered now.

"We could hide, and wait for him."

"No. We made a deal."

"What kind of deal?"

She gave me a real hard stare, or maybe it only looked hard because of the shadows around her eyes and the pitch-dark night behind her. "A deal to get you safe, above all else. We're leaving, right now. You and I. He'll be along behind us, as soon as he's able. Don't worry about him. We don't have time."

I wrapped my arms around myself, feeling slightly deflated. "Do you know how to drive?"

"No, and Simon has the keys anyway. You and I are going to run for the main road."

"And then what?"

She didn't answer right away. She scanned the yard with the lantern, spotted the entry driveway, and shuttered the lantern until we were almost in that perfect dark again. "We have to go now. More are coming—do you hear them?"

"Over that other noise?" My teeth were chattering, and I hated it. "I can't hardly hear a thing, except for you."

I barely saw it, but she frowned at me like I wasn't making any sense. "I don't hear it anymore," she confessed. "Not at all."

I chose not to think too hard about that. I *deliberately* didn't think about it all the way to the edge of the woods, where we found the naked patch that ran between the trees, and we started stumbling down it like our lives depended on it—because, well, they surely did.

"More are coming, yes. *I* can hear them, even if you can't. We just have to outrun them for a little while—we just have to make it to the road—" She wheezed as she said it, and I got the very bad feeling she was trying to convince us both.

"Why? What's waiting at the road?"

"Chief Eagan will be, along with the last decent men in Birmingham," she whispered.

It gave me hope to hear it, even if I didn't know I could believe it.

The lantern swung back and forth in her hand, and the whole forest bent around it, leaning over us, backing away from us, and not helping us one damn bit.

Behind us, a car was coming. We saw its lights bouncing up and down as the tires went over the holes and ruts, and neither of us knew if we should flag it down or run away—it might be the inspector, or someone from Chapelwood sent to catch us.

Lizbeth handed me her axe. "Take this!" she said as she shielded the lantern with her body, then shuttered it completely and took me by the hand to drag me off the beaten path.

I couldn't see where I was going again, and I hated how familiar that feeling had become, but at least I wasn't by myself. I let her draw me back a few feet, into the trees, and then down into a crouch as the car approached. She was wearing a dark dress, but mine was light enough I was afraid I might be spotted—so she pushed me behind her, and traded me the axe for her lantern again.

The car rumbled slowly toward us, and when it was almost even with our hiding spot, it pulled up to a stop. Even in the dark, with just the car's lights pushing forward, and everything else backlit into blackness . . . I could see that it wasn't the inspector's car from the clearing. This was a truck instead, with a short, flat bed behind it. I saw movement in that bed, and spotted three or four of the robed and hooded monsters.

The driver had his hood down, and enough light made it through the truck's windscreen for me to see that it was Nathaniel Barrett. He parked the truck but left it running. His door opened with a low groan and then a squeak as it bounced back onto its hinges, and he stepped out onto the running board. He leaned on that door and it complained a little more. He gazed out at the woods, as far as the lights would show him.

I didn't think he'd see us. I thought we were low enough to the ground and hidden well enough that he'd think we'd gotten away. But I've been wrong before, and I'll be wrong again before my last breath . . .

"Come out, come out . . . wherever you are," he shouted. Little did he know we were right in his line of sight.

One by one, the things in the back of the truck spilled over the sides—they oozed, toppled, and landed on the ground on all fours, some of them. I'd been wrong about how many there were—I wouldn't have thought so many would fit.

Lizbeth had that hard stare again, aimed at Barrett at first, but then she turned it on me. "I told you, Simon and I made a promise. We had a plan."

I whispered back, "What do we do? Do you think Mr. Wolf is coming?"

"Not soon enough." She stood up. I tugged at her dress, but she shrugged me off with a twitch of her hip. She adjusted her hold on the axe, and said, real quiet, "When I engage him, you take the light and make for the road. Whatever happens, don't stop. Keep running, and pray to anyone you think is listening." She took a deep breath. "I'll hold them off until Simon gets here."

"But—"

She didn't give me a chance to argue. Before I could say anything, she stepped out into the truck's light, square in the center of the road, without so much as a glance back in my direction.

All I knew was, there was a plan—and I needed to run.

But I froze up. I was afraid to make a sound. The creatures were milling around the truck—either they couldn't see me, or they were waiting to see what happened with the little old lady wielding an axe.

Once they were talking, I crept away—far smarter than running. I held the lantern up close to my breasts, and it was so hot it almost burned me through my dress. I tiptoed between the trees even farther back, farther away, just a few feet at a time.

I pointed myself in the direction of the road, and told myself I'd make a straight line.

"Give us the girl," I heard Barrett say to Lizbeth.

"It's too late. She's gone already."

"You wouldn't leave her. Not when you've gone to all this trouble."

"You're right—I wouldn't. I told her to leave me. I'm old and slow, and she's young and quick. She's better off running without me."

"She's lying," he said over his shoulder. "Search the trees, and bring her to me."

"You're wasting your time, and theirs." She was cooler than an electric fan, not flinching or sounding desperate at all. She was so calm, so certain, that the robed things hesitated—waiting to see if their boss believed her or not.

"And tell me, madam: Why have you wasted yours? This has never been any business of yours. Why come to Birmingham? Why come to Chapelwood? The numbers tell us you're more than you appear, but how much more?"

"My business is my own, and if your numbers know so much, they can fill you in later. If you survive this meeting."

He laughed at her, but she didn't care. "Are you a spiritualist? A medium, like Ruth? Has some corpse summoned you to Alabama?"

"You're just full of questions, aren't you?"

"And you've answered me with one more. *Disciples . . .* ," he said with a wave of his hand, giving them some sort of directions I didn't understand, but definitely didn't like. They stopped milling around and drifted away from the truck, toward the tree line.

She saw them, and spoke a little too fast. "Then I'll tell you the truth. Or more of the truth, if you prefer."

"Always. I've never sought anything else."

"I'm not here for Chapelwood, or for Ruth Gussman," she told him. "Not for her father, either, or for the priest he murdered. I don't care about your cult, and I don't care about your God—I don't even care if He, or It, or whatever we're speaking of . . . I honestly don't care if you bring about the end of the world."

"Then, pray tell, what *did* bring you here?"

"A woman, missing for thirty years, and the prospect of answers, if not hope. I was looking for a resolution, even if that resolution was something abhorrent. I only wanted to *know.*"

"And do you? Did you find what you were looking for?"

She let out a shaky sigh, the first sign of weakness she'd offered up yet. "I've learned only that I've lost her to some in-between space, where the dead and the living both might linger. Whether I can ever reach her or not . . . there is no answer, and likely there will never be one. But I can live with that now," she added fast, since it looked like he was about to interrupt her with another question. "Because I couldn't save her, my Nance. In the end, I failed her. *I'm* the reason she's gone, or changed, or vanished—whatever eventually became of her, she's beyond help now, and that's on my head. All I can do to redeem myself, to make Nance's loss mean something . . . is save Ruth."

"Who is this Nance?"

"The gray lady," she said. "I believe you know of her."

He shook his head. "I believe I don't. But you present this as if it were a trade of some kind—like you wish to trade one life for another?"

Her eyes narrowed. Maybe it was only the light of the truck bearing down on her, or maybe she was as steely and angry as she looked. "You say you don't know her?"

"I assure you, I have no idea who you're talking about."

She struggled with this for a moment. Then: "It doesn't matter now. She's gone—and yes, I'll trade all of our lives for Ruth's. Mine, yours, theirs. None of it's a fair trade, but it's all I've got to offer."

Whether he believed her or not, he'd gotten his reply. He stepped down off the truck's running board, and then climbed right onto the hood and stood up straight. The engine wiggled beneath his feet, making it look like he was shaking really softly. Holding still but not holding still. Human but not human.

More human than the rest of them, though.

I knew it for sure when something off to Lizbeth's left snarled, then leaped.

It moved like a dog under a blanket, low to the ground and billowing—its robe and hood dangling low and moving in swift waves. It went for her at thigh level—but that was a bad choice. Lizbeth swung without hardly looking at the thing, and caught it up against the head, hard enough to send it falling away—and fast enough to raise the axe again when the next one swooped into the light to take its chances.

I couldn't look away as Lizbeth knocked them back one at a time, then two together—and another one from behind her, caught nearly by accident on the backswing as she brought the axe around again for another pass.

And when the last one (I dearly hoped it was the last one) went down in a pile at her feet, Nathaniel Barrett growled, crouched, and leaped off the hood of that truck . . . I couldn't watch it. Not anymore.

I turned and ran, just like she'd told me. I made a lot of noise, but I was fast. Once I found the road again, I stayed at its edge, ready to dive back into the trees, thinking about that straight line I'd drawn with my brain. I held it in my head, and concentrated as I continued running.

My ankle went a little weak when I hit a hole, and I thought it was going to twist up in pain, but it went cold instead. I tried to keep running, but the cold got a grip on the other foot, too.

I was scared as hell—here I was, having a spell right in the middle of running for my life.

Except this time, the spell didn't hit me all the way. It tangled around my feet, but it didn't rise; it might be better to say that it kept me from falling again. I had to pay attention to my footfalls, and where the road was pitted, gouged, and uneven.

And in the back of my head, the spell spoke in Father Coyle's voice. I didn't see him, but I heard that old familiar whisper filtered through a million miles, on the other side of heaven.

Veer to the right. Go around this tree, don't worry. Stay calm. Only a little farther.

"Easy for you to say," I grumbled at him.

But he continued. *The chief is almost here, and you'll meet him almost at the crossroad, but not quite. Here, look. Here's the highway.*

I drew up to a sudden, none too graceful halt at the edge of a road paved properly. "To the . . . to the right? Are you sure?"

He didn't answer. The cold melted away from my ankles, and when it did, I almost folded up like a chair. I hadn't realized how it'd been holding me up; I only thought it'd slowed me down. My ankle hurt like the devil now, and I guessed I'd sprained it after all, but the father had kept it from bothering me so I could get away.

I started to cry, just a little. I missed him. Without him, I sometimes forgot it. Without him, would I have ever made it back to the road?

Behind me, something roared so loudly it drowned out everything else—and that's when I realized I hadn't heard the weird rumbling noise since Father Coyle started talking. But here it was again, and a thousand times louder. It wasn't alone, either. It came with a rocking shake, an earthquake—I knew that's what it was, even though I'd never been in one myself.

(I'd heard plenty about them from a teacher I'd had once, who'd come from San Francisco. She'd told me that the earth pops up and down, snapping like a sheet flapped across a bed. She said you could watch it, if you were standing in the right place; you could see the ground and the trees rising and falling in waves.)

I wasn't standing in the right place. All I could see was the line of trees behind me, and a ghostly faint glow in the middle where Barrett's truck must be. As I watched, even that glow went away. It winked, shook, and dropped away—and I thought that the headlamps went shooting up to the sky, like the cab had been pushed onto its rear end. But that would have been crazy, right?

Off to my right, just like Father Coyle had told me, there were cars coming. I heard a siren, or a thin thread of one, cutting through the roar that came from Chapelwood, loud like a mountain falling down. I saw the light, and if it wasn't Chief Eagan, I was a dead woman.

But if I tried to go back, I was a dead woman, too. Maybe the inspector was dead, but I couldn't think about that. Maybe Lizbeth was dead, but I couldn't think about that, either. I'd think about it all later, maybe while lying in bed in the weeks that came after, trying to sleep, and wondering where George Ward had gone, what the inspector had seen, what had become of all the people who'd just vanished but didn't die. I'd wonder who Nance was, and why she'd mattered to Lizbeth.

I'd wonder, and wonder, and wonder.

But right then, with the cars coming down the highway, I only wondered if the stars would ever come back.

I missed them.

Inspector Simon Wolf

❧

OCTOBER 4, 1921

I descended the stairs by feel, for although there was a distinct
white glow somewhere at (what I presumed must be) the bottom, it wasn't enough to do my eyes much good. Did I say the
glow was white? Well, to be honest I'm not so sure. It had a white
quality with a yellow undertone; it was white like the sun is
white, though when depicted in art it's often shown in shades of
gold. I'm talking my way around what I mean, but since I can't
pinpoint my precise meaning, this will have to do.

You've asked for a report, so I will give you one. And you
will take what you can get.

That said, I move more smoothly in the dark than people typically expect. It's no secret—I've mentioned it before—that my
eyes are very weak, without the aid of lenses; and it's somewhat less
well known that I had no access to such lenses until I was an adult.

(I don't often speak of my upbringing, but it was not the sort that allowed for recreational visits to an ophthalmologist, I assure you. It was the kind of upbringing where meals were often uncertain, and maybe I have spent the rest of my life in compensation for that early inadequacy. I'm sure some alienist or psychiatrist would have a grand old time deciding it, but I don't care, so I've never asked one's opinion.)

To sum up, I spent a very long time regarding the world without much detail and with no precision at all. To navigate a set of stairs without the aid of my eyes . . . it's not comfortable, but it's familiar. It's something I can do by rote, putting my feet down one after the other, lowering myself toward that glow that did very little except provide that pale absence of color, somewhere far away.

I hoped it wasn't too far. I suspected I would have to climb those stairs again, in order to make an eventual escape. The fewer of them, the better.

In fact, it might have been three or four flights of stairs—I hadn't been counting them, so this is only a lazy estimate. Or not lazy, that's the wrong word. I was hiking them, wasn't I? There was nothing lazy about it. I don't know what's wrong with me, that I'm having such trouble with my vocabulary, when it comes to that night. To that staircase. To that room I found at the bottom.

A *room* . . . well, I can't think of another word for it, so that will have to suffice. It was much larger than any room you can imagine, though. Infinitely larger than anything that ought to have fit underneath Chapelwood, or the entirety of Alabama, for that matter.

Or rather . . . it wasn't infinite in actual size, but it certainly conveyed a *sense* of the infinite. I knew, upon reaching the bottommost stair, that I was quite some distance underground—

thirty or forty feet, at least—but I felt that I was somewhere else entirely.

It might have been the sky's fault, by which I'm trying to say . . . there had been no stars that night, and none the night before, either (now that I consider it). The sky above had been nothing but a thick black curtain covering any source of light that might have reached us from space.

So when I stepped off that bottommost stair, into this chamber ("chamber" is probably a better word), and I looked up to the ceiling . . . I did not see a ceiling. I saw the black expanse of space above me, space without moon or stars. They were all someplace else. They were all gathered together behind the altar.

Wait. Let me explain the altar. Or let me explain the room first.

The room was quite large, as I've said. Wherever the ceiling was, it was high enough overhead that I couldn't dream of touching it; and the floor, smooth as marble—it might have even been marble, black marble as stark as onyx—was marked with designs drawn in salt. These designs were concentric circles, but they were not evenly spaced. It took me a moment to realize that I was looking at the solar system. Each of these rings represented the orbit of a neighboring celestial body, and each of these planets was marked with a tidy little cairn that was lit and burning with incense. I smelled sage and sandalwood, and something sharper (but I couldn't decide what it was). The raw, wet, rotting smell upstairs was wholly absent here, for this place had been purified. The herbs alone wouldn't have done it, but something did.

It was clean, do you understand? Purified. *Holy.* The holiest, if the reverend's assessment could be believed. (And *he* believed it.) The claptrap, altered, added-on-to mansion upstairs was not a church. *This* was a church.

The salt lines swooped across the floors in their lovely arches, untouched by footprints or scuffs, scrapes, or other disturbances. Their sweet-smelling, improvised planets did not line up, so much as they provided a series of stops on the way to the altar at the middle—where the sun ought to be, but a vast white stone sepulcher awaited instead. It was round, yes. Spherical, even— except that the top was flattened, cut off so cleanly it might have been sliced with a razor.

I wanted to stare at it, but I was nearly blinded by the thing after traveling through so much darkness to arrive there. So instead I shifted my gaze along those planets, those cairns that stood for them . . . and I realized that they must be stations. Like the stations of the cross, in any good Catholic establishment. That's *precisely* the purpose they served. They were a map to salvation.

I wondered where the light was coming from. The chamber was illuminated, yes, but the sheer unsullied whiteness of that altar could not have been its source. Or could it? On second (or third, or however many) thought, I can't rule out anything as impossible.

Not after what I saw there. Not after what came next.

I walked those stations, tiny altar to tiny altar, on the way to the great one at the center. I was careful to keep from touching the salt; it felt like sacrilege to consider it, but the toe of my shoe found it tempting, at times, and I was tracking dirt across the pristine place anyway. I told myself that this might be the place where all the dirty things came to be cleaned—literally and symbolically both. But I've told myself a lot of things over the years, and that one makes as little sense as any of them.

So I walked the stations.

At the edge, I passed what stood for Neptune, and past it a

few yards I touched the edge of Uranus and felt the simmering coals; I paid my respects to Saturn, breathing the ashes of its rings; I visited the great giant Jupiter, where I smelled amber and myrrh; I stopped by Mars and smelled only fire, only the chemical warp of sand melting to glass; and then our own home, with a whiff of ocean air and fresh dirt.

I was very close then. Yet still I could hardly bring myself to look up and see the altar, the great Sol at the middle, where all roads led—or all lines encircled. You see? It's awful, how insufficient this vocabulary is. It's embarrassing, how I found myself dazed and moving closer, closer, to something that could not possibly be good.

Here was Venus, cool and smelling of morning mist when the air is nearly frozen. Even though the incense smoldered, when I hovered my hands close to its edge, I felt only a chill.

There was a noise. There had always been a noise, hadn't there? I remembered it from upstairs, from inside the false church and underneath it. I think I'd grown so accustomed to it that I simply hadn't heard it anymore. Unless . . . could the chamber have cleaned the noise away, too? No, that couldn't be right. The smell was gone, the dirt and mildew of the dug-out places were gone, but the sound . . . the sound remained.

There, closer to the center, it was less like a garbled noise. I almost thought it might be a song, but it was no music I'd ever heard; and I cannot say that it was lovely, or grating, or anything an ordinary mortal might use to describe a set of notes. But it was compelling. So compelling, it might have been what drew me forward to that altar, or maybe it was the light that, yes, came from that weird white stone after all.

The vivid white glow emanated from the top, from the flat portion. It projected upward but not very far. It made me think of a lantern behind a sheet of waxed paper, diffuse and present, but not far-reaching.

Mercury. Small and red were the coals, smelling of char and hickory. The cairn was so warm that I couldn't bear to stand beside it long, even to gaze down at the patterns made by the tumbling ashes, rolling over one another as if stirred by a poker.

Only a few feet more. Then three steps, each one's corner sharp as an axe head.

The altar was almost the size of the automobile I'd arrived in. It was white, so very white. So pure that, if it was marble, I've never seen its equal—devoid of flecks, veins, or any speck of color. I don't think it was marble. I don't know what it was, but I do not believe it was of this world, and I will stand by that statement regardless of how it sounds.

I wanted to touch it, and I wanted to run away from it screaming.

I did neither of those things. I stood beside it, and I gazed down into it—for the top was not flat, per se. It was no shelf, no platform. It was a window to something else, and in it, I saw my own reflection. And someone else.

My head jerked up. I was eye to eye with Reverend Davis, robed as black as the floor and ceiling and walls, wherever those walls might actually be hiding. His hands were covered in gloves, but the gloves were too long, or else his fingers were too long—he'd been changed, too, just like everyone else. Not in the same way, I don't suppose. The high priest never dresses like the mere supplicants, after all.

He did not move. He only stood there across from me, this window to another world between us, and the groaning music of some vast machine or entity or instrument filling the air with the incense, the smoke, the simmering hiss of settling coals in the planetary offering places behind me.

"What do you see?" he asked me.

"A madman," I said.

"What else?"

At least he had the decency not to argue with me. "I don't know."

"At least you have the decency not to lie."

"Are you reading my thoughts?" I asked quickly. I know how to tamp them down if I need to; I've spent so long in an office with psychics that it long ago became a necessary skill.

He shook his head. "No. But *He* is. And He tells me what he sees."

"Rather roundabout way of doing things."

"This is no place for mockery." He frowned at me, and I didn't really blame him. But self-restraint has never been my chiefest virtue, now has it?

"And it's no place for a young woman who'd rather be elsewhere."

"This is *exactly* where she ought to be. It's where she will be, sometime before dawn. It's been written in the stars, or in the ledgers that describe them."

I thought of Lizbeth above, and Ruth—who'd already escaped them once tonight. I fervently wished them the best, and I didn't care if this mysterious "He" knew about it. I didn't know where they were. There was nothing It could glean from my optimism.

"We must agree to disagree."

"I'd rather that we come to some kind of . . . understanding."

I wanted to laugh in his face, but I couldn't. I'm not sure why. "I doubt that's possible."

He paused. "No, you don't. You're deathly afraid that it *is*. Look," he urged, gesturing at the perfectly round window in the perfectly spherical altar. "Let me show you what I mean."

I wanted to look away. Or did I? Well, I *couldn't* look away.

I'm sorry. I wish I'd been stronger. (Or do I?)

On the other side of the window I saw the whole universe, and that's the goddamn truth. I saw all the stars that had gone missing over the last couple of nights; and I saw the arms of galaxies undulate like tentacles, like an octopus spinning in a slow, amazing circle. I saw spirals made of light—no, made of stars. Made of suns. I saw the hints and blinking flashes of other spirals, other clusters, other tentacles dancing across the void, which was never a void at all.

I could lie to you, in this report. If I wanted to, I could say that it was all a mirage caused by the mesmerizing powers of that reverend with his slick black hair, his slick black hands (I don't even know if they were gloves at all), his slick black robe that must have been made of silk.

But that wouldn't be true. It wouldn't be true to say that it was only a clever magician's ruse, and that the noise that filled the chamber did not come from something enormous on the other side. I could say that there was no great He, nothing to read minds and speak in numbers. Nothing that waited for an invitation to come through that window and join our world.

Lies, all of it.

Theoretical lies, since I never offered them up as anything else, and since I'm giving you the whole story here, now, and I don't care how it makes me look. Does it make me look mad? Is that what you'll tell me? Save your breath, for I know that already. If you think I've gone around some bend, then you could be forgiven. All I can do is assure you of the contrary.

I didn't know what I was seeing, when it swung into view. I

saw it only in passing as it floated, bobbed, wandered. I sensed that it was more asleep than awake—that the reverend had stumbled upon something with worse than infinite power, and he thought that it was interested in him, in his little human thoughts in his little human church.

But what I saw had no interest in mankind, not in the slightest. What I saw was a slumbering organism of absolute inscrutability and apathy, and if it had some passing fancy to visit Earth, none of us would live long enough to regret the visit.

I saw something that could hold a fistful of galaxies and swallow them, like a man would take an aspirin. It had no shape except every shape; it was too large to describe, and again, my vocabulary fails me anyway.

I was Moses, glimpsing the backside of God for an instant and going blind. And if this astonishing entity can be called Our Father, we are all a terrible accident of stardust and electricity, and there is no meaning for any of us. We may as well let Him swallow us, too, for all that it would matter.

I'd forgotten the reverend was there, until he said, "The portal only goes one way. We can send Him gifts and prayers, but He cannot join us here. Ruth will change that. She will be the door through which He enters, tonight—before the last rumble of His heartbeat fades away."

"That . . . this noise . . . ? It's the beating of that thing's heart?"

"No," he corrected me gently. "It is a single beat, offered once every thousand years. It is His knock upon the door."

A scrap of scripture sprang unwelcome to mind, and I whispered it without meaning to. "Behold, I stand at the door and knock."

He finished it for me. "'If any man hear my voice, and open

that door, I will come in to him, and will sup with him—and he with me.' From Revelations, of course. The last book ever written that ever meant a thing. And tonight is the last night. They will find Ruth, and they will bring her to me. She will serve as the door, and a new world order will begin."

"No."

"You might as well argue with the dawn. You might as well fight against math."

"No," I said again.

A thought bubbled up and I pushed it down; I used all my experience working down the hall from Drake, who reads minds by accident or design, and I shrouded the thought—I buried it with other thoughts, smothering it with my senses. I concentrated on the smell of the curling smoke rising up around us. I concentrated on the salt, and the cold feel of the floor beneath my feet (so cold I could feel it through my shoes). Could I thwart a god? It depended on whether the god was paying attention, and I truly did not think that it was.

"No," I repeated for a third time. "None of that can happen."

"There's nothing you can do to prevent it."

"You're wrong. About everything," I told him. I gazed down through that window, at the wonders of the universe that I surely would never see again, and I concentrated on that, too. Anything to hide what I was really thinking.

Because I was really thinking of grabbing the reverend by the lapels (or whatever bit of robe was there about his throat) and drawing him forward—yanking him off his feet, and throwing him through that one-way portal. I didn't think it, not with the forefront of my brain. I only acted upon it.

It happened fast. We were both surprised.

It happened easy, because I am so heavy and he was a lean

man. I used my weight against him, and I hefted him up off his feet, and I flung him through the window—nearly toppling in after him.

He said nothing. He screamed nothing. And he did not appear on the other side like I might have expected; he only vanished, a tiny dot of nothing that did not rouse his slumbering god in the slightest.

But I . . . I took a moment to regain my balance.

In that moment I was half tempted, against all reason, to let go and fall in after him. Would it have been the worst of endings? To see, in that final glimpse, the wonders of creation, or evolution, or random nonsense that became the glorious cosmos with my own two eyes?

I leaned back and gripped the edges of the lovely white altar. It grew colder beneath my hands. So cold that when I removed them I left some skin behind. Then I was frightened, because the light was dimming. The room was dimming. The little cairns with their scented offerings were dimming, the coals going pink, then white, then gray.

The great chamber shifted beneath me, and I stumbled.

I fell backward down those three stairs and landed on my (now very sore) hands, but I rolled and righted myself—back onto my feet. I'd done something. I didn't quite know what, but I was pretty sure I'd sent the reverend well away from Ruth.

The floor shifted. The salt lines scattered.

A loud crack sounded overhead, and there were the stars. Just like that. The black, smooth nothingness above me was a proper night sky lit up like it damn well ought to be. But that wasn't possible, because I was four stories belowground (at least) and it didn't matter how lifelike the moon and stars appeared, because they couldn't be real. They didn't make sense.

The altar was dimming down to nothingness. In another minute, it'd be as dark as the cold ashes where the planets used to be. The moon and stars (real or false) were the only light I had to show me the way up and out, and even with their help I could barely find my way back to the stairs.

Another loud crack, and the altar went dark.

A third, and the floor heaved violently—flinging me forward onto the stairwell, thank God (whichever one). Again I landed on my hands, which now bled and (I would later learn) one had been broken in two places, but I used them to scramble up the stairs, regardless. The chamber was settling, twisting, and collapsing—and I did not know what became of the moon and stars. Were they ever there with me at all, or was it only some helpful gasp of some lesser deity out to lend a hand?

I climbed for all I was worth, fast as I could, leaning against the wall and holding my injured hand as I stumbled upward. The nearer I got to the top, the louder I heard voices—angry ones, confused ones—swearing and yelling back and forth to one another over the sound of a place collapsing, or a god deciding it was time to move on to other things.

I wanted to yell, too. My left hand was aching and beginning to swell. But my right one was undamaged enough to hold a gun, so I had to quit pitying myself and arm myself instead. I drew the weapon for the last few steps of the flight, though I was panting so hard I couldn't hold it steady enough to fire.

No one noticed at first. No one (or no *thing*) in the smooth dark robes turned to look at the gasping fat man with a gun, and that was all right with me. I pushed myself onward, past the ones who paid me no mind as they debated loudly what was going on. Their arguments sounded as weird as everything else—like they weren't speaking English, or Latin, or any other language known to man. They conversed in hisses and whines, like animals. (Not like angels at all.)

I tried to follow my mental map of how I'd gotten there in the first place, and reverse engineer it back to the surface; it was trickier than it should have been, for now things were not quiet and dark, but loud and dark—and crowded, too. Where did they all come from? How many were there? I couldn't tell, for they were all dressed alike and all had powder-pale faces that were hard to distinguish one from the next, and there was light now—a little, here and there. Someone had a lantern, and someone had some matches, and all the fun of running about in the dark was well and truly over. For me, and for all of them, indistinguishable in the half-light and chaos.

Until I saw *him*.

He was swooping toward me, not recognizing me (I don't think), but running with fury toward the Holiest of Holies, which was no doubt collapsed upon itself by then—if the rocking, thundering, grumbling cacophony could be believed. But then he saw me, and he drew up short. He tried to draw up short, anyway. The motion of the ground flung us both around, and neither one of us was steady at all.

He reached into his robe. Was he going for a firearm? I believed so at the time. He'd already murdered my friend James Coyle, and he'd been prepared to sacrifice his own daughter to the machinations of this church that was never a church.

Would he have killed me? Yes, given half a chance. So it was self-defense, you see, and a matter of timing, that's all. I was holding my gun already. He had to fish his free from the drapes of something ceremonial and impractical.

I did not honestly expect to hit him. I was on the verge of doubling over from exhaustion, and the pain in my left hand was plenty distracting, too. Even if the floors weren't shaking and the walls weren't leaning inward, the odds of me making that shot couldn't have been good.

Would it be preposterous to suggest that I had help?

I might have had help. Before I pulled the trigger there was a chill around my ankles that crept up my side and up to my wrist and fingers. It happened in less than a second, but it steadied me. It was as if some other hand was holding on to mine, and giving it the stability I required to shoot Edwin Stephenson square in the face.

Because that's what happened.

I don't really have to put this here. It's tantamount to a murder confession, and an unnecessary one at that—since they never recovered much in the way of corpses from Chapelwood, least of all *his*. I suppose I'm including it because I want this to be a complete accounting of what occurred, even if I am not cast in an entirely positive light. If anything, should this account become public, perhaps the reader will only assume I've gone mad. Or, in a more just world, this fictional reader will correctly judge that Edwin Stephenson had it coming, and I was simply the method by which it arrived.

Regardless.

It's done. He's dead. His face exploded and I was stunned, but not for long enough to second-guess myself.

I ran.

I kept running.

And when I reached fresh air again, there at ground level, I ran back to the car. It was still there, as I suspected it would be. Lizbeth wasn't there, and neither was Ruth—but I didn't expect them to be. I wished with all my heart that they were well away from that place by then, and that they'd met Chief Eagan at the road, as planned.

The earth rolled and wobbled . . . and sank. A foot or two at a time, then a yard, then a great collapse that began at the center. I scarcely had time to start the car and put it into gear, and even with all my haste—never mind my broken hand—I escaped that place with one tire at the edge of the abyss as it blossomed beneath the earth, swallowing everything behind me, an acre at a time until I finally ran out of running room.

In the middle of that stupid dirt path which passed for a road, someone had abandoned a truck. There was no way around it. There was no one in it, though when I exited my own vehicle and took a quick look, I saw blood on the hood of the thing—and I tried not to consider the implications. (I would later learn from Ruth that this was Nathaniel Barrett's truck, and that she'd last seen Lizbeth there.)

The world was still falling away behind me, after all. The back half of my car was sinking, the front end rising up like a ship about to slide underwater after a long and terrible sinking.

I had no time to consider the implications.

I only had time to trade one set of wheels for another, and praise be—the keys were still in the truck's ignition. For that matter, the thing was still running, so whoever had abandoned it had done so in great haste.

It was my turn for great haste.

The tires spun behind me, peppering the nearby trees with dirt and rocks, but those trees were disappearing anyway, falling over and falling down and falling away, like everything else.

I made it to the road, and found Chief Eagan with Pedro Gussman. Most of the rescue party had left the road already, heading back to town to escape whatever unnatural disaster was taking place at Chapelwood—now that Ruth had been found. She was wrapped in a blanket staring at the trees when I emerged in my borrowed truck, and for a moment her eyes lit up. Then they went dark again.

She and Pedro and the chief were the last ones remaining. They'd stayed despite the quake, the thunder, the violence from the shattering, sinking earth, hoping that Lizbeth would emerge from Chapelwood.

But she never did.

Gaspera Lorino

ST. VINCENT'S HOSPITAL

DECEMBER 25, 1921

(LETTER ADDRESSED TO SIMON WOLF, BOSTON)

On Christmas Eve, my sister brought me new stockings and a cap she knitted, and a gingerbread loaf she baked in our mother's old oven. She sat with me for an hour and took some tea, and she listened patiently while I tried to explain things she would never understand—things I should never attempt to burden her with. It's unfair of me, but I feel like these secrets, these numbers, these mysteries . . . they overflow, and they spill out whether I want them to or not.

I wish poor Leonard had not left me. I wish you would come back. I attempted to write you a letter once before, but the gray lady said that Camille never sent it. She burned it in the oven, where she baked the gingerbread loaf.

I wish I had someone to listen and learn when I tell the truth. So I am trying this again, and I will slip this missive to the orderly, George, for he has always been kind to me. Maybe you will read this. I hope you read this. I hope you write me back, or better yet, return.

In this place, I am going as mad as they think.

The great heart has sounded its beat, and is silent again for another span of lifetimes. The balance is restored, and the pattern is repaired, for now. That uncertain in-between place, that muddled place where the monsters come from, and where the monsters return to—but so do the angels and heroes who tiptoe too close to its edges—that place has never been nearer, or more dangerous.

The gray lady was one of its monsters. Lizbeth Andrew might have become another, but she was lucky—she was strong, and she flew close to that sun but not so close that her wings ever failed her. She kept her balance. She only passed to the other side, where the ordinary dead may wander, yet linger close if they choose.

The two women are separated for infinity. It's not what either of them wanted, but it's what the pattern required.

You need to know, Mr. Wolf—you, too, have touched the middle distance. You spent enough time in the sixth room that you must surely smell of it, to those who know what that clinging miasmic scent must mean. Now you must cling to your sanity and your soul. You might be called upon again one day to put them on the line against some force of unbalance. You and the girl, Ruth. You're the only two who might answer such a call. For I am no longer able, and everyone else is dead, or otherwise gone.

Everyone.

Ruth Stephenson

❧

Pedro understood.

It was never really a love match anyway, though I felt fond enough toward him to live with him. We made a go of it, but it wasn't going anywhere, and we both knew it. Neither one of us was too broke up about it.

I sold my parents' house, and me and Pedro split the money. He said maybe he'd go back to Puerto Rico, but I don't know if he ever did. I said I was going to travel, but I didn't know where. He didn't ask any questions after that. We'd run out of things to talk about, anyway.

I'd lied a little bit, when I told him I didn't know where I'd visit. I knew good and well where I was going. I had a train ticket and everything, but I didn't mention it. From there on out, where I went and what I did was a secret. Nobody's business but my own.

That's what Inspector Wolf told me, when he answered the phone call I made from George Ward's house to that office in Boston. He said to come on out, and he'd meet me at the station. He was as good as his word.

He ran me through the office of their "Quiet Society," as they call it. He introduced me to a man named Drake, and told him that I was the most promising medium they'd brought on board since some lady whose name I didn't recognize or remember. I'm not sure how I feel about being called that. Consorting with spirits is supposed to be bad, and not just for Catholics, but for everyone else, too. Except the spiritualists. I've met a few of them now. They don't seem so bad, but I don't want to join them.

I hope you don't take it too personal, Father, but I'm not sure I want to be a Catholic anymore. I just don't know about God. If He's out there, I don't know if He cares what we do or how we do it. I don't know if it matters.

Inspector Wolf—he says to call him Simon, but I don't find it easy—says that there's a school of thought that says I should believe and practice the faith anyway. If I'm wrong, I've lived a righteous life, and that's the worst that comes of it. If I'm right, I get to go to heaven.

I don't think that's wrong, but I think it's sad.

I would like to see you again. That's one reason I keep wearing the cross, and the little Saint Jude medallion you left me. He's the patron saint of hopeless causes, that's what you told me. I don't think any cause ever got more hopeless than mine.

Simon says I'm too hard on myself.

I guess it's getting easier to call him Simon after all.

Anyway, he took me into his office for something he called "orientation," which just meant that he was telling me who everybody was, what everybody did, and what was expected of me—if I was going to work here. It was overwhelming, but exciting, too.

It's nice to be excited about something again. It's been a while since that happened.

His office is about as big as a bedroom, with bookshelves that go all the way to the ceiling; I bet he can't even reach the top ones without a step stool. All over his desk there are folders and photographs, charts and maps, and all kinds of things held together with paper clips and tape. He has a coffee cup full of pens and pencils, and when he opened his top drawer, it sounded like he had a flask in there and at least a couple of glasses. He didn't offer me anything, and I didn't ask.

"You'll have an office, too. Drake and Evans are having a spot cleared out as we speak."

"Did someone leave?"

"Someone died."

"Close enough," I said.

"I trust you don't mind inheriting a dead man's office . . . ?"

I smiled a little. "If I did, I'd be a shitty medium."

"That's true," he agreed. "But you've said it yourself, that you don't enjoy the work."

"I don't. But I'm doing it, whether I like it or not. You said there's people here who can help me learn to control it, or get used to it. I'd like that. It's awful hard on me when the ghosts come and go. The spells always took a lot out of me. Even Father Coyle's visits weren't always easy, and I loved him very much. All these dead strangers trying to push through the veil . . .

Jesus, they wear me out. I wish they didn't, and if there's any way to make talking to them easier, I want to hear all about it."

"And you will, I promise. Not from me, of course. I don't have that talent. My expertise lies mostly in my bullshit, but it's kept me alive this long."

He was trying to sound lighthearted, I think. He was trying too hard, and I knew why, but we had an understanding that we weren't going to talk about Lizbeth, or whether I'd spoken to her. I hadn't. If she was on the other side, she was leaving me alone. On the one hand, I appreciated it. On the other, I sure do wish I knew what happened to her.

In the end, she was just one more body that nobody ever found.

"Your bullshit is useful bullshit," I told him, trying to be lighthearted back. "You're good at what you do."

"Thank you, dear. One day, I'll retire from all this nonsense, and you can have my office instead of Allen West's broom closet. It's an old storage area they built out when the offices expanded back around 1910."

He drew up short, like he'd said something he shouldn't have. It was one more thing we hadn't talked about, but maybe now was the time. There wasn't much to say, so it wouldn't take long.

I gave him the opening he obviously wanted. "As long as it's not Storage Room Six, I'll be all right."

He cleared his throat and leaned back in his chair. It squeaked underneath him while he bounced slowly, thoughtfully. He opened that drawer and pulled out the flask and glasses I knew were in there, and this time he offered me some. He didn't ask if I wanted any; he just poured a slug into each glass, and pushed one my way.

I took it, downed it like a lady, and said, "You can ask, if you want to."

"All right, since you're allowing it: Whatever happened to George Ward? Did you ever . . . find out?"

"Nobody ever found out. He never went home, and I never heard from him as a ghost, either. Since that's what you're really asking."

"No, no." He sipped his whiskey, and I thought about teasing him about it, but I didn't. "I want to know if he's alive or dead, if he's well or if he needs assistance. It's a frustrating thing, this gift of yours; not everyone who ever dies decides to call you up, so an absence of evidence is merely . . . absence of evidence. Alas."

"What do *you* think happened?" I asked. I wanted to know, too.

"What do I think? I don't know for sure. Maybe no one ever will. But if I were forced to make a guess, literally *compelled* to write something down in a file for the sake of formality . . . I would guess that he stayed in Storage Room Six. I don't think he ever left it. I think that weird room took him wherever it took everything else that vanished. But even if I'm right, there's no proving or disproving it."

"That makes as much sense as anything else. So, you know—not much, but it might be true."

I started to say something else, but he wasn't looking at me. He was staring down at an envelope on top of a stack. It was facedown, and on the back was written "Jefferson Starr," and an address on Trout Street. He pushed it aside, and the next envelope had an Alabama address—which I noticed real quick, but I didn't see who it was from. He gathered up his mail and straightened it by knocking it on the desk. He looked up at me again. "I'm sorry, yes. You're right. Or I'm right, maybe. Perhaps we'll never know."

"Not until we're dead." I said it with a grin, so he'd know I was still playing along. He'd said that the folks at the Society often had a funny sense of humor, and I might as well get used to it. I was game to do that. I was game to join it, too.

The look on his face said he didn't think it was funny, though. He went a little pale, then gave me a shaky grin in return. "That's one thing to look forward to, I suppose."

"Right." I nodded. I hoped I hadn't messed it up already and done something wrong.

He reassured me before I could give it a second thought. "No, don't look worried. I'm sorry. I'm only distracted."

His eyes darted to my neck, and his eyebrows were asking a question about the necklace I was wearing, but he didn't voice it and I don't know why. It was just a little present from Pedro, a good-bye present, you know. Just a round pewter pendant stamped with a constellation: Pisces, for my zodiac sign—since I was leaving to work with the witches, wizards, and spiritualists. Or that was how he put it, anyway.

I don't know why Simon would be distracted by a tiny piece of jewelry like that. It wasn't even hanging down around my bosom, and you have to forgive a man if he glances that way every now and again.

"When will my office be ready?" I asked, by way of changing the subject.

"Tomorrow," he said real fast. "That's what they tell me, and they're usually right. We'll have a case or two for you sometime next week. I'll accompany you at first, but in time you'll investigate these things on your own. Are you prepared for that?"

"I will be. I'll get used to it."

"There will be ghosts, and worse things," he warned. "Possessions, poltergeists, and the like. We'll do what we can to teach you how to handle them. But I must be absolutely clear: We are all flying blind. At its core, this is a place of learning. Success does not always mean a resolution; success means new information, reported responsibly and accurately."

I said I understood, and I was looking forward to the challenge. "If everybody else is learning as they go, then so can I."

"Excellent!" he declared, and with two more fingers of whiskey each, we clinked glasses and did a little toast.

"To new beginnings!" I offered.

He liked that one. Then he added, "To absent friends. To old doctors, and the ocean, and to promises made and kept."

We finished our drinks and I left him alone, because I still had an apartment to unpack and it was getting late. I think he wanted to be left alone. He was getting that faraway look again, and I guess he was really thinking about absent friends, like George and Lizbeth. And probably a dozen others—I don't know; he's a lot older than I am, and I like him a whole lot, but I don't know much about him.

So I took my coat off the back of the chair, put it on, and wished him good evening.

"Have a good night," he said. "I'll see you here first thing in the morning, yes?"

"Eight o'clock sharp. I'm always on time—don't you worry."

"I won't, I won't . . . ," he promised in that faraway voice that said he wasn't paying attention anymore.

He was looking down at a folder someone had left on the edge of his desk. It was tied off with string and finished with a round red wax seal. He ran his fingers over it and smiled softly, like it meant something important to him, but he didn't plan to explain it to me.

That was all right.

It wasn't my business, and anyway, it was just a little imprint of a starfish.